MECH AND MAGIC

The Knack Book 2

By Kim McDougall

This one's for Elaine, for the hard work and for putting up with all my made up words.

1

LET THE WOLF RUN

CONALL LEANED AGAINST THE ANKLE of the giant mech, watching the towers of New Torwood City pass him one by one. In his years as a black market runner, he'd seen many amazing mechs—bejeweled creations worth millions and ancient mechs fueled by powers that modern mages could only dream of. Talos was in a league of his own. The giant metal guardian of the city was a perpetual motion machine, a rustic and stoic piece of art, and as beautiful in his own way as the princess tinker who cared for him.

The giant metal foot lifted, swung forward and slammed to the ground again. Conall swayed and jerked with it. The motion had been less pronounced inside the mech. Out here, Talos's steps had the rhythm of a rolling ship slamming into wave after wave.

Conall had never been a good sailor.

Wolves were meant to run, not swim, said Garou, the wolf in the back of his mind.

Then let's run, brother.

He tapped Talos's leg with the flat of his hand. "Take care of her, old friend."

He leaped, hit the ground hard, then rolled into the shadow of a rocky outcropping before the keepers on the wall spotted him.

As soon as he was on his feet again, he patted himself down, checking for the two gifts Rowan had given him. In his pocket was the key to Talos's lower door so he could return to her one day. He also wore a graphium locket to keep in touch. The locket rested below his breastbone on a chain long enough that it wouldn't hinder his shifting and would fit snugly in the thick ruff of the wolf. His princess had thought of everything.

He was traveling light, only one small pack. He'd left his bow behind because he couldn't carry it when he ran as a wolf. His only weapons for this long journey through monster-infested lands would be his air knives, his teeth, and his claws.

His gaze swept over the vast Meadows, now turning golden under the summer sun. It was right that he was returning to that empty landscape. A lone wolf needed space to hunt. And yet…He turned back to the great city of New Torwood with the northern sun glinting off its walls. He squinted but the tower where he'd left Rowan was already out of sight.

He turned his back on the city. He'd made his choice. As he walked into the Meadows, Garou howled.

I thought you'd be happy to be back on the road, Conall said.

Garou snorted. *Without our mate, our road is barren.*

We'll come back again. Conall believed those words, but he couldn't hide his secrets from the wolf, and they both knew there was a chance they would never return.

And still you run, the wolf groused.

For Nathan and Misha, Conall said, using his brother and his brother's wolf like bait. Garou had mourned their passing as much as he had, but wolves are more pragmatic.

Nathan and Misha are dead. Mate is alive.

Conall had no rebuttal for that, so he kept walking.

The plan was to stay off the road but close to Kanta Highway as it snaked westward. When he reached Old Torwood City, he would turn north and follow Dawson River as far as he could, then find an Ebos scouting party and track them to Benni, the fabled Ebos city.

There were three big flaws in that plan. First, rangers patrolled the highway and the Meadows around it. From his smuggling days, Conall knew they would stop and search anyone they found suspicious.

The second flaw was that he had only a vague idea of Benni's actual location. The Ebos were a nomadic people, but rumor said their only city was somewhere in the far northwest where the Ubruulen Mountains branched into two arms before fading into the sea. Conall had experience chasing rumors. His job tracking down valuable mechs had led him on more than one wild goose chase, but if the Ebos held the secret of what had happened to his brother, Conall had no choice but to chase this goose.

The third obstacle to his plan was Durance—Wildblood territory. He couldn't avoid the shifter enclave. It was huge, spanning nearly a thousand miles of wooded land north of Old Torwood City. It was also where he'd grown up with Nathan and their father and sister. Durance flanked the Dawson River along his direct route to Benni. He'd left there when he was sixteen and never looked back. He wasn't eager to return now, but it seemed inevitable, and somehow fitting. If he was going to seek out the truth about Nathan's death, he should start at home.

The graphium warmed. He pulled on the chain and opened the locket and opened it, marveling that anyone could make a graphium so tiny. The silver exterior was etched with scrollwork vines as delicate as the veins on a dragonfly wing. Inside, the graphium screens were matte blue thera. Rowan held the locket's mate, and for the next few weeks, this mech would be his only connection to her.

The right screen glowed with its first message.

Miss my wolf already, was written in cramped script to fit on the tiny thera chip.

Conall's feet didn't pause in his journey north, but he pulled out the miniature stylus attached to the chain and wrote back, *arooooooo!*

A moment later, Rowan answered with a heart-shaped smiley face.

Conall closed the locket and tucked it away. He had several hours of daylight left and he planned to be far from New Torwood by nightfall.

After a week on the road, his days fell into routine. He slept through the hottest part of the day, and walked through the cooler hours of the long dusk. Keeping the Ikon River and Kanta Highway on his left, he traveled west through the Meadows. It was the height of summer and the grass was tall and cloying, like wading through a knee-high jungle. He left a trail a pup could follow, but he was determined to stay off the highway.

At night, he let Garou out to run on four legs, keeping to the shadows because a wolf wearing a pack would certainly raise suspicions from any humans they encountered. At dawn he would find some shade to hide under. He would shift, eat some rations from his pack, then sleep.

On the eighth day of his travels, he woke from a fitful rest and was suddenly alert. His feet skidded on gravel as he sat upright.

Someone comes, Garou said.

The sun hung low over the mountains. At this time of year, it wouldn't set for another few hours, but its weak light threw long menacing shadows.

Voices traveled over the barren ground—a snatch of conversation, a cut-off laugh.

Conall sat up slowly. He'd been using his pack as a pillow. He lifted it without making a sound and tucked his arms through the straps.

He'd bedded down in a dried out gully next to an old shrine to Jocasta, the miracle healer who came to fame after the Resurgence. The shrine was built over the only spring for miles around. He'd camped here many times in his travels and never run into rangers.

Of course, the voices might not be rangers. There were homesteaders out this way too, and hunters that tracked big game across the Meadows, but Garou hadn't scented any herds in the area. One thing was certain, they weren't Ebos. The elves were silent trackers, but they had a peculiar scent, like overripe fruit. Garou hadn't sensed their trail, and they rarely came this far south.

Conall gauged his options. He could hide in place and hope the strangers didn't know about the shrine or the spring. Or he could sneak into the Meadows and pray they didn't spot him against the halo of the setting sun. Neither option appealed to Garou.

We should run. Two feet can never catch four.

The voices grew louder.

He wished he could let Garou out, but he'd be vulnerable while he shifted. No, he needed to put some distance between him and the strangers first.

He rose and looked around. There was no time to sweep the ground. It would be obvious to anyone with an ounce of tracking ability that someone had slept there recently.

He tucked his knack around him and faded into the Meadows. His boots were leather-soled and made only the faintest crunching sound on the dry ground.

The Meadows were a vast desert of grass and rock with almost no shelter. The land rose and fell in gentle swells. Conall's only chance to evade the strangers was to get over one of those dunes and find some place to hide.

The voices had gone silent. That wasn't a good sign. It meant they were on alert.

The wind shifted, bringing the distinct tang of coyote.

Garou snarled.

Conall ran.

In a fair fight, a wolf could take a coyote, and Conall was confident he could beat a wild pack, but they were nearing Durance now, and the coyotes could be shifters from the Reaver Clan.

The wolves had enough ongoing blood feuds with the Reavers that if a pack of coyotes came upon a lone wolf, they would have no mercy. Conall's bones would feed the scavengers and no one would ever know what happened to him.

Rowan would never know. That thought spurred him to run.

You should not have left our mate, Garou grumbled.

Not helpful. Conall wasn't going to get into that argument again.

Darkness was falling, but not soon enough. He ran north to where the ground was more rocky and uneven. Used to long travels, his heart rate rose, but his breathing remained even. He could only hope the strangers weren't in such good shape. If they were marauders, he'd have a chance. They'd be ill-fed and perpetually hungry. Rangers would be fit and well equipped, and coyotes could run for hours without tiring.

Outcroppings of rock were common in the Meadows. Many had names and were used as landmarks. Conall spotted the Plowman ahead, so called because it was made of two massive stones that resembled a standing man and a plow. He ran for it and ducked into its shadows.

Crouching, he forced himself to breathe evenly, though his lungs wanted to suck in air. He listened to the Meadows over the sound of his pounding heart.

The twilight was painfully silent, then a fox yipped somewhere north of his hiding spot. A woodcock started its repetitive *meep-meep,* and the crickets settled back into their evening song.

Conall relaxed. The animals were telling him he was safe for the moment. He stripped off his clothes and tucked them into his pack along with his boots. The cooler evening air prickled his sweat-slicked skin. He tied the pack securely, then laid it out so Garou could easily slip the straps over his neck. He'd had the bag specially made years ago. The leather was worn to a patina, but the dual strap system was ideal for a traveling shifter.

Crouching naked in the shadows, he listened to the crickets and other night creatures for another long minute before sinking into the change.

It began as an ache in his joints that quickly crested to excruciating pain as his bones reshaped. Some elongated. Others shrank. Muscles stretched. Tendons twanged. His clenched jaw cracked as a muzzle sprouted. Sweat-prickled hairs misted away, replaced by thick, coarse fur.

The change took minutes that felt like a lifetime.

Finally, Garou rose on four legs and shook out his coat. His throat ached to howl, but he was no untrained pup. Those who hunted him could still be close. Instead, he gave in to his other need—to run.

He scooped the straps of the pack over his head and felt it settle into the hollow at the base of his neck, then set his course steadily westward. His padded feet were silent on the dusty ground and his easy stride ate through the miles. He ran until the sun finally set behind the mountains, and then he ran all through the short night.

2

DARK IS THE MARROW

ROWAN KEPT HER EXPRESSION NEUTRAL as she watched Chancellor Olan March, who in turn studied her. Weathered skin and deep wrinkles showed his age, while keen intelligence shone from his gaze. With finger and thumb, he smoothed down his drooping mustache, pulling his lips into a frown. They were seated on opposite sides of a desk in the chancellor's office, a place Rowan knew well. The carpet was still the same, if a little more worn. She'd read most of the books on the shelves behind the desk. On the other side of the room a fire burned in the hearth. It was flanked by two ancient chairs whose cushions held the impressions of ghosts from the past.

A lifetime ago, her father and Olan had spent many evenings in those chairs, talking politics and playing cards. Rowan would sit on the floor by the fire, reading from Olan's library or sorting through a box of old mech bits and building great towers and fortresses. Now that she thought of it, Olan had probably kept that box around just for her.

She breathed in the scent of old cigars and was hit by a sharp pang of longing. Olan smoked the same cigars as her father. A mech timepiece on the wall clicked the passing seconds with a long brass arm. It was the only sound in the room until Phalian shifted on her shoulder with a shuffle of his metal wings.

And still Olan March watched her.

She tried not to squirm like a child while he made up his mind.

Princess Rowan Elizabeth Cecilia Andula, only daughter of the late King Reynar Andula and sister of the heir to the New Torwood City throne, had just laid out her plans to overthrow the government. She hadn't sugar-coated it. She wanted to oust Faustus Atherton and take over as regent, and she needed allies on the council.

Dale Shannock, the current regent's secretary and her childhood friend, was already quietly polling ministers' aides to see which ones might fall on her side of the sword, but they'd both agreed that Olan would be the most likely to offer his support.

Olan had been her father's most loyal advisor, but a lot had changed since Faustus Atherton became regent. Alliances had shifted. New cliques among the nobles had formed. The old king and his cautious, outdated ways of thinking had been forgotten.

She held her breath while she waited for an answer.

It occurred to her—perhaps too late—that Olan could side with Atherton and have her thrown in prison for treason.

"Well, it's about time." Olan let out a breath that riffled through his mustache.

Rowan was so fixated on the fluttering whiskers, she didn't register his words right away. The old chancellor leaned back in his chair and laughed. It was a rough soldier's laugh, but the sparkle in his eyes was full of mischief.

"I thought you'd never take your rightful place as queen."

"Regent," Rowan corrected.

Olan laid a finger against his nose and winked. "For now." He clapped his hands on the desk and rose. "You'll have my support when you need it, Princess. In the mean time, is there anything you want me to do?"

"Actually there is. I would like all thera mechs removed from the royal suites and the West Wing atrium."

Olan was in charge of the palace—everything from security to dinner menus. Removing thera from her suite was a minor request, but odd enough to draw comments from the staff. Rowan didn't care. Since returning from the Meadows, she was wary of using thera. Maybe it was because of what she'd learned about the gaunts, the once-humans that had been turned into monsters through a combination of thera ingestion and a massive spike in natural magic during the Resurgence.

Or maybe it was because of what she'd seen inside the scribe's head. Orson had been cruelly used by the Temple of the Word. His blood had reeked of thera and she suspected that was the cause of his break with reality. He'd been a foul-mouthed killer, but she still felt guilty about her part in erasing his memories. Recent reports from the temple said he wasn't recovering.

Rowan's mech hand was fisted tightly in her lap while she waited for the chancellor to question her reasons for banning thera. How much could she tell him?

He frowned, then his expression lightened. "Your father disliked thera too. You plan to follow his lead, do you? Good thinking. Best to put the right foot forward then." He tweaked his mustache again as he thought through the implications of Rowan's request. "I might have to pull a few things out of storage. Been a while since we had to use oil lamps and candles. But I'll see it done."

"Thank you." She rose and held out her right hand. Olan didn't hesitate to squeeze her mech fingers.

"What ever you need, Princess. It will be good to see an Andula on the throne again."

Rowan left the chancellor's office feeling a little lighter than she had that morning. The burden of her plans still weighed heavily, but with Olan's help, perhaps she could keep it from crushing her.

Minna, her self-appointed honor guard, had been standing outside the chancellor's door and swung into step behind Rowan as they entered the large atrium of the palace's East Wing. Phalian soared up to the domed ceiling that was decorated with elaborate mech works.

The giant clock on the wall struck three with a turning of gears and a booming chime.

Saints, she'd been in meetings most of the day, and she wanted to visit Ethan before his evening nurse came for his bath. She hurried across the marble floor, her soft leather shoes making no sound.

The East Wing was home to the Council Hall and offices for anyone involved in governing. The atrium was full of nobles seeking audiences with ministers, and ministers' aides who liked to mingle with those nobles. All eyes turned to watch the princess and her unusual guard.

Once, Rowan had been mostly ignored by the staff and nobles who didn't know what to make of the princess who dressed in mechanic's overalls and came and went without an escort. These days, Rowan had traded her overalls for something more suitable to court life. She didn't favor the lavishly embroidered gowns of the noble ladies, but her dark blue tunic was elegant and simple. The matching leggings were stitched with silver thread along the outer seams, a minor detail of understated polish. Minna approved of the outfit, since it left her full range of movement in case of a fight.

Her guard was the other reason Rowan was no longer inconspicuous. Minna and her cousin Ferlan were Ebos warriors who'd followed Rowan home from the Meadows. An Ebos elder named Omika had requested that Minna and Ferlan return to the palace as the Evani's personal guard. At the time Rowan hadn't understood why the Evani needed a personal guard. Saints, she still didn't understand why the Ebos had saddled her with the title *Evani,* or what it meant. She was certain that Omika had a personal agenda behind this request, but Rowan was glad to have the Ebos at her back. She could count on one hand the people in the palace she actually trusted.

Of course, the Ebos guards brought complications. Their unusual dress, for one thing. Rowan glanced at Minna. She'd given up the flowing robe she'd worn in the Meadows for a simple leather vest over a tunic and leggings similar to Rowan's, except Minna's were gray and decorated with beads sewn in geometric patterns. On closer inspection, it became obvious the beads were polished bone. Minna wore more bone piercings in her ears and nose. Skewers of bone held her hair in a tight bun—skewers that could become weapons in a pinch.

A group of nobles huddled in the center of the atrium. Rowan nodded to them as she hurried by. One woman put a hand to her mouth so she could whisper to her female companion. Neither tried to hide their stares. The princess had shunned the court for so long that half the nobles had forgotten she existed. The other half believed she was physically deformed or mentally unstable. Regardless of their opinions, they were all curious about the mechanic princess who'd fought monsters in the Meadows. The dark elves she'd brought back only added to the gossip.

The woman gasped and pointed at Minna. Phalian swooped down from the ceiling. Wind from his wings buffeted the noble lady's hair. She shrieked and ducked. Rowan held back a smile. Phalian had become protective of their elf friends. She whistled for the bird. Once he was settled on her shoulder, she nodded to the shocked ladies and kept walking.

It wasn't that the citizens of New Torwood City weren't used to seeing elves. The Enos elves had been a part of the city since its founding, but their cousins, the Ebos or dark elves, were known only from stories whispered around campfires or in pubs after too many cups of ale. The "dark" didn't refer to their appearance. Minna was as blond and fair-skinned as any Enos elf. Dark referred to their preoccupation with death—a myth that Minna's bone embellishments did nothing to dispel.

Omika had seemed adamant that making the Ebos a common sight would sway the New Torwoodians to view them as the gentle people they really were. Rowan wasn't so sure.

She left the atrium through a tall arch and headed toward the West Wing, first passing by the Hall of Rule, with the throne that had stood empty for nearly two decades. She mounted the stairs to the uppermost floor and entered the West Wing by a long hallway with many doors on either side. These were offices for the monarch's personal secretaries and advisors, as well as a butler and housekeeper. Only the last two offices were occupied these days.

Thera lamps glowed pale purple from sconces that were too far apart to fully light the passage. Rowan was learning to hate that purple glow. She was glad that Olan had agreed to retrofit the royal wing and remove all traces of thera. She'd almost forgotten what the warm light of an oil lamp looked like.

Minna sped up. She touched Rowan's arm in a gesture to hold her back, then studied the shadows at the end of the hall. Satisfied that no assassin waited in them, she nodded for Rowan to precede her.

Rowan sighed. "This wing is nearly deserted. You can relax."

"Nearly deserted is the perfect place for an attack, Evani."

Rowan was too tired to argue.

They'd returned from the Meadows two weeks ago. If Regent Atherton wanted to assassinate her, he'd had plenty of opportunities, such as the ball that had kept her up well past midnight last night. With all the nobles in attendance and visiting dignitaries from both the southern cities of Dowchester and Shythe, it would have been a perfect time for an accidental death or even a murder. So many suspects to blame.

Or Atherton could have had her followed when she visited Talos, or ambushed as she took air in the garden. But here she was still alive and kicking down the regime. No, Atherton was biding his time, waiting to find out what she knew and what she planned to do about it.

Earlier in the summer, the council had surprised Rowan by drafting her into Ranger Squad 54. She'd long since given up hope of fulfilling the standard military duties assigned to every youth, but the council had finally approved her request, and they'd sent her into the Meadows on a highly sensitive mission to find a group of scientists from Dowchester.

Squad 54 had driven a thousand miles through the dangerous Meadows only to find all the scientists dead. Then they'd become the target of shadow soldiers who controlled gaunts as if they were dogs on leashes.

Rowan, nine other rangers, and a scribe had set out on that mission. Not all had come home. Her heart still clenched whenever she heard Augie's "Ode to Joy."

The mission hadn't been all terrible though. At least one good thing had come of it: Conall, gone nearly two weeks now. Memories of him already felt like dreams. He'd blown into her life, all bravado and ferocity, and he'd opened a part of her that she hadn't even realized was shuttered. He'd taught her to love. The entire squad had really, but Conall had taught her to love herself. She missed him. She missed them all.

And she would do anything to keep them alive. That meant finding proof that Regent Atherton had been behind the murders of those scientists at the oasis.

Find the proof, then hang him with it.

She dug her fingers into the pulse throbbing at her temples. After the late night, she'd had an early morning breakfast with the ambassador from Dowchester before his party returned south. That hadn't gone well. The ambassador was an old man who had little patience for what he called "flighty children." She'd actually overheard him refer to her that way at the ball. Breakfast had been a silent and awkward affair, then she'd met with other parting dignitaries before her meeting with Olan.

Now she only wanted to head back to bed. Instead, she would spend a couple of hours with Dale, learning about economics, politics, and history so the next time the ambassador visited, she could wow him with her poise and intellect.

But first, she needed to see Ethan.

The hall joined another three-way junction at the Royal Atrium. A single keeper stood with his back to a wall, looking bored. Rowan nodded to him. The keeper's gaze slid from her to Minna, but he was well-trained and kept his opinions about dark elves to himself.

Rowan turned right and headed for the private suites. This hallway was reserved for the royal family. It housed only Rowan, her aunt Bella and her brother Ethan, whose room was the first one on the right. It was a small suite usually reserved for guests, but for the last nineteen years, it had been a sickroom. She left Minna standing just inside the door and immediately crossed the lush carpet to Ethan's bed.

She found him as he always was—pale and lifeless as stone.

Auntie Bella was snoring quietly on a chaise in the corner. Phalian swooped into the room and landed beside her. Rowan sent out a calming vibe and hoped he'd pick up on it.

She sat on the chair beside the bed and lifted Ethan's hand. His skin was dry and his bones felt toddler-soft.

"Hey, bro. Just checking in to let you know the ball last night was as tedious as I expected." She kept her tone light. "You would have hated it."

Actually, the boy she had known would have hated it, but while he'd slept, Ethan had become a man. She had no idea what Ethan the man would like.

Nineteen years ago, he'd wanted to play outside the walls, to pretend that he and Dale were rangers hunting gaunts, and it had nearly cost him his life. Rowan had been an equally impulsive nine-year-old at the time and desperate to prove to the older boys that she could run fast, hunt gaunts, and brave the outside world. Just like them. And it had cost her an arm.

Ethan had been in a coma since then, but she never gave up hope that one day he'd open his eyes and speak to her.

Grant, one of Ethan's army of nurses, came in singing about a meadow lark falling in love with a crow.

"I thought you'd be late today, Princess. I heard that ball went on for all hours last night, so I went ahead and gave him an early bath. He's all ready for you."

"Thank you, Grant." Rowan let Ethan's hand drop to the blankets. A spider crawled across the bed beside his arm—starkly black against the white sheets. Rowan brushed it away with a sigh. Ethan loved spiders, and spiders loved him.

Grant smiled. He was a big man and it was a big smile. "It's a sign, Princess. The spiders come when you stir him up with your stories. Means he's in there, listening to you."

Rowan felt unwelcome tears prickle her eyes.

"Maybe he is." She smoothed Ethan's ginger hair away from his brow. It was still damp and clung to his skin.

Phalian fluttered over and pecked at the spider as it scuttled under the blanket.

Bella snorted and rolled, flinging an arm off the chaise.

"Has she been there all night?" Rowan asked.

"She was on the floor with her head on the couch when I came on shift at noon." Grant smiled. "I settled her and covered her up. Not sure how comfortable she is in that dress, but she hasn't woken since."

The purple gown Bella had worn to the ball poked out from under the blanket. Her elaborate up-do had fallen to one side, and the fake mole she'd painted on her cheek had smeared.

"She'll be fine." Rowan let her aunt sleep. Waking Bella was a mistake she'd learned to avoid. Bella was often cranky and frequently uncharitable, but if disturbed from sleep, she could be downright cruel.

Grant nodded. "I'm just about to head to the laundry, but you should know that I called for Dr. Renata. The prince had an episode this afternoon."

"What kind of episode?"

"I'm not sure." Grant's cheerful expression darkened. "Possibly a seizure. He seemed to be choking. I sat him upright and rubbed his back until he calmed. I wasn't sure what else to do."

Grant was a large black man with biceps that strained his nurse's uniform and hands as wide as cast iron pans. He was a gentle giant and tears glazed his eyes when he thought of Ethan struggling.

Rowan gripped his arm. "Thank you for caring for him. Today and always. I'm sure he'll be fine. Dr. Renata will see to it."

Grant nodded and wiped his eyes before scooping up the dirty linens and heading out.

Rowan sat again. Ethan did look paler than usual and beads of sweat clung to his upper lip. His breathing was shallow too.

"So, do you want to hear about the ball?" She took his hand again and squeezed, always hoping to feel the telltale tightening of a returned grip. There was none. A moth landed on his shoulder and flicked its wings, then another. A beetle crawled across the pillow. Another spider clung to the headboard. That was odd. Ethan's knack attracted insects, but not usually in such profusion. Most days, he slept deeply enough that the insects stayed away. She wondered if the appearance of so many creepy-crawlies had something to do with his seizure.

Then the window began to rattle and the insects scattered. The floor vibrated. Light flared and died in the thera lamp, and the mech clock above the hearth squealed as its gears spun erratically. Rowan gritted her teeth and rode out the wave.

In a moment, the shaking stopped. She glanced at Minna whose face had gone ashen. The Ebos had never experienced a ley-line surge before coming to New Torwood.

The city had been built on a confluence of ley-lines. Once in a while these rivers of magic overflowed. The mages at Jupiter's Temple had issued a proclamation, assuring citizens that the surges weren't dangerous and would subside in a week or two.

"That was a bad one." Rowan grinned.

"They're all bad, Evani."

"Only because you're not used to them. Think of them like meteor showers—exciting and a little frightening, but not dangerous."

"If you say so, Evani."

Rowan brushed away the insects on Ethan's pillow and continued her account of the evening. "Auntie Bella had a bit too much honey wine and she started singing those old bawdy songs that Dad liked. It was pretty funny."

Bella snorted and turned again, squishing her face into the cushion.

"It wasn't all fun though. The ambassador from Dowchester was a pompous ass. He actually called me a frivolous chick with no feathers. I'm not even sure what that means. But don't worry. I got back at him. His driver was advised on a shortcut this morning. It'll take him right through the titan eel swamp."

Rowan rambled on for a few minutes. Another moth found some crack in the walls and landed on Ethan's shoulder. She told him (and the moths) about the guests at the ball, about who was newly engaged, and the brawl that had broken out between squires from Dowchester and Shythe. She detailed the dresses worn by noblewomen, the music that had been too loud, and the food that was cold by the time it was served—because Regent Atherton had arrived two hours late.

"He probably thought it was fashionable to keep us waiting. Pompous ass."

It was inane gossip at best, but if she believed that he could hear her, that meant Ethan was trapped inside his unresponsive body. The boredom of such a prison would drive anyone mad. And so she made a point of trying to entertain him.

She knew Dale did the same, though they read to Ethan instead of gossiping. Grant sang to him. Even Auntie Bella chattered to him when she wasn't passed out. Most days, she spent more time in his room than her own. They all wanted Ethan to come out of the coma one day, and if that didn't happen, they at least wanted him to know he was loved.

Dr. Renata breezed into the room. Her eyes were narrow slits and her mouth was pulled into a tight knot like someone who'd spent years holding back words she ought not to say, and it had left her puckered and peevish.

The doctor laid two fingers against Ethan's throat and felt for his pulse. Phalian chirped from his perch on the headboard. Renata paused in her ministrations to smile at Phalian's antics.

"Such a pretty birdie," she cooed. It was weird. Dr. Renata was a hard woman. Her face had hard lines. Her hair was always pulled into a bun that looked like molten steel. But Phalian's appearance never failed to soften her.

Then the doctor became all brisk and businesslike again.

"Grant tells me he had a bad day."

"Something about a seizure," Rowan said.

Renata unfurled the stethoscope from around her neck and opened Ethan's shirt to listen to his heart. A spider fell from the ceiling and landed on Ethan's cheek. Renata brushed it aside impatiently. After a moment she said, "It's probably nothing. His body shifts from time to time. We saw this when he was growing during his teen years. It's just the body accepting a new normal."

"Okay…" Rowan wasn't convinced. Ethan was thirty-two years old. His body wasn't going to grow anymore. "What aren't you telling me?"

Renata huffed and slung the stethoscope around her neck again. "There is nothing to tell. Ethan is unchanged as always. But it would be natural for him to begin a decline now."

"So this 'new normal' you speak of is his body getting used to the decline?"

"Yes. I told the regent this would happen. It's only a matter of time. I dose him with magic to keep him alive, but his body has to do the rest on its own. And if his body gives up…" She gave a lopsided shrug as if it were too much of a bother to lift both shoulders.

Rowan's mech hand creaked as she made a fist. She had to remind herself that Dr. Renata had selflessly donated her own magic to Ethan for years. It was her knack, this ability to transfer a bit of life's blood to another, and it probably made her a great doctor. That didn't mean she was kind.

The spider returned and jumped onto the pillow. Renata swatted at it, but that only made the pillow bounce and the spider jump and Phalian squawk.

"You should really speak to the housekeeper about these bugs. It's unsanitary."

Rowan ignored the comment just like she did every time Renata made it. Nothing would keep the spiders, moths and beetles from finding Ethan.

Renata glared at Rowan then turned her attention back to Ethan. She laid her hands flat on his chest, closed her eyes and concentrated. The hair on the back of Rowan's neck tingled. Her mech fingers curled into a fist. She couldn't exactly sense magic, but Renata's healing knack always gave her the heebie jeebies.

They stood in that odd tableau for several minutes, until Renata huffed out another breath. "There. I gave him a double dose. That should calm whatever upheavals are going on in there."

"Thank you. Your sacrifice is appreciated more than you know." Rowan meant it. Despite Dr. Renata's other failings, she would always be grateful for her care and for saving Ethan's life.

Renata's pinched lips spread into a taut smile, then she left without another word.

Rowan re-buttoned Ethan's shirt and tucked the blankets in again. The spider was back. So were the moths. They clung to Ethan's pajama shirt, but she left them alone. Insects had never hurt him.

She turned to find Minna peering over her shoulder at the prince.

"It's not right," she said.

Rowan's hackles rose. It wasn't the first time someone had voiced their opinion about keeping the helpless prince alive. But until someone told her that he was truly dead, she wouldn't let him go.

"He's alive," she snapped. "That's all that matters."

"Yes, he lives. That much I can see." Minna smiled and cocked her head. She found amusement in Rowan's ire, but then Minna found amusement in most things.

"But I did not speak about the…the *rightness* of his existence." Minna's English was very good, but once in a while she still struggled to find words. "I speak of the hold that doctor has on him."

"Hold? What do you mean? Dr. Renata is the only reason he *is* alive. She feeds him from her own life-force. She can't heal him, but she can let him live. And I for one still hope for a miracle. One day his body will heal and he will wake up."

"Not so long as you keep letting that doctor near him."

Rowan had been ready to refute the usual argument that she should let Ethan fade away and be at peace. Minna's words stopped her short.

"What do you mean?"

Minna screwed up her face as if she smelled something foul. "It is difficult to explain to a non…*lumina*. A non-mage."

"You're a mage?"

"No, but the lumina power runs deep in my family. My brother Dalkyn is the strongest. He will take over as Evafara one day."

Rowan nodded. She had met Dalkyn in the Meadows. He was a strong mage and also a natural leader. She had no doubt he would become a good—if authoritarian—leader of the Ebos one day.

"I too can sense magic, though its manipulation is beyond my talents." Minna laid a hand on Ethan's arm. "The doctor…she fed him and she allows his bones to live. But she cages him too, like a tightly swaddled baby. Perhaps too tightly." She waved her hand. "As I said. It is difficult to explain."

"Is she hurting him?"

"I can't be sure. I think not, but she holds him." Minna hugged her arms tightly to her chest.

Rowan didn't know what to do with this information. She couldn't go accusing Dr. Renata of mistreating Ethan, not when she had so selflessly aided him all these years. She wanted to trust Minna—she *did* trust Minna—but what if this "holding" was simply part of the spell that kept Ethan alive? She would have to think on it.

"We'll keep an eye on him," she said. "And maybe you can tell me if you sense any changes in him when we visit?"

Minna bowed. "Of course, Evani."

Rowan was rising to leave when another thought occurred to her.

"Can you sense magic all the time?"

Minna smiled mischievously. "If there is magic I cannot sense, how would I know about it?"

"What I mean is, have you sensed other magic in the palace?"

"Of course. The kitchens are full of potions, though the chef calls them sauces. That keeper at the end of the hall wears a talisman on a cord around his neck. I cannot tell for what purpose. Protection perhaps? There were several nobles at the ball last night with spells on them too. Your regent reeks of magic, but of what kind?" Minna shrugged.

That was interesting. Maybe she could use that information somehow.

"Can you tell me the next time you sense magic, whether it's on a person or a mech?"

"Of course, Evani." Minna bowed.

"We should have a code word so they aren't alerted."

"How about *vorha*? It means… magic. But in my language we have many words for the subtle differences of magic, the same way you have multiple words for snow, rain and sleet. Vorha is magic that one feels deep in the bones."

"Vorha. Perfect. And what would you call the magic you sense on Ethan?"

Minna's eyes flicked to the prince. "*Buquor*—murky magic, Evani. We have a saying about buquor. It clouds the mind, but it cannot change the marrow. Let us hope that is true."

Rowan looked at her sleeping brother again with his small menagerie of insects collecting on his pillow.

"Let us hope."

3

OF ALL THE INNS IN ALL THE WORLD

CONALL SLEPT WELL IN THE Meadows. The days were warm and when he lay down, the tall grass cocooned him so he could only see a patch of sky overhead. He'd been following his route parallel to Kanta Highway for over a week when he rose on a clear evening and struck out across the grass. He could just spy the highway to his left. Every now and then a caravan would appear, kicking up dust. Twice he saw mounted patrols of rangers. He was sure they couldn't spot him camouflaged against the backdrop of the Meadows, but he stopped and hid in the knee-high grass until they passed. Better to be safe than sorry. If the patrols had any senior officers, they would recognize the Wolf of Algid Pass. The regent had reluctantly pardoned him for his crimes, and Conall carried his pardon in his pack, but he wasn't optimistic about his chances of producing those papers as proof before someone shot him.

His provisions were nearly gone and he was just thinking about shifting to let Garou hunt when the wolf stirred in the back of his mind. Something had piqued his interest. A scent.

Meat, was all the wolf said. Ten minutes later, Conall could smell it too. Someone was roasting a pig over a fire. And they were close.

Smoke from a chimney appeared next, and then the thatched roof of a roadside inn.

That was odd. He'd passed this way only a few weeks before, when he journeyed from Dowchester to New Torwood City. He didn't remember seeing the inn then.

Intrigued, he risked getting a closer look and waded through the tall grass, approaching the building from the back. It looked grown from the environment itself, like it had been there for generations. Pine log walls were gray with age, and the thatching had seen better days too. The yard behind the inn was bare of grass and muddy where a pump brought water up from an underground spring. Chickens pecked for grubs in the mud and a small vegetable garden was growing along the sheltered side of the inn.

He flattened himself to the ground when a young boy came out the back door to dump a bucket of kitchen scraps into a pen with two fat pigs. The boy stopped at the pump and filled the bucket before returning inside.

Conall was close to the road now. He scanned the highway from horizon to horizon. He should have given the inn a wide berth, but his legs were suddenly propelling him toward it.

Not cool, Conall grumbled. He considered the wolf a brother, and they had a pact. When they ran on two feet, Conall was in control. On four feet, Garou had the reins. But Garou wouldn't let the scent of roasting meat pass them by.

The wind picked up as he circled the inn to find the front door. A wooden sign creaked on two metal chains. A pair of crossed hammers and a mug of ale were etched onto it. The creaking sound scratched at some memory Conall couldn't retrieve.

The inn's door was heavy and it swung shut behind him on well-oiled hinges. Inside, the main room seemed dim, given it was late morning. Six tables and chairs filled most of the small space. A slab of wood on two kegs made a bar along one wall. The air was heavy with old smoke and cooking smells. There were no customers, only the innkeeper standing behind the bar. He wore a dirty white apron over his homespun shirt and pants. His thick nose was red. Bushy eyebrows—more gray than brown—nearly hid his eyes, but Conall could feel the man's gaze on him. He wiped a mug with a ratty towel, then replaced it in a line of similar mugs on the counter. He swung the towel over his shoulder and limped a couple of steps toward the door.

"What can I get you, friend? I have a nice venison stew on the boil. Or I can whip you up a sandwich of cold meat and cheese if you want to take it on the road."

The room spun around him as Conall had a moment of near-debilitating déjà vu. He'd been here before. He was certain of it, but the innkeeper was a stranger. The inn was new to him.

And yet…

Garou whined at the back of his mind. He tried to prod the wolf into being more specific with his concern, but he only retreated from his thoughts. Conall was on his own.

"You look a little lost, friend. Why don't you sit and have a drink?"

Conall nodded and took one of the seats at the bar. He *was* thirsty.

"What's your preference. Got a fresh keg on tap. Or tea brewing in the back." He pointed his thumb over one shoulder.

"Ale, please." The inn felt like the kind of place that needed a mug of ale to appreciate it. "And I'll take you up on that stew."

The innkeeper poured his ale, leaving a thick froth spilling over the side of the mug.

"It won't be a moment." He limped off toward the kitchen.

Conall sipped the drink and contemplated his surroundings. Why did this place feel so familiar? He thought back to all the roadside rest stops he'd made in his time. There were many, and they all looked much the same—dim common rooms, sticky tables, watered ale.

And yet…

The innkeeper returned with a steaming plate of hearty stew with a chunk of black bread on the side.

"I didn't catch your name," Conall said as the plate was laid in front of him.

"Harlowe." The innkeeper didn't reach out a hand for Conall to shake, but his eyes never left him.

"I'm Conall West, formally Commander West of the Ranger Squad 54." He didn't know why he was giving this man so much information, but it felt important, as if he were trying to jar Harlowe into acknowledging a mutual past relationship.

"Good to meet you." Harlowe picked up one of the clean mugs and wiped it again. It seemed a nervous, repetitive gesture, but the man was calm and steady. Perhaps he was just bored.

"I feel like we've met before."

"Could be. If you travel this road, you'll find me right here."

"Right here. Of course. And how long have you been the proprietor here?"

Harlowe leaned in with a grin. "Some days it feels like several lifetimes."

Conall noticed his unusual eyes. They were too blue and flecked with highlights that seemed to swirl around his pupil. The effect was mesmerizing.

"I feel like I should know you. I come this way often, and yet I don't remember…"

The storm in Harlowe's eyes ramped up. Conall couldn't look away. The fork slipped from his fingers and drummed on the wooden plate. Harlowe leaned in closer. Conall could smell his breath, stale like left-over ale.

A fat finger appeared in his sights and his eyes crossed to focus on it.

"Then maybe it's time to remember." That last word echoed in Conall's mind. Harlowe jabbed the finger to his forehead, right between his eyes. Conall felt a jolt go through him and his eyelids suddenly grew heavy.

Garou let out a long, mournful howl.

The innkeeper pulled the plate away as Conall's head fell to the wooden counter.

He slept.

And he dreamed.

INTERLUDE

CONALL PRESSED HIS HANDS TO his ears. He didn't like to hear his mother scream. Garou whined and it came out in his voice.

"Stop that," his father snarled.

Conall fell silent. He clasped his hands in his lap so they wouldn't fly to his ears again.

Garrett grumbled a curse word, then turned his attention back to the bottle on the table. It was nearly empty. He tipped his head back to drain the last of the drink.

Upstairs, Conall's mother moaned.

His aunt and uncle had come for the birth, but the baby was two weeks late, and yesterday they'd had to return to their homestead. Only a midwife from the village stayed with Mum. And his older sister Ianna.

Conall and Nathan weren't allowed upstairs.

Uncle Birch had brought the boys toy cars that he'd carved himself. Nathan had decided that at ten years old, he was beyond toys and he'd given his car to Conall. They both sat in his lap now, but he had no heart to play with them.

Nathan was lying on his stomach reading a book their aunt had brought.

Ianna came into the room, carrying a fresh pile of linens.

"Tell your mother to shut up," Garrett said.

Ianna didn't even pause to acknowledge her father.

"Did you hear me, girl? If I have to listen to—" He was cut off by another sharp scream from the birthing room. He took a sip from the bottle, found it empty and threw it into the hearth. Glass exploded. Nathan let out a yelp as a shard pierced his arm. Conall jumped up to help him, but Nathan plucked it out with a small whimper.

"Don't be such a baby," Garrett said. "It's just a cut."

Nathan held the bloody shard of glass between two fingers. His shoulders were heaving. Conall knew that look. Nathan was angry.

Don't do it, he thought. If Nathan gave into his temper there would be beatings.

Nathan stared at their father for a long minute, while blood dripped from his wound.

Garrett smirked, daring him to say something.

Conall squeezed his eyes shut. *Don't do it. Don't do it.*

Garrett finally tired of the game. "What are you gaping at boy? Go clean up before you get blood on the rug."

It wouldn't be the first time there was blood on the rug.

Conall followed Nathan into the kitchen where a pot of water was always warming on the stove. Nathan washed the wound and found some clean rags to bind it.

"You'll have to help me. I can't do it with one hand."

Conall did his best to wrap his arm. In the other room, Garrett hollered for Ianna to bring him more wine. Upstairs, their mother let out a long, agonized groan.

Ianna found them struggling over the bandage. She didn't ask what happened, but took over with her usual efficiency. Ianna was fourteen, practically a grownup.

Her left eye was red and swollen. It would turn purple by morning. No one mentioned it.

When she was finished with the bandage, Ianna ushered them toward the pantry.

"Take a snack, whatever you want, then go down to the cellar and stay there until I come get you. Got it?"

Something heavy thunked against the wall in the living room. Conall winced.

"Iaaaaanna!" their father bellowed.

"You should come too," Nathan said. "To hell with him." He stuck out his bottom lip in defiance, but Conall knew he was holding back tears.

Ianna brushed the hair from Nathan's forehead, then kissed Conall on the cheek. "You know I can't do that. Mum needs me."

She shoved them into the pantry and closed the door. It was dark, but they didn't need light. Their wolves knew the way.

The door to the cellar opened at their feet. They clambered down and shut it behind them.

In the dark, they waited.

Overhead, Garrett shouted. Ianna shouted back. Their mother screamed.

"We forgot the snacks." Conall's voice sounded way too wobbly in the dark.

"Shush." Nathan reached for his hand and found his knee.

They sat like that for a long time while the storm raged overhead. Their mother's screams became unbearable. Their father ranted, his voice slurred and incomprehensible. New sounds added to the storm. A thud. A crash. A growl. More crashing. Garrett was tearing apart the living room.

Conall whimpered. He'd left his new cars up there. Garrett would smash them or burn them.

Nathan moved around the small space.

"What are you doing?" Conall tried to grab his arm, but missed in the darkness.

"Runes for protection."

Runes were Nathan's knack, but Conall didn't really understand them.

"Will they work?"

"Of course. I read all about it. Feel this." Nathan's hand found Conall's and he led his fingers toward a wooden shelf.

"Can you feel that?"

Conall's fingers traced a long etching.

"Is it a snake?" He jerked his hand away.

"Yeah. That's Salus. She's fierce. She'll protect us."

"Will she bite anyone who comes…comes to hurt us?"

Nathan made a grumbling noise that sounded just like their father.

"That's not exactly how it works, but yeah, no one's coming down here unless Salus says so."

Their mother cried out again, but the sound seemed fainter, like when she'd left for Briar Market last year and called to Conall as she rolled away in a cart.

"Do you think she'll be okay?" Conall asked.

"Yeah. Mothers give birth all the time. You're just too little to remember when Simon was born. It was the same thing."

Simon had lived for only a day. Conall decided now wasn't the time to mention that.

The screaming eventually stopped. Garrett wore himself out too and silence fell on them like a bludgeon.

Conall could feel the damp walls of the cellar wrapping around him. They were too close. Soon they would be on him, suffocating him. He shut his eyes tight, as if he could shut out the silence.

"Nathan?"

"Yeah?"

"Why doesn't Ianna come?"

"She will."

"When?

"Soon."

The darkness seemed to go on forever.

"Let's shift and sleep as wolves," Nathan said. "We can pretend we're camping."

"I can't. I'm scared."

"Yes, you can. I'll help."

Conall felt the push of Nathan's change. Garou reacted to it like he always did and Conall let go. The wolf wasn't afraid of small, dark spaces.

Misha and Garou curled up together, two pups finding comfort while they waited for their sister to come and change their lives forever.

4

WILDBLOODS

For the next three days Conall slept for only a couple of hours at a time. His dreams were bittersweet. Sometimes he spent his sleeping hours in Rowan's arms, reliving the one brief night they'd spent together. Other times his dreamscapes were dark and vaguely threatening as he ran from unseen predators.

Because you run in the wrong direction, Garou said, when they'd been woken by a particularly nasty nightmare. Conall ignored him. Garou voiced his displeasure at leaving their mate behind at least twice a day.

Still, the dreams disturbed him. They came every time he closed his eyes, even when the monotony of loping across the Meadows lulled him into a waking trance. And they weren't just dreams. They were memories meted out in a jumbled timeline. One moment he was a ranger fighting gaunts in the great north; the next he was a child battling demons of another kind.

He'd just woken from one such dream of his childhood home. He was down in the cramped cellar, and though he knew it was only a ten-by-ten foot space, he ran through darkness that went on forever. And in that surreal way of dreams, the cellar morphed into the palace hallways and he was still running, looking for something, not even sure what he'd lost, but desperate to find it.

He woke feeling achy and uneasy. He drank from a stream, then headed west at a manic pace.

Garou nagged him to let the wolf out, and Conall finally relented. The wolf's hearing was better, and when the winds shifted, he could smell human scents even though they could no longer see the highway. He also smelled other animals—fox, deer, rabbits and coyotes. Only that last one worried him.

He ran for hours, until a rabbit caught his attention and Garou veered northward to hunt. He caught the rabbit and a gopher, crunching their soft bones with his powerful teeth and feeling free for the first time since he'd set foot in New Torwood.

Leaving the bones for the scavengers, Garou ran along a trench as the full moon rose, pale against the still-bright sky. In the spring this road would be impassable with snow melt. But they were nearing the end of summer and his paws kicked up loose gravel. The banks rose steadily on either side. They offered shade during the day, and in these deeper shadows, the gully grew damp, then wet.

He trotted up the shallow creek for hours until the water rose past his paws. The night wouldn't get any darker, and the river bank was soft sand, protected from the wind. It was a good place to rest.

He lapped brackish water from upstream. The southward flow was muddy, stirred up by his passing. Until it ran clear again, he'd be easy to track. He lifted his nose above the ledge of the creek bank and tested the air. A gentle wind brought the scent of caribou scat. A herd had stopped to drink at the creek, but the spoor was days old. His nose twitched as he sorted through hundreds of scents commingling in the Meadows air—animal and human. Like the caribou, the human scents were old, probably hunters passing through. Coyotes had been here too, but those scavengers ranged all over like fleas on a sick wolf.

The vague scents were enough to comfort him. They were alone, for now. Conall pounded gently on his thoughts.

Let me out, brother.

Garou considered denying the request. They ran on human feet too often. Conall sent him an image of a small wolf running wild in the forests beside their home. When they were just pups, they'd often gone for days as a wolf, especially in the months after their mother died. Riding shotgun in their mind wasn't a cage; it was rest and comfort.

Garou snorted and shook his mane of black fur. He *was* tired. He'd hunted and filled his belly with water. It was time to sleep.

The shift left Conall writhing on the wet sand beside the creek. Garou had dropped the pack nearby. Conall put on damp clothes. His hands were shaking from exhaustion as he tied the laces of his boots.

The sun broke over the Meadows. It would hover over the edge of the southern horizon all day, working its way west. For now, the creek bank lay in shadow. Conall curled into a ball like a pup and slept.

Dreams of his old homestead plagued him again. This time, he was running along the riverbank below the house. His father, brother and uncle were fishing and Conall had walked too far upstream. Now, no matter how fast he ran, he couldn't find them…

He came suddenly awake. Something had disturbed him, but his groggy mind took precious seconds to recognize it.

A yip came from the trail behind him.

He sat up and the sound of his boots scraping wet sand was inordinately loud. Dangerously loud. Thirst stuck his tongue to the roof of his mouth. The sun had moved and his legs were hot where they protruded from the shade.

He crouched and listened. The late afternoon Meadows were groggy. Bees hovered around the wildflowers growing beside the creek, but most creatures rested during the long sun.

The coyote yipped again. It was ahead of him now. There were more than one. Another sharp cry, closer this time. And then a long howl. They were calling to each other. If he stayed put, they would surround him.

He slung his pack over one shoulder and started running along the river where the rocks would mask his footprints. Not that it would help. If the coyotes had his scent, they didn't need footprints to track him.

They harried him for nearly an hour, until he was certain these weren't a pack of wild coyotes. There were five Wildblood clans. Conall was born into the Black River Clan of wolf shifters. Briar Market, the only real city within Durance, was technically part of their holdings, but the city was open to all clans. It was the site of the great fall trading festival and the seat of the

Wildblood Conclave, the governing body of the land. The foxes of Holt Clan had homesteads south of Briar Market and were mostly trappers. Dawson's Cove Clan were bear shifters and fisher folk to the north. The smallest Clan was Boreal, the cats who kept to the far north.

Of all the clans, the Reavers were most despised. They were scavengers and bullies who tormented other shifters, stealing when they thought they could get away with it, killing for sport, and only pretending to follow the laws of Durance to appease the elders of the Wildblood Conclave, because even the Reavers needed to trade at Briar Market. The Wildblood Conclave put up with their lesser crimes because of their numbers. They bred like rats and were useful when the clans faced outside dangers like raiders or gaunts.

It was just Conall's luck to have a pack of Reavers pick up his scent. He could have outrun wild coyotes. Eventually, they would tire of the chase, and look for easier prey. Reavers wouldn't give up. They knew he was out here. They knew he was alone, and they would run him to ground.

The creek joined with a larger river. Conall forded it in five long strides, soaking his boots and pants. On the other side the ground was soft, and the bank choked by bulrushes already going to seed. He turned back to the water and waded upstream. At first, he moved with ease, but with every step, the current tugged at him, and he tired quickly. He'd been running too long on too little food. Less than a mile from the creek, he left the river. There was no help for it. They would find his tracks on the sandy bank.

The chase had taken him north, away from the highway. That meant he'd missed his chance to buy provisions in the thera camp outside Old Torwood City, but that was the least of his worries now.

He paused, listening. The Reavers called out again. They were closer.

He started to run.

He made his stand as the short night fell.

He was close to the edge of the Meadows, but not close enough. He'd hoped to lose them in the forest that was draped like a blanket of green along

Dawson River. But he'd run out of time. From the sound of their calls, the Reavers would be on him in minutes, and a good mile of open Meadows still stretched before him.

Instead of risking a mad dash to the forest, he'd stopped at a small outcropping of stones. He recognized the place. The Wildbloods called it Castings. Man-sized boulders lay in a rough circle about twenty feet in diameter. Most lay on their sides but three remained upright. The rocks wouldn't protect him, but he liked to have something solid at his back in a fight. He leaned against one of the stones, a blade in each hand.

Garou had agreed the air blades would be their best defense against a pack and so he kept to his human skin. His palms were slick and his knuckles ached from gripping the knives. They were each twelve inches long and slightly curved. A cobalt-blue line of thera was inset along the blade, waiting to be activated.

The Meadows fell utterly silent. Even the crickets knew something was coming. The first coyote leaped into the clearing between standing stones and bared his teeth.

Conall shook the knives to ignite the thera. Air coated blades vibrated at a rate that would easily cut through flesh, bone and even metal. They hummed in a tone beyond human hearing, but the Reaver heard and he howled.

As the echo of the cry died, three more ragged-coated scavengers appeared like wraiths from the shadows. Conall spit at the feet of the first one.

The lead coyote lunged, teeth bared. Conall swiped his knife and sheared whiskers from the side of his muzzle. The coyote dropped to the ground. His haunches bunched and he snarled, ready to spring again. The other Reavers circled, staying just out of reach. Now the stone pillar at his back became his cage. He couldn't run. He couldn't kill all four before they took him down, but he'd make them hurt.

They were at an impasse.

One of the coyotes began to shift. Conall watched from the corner of his eye, not wanting to glance away from the others for even a moment. The shift was quick, not a good sign. That meant the Reaver was strong—both physically and magically.

In seconds a naked male was standing between two of the snarling coyotes.

He was shorter than Conall and wiry. His muscled arms and legs looked like twisted leather left to dry in the sun. Short, dust-colored hair stuck out from his head. Squinty eyes watched him from a pock-marked face.

"Lone wolves ain't welcome here, stranger." His voice drawled. "This is Reaver land. We saw you hunting Reaver hares, drinking Reaver water."

The closest coyote bared his teeth.

"What do we do with outsiders who steal our game, boys?"

One of the coyotes lifted his muzzle and howled. The others followed with a cacophony of yips and howls that prickled the hairs on Conall's nape. He felt suddenly cold, despite the heat. He recognized the feeling; it was anticipation for a fight, tinged with dread. He wasn't afraid, but dread was a healthy part of any battle. Someone was going to die here today.

The Reaver flicked his fingers and one of his pack crept forward, a snarl curling his lips.

Garou responded with a bellow that filled Conall with courage. His hands buzzed with energy vibrating off the knives.

The coyote leaped.

"Stop!" A voice rang out. Conall swiped his arm right and hit the flying coyote on the side of the head. It fell and before it could rise again, a booted foot kicked it.

"I said stop."

Conall dropped his arm even as it rose to strike again. He knew that voice.

The burly man was dressed for travel with a full bedroll kit on his back. He wore a ranger uniform that had seen better days. A dark beard covered most of his face and the rest of his exposed skin was matted with dust from the road.

"You have good timing." Conall deactivated his knives and stowed them in his belt before clasping hands with Lydan Heath, a mountain lion shifter of the Boreal Clan.

"Haven't seen you in these parts for some time." Lydan grinned showing startlingly white teeth beneath the road dust.

The Reavers clustered together in a group, uncertain and unhappy that their prey had suddenly doubled in strength. Lydan turned to the lead coyote who stood with eyes lowered.

"Hoyt, you know the Reavers don't own the Meadows." Lydan's brows lowered over his eyes.

Hoyt scuffed a bare foot in the dirt.

"He ain't from Durance though. He ain't got no rights." He shot a defiant glare at Lydan. "Wildblood law says I can protect my land from outsiders. Even you can't go against the law, *cat*." He spat the last word like an insult.

Lydan leaned back on his heels considering. The other coyotes had stood down, but they watched him sharply, ready for an attack signal from Hoyt.

"The law is the law," Lydan agreed. "But this wolf isn't an outsider. This is Conall West of the Black River Clan. Either you're too young or too stupid to remember that his family has lived in Durance since the Resurgence. Far longer than yours. Hell, his great-great-grandfather was a founding member of the Conclave."

Hoyt's eyes shifted to Conall, then back to Lydan.

"Now you might think a lone wolf is fair game out here, regardless of his family. You might want to use him as an excuse to exercise your bloodlust." He paused to make eye contact with each of the coyotes. "One wolf against four coyotes might be an easy fight, but ol' Conall is an ex-ranger. He fought gaunts in the last uprising. Have you ever fought a gaunt, Hoyt?"

The coyote shook his head, eyes wide.

"Now I'm thinking you could take him on, but he'll do some damage, probably kill at least one of your boys. So which one of your brothers are you willing to give up? Sam?" He kicked dirt at the closest coyote who snorted and backtracked, his face full of dust. "Joss? Or little Pete over there?" Pete slunk back until his butt pressed against a standing stone.

Hoyt mumbled something unintelligible. Lydan nodded as if the coyote had spoken wisely. With the sun behind him, the big man's eyes were shadowed and dark. His beard didn't quite hide his frown.

"Good, good. Now my old friend Conall and I haven't seen each other in years, so we'll be traveling together to Durance. We might just stop at the Reaver's Den to have supper with your daddy. We'll be sure to tell him what a good job his boys are doing out here in the borderlands."

Hoyt made a sound as close to a yip as his human voice could manage, then the coyotes took off at a run, Hoyt lagging behind his furred brothers but not by much.

Sweat trickled down the small of Conall's back, and there was a hollow in his stomach that had nothing to do with hunger.

"Thanks for that. I'm not sure I could beat them."

"Oh, you'd manage it," Lydan said. "But they'd take a few pounds of flesh for your efforts."

"I guess it's my good luck you happened along then."

Lydan's expression didn't give much away. Was he glad to see Conall? Or mad that he'd stayed away for so long? They hadn't spoken in nearly two decades, and their last meeting had been shadowed by death. They hadn't parted well.

Conall looked away, as if he could deny the shame of that memory. He squinted into the sun that hung low over the forest. "You really going to dine with the Reavers?"

"Nah. They'd just as likely poison me." Lydan fished a battered canteen from his pack, took a swig and handed it to Conall. He drank to be polite. It was no small thing to give up your drink in the Meadows where fresh water could be several days travel.

"I can walk with you as far as your old homestead, then I'm heading home." Lydan's clan seat was in the north. He tilted his head sideways considering Conall. "You're going to the old homestead, aren't you?"

The closer Conall got to Black River, the less eager he was to visit the clan house. He took a last sip to hide his hesitation, but Lydan wasn't fooled.

"Ignoring ghosts won't make them go away, my friend."

"I know. It's time to go home." It was a sudden decision, but it felt right, and the vague restlessness he'd been feeling since leaving the city calmed. "But after that, I'm heading north too."

Lydan's brows rose. There was nothing north of Durance except the few Boreal Clan holdings, then miles and miles of desert-like tundra.

"There's a story here, I suspect. You can tell it while we walk." He clapped Conall on the shoulder and they headed away from the standing stones.

5

TEA FOR TWO

ROWAN STUDIED THE MAP. DALE had spread it out on a table in the study attached to Rowan's suite, and was now quizzing her about major land marks and trade routes. The suite door was closed and Minna stood guard outside it. Dale had come in through the servant's door and would leave by it. Until they resigned as secretary to the regent, these study sessions had to be kept secret.

Her finger trailed along the route from Dowchester to New Torwood, stopping to tap the dot that marked Old Torwood. Six hundred years ago, that city had been overrun by gaunts and titans. There was nothing left of it except for a heavily guarded thera farm on the banks of the Ikon River, but Kanta Highway—the only safe route to the southern cities—still ran through it. Avoiding the old city and traveling as the crane flies would cut hundreds of miles off the journey.

"You understand now why the Regent's Council is so determined to get the new road built," Dale said.

"Yes, I see." Rowan tapped the map again. "But why do they need an agreement with Dowchester to do it? Is it just about the funds?"

"Partially. A highway of this length will be exorbitant. But with backing from Theracine Corporation, we could do it." By we, Dale meant New Torwood. The Regent's Council would approve the expansion if it meant a direct route to sell more thera to the magic hungry mech mages in the south.

Rowan frowned. The Theracine Corporation mined thera from the giant nacara mussels found only in the Ikon River. In the last twenty years, thera had become essential to life in New Torwood, and Theracine had expanded production to a second thera mine at Oxeye. They'd also grown in power.

Rowan wasn't comfortable with the influence Theracine had over the council. Dale's quiet inquiries had proven more than half the ministers were on their payroll or were major investors in the company. They were poised for a bloodless coup of New Torwood's government and no one seemed bothered by this fact.

It filled Rowan with a shapeless but gnawing fear.

Putting aside her misgivings about thera, she had to admit that New Torwood City could not presently survive without it. Their lives ran on thera. Every mech in every household was fueled by it. The streetlights glowed with the distinct purple tinge of thera. The city cats were thera-powered vehicles that the average citizen could no longer hope to own. And with the cold Fanfaronade winds already whistling through the city walls, thera would become even more important. New Torwood City was surrounded by tundra. Wood was expensive to burn as a heat source, but thera was clean and relatively cheap. For now.

A city owned by a corporation would be at the whim of profit. Already, the price of thera was inching upwards, even though the city's thera reserve was more than healthy. Dale's contacts noted that citizens of Bailey and Squall's End were grumbling about the price hikes.

"That's it!" Rowan thumped her hand on the map. "That's why we need support from Dowchester. We need lumber to build bridges." She sank back in her chair.

Dale's lips curved downward, but their eyes sparkled. They had a way of frowning and smiling at the same time and it usually meant they were delighted with their star pupil's performance.

"Exactly." Dale traced a new line on the map. "The proposed highway will take serious mileage off the route between cities, but it cuts across dozens of tributaries that run into the Ikon. That's a lot of bridges to build."

"Can't we simply log the lumber as we need it? There must be forests enough near the new route?"

"Some," Dale concurred. "But once we cross the southern border, we'd be logging Dowchester's lumber. They seriously frown upon anyone stealing their resources. Without a formal agreement, they will see it as an act of war, even if the road would ultimately benefit them."

The thera lamps on the walls suddenly bloomed with bright light. They flickered, then went out. The floor shivered and a sound like thunder rumbled in the distance.

Before Rowan could react, the rumbling eased and the lights came on again.

"That was the second surge this week," Dale said.

"Yes, and it reminds me that Chancellor March still hasn't fulfilled my request to have all thera removed from my suite."

"He'll get to it. There's a lot of stuff to go through in the palace storage."

"I suppose that's true." Rowan shoved the map away and rubbed her temples. There was so much to do and so few hours in the day. Dale had been pounding facts, histories, and theories into her head, but the more she learned, the more she realized how badly her education had been lacking. Learning etiquette and poetry hadn't prepared her to lead. And even though her self-taught tinkering had made her resourceful, it didn't give her the all-encompassing education needed to understand the nuances of government.

"So if we need a treaty with Dowchester, you're saying I should cultivate a relationship with the ambassador." Dowdy old Magnus Robson was the last person she wanted to spend an evening with, but she would do it for the good of her city.

"Only if you'd rather let the regent and Theracine make their deals without you," Dale said.

That wasn't an option.

She couldn't yet prove the regent was behind the murders at the oasis, but she'd vowed to stop being a wallflower and take her rightful place on the council as heir to the Andula monarchy. She was determined to reveal Regent Atherton's guilt and remove him from the head of the council. Even better, she'd like to toss him in prison for the remainder of his days.

Her studies were a major component of that plan, but so far, they'd only shown her how tangled the web of corruption was. Council members, nobles, Theracine representatives, and foreign dignitaries—everyone had their own agenda. Everyone was ready to stab their neighbor in the back if it meant stepping up a rung on the ladder of power.

"I'll reach out to Robson," Rowan said, "but it won't do us much good. He hates me."

Dale grinned. "You're in luck there. Magnus Robson isn't coming back to New Torwood. His health is failing. A new agent is already on his way from Dowchester. I hear he's quite charming."

Rowan made a face. "Charm is a great mask to hide behind."

Dale glared at her. She lifted her hands in defeat.

"Fine. I'll make nice with him."

"And you'll study up on these old trade agreements?" Dale pushed a stack of folders toward her.

Rowan held in a sigh. Dale was just doing what she'd asked. No use taking out her frustrations where they weren't warranted.

"Yes. I'll go over these tonight, so I'll be all ready to meet…what's the new ambassador's name anyway?"

"Padgett. Baron Remy Padgett."

"Fine. I'll invite *Baron* Remy Padgett for a breakfast meeting as soon as he arrives and dazzle him with my wit and my extensive knowledge of past trade agreements between our cities. But right now I need a break." Rowan pushed her chair back and rose. "I want to go see Talos anyway." The giant automaton was always in need of some repair, and tinkering with his cogs and gears was the best way she knew to de-stress.

"You taking your guard?" Dale asked.

"Of course. It's not like I could ditch Minna if I wanted to." She turned to the mech valet sitting in the corner. "Roger, may I have Sandra Kane's cachet?"

The mech's wheels whirred as he zoomed forward.

"Roger that!" A compartment opened on his chest and he pulled out a flattened silver disk.

"Thank you." She accepted the disk and Roger spun in place. She'd found him in the Meadows and Conall had confirmed that he was a rare pneuma mech, one that didn't run on thera, but he didn't do much else besides spin and shout "Roger that!"

Rowan turned her attention to the deceased scribe's cachet, turning it over in her hands.

"Any luck with that yet?" Dale asked. Rowan shook her head. She'd been trying to find a way to access its information since they'd returned from the Meadows.

She turned the device over and showed him a small port. When a scribe was active, a cable plugged into that port and then into another at the base of their skull. There had to be a way to offload the data.

"I'm assuming that some device plugs in here, but what?" She glanced around her study. Crates of old mechware brought up from her tinker shop were piled against the bookshelves. "Nothing I have is remotely suitable. And I can't even begin to imagine building such a mech. Where would I even start?" That was the problem with being a self-taught mech mage. She didn't know what she didn't know.

"You need to ask the mages at the Temple of the Word."

"Sure and we know how helpful they'll be." The scribes were notoriously close-lipped when it came to their mechs.

"I might have better luck in the archives," Dale said. "I found an entire section of old records from your father's time that seem to have been forgotten. I plan to go through them soon."

"Good. Can I ask another favor?"

"Anything for my princess." Dale gave a courtly bow and Rowan swatted them on the shoulder. They didn't do courtly. Not when they were alone.

"Can you look into Dr. Renata?"

Dale frowned. "Why? I haven't been able to prove that she's on the Theracine payroll."

"I know. She probably isn't. It's just a gut feeling. For now."

"All right. I'll see what I can find." Dale turned to leave, but Rowan gripped their shoulder.

"When are you going to tell Atherton that you're leaving his service?"

It was a new argument between them. Rowan didn't want to hide her partnership with Dale anymore. She wanted them by her side when she faced the council.

"Soon. I promise." Dale squeezed her hand. "Right now, being Atherton's secretary has its perks. It gives me access to records and to his personal agenda that I won't have once we make the switch."

"I know, but—"

"Give me another couple of weeks, and I'll have all the data we need or at least all the data we're going to get. Then I promise, we'll make this official."

Dale waved the rolled map in the air.

"Fine. Have you at least found anything useful?"

"Only a lot of old trade agreements. I've been over the city charter a hundred times. If there's a loophole that lets us depose Atherton, I'm not smart enough to see it."

Dale was the smartest person she knew. That didn't bode well for their chances of a legal coup.

"I found a batch of old court records," Dale said. "If there's any precedent…" They paused as the study door opened. Minna's face appeared. Worry lines drew her brows together.

"The Regent is here," she whispered. "I showed him to the balcony, but you need to leave!"

Rowan had a strong urge to fling open the door and let the world know that Dale Shannock was her friend, her advisor, and her secretary.

Dale had other ideas. Their eyes went wide and wild, and Rowan decided not to push the confrontation.

"Leave that." Rowan pointed to the map and charts on the table. "And hurry!" She ushered Dale out the study door. They made a quick escape into the dressing room. Rowan walked slowly to the balcony where Atherton stood gazing over the wall at the vast expanse of the Meadows. His hands were clasped behind his back and he fidgeted with a heavy gold ring on his middle finger.

Rowan fixed her face into an innocuous smile and took a deep breath.

"Regent Atherton, how nice of you to visit."

Atherton spun. His black hair was plastered to his head with some kind of balm that shone in the bright light. He wore a three-piece suit in charcoal gray. His ample neck bulged over the tight collar of ruffled lace that almost obscured the Regent's chain of office.

"Won't you come inside?" Rowan offered. "The sun is too hot. Can I offer you tea?"

Atherton nodded curtly and followed her into the sitting room. Minna had already called for refreshments and they waited while a maid poured tea and laid out a selection of cakes and biscuits. Rowan chose her favorite square, a sweet walnut confection that was the cook's signature desert. Atherton filled a plate with half-a-dozen cookies and squares, then sat back in his chair and demolished them.

She watched, sipping her tea as if it were an everyday occurrence to host the regent in her quarters. In truth, she wasn't surprised by the visit, only that it had taken this long to happen.

After several uncomfortable minutes, when Atherton probably thought she was suitably cowed, he wiped his hands together in a criss-cross motion, sending crumbs all over the couch and carpet.

"Well, then." He cleared his throat and tried again. "Let us get right down to business."

Rowan bowed her head. "Let's."

Atherton frowned. "Ah, right. I have had a request from the Bailey Chamber of Commerce for a guest visit from the council. They require a keynote speaker for their annual shareholders' meeting. I suggested you for the part and they were delighted."

"Me?" This wasn't at all how she'd pictured this interview.

"Of course. You are eager to fulfill your role in the council, aren't you? This is what the council does." His smile could have charmed a snake-oil trader.

Rowan put down her teacup and rattled the saucer. She took a moment to calm her nerves. Then, channeling Auntie Bella, she said, "Faustus, you don't give a flying fuck about the Chamber of Commerce. Why are you really here?"

Atherton sniffed the air as if she'd fouled it.

"If you must know, there are some…ah, irregularities in the reports from Squad 54. The council has questions and I thought it best, since this is such a delicate matter, to ask those questions in person."

Translation: Atherton had questions he didn't want anyone else to know the answers to.

"So ask."

Atherton took his time. He selected another shortbread and swallowed it before continuing. "Tell me again how Scribe Orson sustained his injuries."

Oh, saints. Rowan sipped her teas as she thought back to the story they'd concocted to cover up the mess they'd made while erasing Orson's memories. She decided to keep it simple.

"He hit his head on a rock, I'm told. I didn't actually see it happen."

"Yes, strange that. None of the rangers present at the time seemed to have actually witnessed this accident."

"We were fighting for our lives at the time. Gaunts attacked us, but you already know that."

"Right, the gaunts. At the oasis."

They'd had to confess to the first gaunt attack in order to explain Augie's death, but no one on the council could prove they'd been to the Warren, the odd stone maze where Minister Wrede had been experimenting on gaunts.

"Yes, the oasis. Scribe Orson should be able to give you more details."

"Alas, Orson does not seem to be recovering. He's quite ill, so I'm told."

"I'm sorry to hear that." Her mech fingers tightened on her cup and she relaxed them before they shattered the delicate pottery. Phalian felt her agitation and ruffled his metal feathers from the mantle.

Atherton shot the bird a glare, as if it might lunge at him. Rowan thought it was a possibility.

"As you know, the Temple of the Word invests a lot of money and time into the training of each scribe," Atherton continued. "They are very valuable."

Rowan smiled. "I hear they're sacrosanct."

"Indeed. So the Abbot Archivist is quite displeased to lose one of his best scribes. It would help him, and me, if you and the other squad members could put together a more detailed report of the incident. Perhaps you could ask Commander West to oversee it."

"Commander West is no longer in the city." She probably shouldn't have admitted that. There was no record of Conall leaving. She should have let Atherton believe he was still here, looking over his shoulder.

"Ah, well. Perhaps you can ask some of the others."

"We don't really keep in touch."

"Don't you? That's a shame." Atherton rose. "I'll at least expect a report from you then. The Abbot Archivist will be most appreciative of any insight you might have."

I bet. She rose to her feet and extended a hand toward the door. "I'll do my best."

Atherton paused at the door. "You know, I wasn't lying about the

Chamber of Commerce. They are expecting you the day after tomorrow. Try to look…ah, regal." He gave her outfit a look, clearly not impressed with her new style, and left.

Rowan turned to Minna. "Well, that was bracing."

"Next time he comes, I will douse his tea with rhubarb root. It will give him the runs for a week." Minna held open her vest to reveal rows of tiny vials sewn into the lining.

"You know, you can be very scary."

Minna smiled. "Thank you, Evani."

6

A SPY'S LEGACY

DALE SLIPPED THROUGH THE SERVANT'S door at the back of Rowan's dressing room, pausing for a moment with the door ajar. Rowan's greeting to Atherton seemed overly loud. It screamed "Don't look behind the curtain!" She'd never make a good spy. But then, she was a princess. Dale was meant to be her spy, or at least the one who pulled the strings of her spy network. They'd been working to that end even before Rowan took her ill-fated trip into the Meadows.

Closing the door quietly, Dale ran down the narrow servant's hall. Atherton's private quarters were in the East Wing. Taking the public route would have been a ten-minute jog. The servant's tunnels were a twisting maze of hallways, but they would trim a few minutes off the journey. With Atherton occupied, now was the perfect time to search his rooms.

Dale had always known that the day would come when they'd have to side with an Andulan heir against Atherton. That heir was supposed to be Ethan, but Dale was starting to believe that Rowan was the better choice. Even if Ethan woke, which was unlikely, he'd been an impetuous and spiteful child, and would probably be an overbearing adult.

Dale still loved him. There was no helping that. Ethan's spirit had been larger than his short life. Even after all this time Dale's heart was firmly in his corner.

But over the last few weeks, while tutoring Rowan, they'd seen a spark in her—a spark of that intangible quality that all good leaders have. Dale had tried to qualify it—equal parts grit, intelligence and compassion, but also the ability to see a problem from all angles. The only thing she lacked was self-confidence. That would come.

The hallway was dim, lit only by a few thera lamps on the ceiling. It was hot too. Dale loosened their tie and collar. A door opened ahead, forcing them to duck into an alcove. There was no good reason for the regent's personal secretary to use the servant's halls, and if they were found here they'd have to face some uncomfortable questions.

Dale's breath slowed. A maid lugging a basket of sheets walked right past without noticing the lurker in the shadows. When she was gone, Dale continued at a run.

The problem of Rowan's education nagged at them. She was smart and had an agile mind, but the gaps in her basic knowledge were appalling. And she was impatient to learn. She wanted all the knowledge now, as if she could simply etch it into her brain the way mages etched code onto mechs.

In the archives, Dale had found a biography of Rowan's grandfather, written by the old Abbot Archivist in a time before scribes were commonplace. Perhaps Dale would leave it for Rowan to read as inspiration. Part of her still believed that taking the regency from Atherton was a coup. She needed to understand that it was her legacy. The biography would also give her a backdrop for events that had unfolded in her father's reign.

With that decided, Dale left the servants' corridor and let themself into Atherton's suite. They waited, back pressed against the wall until their breathing calmed and they were sure no maids or pages were present. Then they moved through the dressing room into Atherton's main living quarters.

It was less grand than the princess's suite, but it had a good size sitting room, dressing room and bedroom. Most ministers kept palace quarters only for formal occasions, preferring to live and work from their homes in Hightown. Atherton almost never left the palace, which made searching his rooms difficult.

Dale headed for a book shelf beside the hearth. Their hands slipped quickly over each book, looking for papers hidden between or behind volumes.

Nothing.

Moving on to the desk, Dale opened each drawer with little expectation of finding anything useful. Atherton wouldn't leave incriminating evidence in an unlocked desk. The drawers held only stationery, pens, a few thera chips and a graphium. Dale examined that, hoping Atherton's last message was sent to Minister Wrede. That would be helpful. But the graphium screen was bare. Dale set the mech down precisely where they'd found it and scanned the room for a possible hiding place.

It had to be here somewhere.

Dale had been Atherton's secretary for nearly ten years, long enough to have spied some questionable actions by the regent and his cronies. Dale detailed his suspicions and observations in a journal that they kept secreted away in an old cabinet in the archives. Without proof, those observations were useless, and the best proof would be the false ledger of accounts that Atherton kept. The one that Rufus Hayes, Minister of the Purse, never saw. The one that Dale was certain detailed payments from Theracine Corporation to Atherton, Wrede, and possibly others on the council.

Dale had seen the ledger several times, usually at the end of the day, when they'd stuck their head into Atherton's office to wish him a goodnight. The regent would lay his arms across the book or slip it under another folder. So far, Dale's discreet searches for the ledger had proven fruitless.

It had to be in Atherton's private suite.

Dale crouched in front of a side table that held a decanter of honey wine and two glasses. It was marble topped with a rounded cherry wood base. Dale pressed the front and a door opened with a click. The cabinet held more bottles. Dale felt all along the inner sides, looking for a false drawer. There wasn't one.

Standing up, Dale's eye fell on the closed door that led to Atherton's bed chamber. They strode over and tried the handle. Locked. They took several precious seconds to pick it, then shoved the door aside and peered into the murky room.

Dale didn't relish the idea of going through the regent's personal things. But they would do it for Rowan, and for the child Dale had been. The child who had been coerced into tattling on Ethan about their adventures outside the city.

That child had told the old chancellor's secretary about their plans to go under the wall on that fateful day when Ethan had been attacked. The secretary had made them feel like it was their duty to keep Ethan safe. In reality, they'd used Dale to plot their assassinations.

That secretary had been the young Flora Bosman, now CEO of Theracine Corporation. And the old chancellor was Faustus Atherton, who became regent after King Reynar died of a broken heart.

So yes, Dale would risk a lot to find evidence that would bring Atherton to his knees.

They stepped into the bedroom and began to search.

Dark, heavy curtains shut out the afternoon light. The walls were painted in deep purple. The ceiling was black. Carpets with patterns of black, purple and gold were laid over the parquet floor. The coverlet on the bed was also deep purple with a sheen like satin. A dozen black, purple and gold throw pillows smothered the bed. The room was immaculate. No books or trinkets rested on the bedside table. Dale turned to scan the rest of the space. The wall opposite the bed was masked by a curtain.

Odd.

Dale's feet sunk into the plush rug as they crossed the room. Their fingers trailed along the velvet curtain. It hung floor to ceiling, theater style, without any ties or adornments. Pulling it aside revealed a rack of butt plugs. All sizes, shapes and colors.

Huh. Old Atherton had secrets. Excellent. And it was no wonder their spies had turned up so little dirt on the regent. They'd been paying all the wrong whores for information. Dale's mind was already processing how to use this new development.

Pulling the curtain aside further, Dale found another rack of neatly arrayed floggers and a velvet lined case of nipple clamps. A shelf of mech toys came next. Was that...a narwhal?

Jesus, Jupiter and Jocasta. Dale let the curtain fall back into place. Did they really have to search Atherton's den of lust? The thought was nauseating. Not that Dale begrudged anyone their fetishes, but this was Faustus Atherton, Mr. Snooty McSnooty. And their boss and regent.

Dale tried to look at it pragmatically. Would Atherton hide the most important ledgers in the city here, among his dirty little secrets? Probably not, but was Dale willing to let squeamishness get in the way of fulfilling their promise to Rowan? Possibly.

The choice was taken away when a sound from the outer room announced a maid's return.

Damn the saints. They'd dithered too long. Dale pressed an eye to the crack in the door and watched the maid leave a tray of refreshments. As soon as she entered the dressing room, Dale slipped from the regent's boudoir and made an escape.

Atherton would keep his secrets a little longer.

7

HEART OF THE CITY

Commitments, studies, and politics kept Rowan from visiting Talos for another week. The lunch with the Chamber of Commerce in Old Bailey hadn't been the stellar success she'd hoped for. She'd come up against fierce criticism, and not everyone seemed swayed by her princess prestige. The old king had been gone a long time and few of the merchants remembered him. They only knew life under the regent's yoke and it seemed Atherton had little love for merchants outside of Hightown.

During the Q&A after her keynote, she heard a litany of grievances. The council had ignored the cropper guild's request to expand the Old Bailey Market and update the ancient sewers. The blacksmith guild wanted to increase their numbers to better serve the growing population. To do so, they needed to reduce the cost of apprenticeship, but the High Orator from the Temple of Jupiter had blocked that request for three years.

The complaints went on. Rowan had no real way to address them and by the end of the session, she feared the merchants lumped her in with the council's politics. She tried to mollify by promising to be the voice of their concerns, and if they weren't convinced of her power to change anything, they'd at least invited her back for another lunch meeting, a more informal one where she could get a better understanding of their needs. It was a start.

Dale had wholeheartedly agreed with her plan to enlist the backing of the general citizenry, and they'd set up meetings with other guilds. Her lunch times were booked for the foreseeable future.

But on Sunday, she blocked off the morning and told her aides she'd be spending it resting in her rooms.

She needed to visit Talos.

Once the maids were gone, she dressed in old work pants and a shirt. Her best tools were far below in her tinker's shop and she didn't dare fetch them. If she left the royal wing, she was at risk of being cornered by nobles, ministers or any of the lackeys who, since she'd taken her rightful seat on the council, always seemed to need a moment of her time. So she hung her basic tool belt around her hips. Her mission today was only reconnaissance anyway.

She left her room and crossed the hall to the King's Suite. No one guarded this door because the rooms were currently uninhabited, but the keeper at the end of the hall looked her way as she opened the great double doors. She waved to him. The guard shifted as if he might protest, but he had no grounds for it. The princess could go wherever she pleased. He turned his attention back to the atrium.

Ferlan was on duty as her shadow today, and he followed her into the royal suite. He made a quick tour of the rooms before letting Rowan proceed. She paused at a wedding portrait of the future king and queen looking young and regal.

After her father's death, she'd spent many afternoons here, trying to find comfort in the ghosts of her parents. Her mother's spirit was elusive. She'd died during the great rains of 566, when half the city had flooded and a flu swept through the damp streets, killing a tenth of the population. Rowan had been three at the time. She had only vague memories of the woman who'd brought her into the world. A formal portrait of Gwendolyn Andula was on display in the West Wing atrium. Rowan had often stared at it, pretending it was a mirror and she was the great queen with the confident gaze.

Gwendolyn's dressing table remained undisturbed after all these years. As she had often done, Rowan paused to run her fingers over the few strands of blond hair still tangled in the brush's bristles.

Her father was much more present in the room. She could see him standing by the window with hands clasped behind his back or sitting up in bed, startled because she'd woken him in the middle of the night. King or not, he'd never banished her from his room after she'd had a bad dream. She ran her hands across the rust-red quilt trimmed in gold. How many times had he wrapped it around her and pulled her into his arms to soothe away the night terrors? In the end, even her big, strong father hadn't been able to keep away the real monsters.

She turned from the bed and the memories and opened a door to a small study off the main chamber. This had been her father's favorite space. Furnished for comfort rather than ceremony, the room was built into the palace's westernmost tower, known as the King's Tower. The outer wall was bare stone and curved outward. The windows were small and high, but light came in through a set of double glass doors leading to a balcony.

The rapier that her father had worn like a jewel on his hip hung over the mantle next to a small seating area. The rest of the study housed a collection of fine mechs, including a ley-lantern that Rowan coveted. The lamp was a curiosity from a time before thera, when people used tallow candles to light their homes, or if they could afford them, the expensive lanterns that stored magic from a ley-line. When the thera lamps were removed, she'd speak to Olan about moving it to her rooms.

She sat on the couch. Her father's scent clung to the fabric—a blend of cigars, leather, ink and something else that Rowan thought of as sunshine. Sadness thickened in her throat.

Ferlan followed her into the room.

"Evani?"

She smiled and wiped her eyes.

"I'm all right. I just miss my father sometimes."

Ferlan nodded. His English vocabulary was rudimentary, so she wasn't sure he understood, but she chose to believe that his somber expression meant he empathized with her loss.

She rose from the couch, opened the double glass doors, and stepped onto the flagstone balcony.

"Evani!" Ferlan jumped through the door and blocked the way as if he could protect her from the battering wind.

"Don't panic." She smiled and tilted her face to the summer sun. It felt so good on her skin. Ferlan mumbled something in Essian and retreated to the doorway.

Rowan breathed in the fresh air and let herself relax.

The palace was built against the city's north wall, and the King's Tower was a bulwark of that wall. Looking westward, she spotted the next tower. It would be occupied by keepers to protect the privacy of the royal apartments. Not that invasions were common from this vantage point. The wall was sixty feet high. There was a small lip of land at its base for Talos to stride on and for keepers to patrol, but then the ground fell away sharply into a valley that became the Great Meadows. It would be nearly impossible for an army to invade from this angle.

Ferlan made a small growling sound when she hopped up to sit on the balcony's ledge. He was being a worry wart. The ledge was six feet wide. She grinned without remorse for his agitation and stretched out her legs. She released Phalian from his cradle on her wrist. The mouse instantly shifted form, and the bird soared into the sky. Wind buffeted him for a moment, then his metal wings caught the current. He flew toward the keeper's tower, no doubt to make mischief for the guards on duty.

Rowan gazed across the expanse of green stretching all the way to the Ubruulen Mountains. She remembered driving along their foothills, through gullies, sandpits and miraculous tracts of lush greenery. A bison herd grazed in the distance. They were little more than a patch of brown in the green quilt, but the herd probably numbered in the thousands. She'd seen their majestic beauty up close.

A swift and keen pang of longing stabbed her. When she'd been out there, she'd desperately wanted to come home. Now, the dangers and deprivations of the journey had dimmed and all that remained was…what? The freedom? Perhaps. The freedom to be Rowan and not the princess. The freedom to be with Conall. Saints, could she go a day without missing him?

She took out the graphium and scribbled a short note, then closed the locket and clasped it tightly in her human hand, thinking about what Conall's expression would reveal when he read it.

The morning was wearing away, and she didn't need her watch to confirm the time. Talos always rounded the King's Tower at noon. She turned westward, and like clockwork, the shining dome of his head appeared around the bend of the wall.

She stood up.

"Evani!" Ferlan filled that one exclamation with all his outrage and worry.

Talos strode alongside the balcony and Rowan sucked in a breath. His grandeur never failed to fill her with awe. The top of his copper skull crested the wall which was already over sixty feet high. His face was carved from various complementary metals and resembled an old Roman legionary's helmet that she'd seen in a history book. He had deep set eyes and a blunt nose. His mouth had been etched with particular care and it looked like it could open to speak at any moment. Of course, it never did, but Talos spoke to Rowan in other ways.

He was a mech wonder unlike any other that came before or after his creation. Harry Hightower, the most famous of New Torwood's mech mages, had built him to guard the city's walls, but he had become so much more than that. He was a source of city pride, a mascot, and a symbol of endurance and strength.

And he was limping.

Damn the saints. She knew she should have made time for him sooner. When she'd left for the Meadows with the rangers, Talos's upkeep had been shifted to a group of mech mages within the keepers. Upon her return, she'd realized that her days spent tinkering were over, but she saw now that the keepers weren't capable of the meticulous and dedicated care that the ancient mech needed—the care that he *deserved*.

Ferlan's strong fingers gripped her ankle.

"Evani." His tone was uncompromising. She was always amazed how he could make that one word work for him no matter the situation. He could fill it with exasperation, sympathy or formality. This time it was a warning. He wouldn't let her leave the balcony.

Rowan whistled and Phalian returned from his inspection of the tower. He flattened his wings and dove. Ferlan screamed as the metal beak jabbed his hand. He let go.

Rowan pulled her foot free.

"Sorry!"

She turned, ran three steps along the wall, and leaped.

For a dizzying instant she was airborne, then she slammed into Talos's shoulder with a bone-jarring crash. Her mech fingers found the handhold on his neck as her feet skidded on his epaulet. Her grip held and she found her footing. Talos kept moving, oblivious to his new passenger. They were already near the end of King's Tower. She could hear Ferlan cursing from the balcony and had a moment of regret. Minna would reprimand him when she learned that he'd lost the Evani, but the guilt was fleeting.

She rode Talos's shoulder with wind streaming across her cheeks and pulling tears from her eyes until the next tower came into view, then she unlocked the door built into the mech's neck and climbed inside.

A feeling of comfort enveloped her. The usual tang of grease and iron hit her nose, along with another scent—something sweet that she couldn't identify but had come to think of as purely Talos. The sounds of gears grinding, chains wheeling and pneumatic pumps hissing were within normal parameters.

But something was wrong.

The lighting was never good inside Talos, but usually a steady glow from his pneuma heart filled the chamber with an amber cast. Today, the light was dim and had a sickly greenish hue.

Phalian, never a fan of the enclosed space, shifted back to his mouse form and scuttled into her shirt pocket.

Rowan's hands gripped the iron ladder and she began her descent along Talos's chest wall. When her eyes came level with the great beating heart, her suspicions were confirmed. It was noticeably dimmer.

The heart was the real marvel of Harry Hightower's mech. Some mages theorized that Hightower had trapped the force of a ley-line in a gemstone. Other stories told of the great sacrifice he'd made by giving a piece of his own soul to animate the heart. Whatever the truth was, modern mages weren't able to understand his magic, let alone replicate it.

The heart did look like a jewel, or perhaps a jewel encased in amber. The core was too bright to see in any detail, but the amber yolk around it dulled the core's emission. The whole thing was suspended in midair by dozens of tentacle-like arteries that snaked upward or downward, latching onto other vital components inside the mech. They were filled with a golden ichor whose recipe had been lost in time. The ichor circulated the heart's magic in the same way that blood fed oxygen to a human body.

While she hung on the ladder, Rowan's mech hand was already assessing the problem. It sent its knack along the iron railing, into the gears and through the ichor-filled cables, but she already knew what the assessment would be.

Talos's heart was failing. The ichor would stop flowing, and the jewel of New Torwood would fall.

It was Rowan's worst nightmare. She could repair any of the mechanics. She could replace the pneumatic pumps and broken cogs. She could grease Talos's joints to keep them gliding smoothly, or add new rivets when old ones rusted. But she couldn't replace his heart.

She watched it for several minutes. After her eyes adjusted, she wondered if she was overreacting. The light was dimmer, but the heart seemed to be functioning properly. She could hear the hydraulics pumping ichor. Her mech hand picked up some unstable vibrations, but it was probably just a loose gear.

The core at the center of the heart suddenly surged with light. It pulsed pure white, once, twice and again. Then between one of Talos's footfalls and the next, everything went black and silent. Rowan's own heartbeat seemed too loud in her ears. The darkness was as thick as ink. Something deep within Talos shuddered and the amber sac around the heart bloomed with light once again, brighter now.

Talos's stalled foot fell, and he continued his never-ending journey around New Torwood.

Rowan shut her eyes for a moment and thanked the saints of Jupiter who watched over all things mech. It was just a ley-line surge. She studied the heart for several minutes but it seemed no worse for wear. In fact, the surge of ley-line magic seemed to have returned the heart to its usual healthy glow.

Crisis averted.

She descended the ladder, looking for loose rivets and gears that needed grease, and was appalled at the state of her beloved Talos. Rivets were missing all along the outer casing. Songbirds had taken advantage of these holes to bring in nesting material that gummed up the mechanical workings. The gear near his left knee squealed, a sound that only came from metal grinding against metal.

Had the keepers even bothered with the maintenance list she'd left them? Apparently not.

She set to work cleaning, greasing and repairing what she could, but he needed a lot of care. More than she could give in one afternoon.

Two hours later, she mounted the ladder again and let herself out the door on Talos's neck. His slow and steady pace had brought him to the edge of Hightown. She waited until she neared the next keeper tower and leaped the two-foot gap between Talos and the wall.

The council needed to allocate funds to train and properly equip a team of mech mages dedicated to Talos's care. She was so lost in thoughts of how to procure these funds that she didn't see Ferlan until she practically tripped over him. The elf blocked the door to the keeper tower.

Had he run along the wall, chasing Talos this whole time?

"Evani." His arms were crossed over his chest and his brows lowered in irritation.

"I'm sorry, Ferlan. There's really no room for two inside Talos."

He didn't look convinced.

"Oh, come on. It's not like any harm could come to me in there. No one can even reach him."

Ferlan continued to glare.

"Fiiiiine." She drew out the word, sounding peevish even to her own ears. She took a deep breath. "I'm sorry. I won't take off on you again."

Ferlan grunted and stepped aside. Rowan knew she'd get an earful from Minna, but right now, her worry was all for Talos.

How would she convince Atherton and his ministers to spend money on the aging mech?

She needed allies on the council. Chancellor March was firmly on her side. It was time for March to recruit others, starting with Adrian Lind, General of the Keepers and one of two Ministers of Defense. Surely, the man in charge of the city's security would understand the importance of keeping Talos healthy. She could only hope that he wasn't already on Theracine's payroll.

8

RUNNING WILD

As they left the Meadows for the forest, Conall heard Hoyt's pack howl, but they were far away, harassing some other prey. The coyotes weren't afraid of Lydan, but they would only initiate a fight if they were certain of a winning outcome. The cat shifters were the smallest clan, but they had strong voices in the Wildblood Conclave, voices that others listened to. And the coyotes' antics routinely left them one step away from banishment.

He talked as they walked, telling Lydan about Rowan, Squad 54, the dead scientists at the oasis, and their run from the unidentifiable soldiers. He ended with their suspicions about the regent and Minister Wrede building an army of human-controlled gaunts.

Lydan listened to Conall's story without questions until the end. When they stopped at a small creek to drink and fill their canteens, he said, "Sounds like New Torwood is gearing up for war. But with who? The southern cities are the only place to expand their thera market. Doesn't make sense to fight with them."

Conall poured water over his face to wash off the travel dust, then shook droplets off his beard.

"What about when Dowchester and Shythe get tired of paying for their thera? What if they decide to just come and take it?"

Lydan pursed his lips as if sucking on his thoughts. His face was weathered from too many days in the Meadows. Deep lines spread from the outer edges of his eyes as he squinted into the sun.

"An army of monsters would come in handy then, but it isn't right."

"No, it's not." Doubt had been nagging at Conall as he'd told his tale. Now it sat in his stomach like poison.

He'd left Rowan to deal with the council alone. He'd been selfish, putting his needs ahead of hers. And what would this quest bring him anyway? A bit of information about how his brother died? That wouldn't bring Nathan back.

Garou grumbled his opinion, and Conall was starting to agree with him. They should never have left their mate.

"It's a frightening tale," Lydan said. "For you and for the rest of us. Instability in New Torwood will bleed over to the thera mines. Even Durance will feel the effects if New Torwood goes to war with the southerners. Do you think it will come to that?"

"I don't know. It makes no sense to attack scientists from the south. Only time will tell if Dowchester plans to take offense." Conall bent and scooped more water over his face. He desperately wanted a bath, but the creek was too shallow.

They returned to the trail that led into the deep wood. Oak, birch and poplars grew here, but as they headed north, the forest would turn to more coniferous trees. Their feet made no sound on the thick carpet of old leaves. Red squirrels scolded them from the treetops, and the rich smell of pine flung Conall back to his childhood. The dreams that had been plaguing him seemed very close to the surface. He felt like a ghost walking through the silence before a thunderstorm.

The locket suddenly warmed against his chest. He fished it out of his shirt and flicked it open. A message was scrawled on the right side.

Wish I could run with the wolf

To someone else that might seem like an odd sentiment. To Conall it was an anchor that held him to a reality that seemed more and more fragile. He could imagine Rowan standing on her balcony, gazing over the green Meadows. Was she thinking about the days they'd spent walking through it, or the few hours they'd had alone together, hiding in some grotto or other, while they took comfort in each other?

"Your spirit's running wild," Lydan said.

Conall closed the locket and tucked it away. He'd answer Rowan's note later, when he was alone.

"I'm just tired. It's been a long journey."

Lydan gave him a side-eye. "You look like you're used to long journeys."

"I am, but this one's not only a journey made by the feet."

"A pilgrimage is it? You still haven't explained why you're going north," Lydan said.

Conall nodded. He'd been ducking that question.

"While on that mission with Squad 54, an Ebos elder invited me to visit Benni. Said he had a message from Misha."

Lydan's expressive eyebrows rose, widening his eyes. The names that shifters gave their beasts weren't exactly secret, but they were private. Only family and close friends were introduced to them. Certainly, no one outside of Durance would have reason to know the name of Nathan's wolf.

"So you're chasing ghosts," Lydan said. "To what purpose?"

"I don't know." Conall ran his hand over his beard. It was hot and itchy. "Only that the rangers never gave me a solid explanation for his death."

"And that nags at you."

"It does."

"So you're going to travel to the end of the world to find a village that no human or shifter has ever seen, on the off-chance that the elves might know how your brother died?"

Conall let out a rough laugh. "When you say it out loud, it sounds foolish."

"It *is* foolish." Lydan shook his head. "But I would do the same for my brother."

They walked the rest of the way mostly in silence. Conall wasn't the only one chasing ghosts. The crease between Lydan's brows deepened the closer they got to Black River. His family had been allies of Conall's Clan for generations. They met every year at Briar Market where the Wildbloods traded goods and produce before the long winter. Lydan had been engaged to Conall's sister Ianna before she died, and Conall suspected he was reliving his own memories.

They made good time, stopping only once at a Holt Clan homestead. The foxes mostly kept to themselves, but they welcomed Lydan as a respected friend and gave them food and shelter. Despite the luxury of an actual bed,

Conall slept fitfully, and they were on the road again as soon as the short night ended.

The fall meetup at Briar Market was only weeks away and some families were already making the slow trek south to secure a spot at the trading post. Every time they crossed paths with travelers, whether they be foxes, wolves or cats, they would nod respectfully to Lydan and glance warily at Conall. Several shifters greeted Lydan as "Warden Lydan," a rank that meant the lion was an elder on the Wildblood Conclave.

"You've made a solid reputation for yourself," Conall said. "I didn't think you'd ever take up politics."

"Politics has nothing to do with governing."

"Sounds like something a politician would say."

Lydan grunted. A few minutes later, he said, "You know, when you left, you were just a kid. So was I."

Conall nodded. Lydan was six years older, and to sixteen-year-old Conall he'd seemed as adult as all the others who tried to tell him what to do. But looking back at those last days at home, he realized that Lydan had been a kid too. A scared, angry, heartsick kid.

"After…Ianna," Lydan only stumbled briefly over her name, "I went north. Far north. I took over my grandfather's old trapping route. Stayed up there for a year."

"Alone?"

"Alone." Lydan gave him a crooked grin. "I had a lot to think about. A lot to sort out."

"And did you? Sort it out?" Conall couldn't fathom the idea. What was there to sort out? The wardens of the Wildblood Conclave had murdered Ianna. Murdered her and never been held accountable.

Lydan's tone was gruff. "I decided that the conclave wasn't evil, just lazy. And afraid. They feared the backlash if they let Ianna go free. They were weak."

He let that idea sit between them for a beat. "And I decided that what happened to Ianna should never happen again."

Conall closed his eyes, trusting Garou's senses to keep him from stumbling for a few seconds while he processed Lydan's words. He opened them again and said, "So you became a warden."

"I did. It took me ten years."

"And things are different now?"

Lydan shot him a sideways glance. "I'm working on it."

Conall's grunt didn't hide his derision. He believed in Lydan's intentions. He just didn't believe that the pack of elders who'd sat in judgment of his sister would ever admit their wrongdoing. Lydan heard the skepticism in Conall's grunt.

"It's not about revenge or retaliation, little brother. It's about moving forward the right way."

Conall felt his chest tighten when Lydan called him "little brother." When he'd been with Ianna, Lydan had used that moniker to tease Conall, knowing he hated it. Now, it only made him sad for the family that might have been.

Garrett West had been clan chief of the Black River Clan since before Ianna was born. The other wolves respected his reputation for tough but fair judgments when they brought quarrels before him. He'd had a dark side though, and after Conall's mother died, Garrett's anger festered. His addiction worsened, and along with the alcohol, he began ingesting thera. He'd never had a sunny personality, but suddenly even sober Garrett was unmanageable. His moods swung from mania to depression without warning. His default state was belligerence. The wolves started to avoid Garrett. The Reavers took advantage of this weakness and raided homesteads along the edge of Black River holdings.

Twice, Ianna appealed to the wardens. Twice they rejected her claim that Garrett was unfit to rule the clan. Nathan couldn't take it any longer. He'd always been the sensitive one and Garrett picked on him the most. As soon as he turned eighteen, he made plans to go to New Torwood City.

On the day he left, he apologized to Conall.

"I'm sorry. I know he'll turn his eye to you now. But if I stay, I will kill him."

Those were the last words his brother had spoken to him, and they'd been oddly prophetic. A year later Ianna, not Nathan, had been forced to carry out that threat, when Garrett came after Conall in a thera-induced rage.

In front of the wardens, Ianna pleaded self-defense. She had the wounds to prove it because when she'd intervened, Garrett had turned his anger on her. But the elders claimed she'd made a dominance play. They believed Garrett's supporters who'd whispered that Ianna had killed her father in order to take over as chief of the Black River Clan.

Dominance fights had been outlawed by the first Wildblood Conclave.

In the early days after the Resurgence, when shifters left the cities to settle in Durance, dominance fights had been common, and they'd torn the clans apart. Divided, the shifters were weak and easy targets for roaming marauders and packs of gaunts. So the Wildblood Conclave was formed and the first law they passed was to outlaw fights to the death. Changes in clan leadership had to be approved by the Conclave.

They made an example of Ianna, and under the midnight sun after her sentencing, they executed her and left her bones in the Meadows for the scavengers. It was their final insult. No one could claim her, even in death.

As they crossed into Black River lands, these memories bombarded Conall. His childhood had been shaped by his father's drunken rages, but there were other memories too. Good ones. And they haunted this place no less than the nightmares.

By the time they were walking up the road to his old homestead, Conall was rethinking the wisdom of this visit. There was nothing left for him here, and his first look at the house confirmed it.

INTERLUDE

Their father had been drinking again. Conall could see it in the mad glow in his eyes. Why didn't Nathan see it? Why did his brother push and push?

Conall hid in the hallway while they argued. His eyes roamed up the dark stairs to his mother's room, but she wouldn't come out to stop the fighting. She was too sick. Ianna said that mother wasn't sick, that she had lost a baby, but that made no sense to Conall. Baby Bea wasn't lost. They'd placed flowers on her grave that morning. Not Mum, of course. She hadn't left her bedroom in weeks. Conall wondered if Mum was the one who was lost. When he'd asked Ianna about that, she had only sighed in that way that said he was too little to understand.

And where was Ianna?

His sister had gone to trade with their nearest neighbors, the Bormans. If she wasn't back before dark, father would be mad. *More* mad.

"I am old enough to hunt with the clans!" Nathan yelled. "My knack can help too. Father, you have to bring me!"

"Don't tell me what I have to do, you insolent pup!"

The sound of flesh hitting flesh made Conall wince. He ducked back into the shadows.

Nathan always goaded Father. Conall didn't understand why. It was so much easier to keep silent and wait out Garrett's fits. But Nathan couldn't do it. Something in him longed for their father's approval, so he sought out his company, asked questions, tried to be noticed.

It never ended well.

There was a long silence from the great room and Conall dared to peek from behind the stairs.

Nathan looked small standing beside their father. Garrett's face had turned a deep purple. His fist came up and he grabbed Nathan's throat.

"How does your pathetic knack help me?" Garrett snarled. "Show me, pup."

Garrett lifted him until only Nathan's toes touched the floor. Nathan gurgled. Conall's fists clenched. He was going to strangle Nathan. He'd be sorry for it tomorrow, like he always was—weeping about how he shouldn't have hurt them. But he did. And tomorrow it would be too late.

Conall jumped out of the shadows.

"Leave him alone!" He dashed across the room and pummeled Garrett with his fists. Rage blinded him. Snot streamed from his nose. His father's free hand swatted him and he tumbled backward on the hard floor.

He scrambled to his feet, ready to attack again, but Garrett suddenly crumpled to the floor. Nathan fell in a clatter of elbows and knees. His fingers clawed at his throat as he gurgled for air.

Ianna stood over them, gripping the iron fire poker. She let it drop to the floor with a dull clang.

Nathan scuttled backward, putting distance between him and their father.

"Is he…is he dead?" Nathan's voice was rough, like when he'd had that bad sore throat last fall.

Ianna crouched over Garrett. She pressed two fingers to his throat and shook her head.

"No such luck. Even hell doesn't want that bastard." She looked to Nathan. "Are you okay?"

He nodded. "I think so."

"What did you say to him?"

"Nothing! I just asked about the hunt next week."

Ianna sighed. "Why can't you just leave him be when he gets like this?"

Conall tuned out the argument between his brother and sister. It was an old one.

He scooted on his butt until he was right beside his father, and peered at his face. Garrett's mouth hung slack, and the harsh lines around his eyes had relaxed. He looked…fragile. It would be a moment's work to lean over, cover his nose and mouth, and just hang on until the breath stopped.

While his siblings argued and his mother wept upstairs, Conall had the first epiphany of his young life.

His father wasn't a monster. He was just a man.

9

ECHOING BONES

Built by Conall's great-grandfather, the clan house of the Black River wolves had stood for over a hundred years. It was big enough to hold their large family and a handful of guests. In its heyday, the manor was always full. Wolves and other shifters were welcomed when passing through. If they couldn't fit in the house, there was an overflow camp along the river, only a short walk through the trees. Some of Conall's best memories were the times when the camp was full of laughter and games. Those visits had evaporated in the last years, when Garrett's temper became legendary.

Giant red pines, poplars and one prized maple towered above the roof, shading the house in the summer and protecting it from winter winds. In the years since Conall had left, the branches had closed around the structure, making it part of their world.

"I can't believe it's still empty," Conall said.

"Your father cast a big shadow. Some say the place is cursed." Lydan squinted at the upper windows as if looking for life inside. "Give them a generation to forget, then someone will claim it."

Conall didn't know how he felt about that. For the first eight years of his life he'd been happy here. After that, it became filled with sadness and anger.

"Maybe it's best to let it fall down." He felt Lydan's hand gently squeeze his shoulder.

"Take your time, little brother. I'll head to the camp and see if I can lure some fish from the river."

Conall nodded and listened until the sound of Lydan's footsteps faded. He studied the house. The boarded-up windows seemed like blackened eyes watching him in return. The place was eerily silent. Not a ruffle of wind to stir the leaves. No crickets. No birds.

Leaving his pack beside the porch, he walked around the yard. Years of fallen pine needles carpeted the ground and muted his footsteps. He inspected the foundation and the roof line. The house looked solid enough, but too many winters had eroded the stonework around the chimney and it was one strong gust away from crumbling.

The gardens that Ianna had kept in memory of their mother were overgrown. On the far side of the house, a sapling grew through a broken board on the wrap-around porch and vines smothered the railing. A porch board creaked balefully as he mounted the steps.

He approached the front door, careful to avoid rotten planks, and tugged on the door handle. It was locked. He moved on to the bay window. One of the wood slats covering the glass had been chewed by a rodent. He tugged on it and the board snapped in his hands, revealing a broken pane of glass in a rotting frame. A few more tugs had the rest of the boards off. He used one to punch out the glass, and he unlatched the window. It creaked as it swung inward.

Conall stepped over the sill into what his mother used to call the great room. It was a long, wide room where his father heard petitions from clan members. A rustic table sat in one corner. The rest of the furniture was gone, but Conall remembered it. A couch and chair had been clustered around the hearth. On holidays, a feast would be spread on trestle tables along the far wall and smaller tables with chairs were laid out for dining. Later, the room was cleared for dancing.

The empty space echoed with ghostly shouts and laughter.

Conall spied the shadows of two small boys crouched by the hearth. Uncle Birch had brought a bag of marbles from his travels to the southern cities. Conall and Nathan spent hours winging the glass marbles across the great hall's floor, until Garrett tripped on one and confiscated the whole bag. And then beat Nathan for the transgression.

He remembered Garrett asleep on the couch after a clan party, and Ianna daring to pluck away the tumbler of honey wine before it fell to the floor. Mother darning socks before the hearth, humming a quiet song while two wolf pups slept by her feet. Rowdy clan parties and calm evenings when Garrett was away.

All these memories—good and bad—seemed like they were from another life.

The only light came from the broken window, and the hearth at the end of the room was lost in shadow. Conall remembered it was tall enough to stand in and wide enough to roast a boar. On cold winter nights, Conall, Nathan and Ianna had curled up on the warm hearthstones. Nathan would tell stories about far off places. He said he read them in books, but Conall always suspected he made them up.

He turned toward the foyer and the staircase that led up to the bedrooms. A stain on the hardwood floor below the stairs caught his eye. He walked over and rubbed a toe across the blackened floorboards. Garou let out a low rumble as if his hackles were raised. It was Conall's blood. In a rage, Garrett had let out his wolf to attack his son. Conall still had the scars on his upper arm from where his father's fangs had pierced him.

At the time, Conall had been more upset about the stain than the wound. No amount of scrubbing could remove it from the floor. He remembered fuming about it, raging not at his father but at his mother. Why had she died and left him alone to deal with the stain? She would have known how to get blood out of hardwood, but then, if his mother had lived, there wouldn't have been blood spilled in the foyer.

He moved on to the kitchens. The old wood stove remained and the scarred butcher block, but the rest was gone. Sold, scavenged, or given away.

His feet led him right to the pantry. He should have known that he'd end up there. A few bits of broken crockery sat on the pantry shelves, but he ignored those and pulled open the cellar door to reveal stairs. He descended into blackness so complete, it seemed to suck in the only bit of light.

Every creak of the wooden steps was familiar. His feet hit stone and he crouched in the darkness.

The cellar was more of a crawlspace, dug only four feet deep. Conall remembered the first time he'd banged his head on the ceiling. It had taken him by surprise. He'd grown too tall to stand up in the space. Now, as he sat, darkness clawed at his chest and a moment of claustrophobia seized him.

Garou pined for the open Meadows. His whine shivered along Conall's nerves. His breathing quickened, until he closed his eyes and ordered his wolf and his heart to be calm.

After a few moments, the feel of damp cobblestones under his legs anchored him. The smell of earth pressed all around him became a comfort instead of a prison. He lay on his back letting the old memories simply be. There were ghosts here that needed pacifying. Perhaps that was the real reason he'd undertaken this journey.

The darkness was so complete, he couldn't see his hand in front of his face, but he reached backward until his fingers hit the wall. There. Right where he'd known they would be. Nathan's runes still marked their little haven. Salus, the snake god, protector of the innocent. Conall had no idea if the runes had ever been effective, but they'd lived through those years—lived long enough to get away.

He let his hand drop. He didn't know how long he lay on that cold ground in the unfathomable blackness. Garou's worried whine finally brought him back. He sat up. His bones ached from the damp and cold.

I'm too old for this shit, he thought. Garou didn't disagree.

Conall crawled to the far end of the cellar and felt along the floor for that one loose cobble. He had to work at it, scraping away years of dirt and debris, but finally, the stone wiggled. He pried it up with his knife and reached into the hole.

It was still there. A small square tin. He hefted it in his hand. It was heavy for something so small and it rattled when he shook it.

He pocketed the tin, then climbed out of the cellar.

There was nothing else he needed here.

They slept at the camp. Conall preferred the open air, and for the first time in days, his sleep had been undisturbed by dreams.

He rose with the sunrise. Lydan was snoring on his bedroll beside the cold campfire. Conall stoked it with fresh wood and went to check out the camp shed. His old fishing pole leaned against the wall next to a stack of chairs and a folding table. He ignored the pang of nostalgia that hit him when he went through the simple routine of checking the rod and loading the hook with bait.

Standing on the banks of Black River with the current tugging on his line, he felt something ease inside him. The piercing calls of the red-winged blackbirds were the soundtrack of his childhood. The summer sun warmed his back, softening muscles that were always bunched, ready to run or to fight. He even found himself whistling a tune his grandfather had taught him, a song about a young pup who follows the scent of rabbit and gets lost in the woods. At the time, he'd thought the pup was plain stupid. How could one get lost in their own forest? But now he knew that there were many forests in the world and not all roads led home.

He was glad this one had.

After throwing back an undersized trout and catching four more, he reeled in his line, then stripped off his clothes and dunked himself in the icy water, thoroughly soaking his hair. He scratched at his beard, wishing he'd packed a razor. A memory flitted across his thoughts—Rowan's fingers exploring his jawline in the dark after he'd shaved for the first time upon their return from the Meadows. He let the memory linger for a moment, then tucked it carefully away, like something precious.

He shook out his wet mane before donning a fresh shirt. He had only one spare pair of pants, so he put the old ones back on. No point in getting fancy.

Lydan was up when he returned to camp and had chicory coffee brewing over the fire. He took the fish from Conall and handed him a battered tin mug.

"You caught 'em. I'll do the cooking." Lydan expertly filleted the fish and placed them on a hot rock in the fire.

Conall had tasted real coffee in Dowchester. The southerners raved about it, but he preferred their northern brew. The heat from the mug and the fire warmed him after the cold bath. The fish had sizzled and blackened around the edges. Lydan found tin plates in the shed, and he doled out their breakfast, adding a handful of blackberries to sweeten the trout. They ate in silence, each lost in their memories of this place.

After breakfast, they cleaned the dishes in the river, put out the fire and restocked the wood. Unlike the manor house, the camp hadn't been scavenged and Conall realized that clan members still stayed there when they passed through the area.

"I'd like to visit my mother before we leave," he said.

Lydan's lowered brows made him look stern, but he nodded and followed Conall up the path toward the family cemetery. The trail was almost overgrown but deer and other woodland creatures had kept it clear enough to pass.

A few minutes later they entered a clearing. The morning sun filtered through the trees, filling the family cemetery in golden light. The grass was overgrown, but this late in the summer it had dried and shriveled to leave the grave markers exposed. A large stone wolf sat in the middle of the yard. His muzzle was raised to howl at the moon. Graves were ranged around this monument, with the oldest at the front and newer ones near the tree line. Conall's eye immediately went for a large headstone near the back. He remembered the day he and his father had hauled that stone into place over his mother's grave. They'd buried her next to the babies she'd lost.

An unfamiliar stone sat beside his mother's. It wasn't large or fancy. His father's name and the year of his death were etched into its face.

He turned to Lydan. "Who?"

"I did."

"But he killed Ianna." It wasn't true, not logically, but Conall would always blame Garrett for Ianna's death.

"Still he was your father. *Her* father. And pack chieftain. I felt his…passing needed to be noted somehow, because I couldn't…" He let the thought trail away, but Conall wasn't willing to let it go.

"Because you couldn't mark Ianna's passing."

Lydan's head hung low. "No, I couldn't."

Execution wasn't the only punishment for those who defied the ban on dominance fighting. By law, an offender's corpse was not returned to the family. It was given to the Meadows, where the ravens, jackals and vultures would strip the flesh and scatter the bones. Anyone caught trying to bury it would be sentenced to a year of hard labor.

"But I couldn't let her go either. Look." Lydan pointed to a fourth grave. This one was unmarked except for a small cairn of river stones.

"My father suspected I would go after her and he kept watch over me for a month. When I was finally able to get into the Meadows, there wasn't much left. But Raff had her scent imprinted on his heart." Raff was Lydan's lion. "And we found most of her bones. I brought them here." He crouched and laid a hand on the ground before the pile of stones.

Conall didn't know what to say. Emotions warred within him.

He touched the cairn. "Thank you." Rising, he pulled the rusted tin from his pack. The snowflake motif that had once decorated the box was nearly obliterated by rust. He struggled to pry off the lid.

"What's that?" Lydan peered into the tin.

Conall grinned. "Treasure. Father sold nearly everything we had to feed his addictions, but Ianna managed to hide these." He pulled out a small oval frame, ornately carved from wood. A miniature of a pretty blond woman filled the frame. Cora, his mother, painted in her wedding dress with a bouquet of goldenrod. That, he would keep. The next treasure was a thin gold chain with a gold heart inlaid with tiny diamonds. There was a ring to match. They were pretty and delicate, and had belonged to Cora's mother, Conall's grandmother. Garrett had been furious when he couldn't find them. By that point his addiction had burst the banks of good sense, and he'd already sold off every item of worth in the house.

The last piece in the box was a pocket watch. He flicked it open to reveal brass hands that stood out against an onyx background. A tiny window showed the passing of the moon phases. The entire casing was etched with mage work.

Lydan whistled. "That's a beauty."

"It belonged to my great-grandfather."

He handed it to Lydan, who took the watch and peered at the hands. "It's still ticking!"

"It's a pneuma mech." Conall flipped it over. "See that scrollwork? That's a master mage's work. Not a Harry Hightower, but one of the old masters. It won't stop ticking until the end of time."

Lydan cocked his head. "How do you know so much about mechs?"

"I told you, it was my business to trade stuff like this." He pointed to the watch. "It's a good thing Ianna hid it. Garrett would have never been able to sell it for what it's worth. Not around here."

Lydan handed it back, but Conall stopped him with a hand on his wrist. "It's yours."

Lydan's eyes widened even as he frowned. "What do you mean?"

"I mean that Ianna meant to give it to you on your wedding day. She told me as much."

"No, I can't." Lydan pushed the watch toward him again. Conall shoved it back.

"You can. And you will. Please."

Lydan's lip quivered, and for a moment, Conall thought the big man might cry. Then he wiped his eyes and pocketed the watch. "Thank you." He punched Conall on the shoulder in the universal show of brotherhood. "Now let's get on the road. I want to be home by tomorrow."

10

HOW TO INSULT A PRINCESS

Rowan's maid gaped at her as if she'd grown three heads. The girl held out two dresses—one blue and one pink, and both with long skirts and sleeves covered in intricate embroidery. The pink one had frills.

Saints and sinners. How could anyone wear such contraptions? Neither would do for a trip into Grotto.

"I asked for something simple," Rowan snapped. "Not these…these abominations."

She immediately felt badly when the girl turned red and flustered over a few words that never quite made it out of her mouth. She hadn't actually been able to speak in the princess's presence yet. Rowan sighed. It was only the girl's first day. She should cut her some slack.

Her regular maid was used to Rowan's odd requests for loose pants with many pockets or floppy hats that would hide her red hair. Molly was also a whiz at altering dresses and even men's suits to fit Rowan with a style all her own. But Molly had decided to have another baby, and Mrs. Pickney, the housekeeper of the royal wing, had saddled Rowan with this very young and very timid girl. Rowan hadn't even been able to get a name out of her. When she'd asked, the maid had dropped her eyes and mumbled something inaudible.

Now, because the princess was displeased, the maid looked ready to wet herself.

Rowan tried for a softer tone.

"Just put those away and find me something with less color, and simple lines. No embroidery. Nothing gold. Got it?"

Roger thought she was speaking to him. He spun on his wheels and bumped into the table.

"Roger that!"

Phalian said, "SQUAWK."

The maid put a hand to her mouth to hold in a gasp. Rowan realized she hadn't heard a word of the instructions. She touched her sleeve and the girl jumped like a spooked rabbit.

Jesus, Jupiter and Jocasta. They'd sent her a mouse, not a maid.

"Look in the back right side of the dressing closet. There should be some loose pants and a jacket there."

"Pants, milady?" She raised wide eyes brimming with tears.

"Yes, pants. And find me a blouse to go with them. Something white and without lace."

The girl bounced in a half curtsy and rushed into the dressing room with the gowns clutched to her chest.

Rowan turned her attention back to real problems. Two cachets sat on the table in front of her, holding in their secrets. One had been taken forcibly from Orson, the scribe who'd traveled with Squad 54, and the other from Sandra Kane, the scribe who'd died at the oasis. Orson had said Sandra's cachet was scrambled, its data rendered useless. Rowan didn't believe him. Sandra Kane had spent the last moments of her life trying to hide the mech device. It had to be important.

She turned it over in her hand. The cachet was a flattened sphere of silver with no discernible way to open it. The outer casing was etched with mage runes in a pattern so bewildering, it hurt the eye to behold. The only outlet was a port on one end for a plug. Scribes had a similar port embedded into the base of their skulls, and a wire normally linked scribe and cachet. She held the mech to her own skull, where the port would be.

What did that connection feel like? Was it invasive? Did it hurt when scribes recorded information to the cachet ? What drove a person to the Temple of the Word? What trauma in their lives led them to want to be mutilated in such a way?

Maybe she was looking at it all backwards. Maybe recording to the cachet was like talking to a friend. Maybe being connected gave scribes a feeling of euphoria like taking thera as a drug. She would never know because there was no way she would let anyone plug anything into her skull. She shivered at the thought, but short of having an implant put in her brain, she didn't see how she could decode the information.

After worrying over this problem for weeks, she'd decided there was only one place where she might find what she needed to crack the cachet: the Rustworks. It was a junkyard for discarded mechs. Some of the castoffs dated back to the founding of the city. She'd scrounged for parts there before, but it wasn't a place she went to often or willingly.

Even the Rustworks was a long shot. The Temple of the Word kept their mech mages close and their secrets even closer, but the scribes needed to dump their garbage eventually, and maybe she'd find something compatible with the cachets. She hoped so because she was all out of ideas.

The junkyard lay near the foundations of the city, far underground. She'd have to travel through Grotto to get there, which was why she'd requested the simple clothes. She planned to make the journey later that afternoon.

The suite's main door opened and Minna stepped inside. Ferlan's shift had just ended and Minna was taking over. She gave the room a cursory glance as if there might be assassins hiding behind the curtains. When she was satisfied that the room held no new dangers, she approached Rowan.

"A messenger awaits, Evani."

"From who?"

Minna shrugged. "He wears blue and gold."

That was Dowchester livery. It would be the page from this new ambassador, Remy Padgett. Rowan had invited him for breakfast tomorrow.

"Let him in."

Minna nodded and opened the door.

A young man entered and handed her a note, then waited silently with that thousand yard stare that pages everywhere seemed to perfect.

The note said:

To the most excellent Princess Rowan Andula,

I am humbled and elevated by your invitation to break fast
with you in the morning. However, due to the nature of ambas-

sadorial duties, I am, I regret to say, a late riser. Might I be so forward as to suggest dinner instead?

Your humble servant.

Baron Remy Padgett, Ambassador to Dowchester

Humbled and elevated? Great. Dowchester had sent her yet another walking ego in fancy boots. Ambassadorial duties? Jupiter's ass! He was probably planning to play cogs and crowns and drink all night.

She lowered the letter and stared at the page. Roger rolled past him on some errand that only the valet understood. The page's eyes followed him for a moment before snapping back to Rowan.

"So the ambassador won't disturb his beauty sleep," she said. "Not even for the princess—for the hostess of the house he sleeps in." The page flinched and she regretted her words instantly. Not because he was offended, but because she sounded petulant and he would no doubt report them to his master.

She didn't often play the princess card, but this guy irked her. Even his hand writing was overstated—full of curlicues and swooping lines. And the polish on his snub was that he expected her to drop all her plans for the evening and cater to his whims.

Not that she had any plans, other than reading over a new historical biography that Dale had dropped off, but the ambassador didn't know that. She felt like brushing him off, but after yesterday's visit to Talos, she knew she'd have to face Atherton and the council soon to ask for funds to fix the giant mech. Atherton would block the request simply because it came from her. She needed to make an ally of this ambassador. More allies would give her word more weight in council. And if she could impress upon the ambassador the importance of the giant mech, maybe he would put in a good word with the regent.

"Tell the ambassador that I am sorry he is unable to meet for breakfast. I am busy in the evening, but I will be glad to dine with him tomorrow at The Inn. At two in the afternoon. If that's still too early for his excellency then tell him he needs an alarm mech."

There. She'd set boundaries. She wasn't available at his whim.

The Inn was a well-known hotel in Hightown. It was exclusive, expensive and had terrible food, but most people went there to drink and to be seen. It had the added bonus of a fine balcony that overlooked the city wall and at exactly 2:15 Talos would pass it by, making an excellent conversation starter.

She dismissed the page and returned her attention to the cachets on the table. Minna's lip curled when she saw them. Like all Ebos, Minna's dislike for mechs ran deep. She'd become used to Phalian and Roger, or perhaps she'd only resigned herself to their daily presence, but the sight of cachets never failed to disturb her.

"I'm going to Grotto this afternoon." Rowan's mech fingers closed around Sandra Kane's cachet, sensing the untapped magic in its core.

"Do you plan on trying to evade your escort again?" Minna said.

Rowan put down the cachet and looked at her guard. At her friend. Minna's usual placid affability was gone. Annoyance simmered in her eyes.

"So Ferlan told you. I hope you weren't too hard on him. He did manage to keep up with Talos along the wall. That's no mean feat with all those keepers up there."

"Ferlan is not hollow-ribbed." Minna didn't elaborate on that statement, but Rowan was getting used to her bone-related metaphors. They became more frequent when she was irritated or worried.

"Look, I'll take a keeper with me and I promise not to ditch him."

Minna finally turned. Her lips curved in a sardonic smile. "I am certain you will not *ditch* your escort again, Evani, because I will be that escort."

"That's a really bad idea. I'm going to a mech cemetery."

Minna crossed her arms and glared.

"Don't you understand? It will be full of mechs. A mountain of mechs. You cringe at a couple of cachets. No way am I dragging you to the mech Rustworks."

Minna stood a bit taller and her eyes hardened. "Omika has charged me with your safety, Evani. I would see that duty done right."

Rowan gave up.

"Fine. Let me get dressed and we'll leave."

Minna held her hand.

"First, I will finish my sweep of the rooms."

Rowan sighed. "There's no one here but me and the maid. We've been here all morning."

Minna nodded but continued her inspection. Rowan knew it was easier to let her have her way, though it was ridiculous to think an assassin would attack her in her own suite.

Rowan began packing her bag for the afternoon's excursion. She heard Minna open the door to the dressing chamber and then an unholy scream filled the air.

Roger spun around and bumped into her. "Roger that!" Phalian launched from the mantle with a squawk.

The screaming continued. It rose an octave and the maid blundered out of the dressing room. Minna followed her with a tight grin and Rowan suddenly understood the problem.

When she'd come on shift that morning, the maid had entered from the servant's door at the back of the dressing room. She hadn't seen Ferlan on guard duty outside the main doors of the suite. She'd probably never met an Ebos before, but the stories about the dark elves brewing soup out of children's bones had made an impression.

The maid pointed weakly at Minna who stood with one hand on her hip and a grin on her face. Rowan didn't even notice the bone piercings and adornments anymore. Clearly the maid did. She collapsed in a heap of muffled tears.

Omika had sent Minna and Ferlan to the city to protect the Evani, or so he'd said, but his unspoken agenda was to normalize the idea of Ebos in the city. Clearly they had some work to do.

"Go get Mrs. Pickney," Rowan said. "It looks like I'll need a new maid."

Minna shook her head, then left to find the housekeeper.

Rowan discovered the young maid's name when Mrs. Pickney arrived.

"Alice! Pick yourself up! This isn't a resort where you can lounge around all day, swooning with your girlfriends."

"I think she was frightened by Minna's appearance," Rowan said. "Did no one think to warn her about the Ebos in the palace?"

The housekeeper turned a sharp eye on her. Rowan held in a smirk. Mrs. Pickney was a master at the vague scolding technique—where one asked a generalized question that had a very pointed answer—but she didn't like it turned on her.

"This is none of—" Then she seemed to remember she was speaking to the princess. She sucked the words back and the effort puckered her lips.

Mrs. Pickney was fairly new to her job. The regent had installed her in the royal apartments a few months ago, when the old housekeeper finally retired. At the time, Rowan had been content to let Atherton choose her staff. Now she wondered about that decision. At best, Atherton had chosen Mrs. Pickney for her sour personality. At worst, Mrs. Pickney was a spy for the council.

She made a mental note to go over staffing with Dale as soon as possible. They'd probably need to get Chancellor March in on that discussion.

Mrs. Pickney smoothed down the front of her steel-gray dress though it looked ironed to perfection.

"I apologize for Alice's poor judgment." Mrs. Pickney glared at Alice like she was a cockroach that dared to invade the royal chambers. "She is clearly too young for such a demanding post. I will rectify the situation immediately. She'll spend some weeks in the scullery. Maybe she can find sense at the bottom of a pot."

Rowan stifled a protest. If Mrs. Pickney had a mind to, she could put Alice out on the street without a reference. Alice sniffled and cringed when the housekeeper tugged her to her feet and marched her from the room.

"I apologize if my presence has disturbed you, Evani." Minna stood by the dressing room door like a soldier at parade rest.

"It's not your fault. I don't even need a maid, but Mrs. Pickney is a stickler for the proper forms. Just do me a favor and try to find out where poor Alice ends up. I want to be sure they don't dismiss her."

Minna nodded. "Yes, Evani. Do we leave for this Rustworks now? I have preparations to make."

"Of course. Give me ten minutes to dress."

"Yes, Evani."

It took Rowan much longer than ten minutes because she found her dressing room in disarray. It seemed that Alice hadn't been able to find anything suitable for the princess to wear and dresses were piled on every chair. Rowan ignored them all and went for the farthest closet where she kept her work clothes. Either Alice hadn't seen the closet or she'd deemed the worn pants and shirts unacceptable. Rowan would have to train her new maid from the ground up so this didn't happen again.

She chose a pair of dark pants that had many pockets and an unbleached cotton blouse with a leather vest to go over it. The pockets meant she could leave her tool belt behind and still carry everything needed for digging through the junkyard. A wide-brimmed hat completed the outfit. Her hair was starting to grow out after she'd chopped it off earlier in the summer. Left loose it was long enough to touch her shoulders and the fiery red color would make her stand out in a crowd. Instead, she twirled it into a knot and tucked it under the hat.

Back in her sitting room, she filled her many pockets with tools—a screwdriver, pliers and a hammer with grips custom built for her small hands. She tucked Sandra Kane's cachet into a pocket too, but left Orson's behind. She didn't want to weigh herself down, and splitting them up was also a safety precaution. The cachets were her best chance of solving the murders at the oasis. If something happened, she didn't want to lose both of them.

But nothing is going to happen, she assured herself. She was simply going to walk through the most dangerous neighborhood in the city—a neighborhood where even the keepers wouldn't patrol—and then scrounge through a rat-infested mountain of broken mechs until she found something capable of accessing the information on the cachet.

As easy as threading a sunbeam through a needle.

Minna had been making her own preparations. She had a small chest of what she deemed essential magics in the sitting room. Rowan watched her take several pouches from the chest and tuck them into the folds of her robe.

"What are those for?"

"Precautions, Evani. Should you be wounded in this boneyard I would have supplies to heal you."

"No one's getting wounded."

"Yes, Evani." Minna's eyes were hooded, her gaze steady.

"Also, I should warn you that Grotto is underground. Some people find it…disconcerting."

"I assure you I have no trouble being underground. Where you go, I go, Evani."

"Fine. Let's hurry. If I'm going to meet that pompous ambassador tomorrow, I want to have time to go over the new highway proposal."

She headed out the door. Phalian swooped under the lintel with a clack of wings. Roger zoomed after them and banged into the door jamb.

Rowan turned. "You should stay here." She pointed to the corner of the room.

"Roger that!"

But when she turned for the door again, the little valet followed.

"I said stay!"

Maybe she was anthropomorphizing, but his oxidized copper eyes seemed to plead with her.

"Oh, all right. Come along. Maybe we can find something to replace your missing arm."

11

ALL ROADS LEAD DOWN

MECH BIRDS WERE RARE. COLLECTORS of fine mechs like Dr. Renata might have a dipping bird that mimed drinking from a glass, or a clock with a cuckoo, but Phalian was the only flying mech bird she knew of, so Rowan admonished him to stay in his mouse form and hide in her pocket as they headed into the city.

Roger trundled along behind her, exclaiming, "Roger that!" at every new sight, but valets were everywhere on the streets and he got less attention than Minna. The crowd parted around the Ebos. She seemed to prefer that since she could more easily see an attack coming, but Rowan didn't like the gasps and slurs thrown their way, and she glared down more than one goggle-eyed looky-lou.

Rowan didn't get out of Hightown often and she enjoyed the sights—the diversity of people, the mech graffiti and even the peddlers who called to them from every street corner.

She stopped only once, at Temple Jupiter.

Religion had collapsed during the Resurgence and the Dark Age that followed. People had believed in gods, but those gods abandoned them to overwhelming and destructive magic. They were never forgiven.

The city's founders had forbidden divine worship within its walls. Some of the old religions adapted by demoting their deities to saints. New religions popped up after the Resurgence to pay homage to people who did great things during the Dark Age, such as the healer Jocasta.

Temples were founded to revere these new saints, but the city's charter outlined strict rules that all religions must focus on good works. Worship for

89

the sake of worship was banned. Temples must serve the people, rather than have people serve them. The Temple of Jesus fed the poor. Jocasta's healed the sick. Jupiter's temple dedicated itself to industry and innovation, helping small businesses and artisans flourish in the new city. Offshoots of Jupiter specialized, such as the Temple of the Word that trained scribes or Temple Vulcan for mech mages.

As the years passed, the temples grew in wealth and influence. Guilds paid a tithe to Jupiter. New businesses required permits to open shops. Mech mages paid steep fees for their apprenticeships. All this money was meant to go back into the city, to sponsor new business growth. It didn't always work that way. Sometimes the money went to frivolities that glorified the saints.

Temple Jupiter was a good example of such opulence. As Rowan passed the graceful marble columns of the main building, with its manicured gardens and dozens of animated mech statuaries, it was hard to remember that the temple's origins had been humble. Minna eyed the abundance of frivolous mechs with a hooded expression. Rowan stopped to marvel at the famous Jupiter Water Clock. Phalian peeked out of her pocket. For once, Roger stopped his constant jerky movements and gazed at the structure with huge eyes.

Carved from marble, Jupiter towered over the square. His bearded face was tipped toward the sun. One hand cradled a scepter shaped like a lightning bolt. The other arm held a series of twelve metal bowls that seemed to be spilling from his grip. Water filled the first bowl and trickled down with a delicate sound like rain. When the second bowl filled, a mech eagle would pop up to signal the hour. Then it would tip into the third bowl. When that bowl filled, an oak tree suddenly blossomed. The fourth bowl produced a charging bull, and so on.

Rowan's fascination with mechs had begun in childhood when her father brought her to watch the priest mages clean and test the water clock. It was the only time one could see all twelve of the mechs pop up in unison.

She was in a hurry, but she stopped to wait anyway. It was nearly eleven in the morning. A small crowd had gathered as they always did a few minutes before any hour chimed. The crowd's attention was fixated on the water clock, but a murmur rippled through the watchers and a few fingers pointed at Minna. She stalwartly ignored them, so Rowan did too.

Water dripped from the second-to-last bowl making it teeter. With each drip, it tilted farther, until the water sloshed over its side into the last bowl. At the same moment a metal lion popped up from the base of the statue. Its mane was made of overlapping petals of copper and silver. It pawed the air and opened its mouth. A roar like the grinding of a rusty organ emerged, then the lion sank down to its den beneath the statue again.

The crowd cheered. Rowan couldn't help but grin. She glanced at Minna, curious about her reaction to the mech.

Minna shrugged. "About as useful as an eleventh toe."

Rowan hid a grin. Minna could deny it, but she was starting to like city life.

They left Hightown, wound through the streets and passed the market in Old Bailey. By the time they reached Squall's End, people's curiosity about the dark elf dwindled. Residents of Squall's End minded their own business.

Bretta's new ale house, The Glass Boot, was only a couple of blocks away. Rowan realized that she hadn't visited Bretta in over two weeks. Denny, the stray Squad 54 had picked up in the Meadows, worked as a busboy in the tavern. He was hiding until it was safe for him to emerge and tell his story. More guilt weighed her down. Denny was relying on her to bring the murderers of his colleagues to justice. Until then, his life was on hold.

She glanced toward The Glass Boot. The corner of the building was just visible from this distance. The best thing she could do for Denny now was find some way to access the cachet. She turned away from the alehouse.

The entrance to Grotto was a nondescript garage. During the day, the door was rolled up and two old men sat on rickety chairs beside it, smoking thera pipes. They didn't stop anyone from entering, but their eyes were sharp and they took note of everyone who came and went.

The smell hit her as soon as they entered the first tunnel—ammonia, rotting garbage and human waste. It was overpowering. She pulled a scarf over her nose. Minna's expression turned sour.

"You should not go in there, Evani."

"I have to. You can stay here if you like."

She headed into the darkness, knowing Minna would follow.

The sounds of a large crowd going about their daily business floated up from the tunnel ahead, and soon it widened into a market laneway with carts and small shops lining each side.

Minna stopped Rowan with a hand on her sleeve.

"Vorha, Evani."

"Vorha?" Rowan frowned trying to remember the Essian word.

"Yes, there is deep magic in this place. Dark magic." She dug into the supplies on her belt for a leather pouch, indicated that Rowan should hold out her hand, and poured a small amount of dried herbs into her palm.

"Chew this, but don't swallow. Keep it in your cheek until we leave this place."

"What is it?"

"We call it *surrow*. Good for blocking magic. It won't help with a full on assault, but it will temper any passive magic."

"Passive magic?"

"Magic that loosens the tongue, lowers inhibitions, or steals memories. It needs no trigger to work, but lingers on the air. A dirty trick used by market vendors to influence customers and sway the bargaining in their favor."

"Right."

Rowan had no intention of bargaining, but she didn't like the idea of unseen magic affecting her. She stuffed the herb into her mouth and chewed. Her tongue tingled and made extra saliva. She swallowed down the juice that tasted faintly like rosemary, then tucked the wad of chewed herb into her cheek.

Feeling somewhat protected, she took an interest in the ramshackle shops lining the lane that wound downward in a sweeping spiral. Here were the merchants who couldn't afford to pay permit fees to Jupiter. The shops were filled with black market goods. Homesteaders sold vegetables grown outside the city walls and smuggled in without paying duties. Second rate mages sold refurbished mechs. Rag pickers had tables mounded with assorted old clothes. One merchant traded used thera chips for new ones with a ten-to-one ratio. The old chips were no good for fueling mechs, but they'd be ground into powder and sold to thera addicts.

All this trade went on without sanctions from the temples or the palace.

Everyone knew the market existed, but authorities turned a blind eye because it would cost more in manpower to clear out Grotto than it did in lost permit revenues. And the market would simply pop up somewhere else. At least here, the underground neighbors kept to themselves and the crime, poverty and sickness were confined.

Rowan had been to Grotto before, but she'd never looked at it from a governor's perspective. These people needed help. There were no sewers here and waste was thrown into the street, adding to the stench. She stepped over more than one questionable pile of oozing debris. Children wearing little or no clothing ran among the carts. Vendors watched with sharp glares, their faces lined and tired. Some bore wounds that Rowan suspected came from the last gaunt uprising—missing arms and legs or thick scars across the face. Some coughed. Some had weeping sores. All were skeleton thin.

She passed an old woman hunched on a stool before a small table. A fat unlit candle sat on the table next to a pile of worn augury cards. The woman was wrapped in layers of shawls to protect against the chill. She wore an eye patch over a scar that ran from her brow to her chin. The other eye was dark and sharp with intelligence.

"Would you know your future, girl?" Her voice hissed like fire on wet wood.

Rowan hesitated. Part of her wanted to know what lay ahead, but what if the old woman predicted her defeat at the hands of Atherton? What if she never regained her family's seat and honor? Would the crone's words cripple her efforts and cast a shadow over her daring plans?

She shook her head and hurried on. Better not to know.

A glass merchant came after the fortune teller, a tired-looking woman who stood behind a table laden with old glass bottles. Her eyes were wary, flicking from Rowan to Minna and back again. Two children crouched under the table. The whites of their eyes contrasted starkly with their dirty faces. There were many such hungry faces in Grotto.

A new and unfamiliar feeling roiled in Rowan's gut. Shame.

These were her people, the people her family was supposed to protect. What good were trade agreements with foreign ambassadors when the people of New Torwood starved in the dark? Rowan pulled her hat lower on her brow, hoping no one would recognize her as the heir to the throne that had forgotten them.

The market lane continued in its downward helix, but they turned off at a small intersection and headed into one of the many underground caverns that had been excavated by the city's founders. The walls were rough stone. The cavern was lit by several thera lamps, but these did little to fill the big space with light. Dozens of families squatted here. Privacy partitions of hanging blankets sectioned off individual camps. All eyes watched them as they walked the narrow path.

It had been a few years since Rowan came this way, and she didn't remember seeing the poverty and despair that she witnessed today.

"Roger that!" The valet bumped into a woman who lay under a bundle of blankets. She cursed him and he turned, wheels spinning into another camp. Rowan grabbed the mech and turned him toward the tunnel at the far end of the cavern. Then they were heading downward again. Many of the thera chips had burned out in the lamps here and the way was only partially lit.

"Reminds me of home," Minna said quietly. Rowan shot her a sharp look. The elf shrugged one shoulder. "Benni is much dryer and it smells better."

"You must be appalled to see our people living in such a place. I'm disgusted. Now that I see it again, I think all of Grotto should be wiped clean."

"That would be worse for those people, Evani. Then they would be poor *and* homeless."

"Maybe."

"Great leaders don't make sweeping changes. They build infrastructure and let the changes happen."

Rowan huffed out a laugh. "Then clearly I'm not a great leader because I have no idea how to fix something like Grotto."

Minna stopped her and gripped her hands. The elf's gaze was intense.

"Where a good leader plants bone, a legacy of strength takes root. You are a great leader, Evani. Time will test you, and time will tell."

Rowan felt unreasonable tears prickle her eyes. She squeezed Minna's hands. "Thank you. I hope to live up to your confidence in me one day."

They'd come to a crossroads.

"I guess my first test is to find the right road to the Rustworks," Rowan said. She looked left then right. Both tunnels were dark and unwelcoming. The last time she'd been here, she'd come with an off-duty keeper as a guide. He'd known the way because his uncle was a mech mage and taken him to scavenge the Rustworks when he was a child. She spotted a small face carved into the wall. The keeper had told her to look for those.

"This is it." Rowan traced the carving with a finger. It was boxy with antennas sprouting from its head. "Is it just me or does this look like Roger?"

"Roger that!" The valet zoomed forward, bumped into the wall and ran over Minna's foot. The elf swore in Essian and tried to kick the mech, but Roger had already spun away.

They headed down the left tunnel. There were no lamps of any kind here and Rowan asked Roger to light the way. His eyes sparked then glowed. As he trundled along the uneven road, his lamps filled the tunnel with light.

Phalian poked his head from Rowan's pocket, saw they were still underground and retreated. Poor Phalian, he never liked enclosed spaces. Rowan could accept the darkness and the narrow tunnel as long as she didn't let her mind linger on the tons of rock piled above her head.

Minna stopped and listened to the road behind them.

"What's the matter?" Rowan asked.

"I want to be sure we aren't followed."

"Don't worry, no one comes this way. At least no one but a few desperate mech mages. The mechs down here have been stripped of their thera chips and anything useful to the average person."

Minna grunted. She didn't seem excited about that news.

They began to see the first hints of mech debris—heaps of scrap metal bundled like tumbleweeds, broken crates, and an abandoned vehicle stripped down to its metal frame.

The tunnel widened, then gave way to a vast underground cavern. The light from Roger's eyes didn't penetrate far enough to see its end. The stench that permeated the upper markets lessened here, but a new smell hit them. It was hot like burning metal and had a tang of sulfur. Discarded mechs seemed to be piled haphazardly, but a narrow trail snaked through them. It reminded Rowan of the maze inside the Warren. A shudder ran through her. They'd faced gaunts in that warren. Hopefully there wouldn't be anything bigger than rats down here.

Minna scanned the field of mech refuse with a look of distaste on her face. "A boneyard without bones."

Rowan's mech fingers tingled. She fisted and flexed them. "A resting place for old magic. Can't you feel it?"

"Unnatural magic. We call it *hooroo*. It is magic without the coho-ne-teno."

Rowan knew that phrase. Coho-ne-teno was the Ebos idea of a dual spirit—one that moved on to an afterlife and one that stayed behind to aid its family and descendants.

Minna sighed as if resigning herself to this new fate of living among the soulless. Her eyes scanned the piles of debris. "So what should we look for?"

"I'm not sure, but the Blacksmith will know."

"Who?"

"The big man in Grotto, you might say. Some believe he's a myth, but I don't. Someone is keeping law and order up there." Rowan pointed back the way they'd come. "I think that's the Blacksmith. He's supposed to live in the Rustworks like a hermit, buying and selling old mechs. I brought something to trade with." Rowan lifted the leather pouch at her belt. It jangled with the distinct sound of thera chips. Many, many thera chips.

"This tough cookie would have preferred actual cookies to thera." The voice came from the darkness ahead. "But give me your best bargain and we'll see how it goes from there."

A man limped out of the shadows between the piles of garbage.

12

ANYONE. ANYWHERE. ANY WHEN

HE WORE A LEATHER VEST similar to Rowan's, but with no shirt underneath. Gray hair covered his bare chest. The hair on his head and his beard were leaning toward white too.

"You're the Blacksmith?" Rowan's tongue instinctively prodded the wad of surrow weed tucked into her cheek.

"I am. But you can call me Homer."

Rowan squinted, but that didn't help her see him better in the dim light of the boneyard. Something wasn't right. Her head buzzed with a sudden low-grade headache.

"Is that your name?"

"It pleases me."

An answer and not an answer.

The man's stance suggested he was at ease in this place. Corded muscles tensed as he crossed his arms over his chest—the arms and chest of a blacksmith.

They stood ten feet apart in a mech junkyard hundreds of feet underground, and yet the meeting felt intimate somehow. Familiar.

She stepped backward and right into Roger, who was strangely silent.

Beside her, Minna bowed—a full head down, bent at the waist bow—and spoke an Essian word that Rowan didn't catch.

The man gave back a short nod.

The elves were always courteous, and they revered her as the mysterious Evani, but even that title didn't warrant such a greeting. Rowan wanted to know what kind of creature could make an Ebos bow like that.

Rowan turned her attention back to the Blacksmith…to Homer. That name didn't sit right, like it was an ill fitting shirt he'd pulled on at the last minute. Her tongue found the wad of surrow, and the taste of rosemary tingled across her tongue again.

Phalian, who'd been quiet until now, crept out of her pocket and said, "SQUEAK!"

The man smiled and his fierce face transformed into something friendly, into someone she recognized.

"I know you…" The memory unraveled slowly. A smiling man pouring ale. Halleck…or Hartford? From Oxeye. No, Halstead. The innkeeper. And then another face super-imposed on the memory. Or was it the same face? A kindly uncle sitting by her bedside, his touch soothing the phantom ache in her missing arm.

It didn't make sense. She shook her head. Her mech hand was fisted so fiercely that her shoulder twinged, and she shook out her fingers.

"I remember you."

The man grunted. "You shouldn't." He glanced at Minna, who kept her eyes averted. "I didn't account for elf magic." He lifted his nose and scented the air. "Memory wort. Very clever."

"You're Hermie, my…" She stopped short of saying uncle. "You were my father's friend and advisor. And…and Halstead the innkeeper too. You made me forget. Why?" Anger welled in her. How dare he steal memories of her father? They were precious. How many others had he stolen?

Hermie-Halstead-Homer shrugged. "It is my way. Humans live short lives, but some hang around long enough to question how one such as I can go on long after he should be dead."

One such as I.

"You're not human?"

He rubbed his beard. "I suppose there is a spark of humanity in me or a desire for human-ness. Otherwise I would take the form of a bear or a wolf or a snake. But I find opposable thumbs very useful."

He held out his hands and waggled his thumbs.

"But how? How can you be the Blacksmith *and* the innkeeper in Oxeye *and* my father's advisor?"

"Haven't you figured it out yet, Princess? I can be whatever I want. Wherever I want. *When* ever. I can be an advisor to kings, or a reaper on a nacara ship. I can even be a mech mage during the founding of your city." He leaned in toward her. "I can also build mighty mechs to protect that city, mechs unlike any other that will last forever."

Understanding hit Rowan like a blacksmith's hammer.

"You're him. You're Harry Hightower."

He leaned back on his heels, a pleased smile on his face.

"I am."

"And when I leave, you'll make me forget you and everything I learned here again."

"I might."

Her heart sank. He saw her expression and his smile faded. "But I am not all unforgiving. You came here for a reason and I choose to help you. Just like the food you took from my inn at Oxeye, any knowledge you gain here will be yours to keep. But," his bushy brows came together, "don't waste my time. I have many places to be."

Don't waste his time? She had enough questions to fill all of time. Her mind raced. She wanted to know about her father, about her mech arm. She wanted a new arm for Roger, and oh, there was the problem with Talos. Surely his maker would be able to fix him. But the most pressing problem was the cachet. That's what she'd come here to do.

Her human hand fumbled in the deep pocket beside her knee and she pulled out the silver disk. It caught the dim light and seemed to glow.

"Do you know what this is?"

Harry snorted. "'Course I do. It's a cachet, used by those abominations you call scribes."

"I thought you created the first scribe."

"I did. She was a beautiful blend of mech and magic." His eyes rose and focused on a far horizon that was hidden in this underground place. Then he turned back to Rowan and pierced her with a fierce stare. "My scribe used human magic. Not a speck of thera in her. I told them that introducing thera to the delicate mix would only degrade the magic, turn it into something rotten at the core. They didn't listen."

"They? Who? My father?"

Harry shook his head. "No, Reynar was a good man. A smart man. He understood the risks of thera and took measures to limit its use. But after his death, the council could not resist the lure of easy magic. That's when I left. I refused to create anything more for them."

"The council? You mean Regent Atherton?"

"Yes. Atherton fell into bed with those grubbers at Theracine. He would have licked Kenneth Smith's boots." When he spoke the regent's name, his lip curled into a sneer, like he'd just found the regent squashed under his shoe. But it was the other name that Rowan found curious. As far as she knew, Flora Bosman was the head of Theracine. Smith was her secretary.

"There are others on the Theracine payroll," Harry said. "Miron Wrede and Archivist Wiktor. They all played a hand in creating the new and improved scribes. Bah! Just an excuse to peddle thera, if you ask me."

Wrede didn't surprise her, but Wiktor was now Abbot Archivist Wiktor, leader of the Temple of the Word, the man who had single-handedly made scribes an integral part of palace affairs. They were all linked together. How long would that partnership last? Was Theracine pulling Wrede's strings even now? All this time her focus had been on Atherton, but maybe he was the puppet, not the puppeteer.

She turned the cachet over in her hand. It had all the answers.

"I need a way to read the information on this. Can you do that?" She reached out to hand it over, but Harry shook his head.

"Not me, but he can." He pointed to Roger. The little valet had been silent since they arrived at the Rustworks. His face was tilted back, and his eyes fixed on Harry.

"Roger? He doesn't do much more than spin in circles. He can barely speak. Roger, show him."

"Roger that!" The mech spun in a circle.

Harry frowned. "That's not right. Old Cassius here was one of my most sophisticated mechs. Cassius! Stop spinning. Come here!"

The voice command seemed to trigger something in Roger. He locked his wheels and rolled over to Harry who bent down to examine him.

"You've had some rough days, old friend. Missing an arm too. Let's see what we can find to replace it." He turned and strode down a path between piles of mech debris. Roger followed at a good clip and Rowan had to run after them.

A small building appeared like a wraith from the shadows. Its roof slanted toward them. The metal sheeting was buckled and an old tire held down one corner. The rest of the building leaned at an alarming angle, as if a swift kick would send it sprawling. Mech garbage was piled around, blocking the partially open door. Harry squeezed past the debris and disappeared into the building.

Rowan hesitated in the doorway.

"I'll wait out here, Evani." Minna smiled.

"Okay." That was odd. Minna didn't let her go into her dressing room without checking it for assassins, but the elf simply crossed her arms and started scanning the junkyard.

Rowan ducked through the small doorway. She could hear the clank of metal against metal as Harry searched through several crates pushed to one side. Her eyes roamed around the single room. It was dimly lit and seemed bigger than she guessed from the outside. In fact, it was so vast she couldn't see the far end. Crates overflowing with miscellaneous mech parts were piled near the door. Shelves lined the walls as far as her eye could see and they were piled high with tools and more mech discards. Wires hung down from the ceiling. A cat was parked in one corner, its wheels and front hood missing.

She was looking at a tinker's shop, not unlike her own, except this one belonged to Harry Hightower, the most famous mech mage in the history of New Torwood. She was afraid to touch anything.

"Here it is." Harry held up an oblong piece of metal with a plug on one end and a socket on the other. He picked up Roger as if the valet weighed next to nothing and sat him on a work table. Phalian shifted to his bird form and flew over to land beside Roger. He pecked at the rusted bolt that had replaced Roger's arm.

Harry pulled out a lantern and shook it until it emitted a bright yellow glow. Rowan recognized the mech. It was a ley-line lantern, like the one in her father's study, an antique worth a small fortune. She gazed around the workshop, wondering what other treasures it held.

Harry tried to unscrew Roger's arm bolt, but it was rusted firmly in place. He found some oil and worked it into the joint until the bolt finally turned. Once unscrewed, he tossed it aside.

"Cassius here was never meant to be just a valet. He is a sophisticated computation device. Though I lost him before I could really put his full talents to the test. There." He plugged the mech device into the port where Roger's missing arm had been. The new arm was silver and contrasted with Roger's rustic appearance.

"Now, you plug that cachet in there," he pointed to the other end of Roger's new arm. Rowan tried to attach the mech, but the port on the arm didn't match the cachet's port.

"It's missing something. A cable, maybe?" She remembered the cable snaking down from Orson's head to the cachet.

"Of course." Harry rummaged in the bins again until he came up with a silver cable. Rowan plugged in both ends. Nothing happened.

Harry scratched his beard. "Odd. He should be computing now."

"Computing?"

"Scanning and parsing information. He can do it at lightning speed, much faster than you could read or speak it. But something's wrong, I'll have to open him up."

Harry unscrewed the tiny bolts on Roger's chest plate and removed it. Rowan was excited and curious to see the inside of a Harry Hightower creation. The chest cavity was similar to Talos's, but on a smaller scale. Tentacle-like cables clung to a glowing gem at the center. They branched in every direction.

"Is that a ley-stone?" She pointed at the gem. Harry ignored her. "How do the cables move the magic around? Does Roger use ichor too?" Again no answers. After a half-dozen more questions, she fell silent and watched the master at work. Harry mumbled to himself as he pulled various bits from Roger's chest, cleaned them and put them back.

An hour later, Rowan reclined on the only chair in the room. Even Phalian's curiosity had faded and he'd retreated to mouse form again to nestle in her pocket.

"Ah, there it is." Harry held up a small piece of metal between the teeth of pliers. He wore thick spectacles to examine it. "Burned right out. No wonder he's lost most functions." He set the piece of metal aside and turned toward a cabinet on the wall. He fished a key from his pocket and unlocked it.

Rowan's eyes widened when she saw the wonders inside. It was full of fantastic mech creatures—birds like Phalian, cats, dogs, lizards. They were all dormant, but looked like they could wake at any moment. He picked up a lizard-like creature, turned it over and opened a compartment on its belly. He plucked out a piece of metal just like the one he'd removed from Roger.

"This one should have some life left in it." He plugged in the chip and Roger's eyes brightened. His head turned and he said, in a clear voice. "Hello Harry. You've been traveling too long." Then he looked down at his open chest. "Oh, it seems I have been wounded. Is it serious?"

"No, you're all good, my friend." Harry bolted the casing over the valet's chest and patted him. "Cassius I'd like you to meet Rowan. She has a job for you."

Roger—now Cassius—turned his big copper eyes on her. "It is nice to meet you Rowan. I feel like we will be great friends." His voice was deep and had a tinny echo, but his diction was perfect.

"I, uh, would like that. Can you help me read the information on that cachet?"

The device was still dangling from his arm. He lifted it in his other hand. "Of course." His eyes glowed for a moment, then he spoke in a high-pitched voice unlike Roger or Cassius.

*The journal of Sandra Kane novice level one, January twelfth,
in the year 578. This is my first data entry as an official scribe.
Archivist Kinna suggested that I keep it simple to begin with.
Already, the pain behind my eyes is almost unbearable, but she
says that will fade as I get used to off-loading my data.*

*Today, I woke early, excited for the initiation. There were
eighteen in our class. One of the largest classes ever to graduate.
I look forward to serving as scribe, especially now that it seems
certain we will go to war…*

Roger continued the monotonous recounting of a young scribe's daily chores.

"Can he skip ahead?" Rowan said. "How many entries like this are there?"

Harry smiled. "Just ask him. His voice commands are quite nuanced."

Rowan faced the mech. "Roger…I mean Cassius, stop reciting." He fell silent. His eyes seemed expectant, but maybe she was projecting her feelings. She ran a hand over the back of her neck. It was hot in Harry's work room, and she was tired now.

"How many entries are there on the cachet?"

Cassius paused.

"He's calculating," Harry whispered. "His processor is faster than anything that came since."

"There are six thousand, seven hundred and sixty-four voice entries and three hundred and eighty-two data entries," Cassius said. "Would you like me to recite them?"

"Six thousand?" Rowan did a quick mental calculation. "That's over twenty years of journal entries. It will take hours."

"Six hundred and seventy-six hours and fifty-six seconds. I could write them out. That will take one thousand, four hundred and sixty-four hours, seventy-six minutes and forty-two seconds."

Harry looked as proud as a papa watching his son graduate with honors. "There's a stylus attachment for his other arm. I should have one around here somewhere." He started rifling through crates again.

Rowan just stared at Roger. Or Cassius. Or whatever he was. Frustration ate at her already frayed nerves. They were so close to accessing the information she needed to take down Atherton and yet…

"Three hundred hours? That's more than a month, if I do nothing else for twenty-four hours every day! And I rarely get an hour to myself. How am I going to listen to all those journal entries? And what are data entries anyway? How do I access those?"

Harry held up another arm attachment and a stylus.

"With these. Cassius can write out anything you think is important. And don't worry about the number of entries. Cassius can sort and tag them, then start with the most relevant. What keywords would you suggest?"

"Miron Wrede and Faustus Atherton for sure." She banged her fist on the table, thinking. Eklridge Oasis would be too general a term if Sandra worked there. Gaunts and thera too. "The Warren. Or the Academy. Tag those."

Harry turned to face the little mech. "Cassius, sort the data on the cachet using the keywords: Miron Wrede, Faustus Atherton, the Warren and the Academy." He glanced at Rowan, one bushy brow raised. "Anything else?"

She shook her head. Already, Cassius made that faint whirring noise that she was coming to recognize as his processor.

"Cassius, is it okay if I call you Roger?"

Copper eyes turned upward. "Roger that."

"Well, that's all sorted, then," Harry said. "It may take days to sort that data. His processor is fast, but nothing like the computers in the old days."

"The old days? Like before the war?"

"Like before the Resurgence. Back then we had computers that could calculate millions of transactions in the blink of an eye. It was both inspiring and terrifying."

The Resurgence had happened over six-hundred years ago.

Rowan gaped at him, then squinted. "Just how old are you?"

Harry grinned. "Older than god. At least the Christian god that your people demoted to a saint." He leaned in and whispered. "I'm only telling you this because as soon as you walk up that tunnel and back into the city, I'll simply disappear."

Rowan gripped the edge of the table so hard, it creaked. Her tongue flicked to the wad in her cheek. Would it be enough to let her keep her memories?

"What if I need you for something? What if this malfunctions?" She waved her mech hand at him, but he looked unmoved. "The Regent's Council is getting ready to make war with the great southern cities. Don't you care?" Harry stared at her impassively. Rowan pulled out her last card. "What about Bella. You left her alone in the palace with two children to care for. She misses you."

Harry made a growling noise. "You have a lot of your father in you, did you know that? I won't go back to the palace, not while the council is in charge. They took my creations and twisted them for selfish and evil gains.

I won't give them anything more, even if it means…well, never mind. Let me see that hand." He gripped the mech appendage and turned it gently to inspect the seam between mech and flesh.

"Does it pain you at all?"

"No."

"No infections at the connection?"

"No."

He removed her black glove. "Flex your fingers." She did. He grunted, neither approval nor disapproval, then handed her a large metal ball bearing. "Squeeze." She did. Another grunt. "Twist at the wrist. Again, the other way. Any unusual feelings from it? Heat, cold? Anything like that?"

"It tingles sometimes, and you'll think I'm crazy, but it has a knack."

"A what?"

"A knack. When I work with anything mech made, it can sense the inner workings like a map."

"Interesting. I had hoped for a connection to be forged between the mech and your neural pathways, but I was not able to stay long enough to confirm it. That's not the arm's knack. It's yours. The mech is only the conduit."

"That's not possible. I'm a magical dud. They tested me as a child and even the arm's magic didn't manifest until…" Understanding dawned on her. "Until I started tinkering with mechs."

Harry nodded. "You were a late bloomer, but so was your father. And he had the same affinity with mechs. It wasn't exactly a secret, but a king has little use for such a knack."

"Neither does a princess."

Harry smiled. "From what I hear, you've done well with it." He squeezed her hand into a fist and patted it. "Everything looks in working order."

She was being dismissed. "What if I need help with Talos? Will you come? He's been acting weird lately. What if he fails and I need you?"

"All things fail in the end, princess. Even giants like Talos. Even cities. Death gives way to life. Always. I have seen civilizations fall only to be reborn again under a different guise. All will be well."

"That's your advice? Don't sweat the small stuff like the destruction of my city because life goes on?"

"Yes."

She wanted to punch him right in his calmly sanctimonious face.

"Go home, Princess. I have work to do." He turned, walked to the end of the work room and was immediately lost in shadow.

"We're not done here!" She followed him, but when she reached the gloomy end of the room, he was gone.

She whirled and headed back outside. "Roger follow!"

The mech's wheels whirred. They found Minna waiting for them, her eyes still scanning the pathways between heaps of ruined mechs.

"Did he come this way?" Rowan asked.

"No, Evani. The only movement has been rats."

"Damn the saints!"

Rowan took two steps into the Rustworks, then realized the futility of going after a man who could be anywhere or any when.

"You will not find him. Your friend is an *esch*."

"What does that mean?"

Minna frowned. "I do not know your word for it. Someone who is worshiped."

"Like the saints? Harry is a saint?"

Minna made an indecisive humming sound. "Perhaps." Then she changed the subject. "Did you find what you need, Evani?"

"Yes." Rowan sighed. "Let's just hope I remember it when we get home."

13

The Long Way

Conall and Lydan slept one night on the road and the next at Lydan's homestead. The Boreal Clan hunted and trapped all the way from the forested northern edge of Durance to the lowlands of the Ubruulen Mountains. Lydan's family lived in a neat farmhouse tucked into a valley where the forest gave way to grasslands.

His whole family came out to greet them when they arrived—mother, grandfather, sisters, brothers, cousins and a dozen cubs running in their cat forms. The joy on their faces to see the return of their kinsman left a hollow ache in Conall's chest. Revisiting his childhood home had awakened a new yearning in him—a yearning for this. Connections, kinship. Family.

Garou snorted. *There is no such thing as a lone wolf. Only a wolf who has not found his pack.*

Maybe I have found my pack. Conall's thoughts turned to Rowan.

Then why do you run from it?

Conall had no good answer for that. The farther he roamed from New Torwood, the more intangible this quest seemed.

No one thought it amiss that Lydan had brought home a wolf. His mother Nadine begged Conall to stay for a few days.

"Thank you, but the summer is short and I must be on my way as soon as possible."

Nadine was a tall, stout woman with steel gray hair falling out of a bun. She'd raised a pride of lions and didn't easily take no for an answer.

"You must stay for dinner at least. Food, drink and a bed. I insist." She gave him the evil eye. "I mean it. You won't get out my door without it. I'll sit on you and force feed you if I have too."

Lydan laughed. "She means it, little brother. Best to listen."

"Dinner and a rest would be welcomed." Conall smiled. The effort felt odd. His facial muscles were unused to the happy expression.

"It's settled then," Nadine said, as if there had been any question. She herded the pack of children inside and left Lydan to get them settled.

After dinner, Conall and Lydan sat beside the big kitchen hearth, smoking a pipe with Lydan's grandfather, Polrick. The old lion's mind was going, and he liked to ramble about his trapping days while he smoked and rocked in his chair. That suited Conall just fine. He listened without interrupting.

Lydan tried to steer the old man's memories in the right direction with questions like, "Didn't you meet an Ebos tribe one time?" Polrick would nod thoughtfully and say, "Indeed. The elves were the only people I saw for months at a time…" He would continue with tales of how the Ebos came across his snares and prayed for the dead rabbits as if the critters were their kin. He told them about how the snows came early one year, trapping him in a valley for weeks, and Lydan would point him back to the Ebos.

"Tell us, Grandfather, about the time you broke your arm and the Ebos healed you. Didn't you stay in their village?"

Polrick nodded and sucked on his pipe. "I did. I did. They were kind folk and good healers. But I only stayed in one of their camps, not Benni proper." He leaned in and whispered. "It's a secret, you know. Some say it doesn't even exist, but I believe it does." He leaned back with a smile. Then he got lost staring into the flames jumping in the hearth, until Lydan prodded him again.

"So where do you think Benni is?"

"Eh?" Polrick glanced up. "There ain't no Benni. It's a myth." He sucked on his pipe, but it had gone out. While he tapped out the ash and refilled it, Lydan tried to bring his memories full circle again.

"But if it isn't a myth, where do you think it could be?"

Polrick waved his pipe in the air. "Oh, north. Where the mountains begin. That would be my guess. I almost visited once, did you know? That year I fell into a ravine and broke my arm. Amazing healers those elves." His hand dropped the cold pipe to his lap and his head fell against the rocking chair. His eyes closed, and a quiet snore whistled through his mustache.

"I think that's all we'll get out of him tonight," Lydan said.

Conall nodded. It wasn't much, but at least he was heading in the right direction.

After breakfast the following day, Lydan laid a map on the big harvest table in their kitchen. With his finger, he traced a line north to where the Black River petered out in the Meadows.

"There's an old trapper's camp here. You can stop and rest." His finger kept moving north. "The valley extends to here. We call it the Basin."

Conall studied the map. The Basin was a wide open space between the two branches of the Ubruulen Mountains. They were like great arms reaching west toward the sea. About a hundred miles inland, the branches met. The mountain range continued from that point as one line of peaks all the way across the northern edge of the Meadows.

"If I had to guess, I'd say the Ebos village is inside the Basin." Lydan tapped the map. "It's protected from the worst winter storms. It even has its own micro-climate that allows for crops in the summer."

"How long to get there?"

Lydan considered. "Ten days, maybe. A week if you stop only to sleep. We'll give you what provisions you can carry. You may have to hunt along the way. But Conall," Lydan's brows lowered, shading his eyes. "If you haven't found the Ebos by September, you need to abandon this idea and come home. Snow comes early that far north and you don't want to be trapped there all winter. If you don't starve, frostbite will get you." He held up his left hand that was missing the tips off the two smallest fingers.

September. That gave Conall two weeks to find Benni and the Ebos before he would have to abandon this wild goose chase.

Wild goose is a worthy prey, Garou said. *This prey you seek is as foolish as a pup's dream.*

Lydan folded the ancient map and handed it to Conall. He refused to take it. Maps were precious and he wouldn't be able to carry it if he ran as the wolf.

"I don't need it. I'll head north until I hit mountains and follow them west to the Basin. If I end up too far west, I'll swim in the sea." He gave Lydan a rueful smile. "Thanks. I appreciate the provisions and everything you've done." They both knew he was talking about Ianna.

Lydan clapped him on the shoulder. "Stay safe, my friend, and stop here on your way home so we know you're alive."

"I will."

He hefted his pack over one shoulder and left through the kitchen garden. A pack of lion cubs followed him as far as the edge of the Meadows and then he was alone with his thoughts again.

There was no road north of Durance, only a series of connecting trails used mostly by migrating wildlife. After the first day, Conall lost sight of the forest. Looking northward, the grasslands stretched impossibly far, until the lowest peaks of the Ubruulens seemed to melt into the grass. The great sea was somewhere to his left, and if all went well, he wouldn't see it.

He put one foot in front of the other and tried to ignore the gnawing fear that he was leaving behind everyone who'd ever mattered to him. Garou was no help. He grumbled about their slow pace and the poor hunting, though he seemed to take pity on Conall and ceased griping about their lost mate.

A blackened lump sat on the horizon. Conall focused on it, finding satisfaction when it slowly grew bigger. Two hours later, he stood beside a mass that turned out to be an ancient mech vehicle, forgotten and left to rust in the grass. He stopped to rest in its shadow—the only shadow for miles around. Sitting with his back to the rusted hulk, he sipped water, taking care to ration it. There was no telling when he'd have a chance to refill his canteen. He might stumble over a creek winding through the grass or he might have to walk all the way to the Highland River before he found water.

Munching on the trail mix that Nadine had given him, he squinted into the setting sun. The Meadows were busy. Animals that hid from the mid-day heat were out looking for a meal. Insects swarmed in the cooler air. A fox yipped, and the rumbling bellow of a bison carried over the Meadows from miles away.

On the western horizon, two figures mounted on shaggy ponies watched him—stark silhouettes against the setting sun. They weren't trying to hide.

Conall sipped from his canteen and pretended the elves were just another part of the scenery. He'd expected them to monitor his progress north. Nothing happened in their territory without the Ebos knowing about it. He thought about tracking them, but knew it would be impossible. Garou's sensitive nose would easily pick up their trail, but the Ebos roamed all over these parts, and they wouldn't be dumb enough to leave a trail to their village. Not unless they wanted him to follow.

All he could do was keep moving, let himself be seen, and hope they came to him.

A few minutes later, when he looked in their direction again, the elves were gone.

He hefted his pack and kept walking.

He continued steadily north all the next day. Garou was restless in the back of his mind.

We would make better time on four legs.

We're in no hurry, brother. At least not until we know where we're going. And you run too swiftly. We don't want to lose our trackers.

He made frequent stops, finding excuses to fill his canteen from rivulets or dig up cattails along the stream bed to supplement his rations. Twice that day, he spotted the Ebos, always too far away to hail.

Lydan had advised him to look out for the Hangar, a well-known camp used by hunters and trappers. He'd said it was about two days walk from the forest, and on the second afternoon Conall headed steadily toward the only structure on the horizon, figuring it had to be the camp.

The Hangar turned out to be a flat expanse of broken concrete that took up nearly a quarter acre. Tall columns of stone marked three corners, the only remnants of ancient walls. Conall stood at one corner and surveilled the ruins. Grass and small shrubs pushed through the degraded slabs of concrete.

Yellowed vines cloaked the piles of stone. It wasn't much of a camp, but an ancient well pump stood in the sandy yard to one side of the concrete. When Conall cranked the handle, brackish water from a sand point well chugged from the spout. He let it flow for a minute before drinking and filling his canteen.

Wood was scarce in the Meadows and he didn't bother scrounging for the few branches he would find. The moon was already rising and he wouldn't need the light of a fire tonight.

He dropped his pack near one of the rock piles, close enough for it to block the wind, but far enough that he wouldn't be bothered by nesting rodents. With his back against the pack and his ankles crossed, he waited.

The locket warmed. He fished it from under his shirt and read: *Goodnight.*

Conall smiled. Imagining Rowan's face had been his only entertainment for days. He thought about what she might be doing at any given hour. Was she walking on the city wall, getting ready to jump the gap to Talos's shoulder? Or sitting in the council chambers with a barely contained frown on her face as she listened to Old Wind-bag Atherton? He imagined her waking in the morning and rolling over in bed to let the light hit her red hair, turning it to fire. At this hour, she'd probably be returning from a gala event, stripping off the gown she so hated and rubbing her feet that were sore from the fancy shoes.

We should be there to rub her feet, grumbled Garou, and he wasn't wrong.

Most of those memories were manufactured because they'd had so little time together. But other images came to him easily—Rowan fighting with the wind to stake down their cat when they'd been caught in a storm. Rowan sitting in the glow of Murdoch's thera stove, laughing with the rest of Squad 54. Rowan crouching on top of a rock wall in the Warren, her eyes wide while they listened for the gaunts and soldiers who were stalking them.

All these visions flooded him with warmth as he read her tiny message again: *Goodnight.*

He pulled out the branch-shaped stylus and squeezed it between thumb and forefinger. The thera screen was only big enough for a word or two. He thought about what to write for so long, she must have assumed he hadn't seen her message. Finally, on the left side, he scrawled: *miss you.* After a moment, a heart appeared on the right screen.

He closed the locket and tucked it away.

A small white creature emerged from the rock pile and cocked its head, studying the intruder in its terrain. Winged scruffs inhabited the northern reaches of the Meadows. Small and round, its fur was fluffy and white except for where it bled to brown like a mask around its eyes and on its strangely hand-like paws. Long rounded ears protruded through the fluff, pointing straight up, and these were framed by its most distinctive feature, tufts of white fur that mimicked feathers. These "wings" were purely ornamental and though the scruffs could leap great distances they didn't actually fly. Mostly, they scrounged for bugs in the dirt. They'd also been known to invade camps. Their tiny hands were amazingly agile and strong, and if they couldn't open a trash container, they would chew through it.

The scruff stared right at Conall and chirped.

Terrific. Where there was one scruff, there were more, and sure enough, another white head poked from the rubble, then another.

Garou grunted in disgust.

All fur and no meat.

Conall agreed. *That's their best defense against predators. Nothing wants to eat them.*

The lead scruff chirped again. The effort made his whole body jerk. More banded faces appeared.

Saints' sinner. There had to be dozens of the vermin. Conall slowly reached into his pack for his air knives. The scruff's cute chirp turned into a growl and it bared wicked little teeth. They could smell the food in his pack and they weren't going to be deterred by one measly human.

Conall gripped a blade in each hand and flicked his wrists to activate them. The hum of thera made the lead scruff pause even as it started toward him, but two more dashed up from behind and pounced on his pack. He swung his arm backward and they darted away. The lead scruff took this chance for a frontal assault, but jumped away when Conall swung his fist around again. He wasn't really trying to hit them, but if they kept up this mad dance for much longer, he wouldn't feel bad if he skewered one.

A scruff let out a piercing chirp and they all scuttled under the rocks, disappearing as if they'd never been.

Conall looked up to find two Ebos staring down from their mounts. One of the ponies shook its shaggy mane and pranced in place. The elf calmed it with a pat on the neck.

They were dressed in dun-colored tunics. More nondescript fabric wrapped their legs snugly. The one with the jittery mount urged the pony to walk forward until he was only a few steps away. He pushed the cowl away from his face.

"No mech." He pointed at the knives. Conall deactivated the thera, stowed them in his pack and held up his hands to show they were empty.

The Ebos nodded. He was young, with the delicate features of a child, but that meant nothing for an elf. He could be older than Conall, and indeed, the many beadwork necklaces dangling around his shoulders indicated that he was an Ebos of some stature. Conall knew that the beads were carefully carved from bone—animal, Ebos and even human—and they were worn with great pride.

The elf smiled and pointed at the rock pile where dozens of eyes shone from the shadowed crevices.

"*Carrow?*"

Conall shook his head.

"I'm sorry I don't understand."

The elf raised his hands to flank his head in a mimic of the scruff's big ears. "Carrow."

"Scruffs? Yeah, they're a problem."

"Problem, yes." The elf smiled, then spoke quickly. Conall's knowledge of Essian was limited and he just shook his head. The lead elf turned to his companion, spoke several words and the companion rode off.

He turned back to Conall, then pointed to his own chest.

"I am Ailen."

Conall nodded. "Welcome Ailen." He pointed to himself. "I'm Conall."

Ailen nodded and smiled. "Conall."

The scruffs had decided to try their luck again, and several white faces poked through the rocks. Ailen remained silent until his companion returned with a bunch of yellow flowers, which he handed to Ailen.

The elf held them up and said, "*Sicki.*"

Conall nodded. "Sun thistles." The yellow globe flowers grew in rocky terrain all through the Meadows. The leaves were thorny and when in bloom, the flowers gave off a strong and distinctive scent. Garou hated them because they messed up his sense of smell for hours after just one sniff. Wolf pups learned to avoid sun thistles from a young age.

"Sun thi..shel," Ailen said with a smile. He waved the ugly bouquet. The sickly scent wafted over him, and Conall resisted the urge to swipe at his nose like a wolf.

Ailen tossed the flowers on the ground near the rocks. A flood of fur erupted from the cracks, and the scruffs fled into the Meadows. It seemed that wolves weren't the only animals who disliked thistles.

Ailen said something in Essian again and pointed to Conall's pack. He understood. The elf wanted him to carry sun thistles with him to deter the rodents.

"Thank you."

He was trying to find a way to express his desire to visit the Ebos village. Ailen turned his pony to leave and Conall blurted, "I would like to go to Benni!"

The elf stopped and turned on his mount. Maybe invoking the name of their super-secret stronghold wasn't the best idea. Ailen's companion said something sharp, and the elf held up a hand to silence him. Without another word, they swung their mounts around and trotted into the shadows growing across the Meadows.

14

NO SHIRT. NO SHOES

SEVERAL TIMES OVER THE NEXT two days, when the wind suddenly shifted, Garou's nose picked up the peculiar scent of elf. They were tracking him.

Nights were growing longer and Conall took more time to rest. A storm blew up from the mountains and he hunkered down beside the only shelter he could find in the Meadows, a group of rocks that stuck out of the grass like giant fists. He hadn't seen running water in two days, so he rationed what was left in his canteen and chewed the last of the hard tack he'd brought from Durance. He'd have to hunt from here on.

With his back against a rock, he tucked his pack behind his head and crossed his arms over his chest to keep in the warmth. He tried to sleep.

The storm was mostly bluster. Strong winds thrashed around the sky, churning up dark clouds that didn't deliver on their threat of rain. Near dawn, a few drops spattered his face, but the winds had already died.

Since he'd been expecting them, Conall didn't react with alarm when the tip of a spear prodded his leg as he feigned sleep. They must have left the ponies a distance away, but his sensitive hearing had picked up the soft patter of feet. He raised his head and met his assailant's eye.

The elf moved a spear toward his face and barked out an order in Essian. Conall's eyes drifted past him. Ailen watched from about a dozen yards away. Another six Ebos ringed his small camp. They'd brought in reinforcements.

Garou snarled. Being menaced by spear-point was a good excuse for a fight. Conall held him in check, but wolf passion forced his lip to curl.

"Conall." Ailen nodded. He was clearly in charge of this little operation. Conall couldn't figure out if voicing his name was a question, a confirmation, or a demand.

Two more Ebos approached, cautious but not afraid. He didn't protest when they hauled him to his feet or when they bound his hands, though Garou let out an anxious howl.

"Better this way," Ailen said. "Safer."

"Safer for you or for me?" Conall asked.

"Safer for all of us." Ailen proved that his English was better than he'd let on.

Conall didn't argue about the bonds. He needed a way into Benni, and if being carted there as a prisoner was his only choice, he'd take it.

An elf rifled through his pack and started babbling angrily when she spied the air knives. Ailen said something and the elf reluctantly closed Conall's pack and slung it over her shoulder, but her expression of distaste told him that she preferred to ditch the mech. He hoped they wouldn't. The blades were irreplaceable.

Another elf patted Conall down and removed the hunting knife on his belt. He spotted the locket on the chain around his neck, but made no move to take it.

That was interesting. He didn't recognize it as mech.

Conall had learned a thing or two while traveling back to New Torwood City with the Ebos. Only some elves could practice magic. They were called luminas, and were roughly equivalent to human mech mages, though they didn't work with thera. This group of elves had no lumina among them or they would sense that the locket was more than a fine piece of jewelry. A hunting party, then. Or perhaps scouts. Could he dare to hope that the Ebos had been out looking for him? Omika seemed like the sort who put plans into action. He'd planted the idea to find Benni in Conall's mind. It wouldn't surprise him if the old Ebos had sent scouts to watch for him.

That left Conall with the uncomfortable feeling that he was being manipulated, a scenario that became more likely as they set off on the shaggy ponies. Though his hands were bound, he wasn't mistreated. The elves took pains to be sure he was comfortable, muttering over the setup of his reins and saddle pad, but no amount of adjusting could make the ride easy. His mount was no more than twelve hands high, and he was forced to keep his knees slightly bent so his feet didn't drag in the dirt. After a few hours at a fast walk, the tension in his legs turned to pain. A cramp fired up his calf. He groaned and rolled off the saddle.

He was shifting even as he hit the ground.

The Ebos shouted. Hooves churned up dirt as ponies pranced around the horrifying half-man-half-wolf writhing on the ground. His bones elongated. Joints cracked and reshaped. Ropes fell from his paws. The wolf stretched, shucking off human clothes. He ran, taking no time for the usual stretch and shake after a change.

Instinctively, Garou plunged into the tall grass. His long stride ate up the distance, but not fast enough. Humans were crafty. They had weapons that could reach across huge distances—knives, arrows, bolts. He assumed the elves would have such weapons too, so he ran until he could no longer hear shouting or stamping ponies. Then he stopped and crouched. His sides heaved. He sneezed and shook his muzzle. The change had been too fast and too brutal. It left a lingering sense of unease.

You did well, brother. Conall's assurance wasn't needed, and the wolf didn't acknowledge it. *But we have to go back. For Misha.*

Misha. The name filled Garou with an unwelcome ache. Misha had been pack. His first memories were of tumbling with his wolf brother. They'd learned to hunt and fish together. In the deepest cold of winter, they'd slept back-to-back to conserve heat.

If we return they will hunt us, Garou said. *Wolves are not prey.*
We can follow them.
Elves are not prey either.

Garou felt the impatience in his human brother. He often said that Garou didn't understand human ways. Perhaps he was right, but humans sometimes did things for the wrong reasons.

Misha is the right reason, Conall said. *Misha was pack.*

Garou huffed out a breath and rose. He padded back along the scent trail and crouched in the tall grass. The elves were standing in a circle, still mounted on their horses, speaking in low tones. Garou could hear them, but even his human brother didn't understand the words.

He rose. The movement caught the attention of an elf and they all turned in his direction. Garou lifted his nose and let out a howl. One elf dismounted and walked toward him. He had no weapon but his teeth.

Garou let him approach to the edge of striking distance, then he stepped back. The elf stopped.

"Conall?"

Garou stared at him. The elf babbled in his incomprehensible tongue. Garou sat. The elf nodded and returned to his horse.

They rode north and Garou followed at a safe distance.

Garou lengthened his stride to lope ahead of the horses. They'd been traveling all night. The scent of running water drove him onward. Conall might drink from a metal can, but the wolf craved fresh water.

An elf shouted in protest as he increased the distance between them, and Garou's tongue lolled. Their ropes couldn't hold him. Their spears couldn't catch him. Let them remember that he ran with them only because he chose to.

By the time the elves caught up, he was sitting beside a small creek with a belly full of water. He would have to run slower now, but it was worth it to see the elf's agitated face. Conall had called him Ailen. He was leader of his little pack, but Garou sensed that he was new to his role. Command sat uncomfortably on his shoulders, like a barely grown pup who suddenly becomes alpha of the pack.

While the elves filled their water skins, Garou eased his warm muscles by rolling in the grass. He rose and stretched, showing his would-be captors that he did not fear them.

Ailen watched with a frown.

Garou's ears flicked away a fly. Dawn was upon them. The Meadows were alive with the chirps of birds and other small prey. He lifted his nose. The musky scent of bison came from the east.

Ailen barked out an order in his strange tongue and the elves remounted.

Garou ran alongside the horses through the day, stopping only to drink at the few streams that still flowed freely after the long summer. When the shadows began to flatten again, he cut away from the elves and dashed into the tall grass, ignoring the sharp call from Ailen.

It didn't take long to run down a hare. It was mostly fur and bones, but he ate enough to still the hunger in his belly. As he backtracked, he startled a second hare, a juvenile with more energy than sense, and it bolted right into his paws. He grabbed it by the neck and shook it once.

He found the elves camped in the open. There was no shelter here. He laid the hare on the ground beside Ailen. The elf spoke, but his words only skimmed over Garou's ears. He shook his head and did not reach for the hare.

The wolf felt his hackles rise. His gift had been refused.

Calm, brother. He means no offense. Conall had been quiet in his mind all day, but he spoke up now. *Ebos don't eat raw meat and the Meadows provide no wood for a fire.*

Garou let out a huff. Ailen smiled and babbled again, nudging the dead hare forward. Garou picked it up and took his second meal into the grass away from the elves. He didn't know how long they would be running, and a wolf needed his strength.

That night he slept with his back to the Ebos camp and his nose pointing into the night. Glowing moon moss filled the Meadows with dabs of purple light all the way to the mountains in the near distance. Tiny pale stalks sprouted from the moss. They were tipped with star-shaped purple flowers that only opened for the moon. Garou felt Conall stir in the back of his mind as he remembered hunting the rare plant as a child. The memory brought pain. Garou didn't understand the human's propensity to constantly jab at these sore memories.

Lick a wound once to clean it, he said. *Keep licking and you will wear away fur and flesh.*

Conall grumbled in the back of his mind.

Humans. They had no sense of self-preservation.

Already, the nights were chilly this far north. Summer was fading quickly. Wind lifted the fur on Garou's back, making him feel vulnerable.

A wolf howled in the distance.

Garou lifted his nose to greet the night, but the wind was not in his favor. It would fling his scent toward the prowling wolf.

He turned, uncurling to lay his belly flat. His legs tensed under him. He was ready to pounce or run. The unseen predator in the darkness would determine which course he took.

Behind him the elf on watch duty spoke, but her words didn't penetrate Garou's ears.

The wolf called again. It was a command for others to answer and they did. More wolves howled, showing support. Garou counted seven distinct voices, and they were closing on the Ebos camp.

He stood just as a gray wolf stepped into the light of a patch of moon moss, not ten strides away. The wolf fixed his gaze on Garou.

A challenge. Garou puffed out the fur on his neck. His lip trembled as a snarl erupted from him.

He wants you to fight, Conall said. *Do not take the bait. You'll leave the elves vulnerable to attack.*

More wolves slunk out of the shadows to back up their leader.

The rest of the elves were awake now. An arrow hit the ground between the wild wolf's feet. A warning shot.

The wolf danced backwards.

That's right. My pack may run on two legs, but they are not weak.

Another arrow hit the ground in front of a younger wolf. This one yipped and his paws kicked up sand as he tried to flee.

Garou turned on the elf and growled. He would protect the Ebos but he would not see his wild brethren hurt.

Ailen stepped forward. His hand reached out, but stopped just short of resting on Garou's head. "Be calm. Wolves are children of the darkness like us. It is not time for their bones to feed the ground."

The wolves paced along the shadow's edge while their leader confronted the two-leggers and the lone wolf who'd intruded in their territory. Then, without a sound, they slunk back into the night. For a fleeting instant, Garou wanted to run free with them, but they were not his pack. Besides, he had a mission to complete, and he knew how important missions were to humans.

15

LUNCHING ON FAITH

THE HOTEL WAS SIMPLY CALLED The Inn, as if it needed no other advertisement besides its reputation for elegance and opulence. Rowan's heels clicked on the foyer's marble tiles—marble that had been brought to New Torwood City at great expense. More marble flanked the doors to the dining room in the form of Doric columns. Plaster friezes painted in bold hues of bronze, blue and black decorated the walls.

A mech valet emerged from behind a mahogany desk. A second, very human attendant waited by the desk, looking bored. The mech was a beautiful piece of mage-work—boxy but with curving lines below the waist and wheels cleverly hidden beneath a skirt. Humanoid above the waist with fully functional hands and a face designed with pleasing symmetry. It rolled toward her with a faint pneumatic hiss. Rowan's expert eye noted the fluidity of its joints as it held up a hand in greeting.

"May I take your coat?" Its voice module was good for a mech, but since Harry Hightower had unlocked Roger, she had a new standard.

The idea that she had actually met the famous mech-mage still filled her with awe.

She'd left Roger at home. He was deep in a trance as he sorted the scribe's entries. Rowan was so anxious for him to finish, she'd almost blown off this lunch date, but Dale had convinced her that making nice with the new ambassador was a priority. Instead, she'd left Phalian with instructions to find her if Roger woke from his trance.

"I don't have a coat, thank you." She nodded at Minna to wait for her and walked past the valet as it stood with raised arms to receive the garment. The human attendant glided smoothly from behind the desk, proving that the mech was just for show.

"Ambassador Padgett is already seated, Princess. May I show you to your table?"

Rowan nodded and masked her surprise. She didn't visit The Inn often, but they'd recognized her. It was that kind of place. They didn't take reservations, but if the maître d'hôtel didn't recognize you, you didn't belong there.

At the dining room, the marble tiles gave way to carpet plush enough that Rowan's feet sank into it. Tables laid with fine linens weren't crammed into the room for expediency or profit, but spread out to provide privacy to the diners. The room felt hushed and expectant, as if a dome of silence muffled the secrets spilled there.

As the maître d' led her through the room, diners paused their conversations to watch the reclusive princess. She recognized a few nobles. Marilyn Docker, Minister of Guilds, dined with the head of the money-lender's guild. Docker frowned but Rowan didn't give her the benefit of royal attention. She'd be sure to ask Dale about that meeting later though. The maître d' stopped at a table tucked into a dim corner. It was the perfect spot for private conversation and far too intimate for her purposes.

The ambassador stood as she approached. He was tall and ropey with the look of someone who spent a lot of time leaning against a wall with his ankles crossed and a smug expression on his face as he internally catalogued the shortcomings of his peers.

"Princess Rowan, you do me such an honor." He bowed with elegant ease, but didn't bother to hide a smirk. Perhaps he couldn't.

"Would you indulge me, Ambassador Padgett." Rowan pointed to a table by a wall of glass overlooking the gardens. "I do so enjoy The Inn's famous view."

"Of course, of course. But please, call me Remy." He rose. The maître d' took his glass and moved it to the new table. As they settled again, Rowan's eyes roamed to the city wall on the far side of the garden. It had taken her longer to walk across Kingsway to The Inn than she'd thought. Had Talos already passed them by?

"You seem worried, Princess. I hope our rendezvous is not a problem."

"Of course not." She turned her attention to the task at hand and faced the ambassador. Remy was almost too handsome. Black hair fell over his forehead in an orchestrated tousle. His dark eyes glinted with humor, and his wide mouth was made to smile, which he did now as he sensed her appraisal. She wondered how many dignitaries—male or female—had been taken in by that smile.

"I was very grateful and more than a little overwhelmed by your generous invitation." He reached across the table, then stopped. His eyes dropped to rest on her gloved hand. She'd dressed for lunch, not dinner, and chosen a black silk glove to cover the mech.

Padgett realized he was staring. His eyes lifted to her face, and he favored her with another dazzling smile.

"I have heard so many tales of the little princess who hides in the great palace. I am honored that you left your sanctuary to dine with me."

Rowan bobbed her head. She wouldn't satisfy his curiosity by asking about those tales. She knew exactly what the nobles thought of her.

A waiter appeared with a server trailing behind him. The mech carried a tray with cut crystal glasses filled with water and chunks of ice, yet another show of needless opulence.

The waiter served their drinks and took food orders. Rowan waited until he was out of earshot before speaking again.

"Is this your first visit to New Torwood, Ambassador Padgett?"

"Please, I insist. Call me Remy."

She smiled, but didn't offer him the same compliment of using her first name. Remy frowned. It was a feather-light expression that was gone in an instant.

"And yes, this is my first visit," he said smoothly. "I don't know why I have stayed away so long. It is a beautiful city." His eyes locked on hers. "The architecture is most stunning."

"Of course." Rowan had never been to another city, so she had nothing to compare with New Torwood's architecture. He continued to smile and Rowan suddenly felt like a bird locked in a cage.

Remy leaned back in his chair and the move seemed to release his invisible hold on her. Did he have some kind of empathy knack? She found him disarming and, if she was being honest, kind of sexy, which helped her mission since her fragile plan hinged on winning him over with her nonexistent flirtation skills.

"And your mechs are truly inspiring. Never have I seen such mage-work before. The city seems to be run by mechs!" He beamed and pointed to an animated frieze on the opposite wall.

"We are most proud of our mechs," Rowan said. "There is beauty and artistry in such workings, don't you think?"

"Certainly." He finally dove in and lifted her mech hand to his lips. His eyes met hers as he kissed her knuckles. Even through the glove, Rowan felt the heat of the touch like an electrical pulse right up her arm. She gently untangled her fingers from his grip, aware that every eye in the room was locked on them.

His boldness had shattered her composure, and all her careful preparations for winning this man to her cause fled. Then, she spied the brass dome of Talos's head lurching into view above the wall, and sense was restored.

"Oh, look. Here comes our most famous mech. Have you had the chance to study Talos, Ambassador? I mean, Remy?"

Padgett's eyes flicked briefly to the window.

"He's hard to ignore, isn't he? The Talos seems to be everywhere in New Torwood—on flags, signposts, and I even saw his likeness engraved on an ale mug in a tavern."

"You shock me! A man of your breeding in a tavern." She smiled sweetly. Rowan had often taken lunch at one tavern or another in Squall's End after a long day tinkering with Talos. In her mechanic's clothes and with her hair tucked under a hat, no one knew her and she certainly never saw any nobles there. "But yes, we are inordinately proud of Talos. Did you know he was created by Harry Hightower?"

"Yes, I heard that rumor. It's true then?"

"Absolutely. I often go up to the wall to watch him on his daily circuit." She leaned in and spoke softly as if imparting great state secrets. "If you could manage to rise earlier than noon one morning, we could take a late breakfast on my balcony to see him." She batted her eyelashes in a way she'd seen other noblewomen do.

Padgett's eyes sparkled, but his lips pressed into a thin line.

Damn the saints, why didn't her education include flirtation? How hard could it be?

Padgett grinned and leaned back. "I would enjoy such a spectacle, Princess."

The waiter arrived with the mech server again. He served the salad plates with excessive flourish. Rowan stared down at the elaborately curled pieces of carrot with a few shavings of beet and parsnip and sighed.

"You don't approve of salad, Princess?"

"It needs a topper."

"Pepper or cheese?" He raised his hand as if to call the waiter back, but Rowan shook her head.

"I meant more like a steak."

"Ah." A small smile played at the edge of his lips. "I should have guessed that the mysterious princess who hides in her tinker shop would be a carnivore too."

She picked at the vegetable shavings with her fork. "Don't women in Dowchester eat steak?"

"Perhaps in the privacy of their own rooms. Nobody eats unadorned meat in the Dowchester great hall. It's all puff pastries and tiny medallions of roasted bird wrapped in strips of bacon and slathered in sauce. For all I know, we could be eating pigeon."

"Sounds like you could use a bison steak too."

Remy grunted as he lifted the delicate salad to his lips.

The table shook, rattling cutlery and spilling water from the glasses. The floor bucked under their feet. A gasp rose from the other diners as thera lamps flared bright white. The shaking lasted half a minute. The gasps faded to murmurs as it died down. The lamps returned to normal, but the hall suddenly felt dimmer.

Rowan smiled. Remy had a definite look of panic around the eyes.

"Is that your first ley-line surge, Ambassador?"

"Ley-line? That was an earthquake."

"A mild one, yes. Brought on by the ley-lines that converge under the city. It's nothing to worry about."

"This happens often?"

"No. Well, yes. Normal ley-line activity is minor. We might get one noticeable shake every few months. But we're in the middle of what we call a reshaping. Every few years the ley-lines seem to shift or grow. The mages aren't really specific about the details. I'm not sure they really know. But it's nothing to worry about. A few shakes a week for a while, then everything will go back to normal." She lowered her voice. "Thera mechs are most affected. I believe that's why the surges are more noticeable these days." She wiped her lips on her napkin. Should she tell him about her thera theories, about what they'd discovered at Eklridge Oasis? She considered it for only a moment. She didn't know this man, didn't trust him enough. But if she wanted him as an ally, she was going to have to push that trust at some point.

Their next course was served—a pretty plate of puff pastries smothered in gravy. They shared a smile over the southern-style food, then ate in silence for several minutes.

Finally, Remy put down his fork. "As much as I enjoy the company of pretty princesses, I must admit I'm curious about why I'm here. With you."

"Shouldn't you be?"

"Did you ever dine alone with my predecessor?"

Rowan snorted a laugh. "Magnus Robson? Once. Just before he left. He wasn't my biggest fan."

"His loss." Remy sipped at his wine, but his eyes never left her. "So this lunch is for what? To see if I might join the Princess Andula fan club?"

"I hear there's a really good action doll for members. Comes with a detachable arm and everything." She held up her mech arm.

Remy grinned. "I think I'd like to have one of those."

Rowan shoved her plate away. She'd eaten barely half of the small meal, and the food sat like a lump in her stomach.

"I invited you here because I need allies, on and off the council."

"The need for allies implies the desire to effect changes. Do you have changes to propose in New Torwood?"

"I do. The first is a highway that will run from our city to yours. I have created a proposal for this road. It's a good deal for both cities. I would appreciate your support and your time to discuss it with your king and council."

Remy's eyes shone with mischief.

"And where is this proposal?" He feigned looking under the table as if she might be hiding a portfolio.

"If you agree, I will have it delivered to you this afternoon." She looked pointedly at the nobles sitting only a few tables away.

"Of course. You would prefer to be seen as the flighty princess romancing the ambassador instead of a backroom-dealing politician."

"For now."

"And if I agree to consider this highway proposal, how do you plan to implement it without the signature of the regent?"

This was the moment when Rowan had to push that trust in Baron Remy Padgett, a total stranger.

She took a deep breath. "I promise, that if you sign the contract, the regent will sign it too."

"I see." She didn't have to tell him that regent wouldn't be Atherton. This man was shrewd. "And when exactly would the…uh…regent sign it?"

"Before the end of the summer."

"That soon? Honestly, I'm a little shocked. Pleasantly shocked."

He drummed his finger on the table, letting the moment draw itself out. Then he leaned in with a smile. Anyone watching might think he was whispering sweet words.

"You must understand, Princess, I already have a highway proposal from your regent. Atherton brought it to me himself. And it's backed up with money from Theracine Corporation. I can't see any reason to turn it down."

"Atherton is not your friend," she blurted.

He raised an eyebrow. "And you are?"

"I could be." Remy watched her steadily and the words tumbled from her. "What I mean is the regent orchestrated the death of Dowchester citizens. The science team at Eklridge Oasis. They weren't killed by gaunts. They were murdered."

There was a long moment of silence where Rowan could hear her own heart beating.

"You're certain of this?"

Rowan nodded once. "I was there."

"I heard about that. They sent you out into the wilds like a common soldier."

She lifted her chin. "I was proud to serve my city."

"Of course you were."

Remy continued to drum the table until Rowan wanted to smack his hand. Finally, he said, "If I were to bring this new proposal to my king, I would need assurances of its authenticity."

"What kind of assurances?"

"Irrefutable proof that Atherton murdered our people."

"You'll have it." Denny was a Dowchester citizen. If she had to, she'd drag him out of hiding to confirm her story to Remy.

The ambassador still wasn't convinced. "Why would Atherton kill our science team? It was a pet project of our queen, but still, what purpose do these murders serve?"

"I don't know yet. But I will find out. And when I do, I promise you will get a full report." She leaned in and met his eye. "I want the old rivalries between our cities to end. The science delegation was supposed to be a first step in that direction. The highway treaty is another. But if you make the wrong choice here, choose the wrong ally, you may set those rivalries back to the dark ages."

"I will consider your words, Princess." He tapped the table with one hand. "Now, tell me more about this Princess Andula action doll and where I can get one for my nieces."

Rowan rolled her eyes and Remy laughed, but she was glad to be back in flirtation territory.

"I think I have one in my rooms somewhere. I'll send it along with the highway proposal."

"I look forward to seeing them both." Remy's eyes shone with amused delight, and Rowan wondered if she had just gained her first real ally, or made the biggest mistake of her short political career.

16

OLD FRIENDSHIPS AND NEW ALLIES

Dale looked around the sitting room of Gene Hayes's quarters in the palace. It wasn't a large suite, but compared to Dale's cramped little room in the council wing, it was positively roomy. There were no homey touches, no traces of femininity in the decor. Gene's wife and young daughters rarely visited the palace, and he went home to Hightown every evening. That made him a bit of a pariah among the younger nobles who preferred to spend their nights at private clubs.

Dale was happy for him, happy that he'd found the family he'd yearned for.

Gene Hayes was only a year older than Dale. They'd been junior pages together in the palace. Gene was groomed from an early age to succeed his father as Minister of the Purse. Dale's lineage was more modest and they'd never expected to rise higher than secretary. Regardless of the gap in their stations, Gene had always been friendly—kind even. After Ethan's attack, Gene had cautiously reached out to the angry, grieving boy Dale had been. A friendship had been born in that grief.

Dale hoped that friendship hadn't faded too much because they had a big ask.

Gene sat on the couch with one ankle crossed over the other knee and foot dancing to music only he could hear. He was a thin man with blond hair and eyebrows so white, they disappeared against his pale complexion.

Silence stretched between them.

"You sure I can't get you a drink?" Gene asked. Refreshments had already been offered and declined, but Gene's nervous energy had him up and

131

pouring out two snifters of honey wine before Dale could object again.

Dale took the glass, sipped it and set it aside. They'd never favored the sickly sweetness of honey wine.

"So is this a social call?" Gene asked. "Or business?"

"A bit of both. I realized that we haven't caught up in a while." Dale felt a tug of guilt for lying. "How are Rebecca and the girls?"

Gene's entire demeanor changed at the mention of his family. He sat up straighter and a light sparkled in his eyes. "She's expecting again. She's hoping for a boy, but I'll be happy with another girl." He gave a shy smile. "I kinda like being the only guy in the house."

Dale nodded his understanding. Gene had grown up with three older brothers. Two had died in the gaunt uprising. The other was an orator in Jupiter's Temple. That left the family legacy of politics to fall on Gene's shoulders.

"And how's your father?" Dale said.

This brought a scowl to Gene's face. Saints, the man should never play cards. Every emotion that went through his head showed on his face.

"He has good days and bad days."

"More bad than good, I hear."

Gene nodded.

It was no secret that Rufus Hayes was declining. His mind had been sliding into that dark pit of dementia for years. Gene took up the slack where he could. In every way but the actual title, he was the holder of the palace's purse strings.

"People are talking," Dale said carefully. "They say he's no longer fit to serve on the council, that his...condition is actually a danger to the city."

Gene sat up straighter. Two points of pink bloomed on his cheeks. "Who said that?"

Dale waved the question away. "Just rumors. You know, the kind that make noise without much substance."

Gene sank back into the couch and gulped his wine.

"But I believe we should squash those rumors before they grow into something more sinister."

"Yes, yes. Good idea. What do you suggest?"

"Well, you are ostensibly the minister anyway. Other than taking his seat on the council, does Rufus actually perform his duties anymore?"

Gene's lips pressed together as if he could hold back the truth.

Dale decided to approach the problem from a softer side.

"Come on, you know I have your back. You'll be minister one day anyway, so what does it matter?"

Gene grunted an assent.

"All I mean to say, is that you're performing his duties already, so maybe you should take on one more."

Gene sipped his wine and nodded for Dale to go on. Dale took a deep breath. They were relying heavily on the bonds of old friendship here.

"I've been in consultation with Princess Andula, and she has some concerns over the last treasury audit."

"The princess?"

Dale could see the gears and cogs connecting in Gene's mind. Everyone in the palace was wondering what Rowan meant to achieve by taking her seat at the council table.

"Yes, she asked me to go over the books for last year and we're both concerned about some numbers that don't add up." This was a blatant lie. Atherton's ledgers were impeccable—at least the ledgers he allowed the council to see.

"We would like you—and only you—to perform a deep dive audit of the treasury. Make sure the real funds match what's in the books. Can you do this?"

Gene nodded slowly.

"You think someone is embezzling funds from the palace?"

"Not embezzling, exactly, but perhaps making unauthorized payments."

Gene stood up, paced across the room and back again.

"If this is true, my father will take the blame. It will mean he ends his career in disgrace."

Dale knew that Gene had little love for his authoritarian father, but his loyalty ran deep.

"That's why you must do this, and bring the results only to me." Dale stood and gripped Gene's arm. "Think about it. Eventually, these missing funds will come to light. And when that happens, do you think Atherton will even pause for a moment? No. He'll put the blame squarely on Rufus's head. You won't be the next Minister of the Purse. He'll use this as a way to oust your family and put in one of his cronies."

Gene was visibly shaken now. Dale squeezed his arm.

"But we know, Rowan and me and a few others. We know that Atherton has been using your father, exploiting his illness for his own gains. Find the truth. Share it with no one but us, and I promise you, your father's legacy will be honored, not betrayed."

Dale could see Gene's gaze turn inward as he processed this information. It was a lot to take in, a lot to take on faith.

"All right. I'll do it." He drained his glass and slammed it down on a side table.

They shook hands and Dale left the suite, feeling pleased and nervous. Their team was growing. Dale had no doubt that Gene would find discrepancies in the royal treasury. There were always discrepancies. Alone that information wouldn't sway anyone to their cause, but paired with the false ledgers, it would make a good enough case to oust Atherton from the regency.

Now all Dale had to do was find those saints-damned ledgers.

17

CITY WORKINGS

ROWAN WAS THE FIRST TO arrive for the weekly council meeting. In fact, she made sure to be there a good hour before the appointed time. Minna followed her in and stood between the heir's seat and the door with her back to the wall. Rowan had sent a page to fetch Dale, and they trailed in a few minutes later, looking a bit lost, with a mech valet at their heels. Rowan patted the table beside her.

"Sit here, please. Try to look intimidating. Take note of everyone who walks through that door, the time they arrived and in whose company."

Dale frowned. "Won't there be a scribe in attendance?"

"Yes, but people ignore them the way they ignore servants. Hardly intimidating. And every minister knows the hoops one must jump through just to get a transcript from the Temple of the Word. Most don't bother. But having you, as my secretary, taking notes…they'll be thinking about that all day, wondering if I'm poring over their words at night, looking for ways to use them as weapons."

Dale smiled in that upside-down way. "I like it. Subtle and angst-inducing, but I'm not your secretary. Not yet." They took a seat on the other side of the table, leaving a place for Atherton beside Rowan.

She sighed. "You still haven't told him you're leaving." Dale's feet had been dragging over this issue for weeks. She wasn't sure why they stalled. Was it from fear of retaliation from Atherton? Or a simple aversion to confrontation?

Dale touched a button on the valet. A compartment opened to show several files and notebooks. Dale pulled out a large notebook and a stylus and spoke without meeting her eye. "I just need a few more days. I'm working on some things. Plus, I want to finish my sweep of the archives. Once I'm officially your secretary, the archives won't be exactly off limits, but my comings and goings will be noted."

Dale had made this excuse several times already. They'd been friends for twenty years. There wasn't anyone in the castle she trusted more, but she was getting impatient. She wanted to shake Dale until their teeth rattled and the truth fell out.

As they waited for the others to arrive, the only sound was the clicking of the Infinity Clock's gears. The great mech filled the largest wall in the hall. It was the centerpiece of the council chambers, gifted to Rowan's great-great-grandfather by a long-dead high orator of Temple Jupiter. The clock ticked away, counting time, but not the hour. There were no hands for seconds or minutes. Instead, the clock face was a brass and silver sky-scape of the moon, sun and stars. A cloud shaped pendulum rocked back and forth across the sky. Rowan always wondered if it was ticking down to a deadline, and what would happen if its pendulum stilled.

The tedious sound was unbearably loud in the silent room.

A few minutes later, a page stuck her head through the open chamber door. She goggled at the princess sitting serenely at the nearly empty council table and hurried out.

Rowan smiled.

"Right about now, a bunch of ministers are getting notice that the heir called an early start to this meeting and they're already late," she said quietly.

"Your manipulations know no bounds." Dale's expression was impassive. "Look bored and annoyed. There's another page coming."

Sure enough, another young page popped in, then ran out again. A scribe entered next, hurrying to take up their position on the bench in the corner. Rowan's mech fingers clenched impulsively when she spied the cable running from the young woman's neck to a cachet hidden on her belt.

When she was regent…Oh, the changes she would make, and scribes would be the first to go.

Dr. Renata arrived. She scowled at Rowan and sat without a word. Gene Hayes, acting Minister of the Purse, showed up with his shirt buttoned wrong and his hair uncombed. The joint Ministers of Defense came next. Keeper

General Adrian Lind and Ranger General Dobrin Kranson spoke quietly as they took their seats. Chancellor Olan March followed. He winked at Rowan before he sat.

Dale made a notation for each arrival.

Minister of Foreign Affairs Stella Keiffer arrived with Orator Lucian, the minister who liaised with the temples.

The orator favored Rowan with a short bow. "Abbot Archivist Wiktor sends his regrets. There is an emergency at the Temple of the Word that requires his attention."

"I hope it is nothing too serious." Rowan studied him. Lucian was young for such an important job. He facilitated workings between the three main temples and the palace. Considering how much of the palace purse was dedicated to the temples, it was a job that came with much influence.

"A minor outbreak of gangra from all accounts."

Rowan nodded, and a flurry of murmurs went through the waiting ministers. Gangra in the city was ill news. The disease was almost always fatal, and though it wasn't highly contagious, the general populace would panic if news of an outbreak spread within the city walls.

Minister of the Guilds Marilyn Docker arrived next and Flora Bosman, liaison to Theracine Corporation rounded out the table. Flora nodded at Rowan as if her morning schedule hadn't been disrupted. She took the chair at the far end of the table and her secretary, Kenneth Smith, sat beside her.

The room fell silent again. They waited only for the Regent and the Minister of Science. But Miron Wrede wouldn't be coming. As far as anyone knew, he was lost somewhere in the Meadows, perhaps dead.

Faustus Atherton finally arrived, looking displeased. His brows were pinched together and his usually slick hair was misbehaving with a slight curl around the ears. His suit was polished and he wore the chain of the regent's office around his neck. The heavy medallion stamped with the city's emblem—the stylized head of Talos—was askew and it flapped as he walked. It was a minor detail, but for the normally impeccable regent, it was telling.

He made for his seat and stopped when he saw Dale.

"What are you doing here?"

Rowan answered first. "I asked Dale to be here. To act as my secretary until I can find one of my own. You wouldn't begrudge me the use of your secretary, would you?" Rowan favored him with what she thought was a sweet smile. She'd been practicing it in front of Minna for such occasions. Minna said she had too much darkness and not enough mirth in her eyes when she smiled. Rowan wasn't sure what that even meant.

Dale's eyes sparked with defiance, but Rowan had the sinking feeling that defiance was directed at her.

Atherton glared at his secretary then at Rowan. "Well, no. Of course not. But we do have a scribe." He gestured to the black-garmented woman in the corner. Her eyes were already blank with that creepy scribe-stare.

"We do." Rowan confirmed. She left it at that. "I am told there is gangra in the Temple of the Word. I hope our agenda today will address this problem."

"Indeed it does," Atherton said.

"Good. And I have new business to propose, which is why I requested the early start." She heard one of the ministers let out a quiet groan. "But that can wait until this problem with gangra has been resolved."

"Thank you, my lady." Atherton smiled and Rowan frowned. Her title was *Princess* or *Heir Apparent*, not *my lady*. He used the informality as a weapon to undermine her authority. Two could play that game.

"Please, Faustus," she stressed his given name. "Tell us how you plan to address the gangra outbreak." She caught Dale's eye and pointed to the notebook, as if indicating that they should take note. Dale frowned.

"Ah, yes," Atherton began. "In fact, we have a decisive plan for the gangra outbreak in Oxeye, and should the disease become a problem in the city we can implement the same strategies here. General Kranson, won't you walk us through it?"

The General cleared his throat and pushed his chair back so his big frame sat on the edge. Kranson was a ranger through and through. He was a big man who'd shrunk a bit with age. His skin was weathered brown like old leather and it was starting to sag, softening his chiseled features. When he spoke, it was with a voice of authority.

"We isolated the infected. Those with less serious cases are tending to the dying until the Jocastans can get there."

"That seems…harsh," Rowan said.

Kranson fixed her with an unforgiving eye. "It's a harsh disease, Princess. We're doing our best. We lost some good rangers out there."

Rowan nodded her understanding, and he continued. "We brought the Rangers down from Norsap to bury the dead and bring order to Oxeye. Most of the reapers are dead, mind you, so thera production has come to a near standstill."

Flora Bosman leaned in. "We're transferring reapers from the Titan camp, but we're still short of general laborers. Regent Atherton have you given any thought to my suggestion to conscript laborers from Squall's End?"

Atherton's elbow rested on the table and his hand cradled his cheek and jaw. His lips pursed and he ran his middle finger over his mustache as if he were lost deep in thought.

Before he could answer, Rowan spoke to General Kranson. "Please make something clear to me. You moved all the Rangers from Norsap outpost? Doesn't that leave the Algid Pass free for the Taiga to come through? And who's left to watch the gaunts to the north?"

Kranson smiled as if indulging a child who worried about the sky falling.

"We have scouts all along the Ubruulen ridge. We'll know about any mass gatherings of gaunts or Taiga long before they become trouble." He turned his attention back to the Regent, but Rowan wasn't ready to yield the floor.

"Putting aside concerns over security, you can't mean to conscript people. The law strictly prevents that except in times of war." Rowan wasn't sure of this bit of law, but glanced at Dale who nodded.

"We *are* at war," Dr. Renata said with more vehemence than Rowan thought was warranted. "Just because our enemy is a disease, doesn't mean we aren't facing a battle—one that could decimate our army."

"Precisely." This from Flora Bosman. "Theracine Corporation is willing to train and pay all conscripts, but we need bodies in Oxeye as soon as possible."

Rowan didn't like the term *bodies*. It brought back memories of the dead stacked like cordwood outside Oxeye Outpost.

"And we're certain it's gangra?" said Rowan. "How can that be? I thought gangra wasn't contagious."

Dr. Renata sighed as if having to explain was a chore. "Gangra isn't contagious human to human. It is contracted through the consumption of infected nacara mussel meat. However, we hypothesize that the bacteria responsible for gangra is very contagious from one mussel to another."

"And the workers and rangers in the thera camps eat a steady diet of nacara," said Rowan. She turned to Flora Bosman for confirmation.

Flora opened her hands and shrugged. "The meat is cheap and plentiful."

Rowan ground her teeth. People's health shouldn't be compromised by greed.

"I still don't agree with conscription," she said. "And such an act can only be taken by royal decree."

Atherton finally spoke. "Exactly. And I speak for the royal house here, not you, my *lady*." He leaned on that last word. His palm slapped the table. "Conscriptions will begin in a week. Give the order that those who volunteer before then will receive a signing bonus." He looked at Flora Bosman, who nodded. "And then we'll fill in the ranks with conscripts as needed."

"At least we should set an inquiry into the gangra problem at the thera camps!" Rowan wanted to jump up and pound the table just like Atherton, but she kept to her chair. She had to show them she was reasonable and level-headed. Atherton was right. She did not speak for the royal seat. Not yet. "What good is there in throwing more *bodies* at the problem if they're simply going to die?"

"I'm sure Minister Wrede will tackle the problem as soon as he returns." Atherton said. "Moving onto other…"

"Actually, that is exactly my first new business," Rowan cut in. "Minister Wrede has been absent these last three months. I made it quite clear that attendance to council meetings is required, pending some emergency."

"But Minister Wrede is out in the field, doing important research." Flora Bosman smiled. Her thin lips and wide set eyes gave her a reptilian look. Rowan half-expected her tongue to flick out and taste the air.

"Is he?" Rowan asked. "I understand that Minister Wrede had a private laboratory in the Meadows at a place called the Warren, but it has been abandoned."

"Where did you hear this?" Atherton demanded.

"From reports sent to your office. Do you deny it?"

Rowan didn't look at Dale, but she knew they would be fuming. She'd just burned his bridge. Atherton glared at his secretary, then turned to Rowan.

"You go through my private correspondence now?"

"None of those reports should be private." Rowan put the force of her royal lineage behind those words. "You hold your office at the pleasure of this council. That correspondence is for us all." She turned to address the rest of the ministers who watched with expressions ranging from shock to derision.

"Wrede's lab was attacked by gaunts," Rowan said. This was only partially true. There had been gaunts but they'd attacked Squad 54, days after Wrede had abandoned the Warren. "There were no survivors found at the site. In fact, the only account we have of the incident comes from ranger scouts who found traces of blood and a ransacked camp. And since no one here has heard from Minister Wrede in all these weeks, I am sorry to say that we should consider him lost."

She waited for a response to flicker across Atherton's eyes, but they were black and unreadable. Of course she knew that Wrede hadn't been at the Warren when the gaunts attacked. He'd already bugged out, taking his team and research with him.

"You haven't heard from Minister Wrede, have you, Regent? Because if you did, he would be in attendance, wouldn't he?"

"No," Atherton said, curtly. "I haven't heard from the minister or his team."

"Then I propose we need a new Minister of Science, all in favor?" Rowan held her breath. This was a risk. Dale's quiet interviews with the ministers showed they were evenly divided. She might not have the clout to pass this proposal and the loss would set her back.

"Aye," said Chancellor March. General Lind also nodded. His co-minister General Kranson seemed reluctant, but he nodded too. She needed one more vote to push the proposal through. She ignored Atherton and Bosman, knowing she'd get no help there, and looked each of the other ministers in the eye.

Dr. Renata scowled. She didn't seem to have any other expression. Stella Keiffer shook her head. Marylin Docker, Minister of Guilds wouldn't even meet her eye. But one minister surprised her.

"Aye," said Orator Lucian. "We need a minister of science here in the city. Not out gallivanting in the Meadows."

Rowan grinned and looked pointedly at Atherton.

The Regent nodded. "The ayes have it. A search for a new Minister of Science will begin."

"Please, let me find a likely candidate," Rowan said. "Or rather candidates. I wish to be useful to the council." She smiled ingratiatingly at Atherton. "And you will have final approval for the new minister, of course."

Atherton looked like he wanted to spit on her, but it was a reasonable request, and as long as he had the final approval, he had no elegant way to turn her down. He got his expression under control and said, "Of course. Now if there is no new business…"

"Actually, I have one more request," Rowan said. Atherton fought to keep a rebuttal from bursting through his pinched lips and only waved her on.

Rowan hesitated. There were so many things she wanted to change. The people of Grotto needed help. The Bailey Chamber of Commerce wanted sweeping changes. The gangra outbreak was far from settled. But she had to choose her battles wisely and the one that she might actually win was Talos.

"It has come to my attention that the maintenance on Talos has been lacking since the keepers took it over."

General Lind bristled and Rowan smiled at him. "This is not a criticism of your keepers, General. I understand better than anyone, the difficulty of maintaining Talos."

"The mech is a relic of a dead age and should be scrapped," Flora Bosman said.

"Our citizens take great pride in our magnificent mech," Rowan shot back. "No other city, not even the great Dowchester can boast a Harry Hightower mech that guards their walls." She glared at Bosman, urging her to disagree. Bosman crossed her arms and looked away, not willing to take on the fight.

"But in order to maintain this important piece of our history, it's time to care for him properly. I propose a sum of two thousand chips be put aside for labor on Talos. And he will need to be shut down for some time. I estimate two weeks, at least."

Atherton surprised her with a smile. "Once again, my lady, you show your complete ineptitude to govern. Shutting Talos down for more than a few hours would cripple our city."

"I don't understand."

"Of course you don't. Because you are uneducated in the delicate weaves of this city. Talos is more than a monument. His magic is tied directly to the pumps that drive our water supply."

"What?"

Atherton held up a hand to stall anymore comments. "So you see shutting him down for any length of time would put the health of all our citizens at risk. But I agree, something needs to be done. In fact, it has already been done. With the generosity of the Theracine Corporation," he nodded at Flora Bosman. "We are poised to retrofit the city's water pumps with thera burners. The abundance of thera as fuel will mean that Talos will no longer be needed. Perhaps Dr. Renata would like to add him to her collection of exotic mechs?"

"I fear he would fill my entire garden," Renata said. "A more fitting end for Talos might be a dedicated resting place outside the walls where he can be admired by those arriving at our gates. Don't you agree, Princess?"

Atherton didn't wait for her answer, but adjourned the meeting. He rose and left the room, indicating with a sharp jerk of his hand that Dale should follow.

Dale frowned at Rowan, tucked away the notebooks and left without a word.

A few minutes later, Rowan was alone except for Minna waiting by the door. The elf made a fist and tapped her chest.

"When the sky is hollow and the world turns white, follow the bones."

"Am I supposed to know what that means?" Rowan asked.

"One day, Evani."

Rowan covered her face with her hands, as if that could wipe away the embarrassment of this day.

The Infinity Clock's ticking now had an ominous tone.

18

CONFESSIONS

ROWAN BURST INTO HER ROOMS with the bluster of an impending storm. She threw herself on the bed and lay flat, staring at the finely woven threads of her canopy, but she couldn't lie still. Embarrassment—and rage at being embarrassed—made her restless. She rolled off the bed and paced toward the mantle. Staring into the dead hearth did nothing to relax her, and she paced to the double glass doors that led to the patio. The bland overcast sky didn't ease her nerves either.

Roger was tucked into a nook beside the doors. He'd been quiet for nearly a week while his—what did Harry call them? Processors?—while his processors sorted the data on the cachet. She wished she could shake him until the answers she needed fell out.

Minna made a small noise by the door and Rowan turned.

"Will you be going out again, Evani?"

Rowan ignored the question.

"Is it possible? Is Talos really fueling the city's water pumps?"

"Yes and no, Evani. I felt it the first time we came into the city. There is deep magic in his ritual. Talos walks the same road every day. His turning is like a water wheel, only the water is magic. We call it *coku*. You would call it…mimicry magic, perhaps. The act becomes the thing."

Rowan wouldn't call it anything. She had no idea that such a thing was even possible.

"And there is belief too—another powerful magic. We call it *repi*." Minna said.

Rowan stared at her, uncomprehending.

144

"Repi is the most powerful magic of all, Evani. It is the reason your city founders downgraded gods to saints. True belief can break worlds. And the people of New Torwood believe in Talos. He has guarded your city for hundreds of years. He walks the walls as sure as the seasons turn. Children chase him, adults smile when they see the dome of his head over the wall. This I have seen, Evani. They revere him like the sun. All that belief gives weight to each of his footfalls. So yes, Talos may be the thing that runs your city's water."

"So if Talos goes down. The pumps stop working." Rowan leaned her forehead against the cool glass door. "But the council is already planning to replace his magic-fueled pump with one that runs on thera. What happens then to all that belief the people put into him?"

She turned to see Minna shrug. Her bone earrings danced. "It will leave a void perhaps, but the people will find something else to focus their belief on. They always do."

Rowan's thoughts were a jumbled mess, and she worked to sort through them. Talos was inexorably linked to the royal house of Andula. One of the first kings of New Torwood had commissioned him from Harry Hightower. Watching him fall would be like watching her family's legacy collapse.

Which was exactly what the council wanted.

Bringing down Talos wasn't just about replacing the water pumps, it was about replacing the monarchy. She couldn't let that happen.

The door was wrenched open with such force that Minna went into an immediate attack stance. Blades appeared in her hands and her lip curled in a snarl. Then she recognized Dale and relaxed, but only marginally.

"How dare you burn me like that?" Dale's eyes blazed with fury. "I've just spent the last half hour trying to convince Atherton that I'm still on his team."

"You didn't tell me about Talos!" Rowan shot back. "How could you?"

Dale sputtered, face going red. "I've been trying to fill in the gaps in your miserable education, but I'm not a mind reader! It never occurred to me you could be so ignorant."

"And I never realized you had the spine of a meadow snake. When are you finally going to stand up to Atherton?"

They stood face to face, Rowan's head tilted slightly to meet Dale's extra height. Dale's eyes were rimmed in red. From sleepless nights or unshed tears?

How had she not seen the toll stress was taking on her friend?

She let out a big breath and it seemed to deflate her.

"I'm sorry. I should have spoken to you first." She turned to Minna. "Would you please leave us. Make sure we aren't disturbed."

Minna frowned at Dale, then retreated to the hall and shut the door.

Rowan sat on the couch. Dale perched on a chair opposite her. The mech valet that followed Dale everywhere had come in unnoticed and it now waited at the foot of the chair like a loyal dog.

"It was selfish of me," Rowan said. "You kept saying you were going to leave Atherton's service, but then you had one excuse after another not to. I thought," she paused and squeezed her hands together. The mech hand creaked inside the glove. "I thought you'd changed your mind about being my advisor."

"Never!" Dale said with more vehemence than she'd expected. "The only reason I ever went to work for Atherton was to be Ethan's eyes and ears. To try and fix…" The words trailed off with a sigh. "There are things you don't know—things you need to know."

"Tell me."

"I want to." Dale met her gaze, eyes pleading with her. "But you will despise me when I do."

She leaned forward to grip their hand. "Tell me anyway."

Dale sucked in a deep breath and nodded.

"You already know that Ethan wasn't attacked by gaunts. Someone tried to assassinate him."

Rowan nodded slowly. She hated hearing those words out loud.

"Back then, Atherton was part of a conspiracy," Dale continued. "Only he wasn't regent then. He was head of a group of ministers who wanted to oust the monarch altogether."

Rowan's heart felt like it was on fire.

"And you have proof of this?"

Dale nudged the mech valet with a toe. "Memos they thought they'd destroyed. It's all in there. The wording is vague. They tried to cover their tracks but if you read it with hindsight, it's pretty obvious. You were all supposed to die—you, Ethan and your father."

Rowan sucked in a breath. "But they failed."

"Not really."

"How can you say that? Ethan lives. The heir lives!"

"Does he? They might have failed to kill him, but I suspect Atherton got exactly what he wanted."

Rowan's hand went to her mouth as if she could hold in her words. "He wanted to rule."

"Exactly."

"But why not just kill Ethan? Atherton's had years to finish the job."

"Because an incapacitated heir suits his purposes better than a dead heir."

Her thoughts were spiraling now. Minna's words came back to her. There was magic around Ethan, cocooning him, possibly keeping him dormant.

"Think about it," Dale said. "What would happen if Ethan died?"

"I would be heir."

"And if you died?"

"I…I don't know. Auntie Bella would rule, maybe? Cousin Harold? Surely someone would claim the throne."

"Many someones. At best it would start a squabble amongst the nobles. At worst, it would plunge the city into civil war. But in no way would this lead to Atherton ruling."

"And now?"

"And now he's been ruling for nearly two decades. The people accept him. He's got the backing of powerful nobles and the Theracine Corporation which we know has far too much power in the city already."

"All he needs is a clear path to the throne."

Dale nodded. "You need to watch your back, Princess. I've done some digging and he's going to strike soon."

It made sense. The pieces were all in place. Atherton might have waited a bit longer, might have enjoyed his unofficial rule, except for that pesky princess who refused to die in the Meadows like a good girl.

But she'd already known her life was at risk. This wasn't anything new.

"That still doesn't tell me why you've been dragging your feet about the secretary thing. I need you by my side if we're going to navigate these treacherous waters."

Dale pulled away from her grip and looked down. "Because there's something else you don't know. That day at the ruins…" There was a hitch in Dale's voice. Rowan waited, dreading the words that might break a lifetime of friendship.

"That day we went outside the wall," Dale continued, "I told someone where to find us."

"Who?"

Dale's expression was grim. "Flora Bosman."

Rowan searched her memory for the lessons Dale had taught her about recent politics. They'd made her memorize the palace hierarchy going back two centuries. Twenty years ago, Flora Bosman was an up-and-comer at court, and she was secretary to then-chancellor, Faustus Atherton.

Dale's eyes seemed sunken and haunted.

"She came to me more than once and told me how important it was that I keep Ethan out of trouble." Dale laughed harshly. "As if that was ever possible."

Rowan smiled, remembering her brash brother, who always had to climb higher or run faster than anyone else.

"Flora made me report on our adventures, said it was my duty to keep Ethan safe, and if I refused, I would be sent away from the palace."

"That must have been hard for you." Rowan knew that Dale had been orphaned at a young age. The family was minor nobility, so the decision had been made to raise Dale as the prince's companion.

A tear rolled down Dale's cheek. They wouldn't look at her.

"You don't understand! I *told* them where to find Ethan. I *told* them about going to the ruins. They were waiting for us because of me! Don't you see? I betrayed him. I betrayed you! That's why I can't be your secretary! I don't *deserve* it!" Tears flowed freely now. Dale wiped at them with the flat of a hand.

Rowan waited until Dale's heaving breath calmed.

"Of course you told the adults where you were going. You had no reason not to trust them. None of this was your fault. You can't place that weight on the shoulders of a child. And if you would let that child go," she tapped their chest, "you would be able to see that."

Dale looked up, their eyes bleak.

"You don't believe me. Not yet." She patted their hand. "We'll have to work on that. But right now I need to prove to the ministers that I'm capable of making alliances that last. I need you at my side. Can you do that?"

Dale sniffled then sucked in a deep breath. Tipping their head side to side, they stretched and sat straighter. "I can do that."

"So you'll tell Atherton?"

Dale nodded.

"Good. Then I think we need to do something about these new water pumps."

Dale nodded again. "I've been thinking about that. The project is too new for the schematics to be filed in the archives. They have to be in Atherton's office. I'll find them."

"And how are you going to do that if you're not his secretary anymore?" Rowan crossed her arms and glared at him.

Dale smiled ruefully. "I'll tell him. I promise. I'll search the office tomorrow. He'll be out in the afternoon. Then I'll tell him before I leave for the day."

"Snake shake on it." Rowan held out her left hand with her fingers spread wide.

Dale sighed. "I thought we gave up this foolishness when we hit puberty."

"Snake shake!" she demanded.

Dale looped a thumb around hers, then they both waggled their fingers like snakes.

Rowan grinned. It was impossible not to while acting out their childhood buddy pact.

Dale's expression softened too. "You know Ethan was furious with me for showing that to you. Said I violated the brother code."

"Yeah, well, when he wakes up, he can gripe about it then."

"When he wakes." Dale's expression was now determined and Rowan took that as a win.

INTERLUDE

The clan hunted along the Black River. Garou stretched his legs and ran faster than even the pack leaders. Misha couldn't catch him. Only their sister Lark ran faster, and she was ahead, flushing game for others to catch. With the wind whistling through his ears, Garou never wanted to stop running. A hare dashed across his path. He changed course in mid-leap—exalting in the power of his muscles—and crashed down on the hare's back, killing it instantly and mercifully, the way his uncle had taught him.

With the hare dangling from his jaws, he jogged back to the camp, not even winded. It was good to be a wolf.

Garou dropped his offering beside the campfire. There was more game already laid out—hares, weasels, raccoons and a deer. The pack would eat well tonight.

"Is that all? A hare?" The voice grated like gravel in Garou's teeth.

Garrett stood over him with human fists balled at his sides. Garou whined and crouched. Their alpha smelled wrong. It was better when he let his wolf out. Rhys's wolf energy masked some of the sickness in their shared body. But no one had seen Rhys in many moons.

"Get cleaned up, then come and skin these." Garrett kicked dirt and Garou skidded backward. He slunk into the trees and shifted.

Conall rose and stretched. The hunt had been good. He'd needed to burn off some steam. At sixteen, he had energy and rage to burn. Most of that rage was directed at his father.

Garrett's addiction had worsened over the last two years. He was never sober. He would drink himself into a stupor in the evenings, wake and snort thera just to make it through the day. His children tried to hide his weakness from the other wolves, but there would be no hiding it tonight. The Black River Clan had come together to celebrate. They would hunt for a week around the homestead before heading to Briar Market for the yearly gathering of Wildblood Clans.

As Conall pulled on his clothes, he could already hear voices raised in anger. He strode back to camp. Garrett was arguing with Sebastian Boldt, head of a family who lived about forty miles north.

Garrett towered over Boldt, but Boldt wasn't shrinking away. He was short but brawny, and more than one wolf had assumed his stature was a weakness before discovering the power in those shoulders.

The two men were red faced. Boldt raised a fist and shook it. Conall couldn't even tell what the argument was about, but someone needed to intervene, and fast.

If Uncle Birch were still alive, he would have stepped in. Birch was the only one who could calm Garrett when the rages took him. But Birch had died last spring.

"You're not fit to lead!" Boldt shouted.

Garrett spat on him. "I will kill you!" He screamed the words at the sky as if he wanted to drown the world. Tendons stuck out on his neck. They were purple and swollen and throbbed unnaturally. Garrett lowered his gaze and pinned it on Boldt. He looked half-crazed. Dark blotches covered his face, like vivid manifestations of his rage. His eyes were black—pupil and iris fusing as one. He grinned and saliva dripped down his chin.

Boldt stepped back, shocked at the change in Garrett's appearance.

"What is this sorcery?"

Garrett let out an eerie cackle, more rabid than sane.

There were two dozen clan members watching, some human, some wolf, and all still and silent.

Garrett raised a hand. His fingernails were black and pointed. He slashed them across Boldt's face. Boldt staggered backward, his hand going to the bloody gashes on his cheek.

Wildbloods understood what it was like to share their body and mind with another entity, but Garrett's body had been taken over by something ugly and uncanny. Conall, Nathan and Ianna had seen the monster emerge before, but this was the first time Garrett had let it loose among the clan.

The shocked silence spoke volumes.

Conall saw the moment Garrett decided to kill Boldt. His leg muscles tensed, ready to spring. Conall was too far away, but he ran at his father anyway, hoping to intervene before Garrett took things too far.

Nathan beat him to it. He tackled Garrett. They fell hard. Garrett rolled and tried to pin his son. He was taller and stronger than Nathan and lit with the fire of madness. Nathan struck out, catching Garrett's chin with the heel of his hand. Garrett's head snapped back.

He roared and headbutted Nathan.

Blood burst from Nathan's nose. His hands came up to protect his face while Garrett battered him—punch after punch, spittle flying, eyes flashing with savage fire. Nathan's arms took the brunt of the hits, until Garrett landed one on the side of his head. Nathan's arms dropped and he fell unconscious.

During the fight, clan wolves were shouting. Conall was running. Boldt and his sons tried to intervene. Conall reached them and together they managed to haul Garrett off Nathan.

Garrett shook them off and wiped blood from the corner of his mouth. His eyes flashed with dark zeal. He spat blood on the ground and shook his head.

He might have realized he'd gone too far. His eyes flicked to his unconscious son, then to the stunned faces of his clan.

"Get him cleaned up. This party's over." Garrett stalked into the shadows growing under the trees.

Boldt turned to Conall. "He's mad! Completely fucking mad!"

Conall had no answer for that.

Ianna bent over Nathan. "Help me get him into a cabin." She picked up his feet. Conall grabbed his shoulders and they carried their brother away.

The clan left the following day. Ianna and Conall watched from the front porch. Garrett was sleeping off his hangover.

"Will Boldt petition the conclave?" Conall asked.

"I hope so," Ianna said. "The gods know I've tried. Maybe a second voice will make them see reason."

If Boldt made a good case, he could become alpha of the Black River Clan. Then Garrett would have to leave this place, the clan house. They would be homeless. Conall found he didn't care.

Nathan recovered. Two days later, he found Conall on the banks of the river. Conall had come down to fish, but his pole sat on the grass, unused.

"I'm leaving," Nathan said.

Conall nodded, not looking around. A lump in his chest seemed determined to choke him. He would let it. He was sixteen, for love of the wolf. Tears were a weakness he could no longer afford.

Nathan sat beside him.

"I'm sorry. I have to go. If I don't, I'll kill him. And we all know I can't take him in a fair fight. I'll smother him in his sleep or poison his food. It would be murder. The conclave will scatter my bones in the Meadows for it. I won't let him ruin my life."

Conall nodded again. "Where will you go?"

"New Torwood." Nathan had always talked about being a scribe one day and sitting in on the workings of history. "As soon as I'm accepted as a novice at the Temple, I'll send for you. By then, you'll be eighteen, old enough for any apprenticeship you want. Ianna too. We'll make a new life away from all this."

"Okay." There was nothing else to say. Nathan rose, squeezed his shoulder and kissed the top of his head. Conall listened to his brother's footsteps on the trail. Then he sat for a long time, watching the fish jump.

19

THE WEIGHT OF A MOUNTAIN

THE WOLF RAN FOR THREE days and nights. The land changed. It undulated with steep hills and low valleys. Grass gave way to rocks and scrub brush. Nights were growing longer. Moon moss dotted the terrain with purple light. As they moved northward, the blunt ends of the Ubruulens seemed to fizzle out.

Ailen met him as he returned from his evening hunt. He pointed eastward, into the valley between the mountains. "Benni. Soon."

Garou cocked his head. Conall wanted to know how soon, but Garou couldn't ask.

It would be best to meet the elves on two feet, brother, Conall said. *You got us this far. Let me deal with the Ebos now.*

Garou snorted and shook out his mane. For Misha, he would give up his fur and more. He shifted in the shadows, and Conall returned to camp, naked except for the graphium on the long cord around his neck. It felt heavy against his chest. He yearned to open it and find a message from Rowan, but he needed privacy first. And clothes.

The Ebos who'd rifled through his bag on that first night handed him his pack. He'd heard the others call her Kelli. She didn't mask her grin as her eyes swept him from toes to head. He ignored the blatant appraisal and pulled on pants and a shirt. He'd spent too long in his fur coat and without it, the night air was brisk.

After dressing and drinking from his canteen, he joined the elves in their camp. The stunted northern pines and bushy alders provided dead wood for a small fire that lit the Ebos faces gathered around it.

Kelli watched him with a half-grin. She reminded him of Minna who also observed the world with amusement. He didn't know the others by name, only by scent. Beside Kelli crouched a male who looked to be about forty. In Ebos years that could mean he was anywhere from sixty to over a hundred. Garou referred to him as Soot because he smelled like an old pipe. Beside Soot sat Sweat, a nervous young elf with red splotchy skin who wouldn't meet Conall's eye—clearly a new recruit.

An image of Augie—floating and humming—flitted across his memories and Conall's stomach lurched. Hopefully, Ailen could keep his green alive where Conall had failed.

The other three Ebos in the party—two males and a second female— were nearly identical. They favored the fair hair and pale skin of their race. Garou had named them, Scruff, Beetle and Mint, apparently for their unique scents, though Conall's nose couldn't tell one from the other.

Only Ailen stood out. He was taller than the others with tawny hair rather than blond.

His eyes met Conall's and he smiled.

"Conall West. It is pleasing to see you again." Ailen offered him a cup of something warm. Conall sipped it hesitantly, remembering the fermented yenni from his earlier encounters with the Ebos. This drink had a tang he didn't recognize, but it was warm and he didn't detect any alcohol, so he drank it down.

"When will we reach Benni?" he asked.

Ailen tilted his head, considering him. "Tomorrow and tomorrow."

Conall tried to decipher the elf's limited English. "You mean the day after tomorrow?"

Ailen nodded. "Hi."

Conall had been listening enough to understand that *hi* was an all-purpose agreement.

"I won't arrive as a prisoner," he said.

Ailen's brow furrowed. Conall held up his hands and crossed them at the wrists.

"Not prisoner." He pointed to each of the Ebos, then to himself. "We are friends."

There was more babbling in Essian, but no one seemed inclined to bind his hands again. They weren't a talkative lot either, and they soon drank their tea in silence. Then one by one they lay down by the fire to sleep.

The wind picked up, blowing ocean scents over them. Conall wished he'd kept his fur for one more night. He tucked his hands under his arms to keep warm.

Sweat, the youngest scout, was on watch. He sat upright against a rock. Conall lay down with his back to him and pulled out the graphium. He clicked open the locket and found a frowning face on the right screen with one word: *OK?*

Rowan was worried about him. How long had he run as a wolf? The days were blurred together. How many messages had she sent that he ignored? He swiped his finger across the left screen to erase his old message and scrawled out a new one. *OK.* He sketched out a rough wolf head in the small space, hoping that would be enough to make her understand that he'd been unable to answer her.

After a moment, a new message appeared on the right screen: *Say hi to Garou.*

He added one more note—*Love you*—then closed the locket and gripped it fiercely in his fist as if he could send the depth of his need for her by sheer will.

By midmorning Conall spotted the first Ebos sentries hidden among the rocky outcroppings along the path. That could only mean they were nearing a settlement. The sentries hailed Ailen and let the group pass.

The sky was brilliant blue and a light wind tossed Conall's hair. It wasn't the Fanfaronade that heralded winter, but a gentler wind, scented with brine from the ocean.

He hadn't expected to find much life this far north. The herds kept to the plains and the carnivores followed them. Then Ailen turned them east again, and they marched into a valley between the two branches of the mountain range. The Basin, Lydan had called it, and Conall was stunned to find a lush landscape, thriving with wildlife—a landscape that shouldn't be possible this far north.

The trail turned into a dirt road that ran alongside a fast-moving river. Conall tried to remember the map that Lydan had shown him. The river had to be the Highland. It came down the mountains, bringing life-giving irrigation to the valley, then joined with Dawson River before flushing out to sea.

Ducks, geese and other shore birds flocked to the reedy shallows. A forest grew along the far bank—mostly spruce and pine with a few tamaracks and poplars in the mix. But these weren't the stunted trees of the Meadows. They grew tall and still wore their summer greens.

A rabbit darted across the path, waking a sleepy Garou.

There is much prey in these hills.

I don't think we'll stop to hunt again, brother. We must be close to Benni now.

Garou grumped something about city smells and went back to sleep.

Conall remembered Lydan's warning to turn back if he hadn't found Benni by September. His inner calendar was confused after the long run as a wolf, but the green trees told him he'd made the trek with time to spare.

Two hunters broke from the forest and joined their group. Each had a brace of ptarmigans and several rabbits dangling from their packs.

Soon, the terrain transformed again. They lost sight of the river and hiked through a corridor of tall swaying grass. Traffic increased and they passed gatherers carrying baskets that overflowed with end-of-summer wild harvest—mushrooms, tubers and berries. They were joined by fisher folk bringing the morning's catch from the river.

As they moved deeper into the valley, Conall felt like they'd entered another world. The grasslands gave way to cultivated fields with emerald green corn stalks and golden grains growing in great swaths right up the slopes of the mountains. Smaller vegetable gardens were tended by dozens of Ebos, who all looked up from their tasks as the band of scouts and their human visitor passed. A child pointed at Conall. A nearby adult grabbed the child's arm and lowered it, whispering some admonishment into his ear.

Ailen pulled his pony alongside Conall's and pointed to the road ahead.

"Benni." His grin was bigger and brighter than any expression the Ebos had shown so far.

For the next hour, Conall strained his eyes to see the city rise in the distance, but the only indication that they'd arrived were two guards who stood by a natural rock formation that looked like a collapsed archway. Ailen dismounted and indicated to Conall that he should follow. Conall jumped to the ground and held the reins in one hand, unsure about what he should do with them. Kelli spoke quickly, but Conall was starting to understand their language and he thought she used the word for road or ground. She smiled and pointed down, so Conall let the reins drop. The well-trained pony didn't bolt, but just stood with his head slightly bowed as if he might fall into a doze.

Conall followed Ailen toward the stone arch where he was arguing with the guards. There seemed to be some disagreement about the wisdom of letting a human into their home. Eventually, Ailen barked a command at Sweat, who jumped off his pony and took off at a run through the arch.

Minutes passed. While they waited, Conall studied what he could see of the Ebos village from the guard post. It was nestled into the base of a rocky slope where the two arms of the Ubruulens met. He spotted a handful of stone buildings. The ground around them was hard-packed gravel with little greenery.

It wasn't a city. It was barely a village. Stark, isolated and ugly, it lacked any ornamentation and looked like an abandoned homestead. Conall was suddenly uncertain.

"Benni?" He pointed past the two guards who still blocked their way.

Ailen nodded. "Benni."

Conall tried to hide his disappointment. Stories about the great Ebos city had been told and retold by trappers in Durance for generations. The reality of a few stone huts in a dusty clearing made Conall worry that he'd sorely miscalculated the value of this journey. He'd wasted time that could have been better spent by Rowan's side.

I could have told you the rabbit hole was empty before you stuck your nose in.

Conall ignored the comment. Garou was still sore about leaving their mate. As he waited on the dusty road that seemed to go nowhere, Conall was getting pretty sore about it too. A new ire was starting to burn in him. He didn't like being fooled, and it looked like Omika had done exactly that.

The scout eventually returned with another Ebos. Conall recognized him immediately. There was no mistaking Dalkyn as he strode down the road with purpose written in the stiff lines of his shoulders.

Conall owed his life to Dalkyn. The Ebos lumina had helped Squad 54 erase all traces of their battle in the Warren. He'd kept the rangers safe when they were exhausted and injured. He'd even given them horses and an escort back to New Torwood City.

That didn't mean Conall liked him.

"Commander West, welcome to Benni." His clear blue eyes held no warmth. Dalkyn was Minna's brother, but he had none of her charm.

"Thank you. I come at Omika's invitation." Conall's smile was tight and rewarded with a slight quirk of Dalkyn's lips. Dalkyn had once accused him of seeing Omika's words as a threat instead of an invitation.

Dalkyn stepped back, opening the way for Conall to pass. "Our ancestor's bones have been awaiting your tread. And so does the Evafara."

Evafara was the Ebos term for elder or perhaps shaman. The titles weren't clear in Conall's mind, but he knew that Omika was Evafara in Benni and he was well respected. He also knew that Dalkyn was being groomed to take his position when the old Ebos was ready to lay down his bones.

His eyes move like an eagle's, Garou said, *with no humor and only one purpose—to seek out prey.*

Conall didn't disagree with the wolf's assessment, but he hoped Dalkyn had more to him, if only for the sake of the Ebos he would one day lead.

Dalkyn's hand fell on his arm as Conall headed through the archway.

"You must give up all mech to stand before the Evafara."

"Ailen has already taken my mech." Conall pointed to the pack that was tied to the saddlebag of his pony.

Dalkyn pursed his lips and looked pointedly at Conall's chest.

Ailen's scouts had searched him, but they weren't luminas. Dalkyn's keen sense of magic had immediately detected the tiny thera chip inside his graphium.

Conall smiled. He should have known he couldn't fool the Evafara-in-training. He took off the locket and wound the chain around it before tucking the whole thing into his pack.

Dalkyn spoke sharply to Ailen who seemed embarrassed. The scout had just been dressed down for letting the mech go unnoticed. In his position, Conall would have done the same, but that didn't make him like Dalkyn any better.

They walked down the desolate street. Gravel crackled under their boots, unnaturally loud in the quiet village. As they passed the first stone hut, Conall tried to peer into a window. It seemed abandoned. In fact the village seemed staged to look like a ghost town. If Conall had been traveling through, he wouldn't have even stopped.

Perhaps that is the point. Let the enemy search an old den while the pups are safe in a new one.

Garou's logic was sound, but that still begged the question: where was Benni?

Dalkyn led him toward the largest building, built right into the rock face at the far end of the village. Two Ebos emerged from its open doorway. They startled when they saw Conall, then spied Dalkyn and hurried on their way without another word.

The building was large, but not large enough to house a city's worth of people. Conall revised his estimation of Benni. Perhaps the farmers, hunters and fisher folk lived in homesteads outside the village?

Too many scents, Garou observed. *Many people come this way. Regularly. Maybe it's a meeting hall?*

Garou made a noncommittal grunt. He wasn't convinced.

As they entered the building, Conall expected to find a grand hall with space for the Ebos to meet, but after the bright sunlight, he found only darkness. He held back until his eyes adjusted. Dalkyn urged him onward and a growl escaped Conall's throat.

He didn't like closed-in spaces and the interior of this building was stifling. With no windows and a low ceiling, darkness spread before them like a tunnel through an abyss. Indistinct voices trickled from that darkness, many voices, like the murmurs of a large crowd.

"What is this place?" Conall's voice was rough. The wolf was close to the surface.

"It is a doorway. Be at ease, Wolf. All will be clear." Dalkyn's hand rested on Conall's arm. Ailen and another scout were at his back. He had nowhere to run.

He gritted his teeth and walked onward. Better to arrive under his own steam than to be dragged before Omika like a prisoner. His eyes were adjusting and he could see a faint light in the distance.

They reached the far wall and another stone archway. It wasn't built of blocks of stone, but cut right out of the rock face and decorated with carvings.

A single torch illuminated what Garou's nose already told him. Those weren't carvings of stone. They were elaborate designs made from thousands of small bones that radiated from the arch like the rays of the sun.

Through the doorway, he spied a tunnel leading deep into the mountain. This building was nothing more than a portico for whatever was at the end of that tunnel.

Dalkyn led them into the deeper darkness. The tunnel veered sharply right and fell into a steep slope. The voices were louder here. Torches guttered at intervals along the wall, only bright enough to enhance the shadows rather than light the way.

Dalkyn strode onward.

Garou whined in the back of Conall's mind.

"Commander." Dalkyn's tone was a rebuke. Conall had stalled at the top of the ramp. He didn't want to go down there. The thought of all that rock weighing on them made his heart race.

Ailen tucked his arm under Conall's elbow. The slight pressure was reassuring, and Conall reluctantly let the elf lead him into the darkness.

As they plunged into the shadows between the sconces, he was suddenly thrown back to his days as a pup, frightened and alone, hungry and thirsty, and cowering in the dark cellar while his drunken father raged overhead. By the time they reached the end of the ramp the old wound in Conall's jaw ached from gritting his teeth.

The voices grew in volume. Ahead, Dalkyn turned yet another corner. By Conall's calculations they were heading even deeper into the mountain.

Run, brother! Flee!

His skin prickled with the need to shift. Then he rounded the corner and stopped in his tracks. The elf behind him stumbled into his back as Conall's eyes roamed up and up. And up.

He stood in the entrance to a grand cavern. The air was cool and clear. Instead of torches, white lamps hung on the walls and ceiling. They were bright enough to fill the massive space with light.

The smothering claustrophobia waned and Garou settled into an uneasy quiet.

They were standing in a market. Trestle tables were laden with fruits and vegetables. Trappers offered tanned hides and furs. He spotted an herbalist with bunches of dried greenery hanging on a rope above her cart. Tables and stools were clustered outside a makeshift pub, where several Ebos lounged, drinking from bone cups.

Conall turned to take in the archway they'd just come through. The horns of a titan caribou hung above it like a trophy with an array of smaller bones spread out behind them. More bones rose in a tower in the middle of the market square. As they neared it, he saw they were human scapulas, then realized, no, that would be ridiculous. They were Ebos scapulas. A shrine to their ancestors.

Conversations stilled and recovered as they passed through the crowd, like a titan eel through a school of fish.

A tinker's shop selling metal pots and pans caught his eye. The pots were displayed on little stands made of bone. The decorations above a trapper's stall were particularly intricate—a woven pattern of small animal bones. Bone necklaces dangled from every throat. Buttons on shirtfronts shone a dull white. Delicate bone combs were woven into hairstyles. There were bone piercings and bone beadwork. Everywhere he turned, Conall was faced with the dead.

They don't just revere bones, he thought. *They integrate them into everyday life.*

Perhaps they believe this keeps the spirit of the dead with them, Garou said.

Conall remembered Minna explaining the theory of *coho-ne-teno* when they buried Augie. The dual spirit. It had seemed contradictory to him, but the saints knew religion wasn't about logic. When the founders of New Torwood City had outlawed the worship of gods, and the devout had simply shifted their prayer to saints, neither the priests nor the ruling kings of the time seemed to find that hypocritical. So why not believe in a spirit that could fly to heaven and remain on earth at the same time?

Are we not proof that dual spirits exist? Garou asked.

Conall grinned and shook his head. The wolf's thoughts rarely ran deeper than his next meal, but once in a while Garou surprised him.

They wove their way through the market along a main thoroughfare. Smaller alleys branched from it, leading down dimmer tunnels. Conall could only guess that these led to living quarters. There had to be hundreds, if not thousands of Ebos living here. The legends of Benni were true, but it was not what he'd expected.

Dalkyn turned down one of those branching tunnels. Conall braced himself for claustrophobia to hit again. He knew it was irrational. The Ebos had clearly been living here safely for generations. The mountain wouldn't fall today. But his dislike of small closed-in spaces wasn't rational.

Thankfully, the alley that Dalkyn chose was broad and well lit. If Conall ignored the rough stone walls, he could almost forget that he was traveling into the heart of a mountain. Almost.

They reached two closed doors with guards on either side. Dalkyn didn't hesitate. He opened one of the doors and headed through it. Ailen and the scout stopped at the threshold. Conall paused to glance back, but Ailen gave him an encouraging smile and waved him forward.

Conall followed Dalkyn. Their footsteps echoed on the stone floor in a vast empty hall. It looked like a throne room, though there was no throne, only an empty dais at the far end.

Dalkyn continued through the hall to a small door behind the dais. Conall had to quicken his step to keep up. Through the door, they found another long hallway. It was dimly lit, but it felt like any other hall in any other castle, and Conall's phobia had dwindled to nothing more than the usual itch he felt being within a city instead of roaming free in the Meadows.

There were Ebos working in offices and Conall spied a library through one open doorway. Nobody stopped them, but all eyes followed the stranger in their midst.

After a walk that seemed like it would never end, they came to another door with two more guards flanking it. Dalkyn held the door open.

"I leave you here, Wolf. May you find what you have been searching for."

Dalkyn closed the door behind him, leaving Conall in a dimly lit den.

A large desk laden with books and scrolls took up one end of the room. The walls were lined with shelves that held more books, pottery, bone sculptures and other oddities. The room was big enough that the far end behind the desk was lost in shadow.

Closer to the door, two chairs with side tables sat on either side of a hearth-like structure. No fire burned in it. Instead, there was a metal grate in the floor. On a stand above the grate sat a bowl with three glowing stones. Conall waved his hands over the bowl and was met with warm air flowing up from the vent.

"Geothermic heat," said a voice from the shadows at the far end of the room. A figure appeared as if from nowhere, and Omika stepped into the light.

"The heart of the mountain heats us even in the coldest winter. It is the only way we can survive out here."

Omika looked more regal than Conall remembered. He wore a blue robe heavily embroidered with bone beads. An elaborate bone crown rested on his nearly bald head. He also looked tired, as if the few weeks since their last meeting had aged him by years.

The elder smiled. "I am pleased that you found your way to our hearth, Commander West." His English was near perfect, with only a hint of the Ebos accent.

"I'm glad to be welcomed here."

Omika lifted the crown from his head and laid in on a shelf. It left red indentations on his brow. The heavy robe opened like a cloak. He shucked it off and hung it from a bone hook on the wall.

He sighed. "Good. I have only a few minutes before I must prepare for another service, so let us speak plainly." He poured something steaming from a small pot on the desk into two bone cups and handed one to Conall. Then he sat in a chair with a grunt that suggested achy muscles. Conall stood for a moment longer gripping his cup, then he sat on the second chair. It was sized for an elf, and he felt like an oaf trying to sit in a doll house.

He sipped from the cup and was glad to find tea and not something stronger. Omika let his eyes close for a moment. Without his outer cloak,

Conall could see his thin chest rise and fall under his shirt. His hands shook as he raised the cup to his lips.

"Your hearth is remarkable," Conall said to break the silence. "I've never seen stones that give off such pure light. Are they the same stones that light your lamps?"

Omika nodded. "Your people call them ley-stones, but they are actually crystals. The first Ebos clans who came through the rift to this world brought the crystal seeds with them. Our luminas grow them in the heart of magic."

"The heart of magic. You mean a ley-line? Like the one that runs under New Torwood?"

"Yes. Like yours, our ancestors were wise in the ways of tapping such power."

Conall didn't know enough about magic theory to comment. He sipped his tea. Omika seemed content to drink and rest with his head against the high back of the chair. The room was utterly silent. Clearly, the old Ebos wasn't going to make this easy for him.

Conall cleared his throat and set down his tea.. "I…uh…came here because the last time we met, you mentioned the name of my brother's wolf."

Omika nodded as if Conall had spoken some great wisdom, but he didn't respond.

The ire that had started to burn at the gates of Benni was now flaring hotly inside Conall. He'd traveled a long way, left Rowan, been harassed by coyotes, forced to confront memories he'd rather let alone, been treated as a prisoner, and now he was stuck under tons of rock trying to pry information from a half-senile Ebos elder. His hands closed over the arms of the chair and squeezed. The wood creaked.

Omika watched him with a flicker of amusement in his eyes.

Conall fought to keep his tone level. "I would like to know where you heard that name."

Omika leaned forward. "From your brother, of course."

"You met Nathan? When? Was he here?"

"All in good time, my friend."

Conall shot to his feet. The wolf was so close to the surface, he could feel his whiskers twitch. "I want answers. Why are you stalling?"

"I am not stalling. I am waiting for our guest to arrive."

A sound from the shadows behind the desk had Conall spinning. A figure entered the ring of light from the hearth.

He was thinner and older, but Conall recognized him immediately.

"Hello, brother," Nathan said.

Garou howled.

20

The Memory of a Wolf

THE FURY BOILING JUST BENEATH Conall's skin erupted. He leaped over the table and threw a punch at his brother. Nathan had always been more nimble. He sidestepped the jab and slammed his elbow into Conall's ribs. But Conall was bigger and stronger. He bent in two and rammed his head into Nathan's gut. The brothers crashed into a bookshelf, sending scrolls tumbling to the floor.

Conall pinned Nathan. A growl emanated from Nathan's throat, and Conall realized too late that he was shifting. Garou responded with a howl that started in his hindbrain and ended in his throat. It was nearly impossible to ignore the primal urge when another pack member shifted. And Nathan was pack, despite all the years and distance between them.

Conall gritted his teeth and fisted his hands as he fought the shift and failed. He collapsed sideways, bones, muscles and tendons already reshaping.

The commotion brought guards running into the room, and when Garou finally stood on four paws, panting and shaking, he was faced with the point of a spear.

Omika spoke sharply in Essian. The spear lowered and the guards left.

Misha sat calmly. Like Garou, he was mostly black, but his accents faded to gray instead of bronze. Garou paced around the small room. Conall was raging in the back of his mind. He cursed Nathan for cheating, for faking his death, for abandoning him, but these were human concerns that didn't ruffle a wolf's fur.

Garou felt the urgency of the fight fade away. He licked his lips and sat. Misha sneezed and shook his muzzle, then stuck it under Garou's chin, taking in his scent from the most vulnerable part of his neck. A whine escaped

Garou's throat. Misha fell to the floor, rolled and exposed his underbelly.

Omika stepped forward. "Now that you boys have been reacquainted, perhaps you can take your human forms again. We must talk."

The explosive shift had left Conall's shirt in shreds, and his pack was still with Ailen's scouts, so he sat in the chair by Omika's fireless hearth wearing only his dusty pants and boots. After dressing, Nathan pulled a chair from behind the desk to join them. He wore the dun-colored tunic and leggings of an Ebos scout but without bone adornments. His hair had darkened and it was cropped short. There were creases around his eyes. With his head lowered, he lifted his gaze to study his brother with a secretive grin. The expression was pure Nathan and Conall felt emotion fill his throat.

During their teen years, Nathan had kept his head down. He'd watched and studied from beneath lowered lashes. He'd waited for others to speak first, though Conall knew his opinions ran deep.

And now he waited for his brother to begin.

Conall had questions. Many questions. But most were too personal to air in front of Omika, so he said, "How did you get here?"

Nathan lowered his brows, confused.

"Into this room, I mean. You didn't come through the door. Were you hiding under the desk?"

Omika answered. "There is a passageway in the closet." He pointed to the shadowed end of the room. "It's hidden and secret. Mostly. Only my most trusted advisors know of its existence. When you leave here, you will go out the door you came in. Too many people saw you walk through the market. They will be watching for you to leave."

Conall digested that. There was a lot to unpack—the need for a hidden escape route, the idea of eyes watching him in the market, and the fact that Nathan was part of the elder's inner circle.

He turned back to his brother. "So you lurked in the shadows to ambush me."

Nathan spread his hands in defeat. "I hoped it would be a happy surprise."

Conall crossed his arms. He felt unreasonably vulnerable without his shirt. The anger had faded but it left him restless and ill-tempered.

"How long?"

"How long what?"

"How long have you been living with the Ebos?"

"Since the last year of the war."

Ten years. His brother had been alive and living safely here for ten years without making contact. Silence fell between them.

"Did you ever think to let me know?"

Nathan ran a hand over his face and down the back of his head. It was their father's gesture, one that Conall knew he imitated too.

"At first, I was too injured," Nathan said. "Later…you'd left the rangers. I made discreet inquiries, but no one knew where you'd gone."

"Discreet inquiries?"

"I was in hiding. I still am." Nathan leaned forward, resting his elbows on his knees. "I want to tell you everything. I will. It's the reason we brought you here."

"No one brought me. I came on my own steam."

Nathan glanced at Omika. There was something going on here, something bigger than a long-lost sibling.

A gong sounded deep in the mountain. Omika rose.

"I am needed for service. Nathan, take your brother home to meet your lovely wife. Tell him…tell him everything."

"Yes, Evafara." Nathan rose and bowed. He headed for the door. Conall stood and faced Omika. The old Ebos smiled faintly, but gave no indication that he was going to shed light on this mystery. Instead, he turned away and reached for the heavy robe he'd hung on the wall.

Conall grabbed Nathan's arm as he reached the door. "Wife?"

Nathan gave him his first genuine smile. "Yes. Soffi. She's waiting for us. Come on."

Conall's thoughts were too numb to react. His brother had just come back from the dead and now a sister?

The lone wolf gathers a pack. Garou seemed pleased.

Conall wasn't ready to go that far, but he followed his brother out the door and back down the long hallway. The market that had been bustling with activity an hour ago was much quieter. The empty boulevard seemed wider without the foot traffic.

"Where is everyone?" Conall asked.

"At vigil. Omika is giving the service today. He gets a bigger than normal draw."

A few merchants remained in the market. One woman was hanging bundles of herbs when they passed. She saw the brothers and gasped before ducking through a beaded curtain into her shop.

Conall's first walk through the market had caused a stir, but the herbalist's reaction seemed less surprise and more fear. And she wasn't the only one to react this way. An old Ebos sweeping the street stopped his chore and turned his face away until they passed. Others hid or lowered their eyes. One merchant bowed. Nathan ignored them all and kept walking.

He brought Conall back to the main arch outside the decoy town. One of the guards on duty nodded at Nathan. The other bowed deeply and said, "*Irivu.*" He touched a bone disk on his necklace to his lips.

Nathan smiled and acknowledged the odd greeting.

The afternoon sun was blazing and Conall was happy to find his backpack waiting for him at the guard outpost. He donned a fresh shirt, then searched the pack until he found the air knives and Rowan's locket. Relief washed over him. Losing the air knives would be inconvenient, but losing his one tie to Rowan had begun the irrational rage in him—the rage that had culminated in attacking his brother.

He glanced at Nathan who watched him with his half-smile. Yes, the anger was still simmering inside, but Garou's no-nonsense wolf equilibrium was tempering it.

He dropped the locket over his head and glared at Nathan, daring him to protest the mech. Nathan just shrugged and turned for a trail that ran along the base of the mountain.

Conall caught up to him.

"What's with the blessings or whatever. Some of those people seemed afraid of you."

Nathan slowed until Conall walked beside him on the narrow trail.

"I am part of a group known as the Rati-Irivu."

"What are they? Priests? Assassins? Or, I know, assassin-priests?" Conall was being a smart ass, but Nathan's reticence irked him.

Nathan rolled his jaw side-to-side. "Neither. Not exactly. It's hard to explain. Better that I show you. It isn't far now."

They followed a dusty track, barely wide enough for a goat. It curved around the mountain until they came to another village nestled against the hillside. A dozen stone huts were clustered around a clearing. Small vegetable gardens filled the spaces between the huts and the mountain. The gardens were lush with end-of-summer produce—squash, beans and root vegetables.

Like in Benni, a larger stone building was built against the mountainside, and Conall suspected it was the foyer for another underground settlement. He was glad when Nathan turned off the path for one of the cottages. His nerves were raw and he didn't think he could take another adventure underground just yet.

The door opened and a woman emerged from the cottage, holding a child on her hip. She was tall for an elf, but still small compared to human women. Her blond hair was pulled back from her face and held in place with bone combs. The child, barely out of infancy, sucked on her fingers while the other hand gripped a loose lock of her mother's hair. There was jam on her cheek.

Nathan took the baby, swung her upward to childish squeals of delight, then tucked her into the crook of his elbow.

"Conall, this is my wife, Soffi, and our daughter, Jula."

"Welcome, brother." Soffi reached out a hand. Conall leaned forward to grasp it. Her eyes widened when she saw the graphium locket, but she hesitated for only a moment before gripping his hand.

That was interesting. Soffi had some mage talent. She was able to sense the thera magic, but she didn't shy away from it like other Ebos.

The child squealed and pouted.

"Please, husband, bring our brother inside and serve him tea while I tidy Jula." Soffi's English was lightly accented.

"We're just stopping to say hello."

"Will you not offer your brother the comfort of food?"

"I'm not hungry," Conall said. "But perhaps a sip of water would do."

Nathan kissed her cheek, then dabbed at the jam on his daughter's face. "I'm taking Conall to see the Pit. We'll be back in time to help with dinner."

Soffi smiled. "Do not rush…*Fenna* is already prepared. I will wait for your return."

Conall didn't know what *fenna* was, but by the savory smells coming from inside the cottage, he was already looking forward to it after weeks of hard tack and raw rabbits.

Soffi took Jula inside. Nathan and Conall followed, leaving the door open. The cottage was little more than a large main room with a kitchen, table, and a hearth with two chairs. A curtained doorway led to a second room, presumably a bedroom. Conall could hear Soffi's low voice singing to the baby.

Nathan led him through the kitchen and out the back door to a well in the yard. A horn cup sat on a stone beside a manual pump. Nathan filled the cup and handed it to Conall, who drank it all down.

Nathan tilted his head back to feel the sun on his face.

"We won't have many more fine days like these."

Conall filled the cup and drank it down again.

"Are you ever going to tell me what in the saints you're doing here? What I'm doing here?" His tone was harsh.

Nathan sighed. "This place is called Rivu. It's set apart from Benni for reasons that will become clear. I live here with the Rati-Irivu. That means the *banished of Rivu*." Nathan ducked his head and looked up at Conall with a smile. Conall had questions, but he would hold his tongue until Nathan finished.

"The Rati found me in the Meadows ten years ago. I was near death. Without their medicine and the intervention of their luminas, I wouldn't have survived." His gaze turned inward as if reliving those pain-filled days. "Before that, I was a ranger, just like you."

Conall shook his head. "I never understood how that happened. I thought you left Durance to become a scribe."

Nathan smiled sadly. "That's a story for another day, but suffice it to say that I didn't have the makings of a scribe. It turns out that shifter magic is incompatible with their mech."

"Hmmm." Conall had many thoughts about scribes and their abhorrent magic, but he nodded for Nathan to continue.

"After I left the Temple of the Word, I was immediately conscripted. I wanted to serve my term as a keeper, but news of gaunts massing in the mountains was already making the generals wary. I was given a ranger's uniform and sent to the far north. I traveled there with Miron Wrede and spent many nights on the road talking mech theory with the minister and his aides."

Wrede's name brought a sharp intake of breath from Conall. Why wasn't he surprised? He'd never met the man. He was a wraith, and yet he seemed to infiltrate every part of Conall's life.

"The minister liked me. He said I had a brain for science, and he offered me a position in his entourage. At the time, I was flattered and relieved that I wouldn't be sent to the far north. Later, I understood that Wrede wanted my insight into scribe mech. I was an oddity. Neophytes in the Temple of the Word either become scribes or they die trying. No one ever leaves the temple. And they keep their secrets close—secrets that Wrede desperately wanted. But I only learned that later. Too late."

"I've had a run-in with Wrede," Conall said. "Sort of. I met some of his cronies on the road."

Nathan nodded. "Dalkyn spoke of it to the *Ossvara*, the, uh…circle of elders, I guess you'd call them." He paused for a long moment, then continued. "I'm sorry you've been caught up in all this."

"Caught up in what exactly?"

Nathan hesitated again, either deciding how much truth to give or where to start.

"When the Ebos scouts found me dying in the Meadows, my wounds weren't from gaunts. I never saw battle."

"But the records…I asked. The official report said you died in a gaunt raid."

"That was a lie to cover up Wrede's attempted murder."

Conall could feel that rage building in him again, partly because his brother had been so ill-used, and partly because that same brother seemed bent on doling out his story, one truth bomb at a time. Nathan must have seen the rage warring with confusion in his expression because he sighed and held out his hands as if in surrender.

"I'm not trying to be enigmatic. There's just so much to tell you." He took the cup from Conall and worked the pump to fill it again.

"Dalkyn filled me in about your adventures at the Warren. That was Wrede's second work site. He had another set up in the foothills of the Ubruulens, far east of the Warren, far from any trade routes and the war in the west. For years, he experimented with blending mechs and animal DNA."

"DNA?" Conall thought back to his murky lessons in school. "Isn't that a molecule. To do with cell biology, or something like that?"

"Yes. It's the basic building block of all living things. Wrede had some ancient books that outline its purpose, and he found a scientist who's able to sense matter at the molecular level, better than any mech scope. She's instrumental to his work. Or was. The Rati have information that says she died last year." Nathan shrugged. "Maybe she didn't matter that much. Wrede kept his operation going without her." He sighed and splashed water over his face.

As Nathan continued his impossible tale, Conall began to understand that something more than fate had brought him hundreds of miles into the north.

"This all goes back years, long before the war. The Regent's Council gave him their blessing and their funding because he was the golden boy who'd discovered how to take the potential magic in thera and turn it into a practical fuel. Twenty years ago, that discovery revolutionized New Torwood City, and the council looked to him to win the war.

"At first his experiments were more biological. He tried to breed gaunts with humans." Nathan's eyes looked haunted. "These failed as horrifically as you can imagine."

Conall remembered the murdered gaunts in the oasis and his empty stomach turned sour.

"That was when his black site and his experiments came to the attention of my friends, the Rati. Wrede captured Taiga women from the raiders that came over the mountains. He used them as breeding stock. The Ebos trade with the Taiga on occasion and word got back to us."

"Did you stop him?"

"Not me. This was before my time here, but yes, the Ebos elders sent warriors to wipe out Wrede's lab. They found the Taiga already there, but they lent their blades and bows to the attack that wiped out Wrede's operations. The attack made a statement, but it didn't help in the long run. Wrede simply rebuilt at a new site, one that was almost impenetrable. He called it the Academy."

"The Warren," Conall said. He remembered Denny describing it as the Academy.

Nathan nodded. "And he switched his focus. He began to experiment on infant gaunts. That's where I came in. He wanted to understand the scribe mech, to see if their implants could modify behavior and if they could be used on gaunts.

"I'm ashamed to say that I gave him everything I had. It wasn't much because my training ended before I was initiated into any real secrets, but it was enough for him to get started. He created a device that controls gaunt behavior through punishment and reward—a tiny device that stimulates the pain and pleasure centers—but gaunts had to be trained from a young age for it to work."

"I think we met some of his test subjects."

Nathan nodded. "The second generation. They would have been babies when I left."

"And why did you leave?"

"Because I learned that Wrede had never stopped experimenting on humans. He tried to keep it secret because he knew even the council wouldn't sanction such barbaric tactics. The thought still sickens me."

Nathan rubbed a hand over his eyes. "I don't know how much you understand about scribes, but their blood is different."

Rowan had tried to explain the alienness they'd found inside Orson when she'd linked with Noah and Denny to wipe his memories.

"I understand enough."

Nathan nodded. "Dalkyn told me what happened with your scribe."

Not what happened. What we did to him. Garou's intrusion was as unwelcome as it was true. Rowan believed it was the just thing, but Orson had been left an empty shell after they'd rifled through his mind. Killing him would have been safer and kinder.

"Wrede was feeding thera to soldiers," Nathan said, "trying to mimic the mech reaction in their blood. The men began to change, physically and mentally. Most died. Those who didn't became irrational and aggressive. I'm not embarrassed to say they scared the saints out of me."

"They were addicted," Conall said.

"Nathan nodded. "Their reactions were so like father's—the ranting, the monstrous changes…" He trailed off. His gaze was fixed on long ago.

"By this time, I was working closely with Wrede. We shared everything. Or at least I thought we did. He was a mentor—a *trusted* mentor. And when I objected to the new line of experiments, he promised to stop. But later…I discovered that he'd kidnapped a scribe. They dissected her like an animal… all to understand how thera connected the mech to her blood."

Nathan's eyes were haunted.

"I could no longer continue the work in good faith. The saints know I allowed some horrible things to happen in that lab, but this was too much. I sent a graphium to my old mentor at the Temple of the Word."

Nathan let out a gruff laugh. "I was so stupid. Of course Wrede would be monitoring all communications. That night, I was dragged from my bed, tied up, gagged and blindfolded. They drugged me so I couldn't shift and drove me into the Meadows where they slit my throat and left me to die. But I didn't die. Wrede had sent a couple of greens to do the job and they panicked. They missed the artery. Still, I would have bled out if the Ebos hadn't found me. They were a Rati scout force who'd been watching Wrede's lab. They brought me here to Benni to recover, and I learned of the vitally important work they're doing. I never left."

"And what is that work exactly?"

Nathan smiled. "That's what I'm going to show you. Come on."

After Benni, Conall wasn't surprised to find the building constructed against the rock face was little more than an atrium.

"I don't know how you can live under a mountain," Conall muttered as they headed through the darkened chamber.

Nathan squeezed his shoulder. "Breathe. It's perfectly safe."

And just like when they were kids, the simple presence of his big brother eased him.

There was no grand archway at the end of this atrium, just a narrow doorway knocked out of solid rock. They pushed through it and Conall stopped on the other side.

Nathan swept his hand forward to encompass the large cavern.

"Welcome to the Pit."

21

ALL ROADS LEAD TO TREASON

MAYBE IT WAS BECAUSE HIDING the truth had become wearisome. Maybe Rowan's forgiveness—though unwarranted—had loosened something inside Dale. Or maybe Atherton just didn't have that same gravitas after Dale had spied his secret love nest, but Dale was suddenly tired of keeping up the charade of obedience to the regent's office.

Besides, a promise to Rowan was worth keeping.

Dale left the tiny office that had been their sanctuary for the last ten years. They'd always kept it neat, so no one would notice that all personal items were missing. Dale had already moved most of the stuff to new offices Rowan had set up in the royal wing. Now they had one more task before vacating the council wing for good.

Atherton had a morning meeting in the city, then he planned to take a late lunch at his favorite club. That meant he wouldn't be returning today. He'd probably drink too much with his cronies and head straight for his private suite sometime before the midnight sun set.

Dale had waited for lunch hour before venturing down the hall toward Atherton's office. The other offices were empty and dark. The junior secretaries knew about Atherton's habits when he went out to play. They would take advantage of his absence. Many might not return for the rest of the afternoon. A year ago, Dale would have sent out reprimands to those slackers. Now they didn't care.

Slipping into Atherton's office was easy. Dale had the only spare key. They shut the door and lit a small thera lamp because the curtains were drawn.

The first thing they did was leave a folded letter on the desk. It was sealed

178

with wax and stamped with Dale's family crest. Inside was a simply worded resignation. Dale hadn't given any reasons or excuses. There was no point. Atherton would soon learn they'd defected to Rowan's camp.

The battle lines between regent and heir were being drawn. Dale had spent the last few weeks quietly shoring up support for Rowan, while sowing seeds of discontent for the status quo.

Still hoping to find the second ledger, Dale opened the desk drawer, felt around the inside for a false bottom panel, but couldn't find any triggers or gaps. As they were about to close the drawer, Dale caught sight of a small metal disk tucked into the corner. It had a hole near one end as if it might hang on a cord. One side was blank. The other was engraved with a stylized face of a dog with large fangs.

Odd. The image struck a memory chord. They'd seen this icon before, but where?

Dale tucked the medallion into a pocket. They would make inquiries later, maybe check the archives for any references to the icon.

Time was wearing away. One of the junior secretaries could return from their extended lunch at any time.

Dale's attention turned to the work table set up beside the bookshelves. Schematics for the new water pumps were unrolled on the table and held in place with stone weights.

Dale had been present for the negotiations between Theracine and the regent, but they hadn't studied the schematics. Mech-magery wasn't their forte. They studied them now though. There was no time to copy the plans, but Dale tried to commit details to memory so he could fill Rowan in.

The door was thrust open. Atherton paused when he saw Dale leaning over the schematics.

"What are you doing here?"

Dale thought about making up a lie, but there was no point.

Gesturing to the drawing of the proposed water pump, they said, "You know this is a bad deal for the city, don't you. But it's a good deal for you, and that's all that matters, isn't it?"

Atherton squinted. His hair fell across his forehead in a tangled mess. His jacket dangled by one finger over his shoulder, and sweat stained his shirt from underarms all the way down his chest.

"Get out." He threw his jacket onto the chair and spotted the letter on the desk. With a frown he broke the seal and read it. His lip curled and he crumpled the sheet in one hand before flinging it into the cold hearth.

"You lied to me. You're working for her, aren't you?" In a flash Atherton was around the desk and shoving Dale against the bookcase. Atherton wasn't a strong man, but he was several inches taller and fifty pounds heavier than Dale. With his face only inches away, the smell of alcohol on his breath was nauseating.

Dale didn't struggle. They let their limbs hang loose so Atherton had to take all their weight. They stared into his red-rimmed eyes—eyes that seemed desperate rather than angry—and didn't flinch.

Atherton thrust them away.

"I want you out of my office and out of the council wing. If I find you in here again, I'll have you arrested. Your princess won't be able to help you. And if I find that you've stolen state secrets in her name, I will have her put on trial for treason too."

Dale stepped into the doorway and paused. Ten years of living in this man's shadow had been enough. They stood straighter and spoke clearly.

"Try it, Atherton. You can't be the secretary to a criminal for ten years without learning where the bodies are buried. I have insurance. You come after me, or you hurt her, and I'll use it."

Atherton's expression showed one satisfying instant of surprise, before it turned to rage.

Dale whistled as they headed toward the royal wing, a new office, and a long-postponed mission. With a hand in their pocket, they fiddled with the medallion etched with the face of a dog.

22

The Weight of Waiting

Rowan took more time than usual to get ready for bed. She dismissed the new maid and brushed her own hair. It was growing out after she'd hacked it off. Her ranger cap hung on a hook beside her dressing table. She tried it on, remembering how she'd felt so out of place the first time she'd worn it and now, despite the monsters, the storms, and the murderers, she wished she could ride into the Meadows with Squad 54 again.

She hung up the hat and pulled on a robe, belting it at the waist. Her hands slipped into the robe's pockets and gripped two small knives.

"Evani?" A voice came from the other room. Rowan took a deep breath and went into the bed chamber. Minna's face was unusually somber.

"I have secured the room. Shall I close the doors?" The elf nodded to the balcony doors where a stiff breeze ruffled the curtains. Thunder rolled somewhere out in the Meadows.

"Leave them for now." Rowan breathed in the fresh air blowing off the Meadows.

Phalian was zipping around the room. His wings clacked and tiny squawks escaped him as he flew.

"You won't get any sleep with that racket, Evani."

"It's the storm," Rowan said. "He can feel it."

"We all feel it." Minna's eyes locked on hers, and she nodded. "Are you certain you don't want me to stay?"

"I'm perfectly safe in my own room." Rowan lifted her chin. "You must be exhausted too. Get some sleep."

"As you say, Evani." Minna bowed and left.

Rowan stood by the open balcony doors for a few minutes. The air smelled of impending rain. Ferlan was hidden somewhere in the outside shadows, watching. Wind ruffled her hair. She pulled the robe more tightly about herself and returned to her bed.

"Phalian!" She gave a short whistle and the mech bird landed on her shoulder.

"SQUAWK!"

She patted him and made soothing noises.

"Come on now. Time to sleep." He shifted and little mech feet scampered down her arm. He locked onto the charging port on her wrist.

Rowan sat on the edge of the bed and propped up the pillows. She slipped the knives from her pockets and hid them in the bed clothes before tossing the robe to a nearby chair. Tucking her feet under the covers, she leaned against the pillows. Her hand itched to retrieve the knives. Instead, she opened the book on her bedside table and began to read. It was a modern retelling of stories she'd learned as a child, parables written by Saint Jocasta, the miracle healer who'd come to prominence after the Resurgence. The stories didn't hold her interest tonight, and after rereading the same page several times, she leaned over and twisted the knob on the ley-lamp.

Olan March had finally kept his promise and cleared all the thera mechs from her room. She'd filched this lamp from her father's study. Her eyes slowly adjusted to the dim light. It was never truly dark in the royal suites. Even on a cloudy night, lights from the towers on the wall filtered into the room. She could just make out the shapes of furniture and the flapping curtain.

She leaned her back against the headboard, a picture of repose. Under the blankets, her hands gripped the blades. Phalian crept from his cradle and crawled up her arm to rest on her shoulder.

They waited.

Rowan could hear her own breathing. Her hand went to her neck. The bruises from Orson's attack had faded on the skin, but not in her memory. As she traced the line of her collar bone, his bulging eyes appeared before her, intent with madness and the need to extinguish her life.

Her breathing hitched and bucked. Suddenly the room was too hot and airless. Her human fingers were digging into her chest as if she could squeeze her heart. They brushed against the graphium's chain and she grabbed the locket in her fist. She breathed in and out in steady, deliberate breaths until the panic eased.

Saints, she wished Conall was here. She took in another deep breath and let it out slowly.

The night felt like it would never end.

Sinking back into the pillows, she stared at the light coming in from the storm, and…

She woke with a start. She hadn't meant to doze off. The room was exactly as she'd left it. Her neck ached from sleeping while sitting upright. She tilted her head side to side, listening to her bones creak, listening for whatever had woken her.

Lightning cracked across the sky, searing her eyes with a fragment of a vision.

Something moved.

The curtains fluttered.

Rowan's left hand still gripped the handle of a knife, but the other blade was lost somewhere in the blankets. Phalian had shifted to his bird form and remained vigilant while she slept. His tiny claws scraped her shoulder through the thin fabric of her nightdress. Blood thumped in Rowan's ears. She tried to mimic sleep, but she was sure her pounding heart could be heard over the storm.

Lightning flashed again. Something definitely moved beside the couch.

Rowan slammed her hand to the thera lamp to ignite it, then remembered that all the thera mechs were gone. Her frantic swatting knocked over the ley-lamp.

Something hissed.

"SQUAWK!"

Phalian launched from her shoulder as a shadow landed on her bed. A yowl filled the dark.

Light from the patio doors revealed a cat crouching in the middle of her bed, its ears back and hair standing on end. It spit and hissed as Phalian dove for another strike. The cat's bronze-colored fur was dotted with black rosettes. This was no ordinary house cat. It looked more like a meadow cat with bared teeth long enough to take down a small elk. Inch-long claws dug into the coverlet as it ducked away from the dive-bombing mech.

Ferlan appeared in the open doorway from the balcony. He threw a dagger. The hilt of the blade ricocheted off the beast. The cat howled and flattened to the bed. A threatening growl filled the room. Minna ran through the main suite doors. She hadn't gone to bed, but had been waiting in the hall.

The cat, seeing it was surrounded, made one last attempt. It leaped across the coverlet at Rowan. She raised both hands. Her human hand held the blade, but her mech hand had the power. Instinct flushed through her and galvanic magic surged down her arm. The cat's teeth clamped onto her mech. She let the magic loose. The cat howled and fell away, tumbling off the bed. Fur smoked. Its mouth hung open and ribs rose and fell in a quick pant.

Rowan croaked out a curse to the saints. "Minna look for someone controlling it!" The cat had to be spelled with magic.

Minna stood over the beast and shook her head.

"No, Evani. Look."

Fur rose and melted away like fog burning off a summer field. The body elongated and joints popped as the creature shifted back into its human form. In seconds a young woman lay on the rug, her hair still smoking.

A dead woman, a kid really. She couldn't be out of her teens.

"A shifter!" Rowan gasped. Or was it? The girl was fully dressed in a black tunic and leggings. Her dark hair was braided down her back. A knife holster hung from a belt around her waist.

Rowan's mind reeled. She was no expert, but she'd seen shifters change during her time with Squad 54. Neither Conall nor Bretta kept their clothes when they shifted. What kind of sorcery was this?

"Minna, get Dale. Now."

"Yes, Evani, but first we must secure the room."

Minna and Ferlan swept the suite for more intruders but the shifter assassin had been alone.

"The servants' door is unlocked, Evani," said Minna. "I locked it myself not two hours ago."

Rowan nodded. Minna had told her this hidden door was a risk, but she hadn't listened. Ferlan left to find Dale and Rowan quickly dressed in pants and a loose blouse. Her eyes never left the body on the floor as if it might come back to life and attack again. Her fingers shook on the blouse's buttons. Phalian continued to swoop around the room. Until she could calm her own nerves, he would react to her agitation.

She fell heavily onto the couch. Atherton wanted her dead. And she'd killed a person. The double weight of those truths was suddenly overwhelming.

Dale found her there, with her knees drawn up to her chin, and tears leaking down her cheeks. Phalian swooped once as Dale sat and put their arms around Rowan.

"Get away, you damned pile of bolts." They swatted at Phalian, then murmured to Rowan. "Tell me. What happened?"

She gave a little hiccuping laugh. "It was a cat. Isn't that ridiculous? Who sends a cat to kill someone?"

Dale rose and stepped over to the corpse to examine it. They pulled a cord from under the girl's shirt. A medallion hung on it. Rowan didn't have to look closely to know it would be carved with the head of a fanged dog.

"It's the Pincer. The contract has been activated." Dale let the medallion drop to the girl's chest.

"Assassin." Rowan squeezed her eyes shut until lights burned behind her eyelids. Dale had come to her yesterday with the medallion he'd found in Atherton's office. They'd done some digging and matched the dog symbol to a shadow group of assassins known as the Pincers. Rowan had scoffed at the idea. The Pincers weren't real. They were a story that young pages told to scare each other.

Legend said the Pincers were once a sect of priests in Jupiter's temple, the strong arms who dealt with guilds and apprentices who didn't pay their fees. They eventually broke away from the temple and went underground, morphing into something darker, more dangerous and more secret.

Dale had warned her what the medallion found in Atherton's desk meant. Their network of informants had confirmed it. Atherton's patience had worn out. He'd made a deal with the Pincers. The contract was new and the attack had been imminent. Even though they'd taken precautions, she hadn't wanted to believe.

When she opened her eyes, the corpse was still there. So was the cold dread in her stomach. Even after everything they'd been through in the Meadows—she hadn't wanted to believe that Atherton would stoop to such a level.

"They won't stop at one assassin," Dale said. "I did a lot of reading this afternoon. There are full reports on Pincer contracts going back hundreds of years. They get away with charging exorbitant fees because they always hit their mark. If one Pincer fails, another will take its place until the job's done."

"Can we prove Atherton sent her?"

"No." Dale was patting down the assassin's pockets, but found nothing. They rose and studied her with a scowl. "The medallion found in his desk is proof of a contract, but Atherton could be targeting anyone in the city. And the Pincers have been known to have ties as far south as Dowchester. She could have been sent by anyone."

Rowan sank back against the couch feeling deflated. "So we're back to where we started, jumping at shadows and with no proof against whoever sent…that." She waved a hand at the corpse.

Dale scooped up the body, cradling the assassin like she was a sleeping child.

"What are you going to do?"

Dale thew her a feral grin. "I'm going to interrogate our assassin."

23

THE LURE OF THE SPIRIT

DALE STOPPED AT THE DOOR to the princess's suite. The dead girl weighed nothing, but she stank of burning hair. Rowan had been following closely behind, and she bumped into their back.

"You should stay here," Dale said.

Rowan crossed her arms and her lips pressed flat. Dale knew that look. She was already digging in her heels. She would contradict anything they said next.

"It's not safe."

"And it's safe here? I was almost assassinated!"

"Ferlan will stay with you."

"We will both stay," Minna said.

Dale hefted the dead girl and her head lolled. "No, I need you."

Minna cocked her head, not understanding.

"You're Dale's insurance," Rowan bit out. "They're going to let the spirit of the assassin possess them. If things go badly with the interrogation, someone needs to kill them. They don't think I would do it."

"I know you wouldn't," Dale said. They stood face-to-face. Dale had a fleeting image of the fierce little girl Rowan had been. She'd grown into an even fiercer woman, but her heart was too soft to kill outright. She hadn't even been able to kill that scribe in the Meadows, and they suspected the tears she'd shed on the couch were for the life she'd taken in self-defense rather than fear for her own life.

She couldn't be part of what came next, but she'd be vulnerable in her rooms too. Pincers worked alone, but there were others in the city. As soon as they learned the contract had failed, another assassin would take it up.

Minna stepped between them. "Is this interrogation necessary right now?"

Dale looked down to meet her eye. "We have only a few hours before her spirit moves on. If we want answers, it needs to be now."

"Then we all go." Minna motioned them into the hallway and waved at Ferlan to follow. Phalian zipped out the door with a chirp and click of wings.

"Keep that thing quiet," Dale snapped. Rowan whistled softly and the mech settled on her shoulder.

Dale peered down the hallway toward the atrium at the head of the royal wing. At least one keeper should be on duty, but no one came to investigate the noise they'd made leaving the suite.

Dale shifted the dead weight and peered toward the atrium. They should investigate the lack of guards. What if the assassin had incapacitated them? But time was wasting and alerting the guards would only raise questions. Why are you carrying a dead woman? Who is she? How did she get into the royal suite? Questions they had no time to answer.

Still, it was irregular that the keepers hadn't heard Phalian and at least peered down the hallway.

Minna saw the problem right away. She whispered a word to Ferlan and the other elf loped toward the atrium. He returned in mere seconds.

"Two keepers," he said. "Dead."

"Damn the saints. That gives us less time. Hurry now!" Dale dashed across the hall to the King's Suite.

As naturally curious boys with too much time and imagination, Ethan and Dale had run through this palace discovering many of its secrets, including a network of hidden doors and hallways. Some were used by the servants, but others were festooned in cobwebs, suggesting they'd been forgotten.

When Dale began work as secretary to the regent and gained access to the archives, they'd studied the palace's original plans and those for various upgrades over the centuries. There wasn't a room, door or passage that Dale didn't know about.

They dashed into the King's Suite with Rowan and Minna right behind and Ferlan bringing up the rear. The suite was dark, with only light from outside to fill the deep shadows. As they passed into the study something stirred on the couch. Dale froze.

"Wha—who are you?" said a tremulous voice.

"Auntie!" Rowan dropped to her knees beside the couch. "What are you doing here?"

Princess Bella sat up and righted her towering mass of hair. She wiped the back of her hand across her cheek and smeared a bit of sleep drool.

"I…I came for that." She pointed to the decanter of spirits on the table before the couch. A glass half-filled with amber liquid rested on the table beside it. "And for that." She pointed to a silent theragraph in the corner with a pile of thera disks beside it. "Sometimes I like to come and listen to the music we favored as children. I never hear it at court anymore. So much has changed…" Her eyes came to rest on the assassin's arm dangling from Dale's grip.

"Is she…dead?" Bella asked.

"Quite," Dale said. "She's a Pincer."

"Assassin? In our home?" Bella sat upright, now fully alert.

Rowan gripped her hands tightly. "We're going to find out where she came from, Auntie. And who hired her."

"How?"

"Dale can…" She trailed off.

Bella's sharp eye fixed on Dale. "The rumors are true then. You come from a family of thano mages."

Dale nodded and shifted the dead girl's weight.

"The guards at the atrium are dead," Rowan said. "As soon as replacements come, there will be an uproar. Stay here and stay out of sight."

"Nonsense, child. I'm coming with you."

"You can't."

"I can help."

"We don't have time for this," Dale said. The dead girl was getting heavy and they had a long way to go. Dale turned toward the bookcase, eyes scanning for the right volume. There it was. An unassuming book bound in brown leather with a title that discouraged reading: *A Study of Sewage Through the Ages*. Pressing the book's spine produced a loud click as the latch to the secret door gave way. A three foot panel of shelving swung into the room, revealing a pitch black passageway.

"Stay or come with me. I don't care." Dale walked into the darkness.

In the bowels of the palace, there was a small room, nearly forgotten by all those living above it—remembered only because Ethan and Dale had ferreted out all these lower rooms, pretending they were keepers fighting gaunts through mountain caves, or prisoners in a dungeon, or warlocks in their sorcerer's lair, or a dozen other scenarios that came easily to inventive boys. Only as an adult, when researching the history of the palace, did Dale realize how close the warlock assumption had been to reality.

Dale laid the dead assassin on a large stone table that nearly filled the room. The hairs on their neck felt like they were crawling.

Minna felt it too. "Vorha, Evani. There is magic in this place."

Rowan nodded. Her face had gone gray and had an unhealthy sheen. Dale hoped she wasn't going into shock.

Minna set her back against the wall beside the door and held her knife at the ready. She pointed to the stone altar. "There is blood on it. I can smell it."

"It's a ley-line marker," Dale said. "If there's blood, it's ancient. This place hasn't been used for sacrifices since the founding of the city."

Dale was almost certain that was true. At least as far as the archival records showed. Hundreds of years ago, mages had worked big magics here to secure the first foundation stones of New Torwood City. It was possible but unlikely that someone else had mapped these ancient and forgotten halls and used the altar for their own means.

"Two ley-lines intersect right at this point," Dale said. "It's a potent source of magic, and the reason the city was built on this site. Now help me remove her clothes."

"Just what kind of ritual is this?" Bella's voice rose sharply and Rowan shushed her.

"Trust Dale, Auntie. They know what they're doing."

The old princess harrumphed. She stayed in the doorway, leaning against the jamb as if her legs might fail her. Ferlan stood guard out in the corridor.

Rowan began pulling off the assassin's shirt. Dale tugged at her boots and chucked them aside. They wouldn't fit. Her pants would be a tight fit too. She was tall, but lean. Dale slipped one pant leg over the leggings they wore and then the other, not bothering to tie up the fly. This wasn't a fashion show.

"The last time you did this, you were twelve and it was a bird. You only had to wear its feathers as a head dress." Rowan handed over the black shirt.

"Birds are easier. Their souls fight less." Dale pulled the shirt over their head. It smelled like burned hair, and they swallowed down a surge of reflux before plunging their arms into the sleeves.

Standing in the assassin's restrictive clothes, Dale wondered if this was a bad idea. They swallowed down that doubt too.

"For a human, I'll need all the help I can get. Cut off her hair. As much as you can."

Rowan hesitated. "Have you…done this spell on a human?"

"Once." Dale didn't elaborate. The thano mage knack ran in their family but they didn't have much opportunity to practice. Before his death, Dale's father forbade it. When their mother died, Dale's older brother had made Dale the guinea pig to test the knack. Dale still had nightmares about speaking in their mother's voice. A few weeks after that mishap, Dale had been sent to the palace to be Ethan's companion.

Rowan handed over a long braid hacked from the assassin. Dale set it on the stone, pulled out a thera lighter and tried to set it on fire. Their hands shook and the glowing thera at the tip of the lighter wouldn't connect with the braid.

"Let me." Rowan's mech hand stilled their attempts and Dale shied away from that touch. Not that they had any real dislike of the mech, only that every time it touched them, Dale was reminded of the day it happened, of their own failure to protect Ethan and Rowan.

The princess smiled. She knew Dale shied from her mech, and like their other shortcomings, she forgave them.

A short blast of galvanic magic from Rowan and the hair went up in flames, filling the small room with acrid smoke.

"You're getting better at that," Dale said.

"I've had reason to practice lately." Rowan stood back as the flame fizzled out, leaving mostly ash and about two inches of singed braid.

"Again?" She poised her hand, ready to blast it a second time.

"No. That's enough." Dale tested the ash with a finger. It was warm, but not hot. They dipped two fingers into it and smeared it across their cheeks, around the eyes and over the bridge of the nose.

Dale leaned over the assassin. With her face uncovered, hair shorn and wearing only her underclothes, she looked vulnerable. She was barely more than a child. Dale knew the Pincers took in orphans and trained them from a young age, but the sheer waste of such a young life choked them with rage.

Minna was suddenly at their side. "Breathe," she urged. "Let the *coho-ne-teno* flow. I will be your anchor, yes?"

Dale nodded. An anchor was good, but they hadn't wanted to ask Rowan. An anchor could keep Dale's spirit from getting lost in the ether if the possession didn't work.

Dale sucked in a rough breath and let it out in a shaky exhale. "If my spirit gets lost, it will leave room for something else to take over my body. Something worse. My grandmother called it a demon, if you believe in such things. Do you understand?"

Minna nodded. Her eyes were black pools.

"If that happens, you'll know. The demon can't hide. Don't hesitate. It will only get stronger the longer it stays on our plane. Kill me…and it. Fast."

Minna bowed.

"Dale, you shouldn't do this," Rowan said. "It's not necessary."

"It is." Dale's voice was firm. They all knew they were at a dead end with Atherton and the council. They were biding their time, hoping to come up with proof to condemn him, but if Atherton was going on the offensive, they needed to do the same.

Dale leaned over the girl, filling their senses with the sight of her dead face and the smell of her burned skin. The mantra Dale's brother had taught them came back easily. Two words: *I am.* Dale chanted them aloud for a few minutes then turned the chant inward. The girl's face seemed to glow, then grow—filling their entire perception.

I am. I am. I am.

The words were meant as an affirmation, a reminder to keep a small part of oneself carefully locked away. For Dale, the mantra filled the void of their mind, pushing out intrusive thoughts, making a space for the girl's spirit to enter, and hopefully, blocking any malignant spirits that lingered nearby.

I am. I am. I am.

The words gonged and reverberated making ripples like a rock thrown into a pool. Dale sent those ripples crashing over the assassin's defenses. Their magic dangled like a lure on a fishing line. Once bitten, Dale would drag the assassin's spirit into their own mind. It wouldn't last. The spirit was already dissipating into the ether, but they would have a few minutes to peer right into that murderous psyche.

The gong sounded. The magic rippled. The lure trembled.

Nothing. The assassin's spirit didn't take the bait.

A new sensation shook Dale. It felt like flaming fingertips, scorching their arm. Dale's eyes cracked open to find Bella at their side. The fire from her touch settled to a comforting warmth and Dale realized that she was boosting their magic.

Saints! The old princess had a deep well of power behind her knack, and apparently she couldn't manipulate magic like a mage, but she could lend that power to anyone to wield as a tool, a suture or a weapon.

With Bella's magic boost Dale latched onto the assassin's dying spirit. It was faint and cooling, like a smoking campfire after rain.

WHY?

The voice reverberated through their mind. Dale's lips opened and a breathy voice said, "Why do you keep me from the rest that I earned?"

Dale felt that sickening sensation of having someone else look through their eyes. The assassin turned their gaze toward Rowan. She evaluated the princess for weakness, looking for a way to finish the job that death had cut short. Dale's fingers flexed as if looking for a neck to strangle, and they forced the muscles to relax. The Pincer might see through their eyes and speak through their mouth, but she wouldn't get full access to their brain and body.

The girl seemed to realize that her control was limited. Her eyes came to rest on her body splayed across the stone table, and she pouted. "Let me go."

Minna stepped in front of them. "We will. Be easy spirit. Your coho-ne-teno will join with your ancestors. As soon as you answer our questions."

Her gaze rested on the body. "Ask me."

"You are a Pincer, yes?"

Dale's head nodded. "Yes."

"Who holds the contract for the princess's murder?"

Dale felt the spirit fill with mirth. Their eyes fell on Rowan, then turned to Bella. "Which princess?"

Bella took a step backward, breaking the connection of her magic. Dale's lips turned upward in a grin. They couldn't stop it. They were losing control.

Minna hesitated.

Was there more than one assassination contract? Were both princesses at risk? What about Ethan? Dale was wondering all these things too when Minna forged ahead.

"Who hired you to kill Princess Rowan?"

"I go where the Pincer points me," said the breathy voice.

"But you know who hired the Pincer."

"Yes."

"Who? Tell me." Minna leaned on the command. She held a blade to their throat and her eyes bore into them. There was magic in that gaze, magic that held Dale and the assassin immobile. She squirmed under that hold, while Dale welcomed it. Minna could control the spirit, and Dale slowly resumed command of their body.

"Tell me," Minna urged.

The spirit struggled. Dale increased the pressure from within, squeezing her into a small part of their mind until she squeaked with pain.

Sweat ran down their forehead and burned their eyes.

"I…the contract was from the palace…Keiffer…minister of foreign affairs."

Dale let go. Minna stepped back. The spirit relaxed, then an inhuman giggle erupted from Dale's lips.

"Fools!" The spirit grabbed Minna's blade and lunged at Rowan before Dale could react. Rowan screamed and a blast of white hot galvanic magic hit them in the chest. Dale gasped and the dim room faded to black as they crumpled to the floor.

Shouting hurt their ears and Dale couldn't tell if it came from within or without. They squeezed their eyes shut and pushed with everything they had. The spirit clung to their psyche like the last leaf on a winter tree.

"Tell that bitch to get lost."

Dale's eyes opened to find Bella's grinning face. Her hand touched the sore spot on their chest and it warmed. Dale screamed as the touch went deeper. So did the spirit. Bella's touch *hurt*! The Pincer's scream was shrill, and it tore at Dale's soul.

And then it was gone. They were once more alone in their bruised mind.

Dale's last sight before passing out was Minna bowed over the corpse.

"The marrow feeds the spirit, long after the meat is gone." Her knife flicked out to take a finger from the hand of the dead girl.

24

RATI-IRIVU

THE PIT WASN'T AS BIG as Benni's market square, but the ceiling vaulted high enough to be lost in shadow. It took Conall a moment to understand what he was seeing. There were workstations everywhere. That was the only word that came to mind, but they were unlike any workstations he'd ever seen. Dozens of Ebos sat at desks fashioned from metal, glass and other substances he couldn't even describe. A few looked up when they entered, but most were intent on the mechs before them.

And there were mechs everywhere. Some were lit by flashing buttons. Others hummed and clicked. Ebos men and women sat in chairs before their stations, reading words and diagrams on what appeared to be massive graphium screens. Mechs of unknown purpose sat on every desk and side table. Cables curled from one mech to another like the tentacles of a sea titan. A kind of mimeo mech droned and clacked in one corner, spitting out sheets of printed paper. A valet retrieved those sheets and dispersed them to different stations. The whir of its wheels added to the hushed sounds coming from all directions.

Garou snorted at the odd smell, like burned metal and the zing of lightning after a storm. The last time Conall had smelled that was when Rowan zapped the walrus titan.

Galvanic magic. The room hummed with it.

They stepped over cables and around stacks of metal mechs that beeped and flashed lights of different colors. Ebos looked up from their work to nod as they passed. The screens lit their faces with an unearthly glow.

Nathan tapped a box with one such screen and said, "This is a monitor."

He explained other devices as they walked, but Conall understood only one word in three, and even those words were used in a context that was beyond him—words like *network, compute* and *processor*. Nathan spoke of *technology* and *electricity* and *plastic*—words Conall had only read about in ancient novels that were scavenged from old ruins and passed around the Briar Market.

At the far end of the room, they stopped at an alcove cut into the mountain. It was no bigger than a hearth and filled with glowing ley-stones. Two Ebos wearing white robes knelt on the floor before this hearth. Eyes closed and heads bowed, they were lost in meditation.

Conall's sensitivity to magic was as good as any shifter's and he could feel the heat of power coming off those crystals and bathing the meditating Ebos.

"Who are they?"

"Luminas," Nathan said. "Mages trained to track magic emanating from the mountain. We sit on a ley-line. The stones act as a focal point for that power. After a few weeks, they are ultra-charged and can be used as fuel."

Conall nodded. "I saw those stones in Omika's hearth."

"It's a simple, renewable energy." A hint of a shadow darkened Nathan's eyes. "At least as long as the ley-line holds out."

"Is there any reason it shouldn't?"

"I don't know. Maybe. The elders will talk about the circle of bones and how all things have their season. To be honest, I don't understand most of it, but the luminas devote their lives to finding that understanding."

Conall turned and took in the space. There was a busy hush in the room, punctuated by small sounds of working mechs.

"I'm glad there is something you don't understand in all this because I'm at a complete loss." He squeezed the tendons at the back of his neck, trying to relieve pressure.

Nathan grinned. "It is pretty amazing. I remember when I first stepped in here."

"More overwhelming than amazing. What are all these mechs?"

"Computers."

"Computers." Conall rolled the word around his tongue. It hit his thoughts like a memory, lost on the edge of awareness. "And what exactly do these computers…compute?"

Nathan's lips were flattened into a serious line, but a spark of excitement lit his eyes.

"They gather information. They track, calculate and design. Anything we need. They even extrapolate possible futures. But most importantly, they spy on our enemies."

"Is this why you lured me here all the way from New Torwood City?"

Nathan smiled. "Partly. But maybe I just wanted to see my baby brother again."

Conall shook his head and frowned. He was happy to see Nathan, but he wasn't yet ready to forgive those missing years.

Garou snorted. *Wolves have no use for a grudge. It is like the shit of your enemy. You can't eat it, and keeping it around only mucks up your senses.*

"I have something else to show you." Nathan seemed reluctant and uncertain. "You're not going to like it."

"I want to see anyway." Conall shook his head. None of this was easy. It was so far from the realm of easy that he didn't even have language to express how wrong this hidden world felt. But he needed to see whatever other wonders these Ebos were hiding inside their mountain. He needed to see it all.

"Show me."

Nathan beckoned him toward a particular workstation where a male Ebos was staring at a monitor. Nathan laid a hand on his shoulder.

"This is Rudi. He is a *lochi*, the Rati version of a mech mage. One of our best."

A light flashed on the screen, then Rudi sat back and smiled at Conall. "Hiya. Nice to meet you."

He was short, even for an elf, with owlish eyes that peered from a round face. Light from the screen tinged his skin green. His blond hair was long and unkempt and fell around his face in tangled hanks. Conall suddenly realized that none of these Rati wore the traditional bone ornamentations.

Conall nodded a greeting. "How is a lochi different from a lumina?" He glanced toward the far end of the cavern where the mages were still deep in their trance.

"Luminas wield magic, yes? Yes." Rudi said. "I wield mech. In another age, I would be a technician. Maybe that makes me mechnician." He grinned, pleased with his joke. Then his expression turned somber and he tapped the screen before him.

"Now I scan for spikes in thera." He pointed to the screen. Conall leaned over the Rati's shoulder for a better view. It was a topographical map of the Meadows. He recognized a few natural landmarks, the spine of the Ubruulens to the north and the winding tail of the great Ikon River in the south. Numerals scrolled down the screen too quickly for him to read.

"See, thera here. Thera there." Rudi pointed to a couple of red dots on the map. "All expected, yes? Yes."

Conall recognized the locations. They were ranger outposts. It made sense that they would use thera.

"This one not natural." Rudi pointed to a spot in the far northeast. "A gaunt cluster? Maybe yes, maybe no." He shrugged and tilted his head from side to side.

"But how is that possible? How do you track something so far away?"

"For years we plant surveillance mechs. We track movements of herds, gaunts and Taiga."

"And Wrede and his men to some extent," Nathan said.

Rudi pointed to a red dot flaring on the map. "Here, again! Look, look! I watch all day, yes? Yes. Thera spikes. Exactly two minutes every hour. Right there, then gone. Watch."

They waited, and in a few moments, the flickering light on the screen died. Rudi swiveled in his chair and grinned.

Conall studied the map. "That's the Warren."

Rudi nodded. "Once it lit up the screen with huge amounts of thera magic. Huge! Then Wrede shut it down. Or so we thought."

"There's nothing left of Wrede's operations," Conall said. "I was there."

"Nothing? Maybe yes. Maybe no." Rudi tapped the screen.

"Could it be residual magic from their mech? The place was trashed when I saw it, but it didn't look like they left anything behind, except…"

His mind raced back to that night when he and Clem had found Wrede's lair and then fought their way out.

"There was an underground room we didn't have a chance to investigate.

But that doesn't make sense. It's been weeks. Any mechs left behind would have died by now." Thera chips didn't last that long.

"If they were left on, yes? Yes." Rudi jabbed the screen with a finger. "But this signal is…Beep! Then gone." He opened his hands as if they'd exploded.

"It's intermittent. Like someone is turning it on and off?"

"Or it's on a timer," Nathan said. "Either way, it's worth investigating. We were already planning a trip to the Warren when we got word of your arrival."

"I'm going with you." Conall needed to finish what Squad 54 had started. And Rowan needed answers. If that meant another trip into that hell hole, he would do it.

"I have more," Rudi swung around in his chair and tucked his legs under him. "The signal flashes, yes? What you humans call Morse code, yes? Could not be sure at first. Something interferes with the signal." He frowned. "If underground…that would explain, yes? Possible to amplify with a quantum booster…" His eyes went glassy as his thoughts turned inward. Conall wanted to shake him, then Nathan *did* shake him.

"Rudi, the signal."

"Huh?"

"What does it say?"

"Oh, yes. Yes! It says *Eklridge.*" He gave Nathan a small smile. Nathan looked like he'd been punched in the stomach.

"Eklridge?" Conall said. "That's the oasis where all the scientists died."

Nathan nodded. "We had two contacts in their camp. Both went dark after the attack."

"But now you think one may be alive?"

"Maybe."

Something had always seemed off about the massacre at the oasis—some detail they weren't grasping. Missing bodies. The scribe burying her cachet. The burned out ward.

"Who were your contacts?"

Nathan screwed up his lips as if he didn't want to say.

"Sandra Kane," Conall suggested. "The scribe was working for you."

Nathan nodded. It made sense. He had contacts at the Temple of the Word. And Kane had been desperate to keep her cachet out of Wrede's hands.

"And Dr. Banerjee," Nathan said.

Whoa. Conall hadn't expected that, but it made sense too. Banerjee, his assistant Elsie Myer, and one maintenance worker had been the only bodies unaccounted for.

"The scribe is dead. I saw her body myself."

"That leaves Banerjee," Nathan said.

"We should leave now. As soon as possible." Conall was already turning toward the door. There were answers out there, answers that he needed in order to keep Rowan safe.

"Slow down, brother. We can't just run into the Meadows unprepared."

Conall grabbed his shirt front and jerked it upward. A wolfish snarl escaped his lips. "Don't screw with me, Nathan. I'm tired of your games."

Rudi watched the brothers with one eyebrow raised. Nathan looked amused. He squeezed Conall's fingers until he let go, then smoothed down his shirt.

"It must be dinner time," he said with a grin. "You always were cranky when hungry. I promise we're going to find out what that signal means. But I meant what I said. We need to prepare. Horses, supplies, weapons. We can leave tomorrow or the next day at the latest."

Conall forced himself to relax. Nathan was right. Normal people didn't rush into the Meadows unprepared. He'd been running as a lone wolf for so long, he'd forgotten that.

Nathan squeezed his arm. "For now, let's leave the Rati to do their jobs. We'll go home for supper. Soffi made caribou steak and ale pie."

I like caribou, Garou said.

Conall nodded.

"And you can tell me more about your mission at the Warren," Nathan said. "I've got questions."

"So do I. A lot of questions."

"An answer for an answer then. We'll trade and I'll supply the yenni." Nathan clapped him on the back. "Come on home. Let's get you fed."

25

The Shadow of Missing Years

Dinner was the best thing Conall had eaten since…forever. The pie was hearty with a thick gravy and chunks of caribou, turnip, and carrots. They'd emptied a jug of sweet, dark wine, and Garou was making little satisfied grunting noises in his mind.

"You've been on the road too long." Nathan watched him mop up gravy with a dark stone-ground bread. "Your muscles are ropey and you look like a half starved stray."

"And you look like a cleric. Someone who spends too much time at a desk." Conall poked Nathan's waist. He wasn't fat exactly. Just soft.

Nathan laughed. "That's what a happy home life will do. You should try it." He squeezed Soffi's hand and she smiled. Little Jula was perched in her lap. She cooed and tried to grab her father's fists, then switched direction and rubbed her eyes, mashing gravy into her hair.

Soffi kissed the top of her curls. "She needs a bath and her bed," Soffi said. "I will let you get out of bath duty tonight, my love, but only because we have a special guest. And you will owe me." She leaned down to kiss his forehead.

Nathan pecked Jula on the cheek. "I'll make it up to both of you. Bath duty and story time for a week. At least."

Conall watched them retire to the small room off the kitchen.

"How is that possible?" He kept his voice low, not wanting to offend his sister-in-law. Ebos and humans could not procreate. It was a well known fact. They were different species.

"You mean how is it possible that such an amazing and beautiful woman would love your wreck of an older brother?" A spark of amusement glinted in Nathan's eye.

"You know that's not what I mean."

"She's not my child." He watched Conall with that familiar lowered look and half-grin. "Not biologically, but she's my daughter in every other way. She was orphaned. Her father was my colleague, another Rati. He died a month before she was born. Her mother died in childbirth."

"I'm sorry to hear that."

"Life is harsh in the north."

In Conall's experience, life was harsh everywhere.

"Her father Tiri was a good friend. There was no question about taking in Jula. Soffi was meant to be a mother."

"And how about you? How does it feel to be a father?"

Nathan looked down at the remains of their dinner, and Conall could have kicked himself for bringing up the darkness that was their childhood. Then Nathan raised his head and smiled.

"It feels amazing. There is nothing quite like holding your child, watching her take her first bite of food, her first steps. It makes me think that our father must have experienced those joys. I can only wonder how he forgot them. And I hope..."

Nathan's eyes shone. Conall gripped his arm. Nathan had always been the older brother, the one who consoled. The one who told Conall stories in the dark while their father ranted through his latest drunken binge. As a child Conall had thought he was so brave, but looking back now, he realized that Nathan had been a scared kid too.

"You won't ever forget," he said. "You are not our father."

Nathan smiled and thumped the table. "Help me with these dishes and then we can take a nightcap in the garden."

"Wait. I have something for you." Conall found his pack by the front door and took out their grandmother's ring and the necklace.

"Soffi should have these."

Nathan's eyes widened when Conall dropped them into his open palm. The light from the hearth caught the diamonds and they glittered.

"How?" Then he looked sharply at Conall. "You went home. When?"

"I met Lydan on the road. He sort of insisted that we stop at the old homestead. And I'm glad I did."

Nathan closed his fist around the jewelry and held it toward Conall. "You should keep them. I hear there's a princess in your future."

Conall pushed the fist back at him. "Ianna would have wanted you to have them. She would have loved Soffi. And one day you can give them to Jula."

Nathan's eyes shone with unshed tears, but he nodded.

Conall gathered up the used dishes while Nathan got water from the well. There was already a pot of warm water hanging over the ley-stones in the hearth, and Conall used it to fill a wooden basin.

Nathan returned and they worked quietly for a few minutes. Conall's mind was sorting through everything he'd seen that day.

When the kitchen was tidy, Nathan grabbed a ceramic jug and two cups from a high shelf.

"Let's sit outside. The night is warm enough."

The garden path was lined with herbs and their feet stirred up the scent of thyme as they made their way to a couple of stone benches near the bottom of the garden. They sat and Nathan poured milky draughts into the cups. He handed one to Conall.

"Go easy. It has a kick to it."

"I've had the pleasure of tasting yenni before." Conall sipped the fermented caribou milk flavored with elderberries. It was sour and tangy and sharp enough that it felt like a snake bite on his tongue. His eyes watered. Garou growled. He was never one for self-imposed poisons.

"Now I know my little brother doesn't cry. Not ever. So I'm going to assume those tears are from the dry wind."

"It's this yak spit." Conall thumped his cup on the bench.

Nathan grinned. "It's milk not spit." When Conall didn't answer he sighed. "Okay. A question for a question. You go first."

They were well into the evening, but the sun wouldn't set for another hour. Conall watched a bird fly overhead. The ever-present predator in his mind catalogued it as a Long-Tailed Jaeger. Not enough meat to get excited about.

"I guess my biggest question is about the Pit," he said slowly. "I thought the Ebos abhorred mech. So, explain to me in simple words, what in the saints was all that?"

"They do abhor it," Nathan said, "and with good reason. The Ebos fear and despise mech because it nearly destroyed them once. Six hundred years after the first elves came through a rift to our world, the Ebos elders still teach their children about how mechs became too powerful on their home world, Essa. These Ebos and the Enos who live in the city were once all Essians. The divide happened only when they came here. The Ebos vowed to live simply and worship the coho-ne-teno as their ancestors did. The Enos embraced human civilization and everything that came with it, such as mechs."

"That still doesn't explain…that." Conall waved in the general direction of the Pit.

"I'm getting there." Nathan took a sip of his drink. "The Ebos vowed to live simply, but they never forgot the lessons of the past. They also vowed never to let technology overpower common sense again. The Rati are watchdogs. They were formed with a single intent: to monitor the rise of mech. That's why the Ebos reacted to me as they did in the market. They both fear and revere the Rati. We are heroes but also tainted by our constant proximity to mech. Necessary evils. It's why we live apart in Rivu."

The picture and scope of the Rati's purpose was starting to come clear.

"So all that mech is from another world? From Essa?"

"Most of it. Some is Earth technology from before. From what we've discovered, it seems that humans were on the verge of a mech apocalypse similar to what happened on Essa. Then the Resurgence happened. I choose to believe that's not a coincidence. Now I have a question for you."

"Go on."

"From the reports, mostly brought back by Dalkyn—and by the way he doesn't like you much."

"Yeah, I get the feeling Dalkyn doesn't like anyone over five feet tall."

"True enough." Nathan laughed. "Anyway, Dalkyn's report was very useful. He showed us how you and your princess friend carved out homing devices from the gaunts you killed. After you left Eklridge Oasis, our team went in and retrieved one of the dead gaunts there. They brought it back here for a…uh, closer examination. It had a tracker too. If not for Dalkyn's intel, Wrede would have tracked us right to Benni."

"That was lucky."

Nathan smiled, but there was a grim edge to it. "Yes, it made us reevaluate how we do things. Clearly we need more distance between the Rati and Benni before this war escalates."

Conall didn't argue with his assessment. They *were* at war.

"We're making arrangements to move our operations. Omika seems to think our base should be in New Torwood City."

Conall let out a rough laugh. "I knew that old puppet master had an agenda."

Nathan let the comment go. "We also understand that Wrede was able to control these gaunts. For years we believed it was simply a matter of training. He takes them when they are infants and rears them on a strict diet of punishment and reward. Barring that, we assumed some kind of magic was involved, similar to the scribe mech, but we were never able to determine what kind or how deeply it was rooted in the gaunt's brain.

"Dalkyn told us of a device the soldiers used to control the gaunts that attacked you. At first we thought this remote control linked to the homing device, but scans of the beast show something different. They show thera throughout its system, and we wonder if the controlling device reacts to that."

"Scans? What kind of scans."

"Different kinds. We have an empathic medic who's able to delve into a living body without cutting it open."

Conall nodded. Both Denny and Noah had such abilities to some extent. It's what enabled them to wipe Orson's memories.

"But we use other types of scans too. Digital scans that show us the gaunt's blood, tissue and bone, down to a molecular level."

There he went using that language again. Digital. Molecular. They weren't foreign words, but their meanings were so shrouded in lost time that they might as well be.

"I still don't understand what you want from me."

Nathan ran his hand over his hair and gripped the back of his neck. "So many things," he laughed. "We need a foothold in New Torwood. We need help from the humans and even the Wildbloods if we are to find Wrede's new lab. And Dalkyn says that you had one of those controllers, taken from a dead gaunt in the Warren. We need that device so we can reverse engineer it and possibly understand how Wrede is controlling them."

"I did have one." Conall was reluctant to say more. Rowan had the controller. He trusted his brother not to hurt her, but he didn't know these Rati-Irivu, didn't know how far they would go in their fanaticism to track and understand all things mech. After a long moment, he sighed. Who was he kidding? Rowan would be the first to help these strange Ebos with their dangerous mission.

"It's in New Torwood."

"Then I propose we go to the Warren, find where that signal is coming from, then head south to the city."

If Conall hesitated, it was only for a fraction of a second. "And what do you plan to do once you, how did you put it? Reverse engineer the controller?"

"Destroy the gaunts. Maybe turn them against Wrede, if we can, before we wipe them out. They're abominations." Nathan's grin was sharp and bleak. The cold look in his eyes sent a shiver up Conall's spine.

Conall gazed at the sky for a long moment before coming to a decision.

"There's more you need to know."

As the midnight sun finally set, Conall spoke. He told Nathan about what they'd found at the oasis, about Denny's survival and how the junior scientist had filled them in on Banerjee's work with gaunts. He told about the new findings that gaunts were once human, twisted by a combination of thera ingestion and the massive spike in magic during the Resurgence.

In turn, Nathan told him about his time with the scribes and his early days at Benni.

For hours the brothers spoke, heads bent and voices low.

When the questions and answers were finally exhausted, the missing ten years didn't seem so dark anymore.

Nathan rose and drained the last drop from his cup. "I can make you a bed by the hearth. I'm sorry I don't have anything more comfortable."

"I take my comfort from the open sky. I'll sleep out here tonight."

"Are you sure?"

"It feels like I've been on the road forever. I'm more comfortable with the stars overhead than a roof. If the night turns cold, I'll come inside."

"Suit yourself." Nathan went into the cottage and returned with a small embroidered pillow and a quilt. "At least take these."

Conall accepted the offer, but as soon as Nathan left, he set them aside. Someone had put a lot of effort into the pillow and quilt. He wouldn't sully them with garden dirt just for his comfort.

He leaned back on the bench. His hand found the locket under his shirt. Flicking it open, he was disappointed to find the left side empty. He took the stylus and wrote on the right side: *At Benni. Love you.* It was all he could manage on the tiny graphium. He hoped it was enough.

He dropped the locket back into his shirt and then tucked his hands under his armpits to keep them warm. Eventually, he gave in and draped the quilt over his legs, but it was a long time before sleep finally found him.

26

Finding Wisdom at the Bottom of a Pot

Rowan sat in the study off her bedroom. She preferred to take breakfast outside, gazing at the big sky and green Meadows, but a storm had blown in overnight and the menacing clouds lingered. Thunder rumbled in the distance and the sky was low, black and heavy with rain. The study was dark, but she hadn't bothered to light a lamp. She sat on the couch, still wearing her dressing robe, and watched Roger who sat unmoving in one corner.

She opened her graphium locket and looked at Conall's message again. He'd made it to Benni. She was happy that he would find the answers he needed, but sad that he was so far away. Twice that morning, she'd picked up the stylus to answer him, and twice she'd abandoned that idea.

Should she tell him about the Pincer? The graphium was so small. What could she say in a few words?

A tried to kill me. Didn't work.

"A" stood for Atherton because even if the dead assassin had pointed to Minister Docker, Rowan's heart knew that Atherton was part of the scheme. He'd probably orchestrated it and used Docker to cover his ass.

Still, she couldn't bring herself to write the message. That would send Conall into a fit of rage and worry. She would save that news for when he returned. If he returned.

She picked up the tiny stylus again and wrote, *My best to Omika.* She tucked the locket under her shirt and turned her attention to Roger.

It had been nine days since they'd descended into Grotto—nine days during which time Roger had sat in the corner as still as one of the Rustwork's discarded mechs. He wasn't dead, just occupied. At least once a day, she put her ear to his chest and listened to the faint whirring of his internal processors as they shifted through all the data on Sandra Kane's cachet.

Harry Hightower—she still had to pinch herself when she thought about meeting the famous mech mage—had said Roger would take a few days to process the data. Rowan's impatience had her questioning that timeline. How many was a few? Three? Five? Twenty? She kept expecting Roger to wake, and she wanted to be here when he did.

They desperately needed the information on that cachet. The attempt on her life was proof that her enemies were getting restless or scared. Or both. She could still see the staring eyes of the dead girl. Assassin. She had to call her what she was because every time she remembered how young she'd been, Rowan's heart squeezed painfully in her chest. What kind of monsters turn teenagers into assassins? The really smart kind. Who would question a young girl in the palace? She'd probably posed as a maid to use the servants' stairs.

That reminded Rowan of Alice, the poor girl who'd been banished for falling to pieces at the sight of Minna. She thought about asking Mrs. Pickney what had become of her, but she didn't trust the housekeeper to tell the truth.

Maybe she could send Minna to the kitchens to see if the girl had really been sent to scrub pots. But Minna and Ferlan had also been up all night. They were resting now, and she didn't want to disturb them.

They couldn't go on as they were. Minna had warned her that she needed a full guard as entourage. It was a princess's right. Up until now, she'd been avoiding that because…she didn't really know why. Perhaps it was simply habit. For so long she'd been a ghost in the palace, hiding in plain sight by eschewing the noble dress code and spending all her time in her tinker shop or on the wall. Now she had to learn how to be a princess with all the drawbacks and benefits that came with the job. And that meant a full honor guard.

She despised the idea of having keepers trail after her everywhere she went, but she could no longer rely solely on Minna and Ferlan. It wasn't fair to them. And it wasn't safe. She would do something about that. Soon.

She glanced at Roger. He still hadn't moved.

She read Conall's message again. It made her heart hurt. With Conall at her side, she knew she could be a princess, a tinker, a woman…anything the world needed from her.

Hurry home, my love. She squeezed the locket, then tucked it away.

She needed to get up and get dressed. She needed food and fresh air. And she really needed to stop feeling sorry for herself. This wool gathering was doing her no good. She swung her legs around, rose on bare feet and headed to her dressing room.

By the time she emerged, dressed in a simple but elegant tunic, Minna was awake and taking her breakfast at the table by the balcony doors.

"I'm going to the kitchens," Rowan said. "I won't be long. Stay here and finish your breakfast."

"Yes, Evani." Minna wiped her mouth on a napkin and followed her to the door.

Rowan sighed. "There's nothing I can say to make you stay here and rest, is there?"

"No, Evani."

"Fine, but when this business is done, I'm coming back here for a nap before lunch if only so that you can rest too."

"Yes, Evani."

The palace kitchens had always been a haven to Rowan. They spanned three large rooms with pantries, cold rooms, and other storage added on, along with a large eating area for staff. This area was set up like the keepers' mess hall but on a smaller scale. Two long tables with benches filled the room. A sideboard offered hot tea, fresh water, and an assortment of pastries all day long. Kitchen staff and maids could sit and refresh for a few minutes on their breaks. This was where a lonely young princess had learned to bet at cogs and crowns. She'd learned other useful skills here too. The maids had shown her how to sew on buttons and hem skirts, patiently waiting while her mech fingers learned the fine dexterity required for needle work. She'd listened to stories told after supper when all the work was done. She'd even learned to cook simple things like scrambled eggs and cottage pudding.

When she hit her teen years and the regent began expecting her to participate in galas and dinners, the kitchen staff started looking at her differently. She was no longer the cute kid with the mech hand. She was suddenly a royal.

Later, when she rebelled against this label and turned to tinkering, the staff, like the nobles, didn't know what to make of the grubby young woman who preferred to dress in men's clothing instead of gowns.

There was one who never gave up on Rowan. Marjory Gorrie had been the cook's assistant during her father's time. She'd seemed ancient then. When the old cook retired, so did Marjory, but since she had no home of her own, the chancellor had made a place for her in the kitchens.

Rowan found her in the corner of the mess hall near the wood stove. The day was warm, but Marjory sat in a rocking chair with a shawl over her legs anyway. A basket of yarn perched on the hearth by her feet and her hands worked at knitting something gray and shapeless.

"Good morning, Marjory." Rowan had snatched a flower from one of the many vases in the palace atriums and handed it over. Marjory took it with a trembling hand. Arthritis bent her index finger at a painful angle. She stared at the yellow burst of petals with rheumy eyes, then sniffed it.

"Mmmm. Salsify. Edible but bitter at this time of year. Good for loosening the bowels."

"I'll try to remember that." Rowan smiled. It had been their favorite game. Rowan would bring herbs, flowers and weeds from all over the palace grounds and Marjory would tell her their various uses.

Marjory bit off a couple of petals and chewed. Her round cheeks pumped and Rowan imagined gears inside them, cranking her jaws. She tipped her head to peer around Rowan and blinked when she saw Minna.

"You're keeping odd company these days."

"You could say that. How are things down here?"

"Same as always. That new cook, Taggart. Bah!" She puffed out an exasperated breath. "He screams out his orders and Dru screams right back at 'im."

Taggart was new only to Marjory, whose world seemed stuck in the past.

A shout came from the main kitchen, then the sound of a pot clattering to the floor. And more shouts.

"Sounds like he's in a temper today," Rowan said.

"Must be a Saint's day." Marjory grunted and went back to her knitting. Rowan held in a smirk. There were hundreds of lesser saints and every day of the year was named for one or another.

"I'm looking for a maid. She's very young. Her name is Alice. Have you seen her?"

"Thin little waif with flaxen hair and the look of a scared rabbit?"

"That's the one."

Marjory pointed with her knitting needles. "In the scullery, probably with 'er head in a pot."

"Thanks." Rowan turned away and paused. "Are they treating you well here?"

Marjory's hands didn't stop, but she glanced over her knitting. "Well enough. Stove is warm. Tea is good. I could use more yarn. Have to undo my stitches each night just so I'll have a reason to keep my fingers busy."

"Good." Rowan had thought about moving Marjory into the West Wing, but she knew the old cook would miss the action and gossip of the kitchen. Instead, she made a mental note to find some yarn.

She headed into the main kitchen. It was a chaotic place, with a dozen sous chefs preparing food for all the nobles in residence. Smoke and steam filled the air. Mechs mixed and chopped. Other mechs rolled about, bringing ingredients to cooks.

In the middle of this frenzy, Taggart and Dru were having a philosophical debate about whether parsley was an herb or a garnish. The philosophy included the throwing of pots and a raised butcher knife.

Rowan was certain that Taggart wouldn't kill Dru. Fairly certain.

"Get out of my way!" the cook blustered. "I'll ruin her just like she ruined my béchamel with her nasty greens."

"You wouldn't know a vitamin if it bit you in the ass!" Dru flung a handful of greenery at him and Taggart lunged with the knife held high.

"Stop!" Rowan stepped between them. She turned to Dru. "Go find Alice, the scullery maid. Bring her to me."

Dru scowled, but she stepped away from the confrontation. Rowan turned to Taggart. He was a big man. Tall and broad across the chest with hands that could each wrap around a ham. His face was red from the heat of the ovens or overexertion.

"She acts like a spoiled princess!" His face went even redder when he realized what he'd said.

"Do you know many spoiled princesses, then?" Rowan asked. "Because I don't. There certainly aren't any in this palace."

Cook mumbled something like "saints take her" under his breath and turned back to his hearth.

"I have some requests," Rowan said, catching his attention again.

"Your breakfast not up to your tastes, Princess?" His lip trembled with the need to sneer. "Should I add a lump of parsley to your porridge?"

"Breakfast is just fine."

"I would like an allocation of yarn given to Marjory every month. She's knitting blankets for Jocasta's Temple. At my request."

Rowan could have spoken to the quartermaster directly for the yarn, but Marjory—retired or not—fell under Taggart's domain. By asking him, she showed that she respected his authority.

Taggart's nose twitched. "Fine. I'll see to it. Anything else?"

"Yes. The maid, Alice. She was banished here, I'm told. I would like to take her on as my page."

"Alice?" Taggart laughed. "You can have her and good riddance."

Dru returned, shoving the girl ahead of her. Alice was grimy from head to foot. She looked like she'd scrubbed pots with the curls on her head.

Rowan smiled. "Hello, Alice."

The girl bobbed a curtsy.

"Are you happy here in the kitchen?"

"Yes, my lady, I mean, Princess." Alice's eyes darted to Taggart who was already back to haranguing another assistant.

"Would you rather work for me again, in the royal suites?"

"As your ladies' maid?"

Rowan thought of the mess Alice had made of her clothes and shook her head.

"As my page. You would deliver messages and take on other small jobs for me."

Alice screwed up her face. She was either thinking it over or about to cry. Finally, she took a deep breath. "Yes, milady. Princess, I mean. I would like that."

"There's just one thing." Rowan stepped aside to reveal Minna who stood near the kitchen doors watching all the blades chop as if they might suddenly fly at Rowan's head.

Alice's eyes widened. Rowan gripped her hand in case she decided to flee. "You need not be afraid of Minna."

Alice smiled and Rowan caught a glimpse of the pretty woman she might become.

"I know, Princess. My new friend Elias explained it to me. He's an elf too. Not the dark kind, but he explained how the dark isn't really so dark after all, so I guess it's all okay now." She finished with a gasp as if that reasoning had taken all her breath.

"Elias Horora? He's here?"

Alice nodded. "He's been scrubbing pots with me. Showed me how to get tarnish off silver too. Elias knows everything about…"

Rowan cut the girl off. "Take me to him."

Alice shrugged and led her through the kitchen to a back room near the outer yard where tables were piled high with dirty dishes. A large thera stove boiled water in one corner. Steam filled the room, making the warm day unbearable. And there, elbow deep in a sink full of dishes was Elias.

Minna stepped forward. "Hey, handsome. Remember me?"

Elias shook soap from his hands and grinned.

The following morning, Rowan dressed for a day in the city. Instead of her usual tunic and leggings, she wore a simple dress with clean lines that barely cinched her waist. It was deep blue and contrasted nicely with her strawberry curls.

Rowan had been furious to find the smart, resourceful elf working in the kitchen scullery. When Elias had been released from Squad 54, the palace quartermaster had assigned him to the kitchens. Rowan wanted to march into the quartermaster's office and berate him for wasting good talent, but she was learning to choose her battles more wisely. Instead, she offered Elias a job as her guard and sent him with Alice to get cleaned up and outfitted for their new posts.

With three guards, each doing eight-hour shifts, they could all get some rest. Until she selected her full honor guard, it would do.

Elias was ready to take on his new role, and for once, Minna was relaxed enough to let him. She'd informed Elias about the assassination attempt and instructed him not to let Rowan out of his sight for a moment.

"We're going to Jocasta's temple," Rowan said. "How much trouble can we find there?"

"If there's trouble, you'll run headlong into it," Minna grumbled. Elias grinned.

"And what should I do while you're away, Evani?" Alice had taken to calling her by the Ebos title since she never could decide between "my lady" and "princess."

After cleaning up and donning the simple uniform of a page, Alice looked both older and younger somehow. Her wispy blond curls gave her a childish air, but her solemn expression was very grown up.

Rowan looked around the suites for something to keep her occupied, and her gaze landed on Roger who still sat immobile in the corner.

"See that valet?" she asked. Alice nodded. "He's very special. Right now he's…sleeping." She didn't want to get into the whole explanation of data and processors. "But he's going to wake up soon. And I need to know the minute he does. Can you do that? Stay here and watch him. Come get me at the temple as soon as he wakes."

"Of course, Evani. Is there anything I can do while I wait?" She looked around the room as if searching for something to clean. That was good. It showed the girl had a strong mind that didn't like being idle.

"How's your reading?"

"Good, Evani. I was at the top of my class before I had to leave school."

"And when was that? What year did you finish?"

"Grade five, Evani. That was the year my ma died and I had to find work."

Grade five. Rowan scanned her bookshelves, pulled down a slim volume and handed it to the girl.

Alice read the title slowly. "The Founding of a ca…a City."

"It has some interesting drawings too. I think you'll like it."

"You want me to read a whole book?"

"Yes. And I'll be quizzing you on it later. You can read it aloud to Phalian. He likes a good history."

Phalian said, "SQUAWK!" and landed on the bookshelf.

Alice's eyes grew huge and she hugged the book to her chest.

"Yes, Evani."

Rowan nodded. If the girl proved to be a good student, she might make a decent secretary one day when Dale was promoted to first advisor to the regent. Or to the queen. Rowan checked that thought as if simply thinking it was a jinx. But she did need to plan ahead and watching Alice devour the first page of New Torwood's history was satisfying.

"Come on," she said to Elias. "I told Noah we'd be at the temple by noon."

27

IN SERVICE TO THE SAINTS

NOAH'S MESSAGE LEFT OUT MORE than it said.

Meet me at the Old Bailey? I'd love to catch up about old friends.

Rowan hadn't seen him since returning to the city, but if he'd wanted to chat and be with old friends they could meet at The Glass Boot, Bretta's new alehouse. The fact that he wanted to see her at the temple hospital meant something was up.

It was nearly noon and the traffic tried her patience. The market in Bailey had been open since sunrise. Vendors were taking a break before they packed up their wares for the day. Rowan hurried through the maze of carts and a few straggling shoppers, stopping for a messenger mech that zoomed by with little regard for pedestrian traffic.

Elias followed at a discreet distance. Taking him into the city rather than Minna or Ferlan let her pass unnoticed, and she reached the hospital known simply as Old Bailey in good time.

The building was a square, gray stone structure with wide stairs leading to double doors that were always left open. A few people lingered on the stairs, either current patients taking some air or new patients waiting to be seen by the busy healers within.

"Wait here for me." Rowan said, and Elias frowned. "No one would dare attempt anything inside the temple." Saint Jocasta had abhorred violence of all kinds and her temple was a sanctuary. Elias still didn't look convinced. "I'll be with Noah anyway. You don't have to worry."

Elias crossed his arms. "I worry more about facing Minna when you get assaulted in the temple mall."

Rowan could see his point. "Fine. Come along."

They entered the dim foyer. This main entrance had been the barracks for the original bailey that had stood here. Once the main city walls and fortifications had been built, the bailey was abandoned. Jocasta's doctors took it over. The rest of the hospital was built later as an annex. The foyer was cramped, empty and dark. It led directly into a concourse that couldn't be more different. The concourse stretched away farther than the eye could see, with a soaring ceiling and arching windows that bathed the space in sunlight. Rowan walked through a long corridor of columns made of wood and carved with vines and woodland creatures. It felt like walking in a forest. Small pools of water with discreet fountains appeared at intervals. They were edged with stone benches for supplicants to sit and contemplate Jocasta's benevolence.

Rowan stopped at one. Trailing plants were arranged around the pool to look natural, if artful. In the middle of the water stood a statue of Jocasta holding the paw of a wolf as she healed it. The wolf's muzzle was raised to the sky as if it might howl at any moment. Jocasta's smile was serene. Calming.

Unlike the other saints, Jocasta had never been a god. She was a simple woman with a knack for healing who lived through the last years of the Dark Age by traveling through the monster-infested Meadows to heal anyone who needed it. She asked for nothing in return. When the first king Andula found her in a village treating an outbreak of the pox, he enticed her to join him in the new city by promising to build her a hospital and fund it from the royal purse.

That's how Old Bailey became the first temple in New Torwood. It was still partially funded by the palace, but it had other sources of income too. Everyone paid for their healing, whatever they could. The poor might give a dozen eggs to have a broken arm mended. The rich would give a bag of thera chips for the same. There was an unspoken rule that anyone who visited the temple should donate something—money, time or goods.

Rowan dipped her hands into the pool, washing them with water blessed by Jocasta's doctors. Her mech fingers tingled from the magic. The bottom of the pool was lined with thera chips. She gave thanks for the people in her life, people she hadn't known she needed until just a few weeks ago. Then she tossed in her own chip.

After the concourse came the mall. This was the temple's other source of income. Jocasta profited from the permits for all medical practitioners and purveyors of medicine who set up shop in the city, but the temple's apothecaries also made medicines which they sold for profit in the mall.

It was a space as large as the outdoor market she'd passed through earlier. Entire sections held tables piled high with bags of dried herbs. One wall held hundreds of jugs of tinctures, all lined up on metal relays that hooked up to a mech dispenser to dole out portions by the ounce.

Another wall was given over entirely to a display of crutches, wheeled chairs and mech walkers that had been abandoned by people healed through the saint's benedictions. A large sign posted above this exhibit said: *Dedicated to those healed by Jocasta's grace.* It was an impressive display, but Rowan thought the saint's healers—and not prayers—probably had more to do with these miraculous cures.

The apothecary mall was busy. Mechs weighed pouches of herbs. A valet offered samples of an emollient used for dry skin. Rowan waved it away when the mech tried to slather some on her arm. Another sprayed her with a fine mist of something that smelled of pine and camphor.

"Breath balm," droned the mech. "To open lungs. Only four chips per bottle." She pushed past it and came up against another mech selling another balm.

Elias wasn't as stealthy at avoiding the mech samplers and by the time they reached the end of the mall, he'd been slathered and anointed by a dozen balms and sprays.

"I stink like a whore's boudoir," he grumbled.

"And how would you know what such a boudoir smells like?" Rowan teased.

"I can imagine." Elias turned red. He was an easy mark.

She had to admire the Jocastans. Every patient entering the hospital was forced to walk through the concourse with its many reflecting pools, where a chip for good luck was a common donation, then through the mall, where eager mechs enticed them to part with even more chips. She couldn't really begrudge them for trying to make a profit. Stocking and manning a hospital was expensive and the care given by Jocastan doctors and healers was top notch.

They finally entered the hospital section of the temple. It was by far the largest wing and was bracketed by the mall on one end and cloisters for offices and staff rooms on the other.

Unlike the other temples, Jocasta's didn't have priests, archivists or orators. It had doctors, healers and medicos. The healers made up the bulk of the workers. They performed minor healings and diagnostics. Doctors had undergone extra schooling to be able to perform rites in the name of Jocasta. They were surgeons and physicians but also administrators and liaisons with the palace, the guilds, and other temples. Medicos were students in training and they lived in the cloisters.

She waited in the triage center where patients were tended by the medicos before being assigned a doctor or a healer. The medicos and healers all wore unbleached homespun linen. Rowan supposed it was easy to clean and disposable if it became too soiled. Doctors were distinguished by their white coats.

She stopped one young medico and asked for Healer Noah Sommerton.

The girl frowned. "I don't know them." She couldn't have been older than fifteen, but she had the solemn expression of someone wiser than her years, a good face for a future doctor.

"He's new. He'll be expecting me."

"Please wait here. I will send a runner to find him."

"Thank you."

For the next fifteen minutes she watched the young medicos stabilize broken bones, stop a head wound from bleeding and induce vomiting in a child suspected of eating poison. The flow of orderlies, patients and visiting families never stopped.

Rowan spied Doctor Renata conferring with another senior doctor at the main triage desk. She looked smaller and less severe in her doctor's coat. Rowan turned away and hid among the patients waiting to be seen before the minister recognized her.

Noah finally came through the door that led into the hospital proper. He looked rushed and frazzled. He was thinner than she remembered and a deep line creased his forehead. He saw Rowan and waved her through the doors.

"Come on, this way." He turned his back and led them down a clean bright corridor. Small rooms on either side held beds with patients. Rowan caught his arm. She could feel the tension in his muscles.

"Noah, stop."

He paused.

"Don't you even say hello?"

His shoulders sagged and he turned.

"I'm sorry. Hello."

Rowan leaned in and hugged him. He was stiff but he endured it. When he pulled away he held out a hand for Elias. The elf ignored it and threw his arms around Noah. The crease on Noah's brow eased as surprise took him, and he patted Elias's back.

"It's good to see you too."

Elias stood back and sniffled.

"You said you wanted to talk about old friends," Rowan said, "so I brought one along."

"That's good." Noah's smile didn't reach his eyes, but then, it never did. He was not someone who embraced happiness.

"So what's this all about?" she asked.

"Not here. I have something to show you first."

Noah led them down winding corridors with treatment and recovery rooms on either side. The halls were spotless. A fleet of janitor mechs mopped and wiped down every surface under the watchful eyes of human supervisors. They walked in silence until they passed under an archway with a sign that read, "Hospice Ward." This corridor was shorter, quieter and less bright. Gone were the individual rooms. They passed open wards with ten to twenty cots each.

Noah led them to the farthest ward and ushered them inside. The room held about thirty cots in three rows. There were no families sitting at the bedsides here. No flowers on the side tables to brighten the place. A single janitor mech trundled up one row of beds and down the next, its mop rotating in a dull hum that added to the white noise of the fans on the ceiling.

Every bed was full. Several were isolated by curtains. In the nearest bed a young woman was sleeping. She had a severe disfigurement. Her nose seemed to have melted into a red, viscous ball. Beside her was an older man with half his face blackened as if burned.

"Is this a gangra outbreak?" Rowan had never seen such severe cases, but she'd heard that gangra could disfigure in this way.

"No. These patients are all thera addicts." Noah pinched his lips into an angry ball. "But don't they look just like that poor kid we saw at the gate in Oxeye, the one dying of gangra?"

Rowan shuddered, remembering the young ranger who had barred them from entering the fort at Oxeye. The ranger outpost and thera camp had been restricted due to the gangra outbreak. Despite his own illness, the young ranger had kept to the strict quarantine. His face had been disfigured in a similar way.

They walked down one aisle. Every patient was deformed or damaged in some way—fingers missing, faces blackened.

"Will they recover?" Rowan whispered.

Noah pulled her aside. "Probably not. There is no treatment for thera overdose. The protocol is to keep them comfortable. This means administering small doses of thera every day. Otherwise the withdrawal is excruciating."

"And you don't agree with this." She could already tell by the scowl on his face.

"No. It's not a treatment. It's a death sentence. But there's something else." He pulled her to one of the two windows in the room, where a desk for the healer or doctor on duty sat unused. Noah turned his back to the ward as if afraid someone might read his lips. When he spoke, his voice was barely above a murmur.

"The thing is, no one dies here. At least not on my watch. And I've been here for two weeks."

"So they just linger on like that?"

"No. You don't get it. They die, just not here. Every time I come on shift, patients are missing. When I question it, I'm told they died in the night. Or while I was working another ward. But I checked the morgue." He glanced around again to be sure they weren't overheard. "They have no record of the last three patients who were taken away."

He watched her with a stern expression while she worked out the implications of his words.

"You think someone is stealing your patients? For what? To experiment on them?"

Noah shook his head. "Maybe. Or maybe someone is trying to hide the effects of thera addiction. Look at this." He pulled her over to another patient bed. This one held a young man. His face was unmarked and he looked like he could simply be asleep, but when Noah pulled back his blankets, he didn't stir.

Rowan's hand went to her mouth to hold back a gasp when she saw his arms. From wrist to shoulder, they were gray and scaled. Just like the armored plating of a gaunt.

"I think thera induces this change. Not in everyone, but one in ten patients show this mottling of skin." He tapped the man's arm to show it was as hard as plating. "And I think no one wants us to know about it. I think the worst cases are taken away before they turn into monsters before our eyes."

A dozen thoughts fought for space in her brain. Gaunts were once human. Denny had confirmed that, but this? This wasn't a theory. It was happening now, right before their eyes.

"Denny made it sound like that mutation had been a one-time thing. Thera was part of it, but it had taken massive doses of magic too, the kind of magic that only happened during the Resurgence."

Noah watched her with his lips pressed thin as she worked the logic to its natural conclusion. When she did, her hand went to her mouth as if she could hold in the next words.

"It *is* the thera. But thera ingested over time."

Noah nodded.

"But why? Why now, I mean?"

"Because until twenty years ago, thera was relatively unknown."

"And now it's everywhere."

Denny and the scientists had been wrong. It wasn't a one-time mutation.

"Oh, saints, Noah. The regent is installing a thera water pump for the city. Water will run through pipes laced with the stuff."

Noah just shook his head.

"We should have seen this coming. Thera addicts have been showing odd symptoms for years, but no one cares about them."

"The temple doctors must know." Renata was a prime doctor and palace liaison. She must have known, and still she voted for the thera pump.

Then a worse thought hit her.

Noah took thera to manage the backlash from his knack.

She gripped his arm. "Are you okay? I mean, you've taken thera before. You haven't…"

"I'm fine," he assured her.

"You must stop taking it."

"I have. You don't have to worry about me. We have enough to think about." He beckoned for her to follow again. This time he swept back the curtain that secluded a bed in the farthest corner from the door. He motioned for her to approach the bed so he could close the curtain, while Elias stood watch outside the flimsy barrier.

Orson slept in the bed.

"They said they couldn't care for him at the Temple of the Word anymore. He started having manic fits that turned violent. He's sedated now."

They'd done this to him. Orson's memory wipe had been necessary, but when Rowan looked too hard at their actions that day in the Meadows, guilt burned in her stomach like acid. The fact that he'd tried to kill her made her feel only marginally better.

Conall had wanted him dead. She'd refused because Orson had been brainwashed. Denny had called it programming, but the logistics of it were lost on Rowan. All she knew was that Orson hadn't acted in his right mind. He was despicable, yes. When they'd linked to wipe his memories, Noah, Denny and Rowan had witnessed the extent of his hatred and the pure malevolence that his mind was steeped in. But he was also a human being and deserved compassion. And this is where her compassion had led.

Orson and Augie weren't the only casualties of that mission. Everyone on Squad 54 had returned from the Meadows a different person.

"Denny said the effects of losing his memories would wear off, that together we could target the specific timeline and leave the rest of his memories intact."

Conall didn't trust Denny, but Rowan had. There was an innocence about him that she found endearing. But what if Denny had been wrong? Or worse. What if he'd misled them?

"Denny also said that he had never seen anything like those particles in Orson's blood," Noah said. "It was a long shot."

Rowan's mech fingers squeezed the blankets. "It would have been kinder to kill him."

"Maybe. But I think he was already on the road to…something. Illness, insanity or even death. We just sped things up. Look."

Noah turned down the bedding and pulled up the thin hospital gown. Orson's stomach was gray and plated. Now that she was looking for it, she saw spots of gray at his temples and inside the crook of his elbow too.

"Saints help us. He looks half gaunt already," Rowan said.

Noah nodded solemnly. "It's the thera. It has to be." They'd all felt it when they joined together to examine him. Thera was at the heart of scribe magic, and Orson's blood and bones were full of it.

"Are there more scribes here?"

"At least five. And two of the bodies that disappeared were scribes."

"So what do we do about it?"

"I have no idea, but I thought you should know." Noah's attention shifted when a doctor came into the ward to make her rounds. He made his excuses to Rowan and promised to visit Bretta at the Glass Boot, then hurried away to attend the doctor.

Rowan sat by Orson's bedside for a while. She didn't hold his hand—couldn't bring herself to touch him. The panic attacks were less frequent now, but she still found it hard to sleep some nights. Her breath would come in fits for a few moments until she convinced herself that she was safe and memories couldn't hurt her.

Seeing Orson lying there should have made her feel better. It didn't. She had more questions than ever, and no place to begin looking for answers. Or did she?

Harry Hightower.

The mysterious mech mage was at the heart of all this mess. Hadn't he mentioned his disgust for scribes? Maybe he'd known it would turn out this way, with scribes falling to thera addiction and a percentage of those addicts turning into gaunts.

She needed to speak to him again.

Noah was still busy with the doctor and she didn't want to draw attention to herself, so she quietly left the ward, headed back into the maze of hallways, and immediately became hopelessly lost.

"This way, Evani." Elias pointed down a corridor that looked like all the others.

"You're sure?"

He nodded. Elias had proven to be a reliable tracker in the Meadows. His sense of direction had to be better than hers.

Ten minutes later they were through the mall and concourse and back outside. A thin figure was sitting on the stairs in front of the hospital. She jumped up and ran toward them. It took a moment for Rowan to recognize Alice as she wore a scarf over her head like a cowl.

"Princess! Princess!" The girl bounced on her toes.

"Shhh!" Rowan took her hand. "Don't call me that here!"

All she needed was a swarm of well-wishers and gawkers to find her. Then the keepers would have to be involved and the whole outing would become an affair.

Alice looked chagrined. "Sorry, prin…I mean, Evani."

"What are you doing here?"

"It's the mech." She bounced on her toes. "The valet you asked me to watch. He's awake!"

28

A CURSED BENEDICTION

Soffi held Jula too tightly against her chest as if the child could shield her from grief and worry. Jula's biological father had been Rati, and he'd died on a mission into the Meadows. Conall suspected that Soffi worried every time the Rati left the safety of Rivu. Nathan wrapped his arms around his wife and child, cocooning them in a world of private words and reassurance.

Conall turned away. The sharp pang of envy in his chest startled him.

You are no longer a lone wolf brother, Garou said. *You just don't know it yet.*

Conall ignored him and went to check on their horses. Ailen was joining their crew as a guide, along with Kelli and another scout named Cob. They weren't Nathan's men but fighters sent to protect the precious Rati-Irivu who'd been tasked with a job that was considered abhorrent but necessary. Rudi was coming too and a lumina named Irva rounded out the group. Conall recognized her from his visit to the Pit. She'd been deep in meditation beside the ley-stones. He realized that she was older than the others. Since Ebos tended to look younger than their age, she could be nearly a century old. He worried that she would find the long journey difficult, until she leaped onto her pony without any help, spry as a youth. She grinned at him, as if his thoughts were transparent.

Ailen handed over the reins of a good sized bay and spoke a few words in Essian. Conall recognized only the word for horse: *ko.*

Irva approached on horseback. "He says he chose the biggest horse he could find for you." The elf eyed Conall up and down. "It is still not as tall as you are used to, but your legs will not drag on the ground."

"Thank you."

Irva smiled and bowed, then straightened when she caught sight of a figure moving slowly up the path toward them. It took Conall a moment to recognize Omika. He seemed to appear from nowhere, then Conall remembered the tunnel between Omika's office and the Pit. He must have come underground.

The elder walked alone and wore a simple unbleached robe, the kind Ebos scouts wore to blend into the Meadows. Only a single strand of bone beads hung around his neck.

The Evafara was going incognito.

As he approached, he pulled back the cowl on his robe and the morning sun reflected off his few wisps of white hair.

The Rati bowed deeply. Even Nathan lowered his head in deference. Omika squeezed his arm, though the gesture might have been to steady himself.

In the harsh light, Omika looked ancient.

"Be at ease. I am not here for ceremony, and I have only a few minutes before my babysitters realize I am gone. They panic so easily when I wander." His eyes twinkled.

"I came to give you all the blessing of the bones, for your road will be hard. Remember, wind and rain may strip the flesh, but bone endures. Come back to us in whatever way you can."

That's not ominous. Not at all. Conall knew that talk of bones meant something different to the Ebos, but he couldn't help thinking Omika's blessing sounded more like a curse.

The Rati lined up to file past him. One by one, Omika laid a hand on each elf's shoulder and spoke a quiet word. Conall stood back with Soffi who was trying to hold on to a squirming child. He didn't want to intrude on what was clearly a private moment between the Evafara and his followers. But Omika had other ideas. He beckoned and Conall found himself standing before him with as much humility as any Ebos. Omika's serene humor woke some unidentified emotion from deep within. Even Garou stirred when they met his blue eyes.

"I drew you here for selfish reasons, using the love for your brother as bait. And for that I apologize. But the work that Nathan and the Rati do is more important than any one person's feelings."

"I don't blame you," Conall murmured. "I'm glad to find my brother alive and well. And if the Rati can help me understand certain…recent events, then I am doubly glad to have found them."

Omika patted his arm. His touch was hot and dry. "And how is your lady princess?"

Conall frowned. "She's not my lady. At least not yet. But Rowan was well when I last saw her."

"Good, good. I sent Minna and Ferlan to guard her, but in truth they are more than guards. They are ambassadors. The time is coming when the Ebos can no longer live apart from the world. We must go south to New Torwood City and perhaps even to the great cities beyond. I fear that soon we will have to fight our old enemy."

Conall felt every muscle in his body tense. "What enemy is that?"

"Progress." Omika frowned and the wrinkles around his mouth and eyes deepened. "A deceptive word, progress. It shines a positive light, but in practice it is the shadow that conceals greed and suffering."

Conall's gaze was locked on Omika's and he felt the first flutters of enthrallment looking into those eyes. Garou howled, but Conall could not look away. Omika's tone was pitched low, for his ears only.

"Tell the Evani that I will come if she calls. The Ebos will come."

Omika clapped his hands and stood back, breaking the spell he'd been weaving. Conall shook his head. Garou whimpered.

"I wish you all an easy road. May your ancestors walk with you, and may your coho-ne-teno find peace wherever that road takes you."

"Still more curse than blessing," Conall mumbled. Nathan eyed him sharply and he shook his head.

As they rode off, Conall twisted in his saddle to see Omika standing beside Soffi, watching the party leave while Jula pulled on the strand of bone beads around his neck.

29

GHOSTS OF ALGID PASS

CONALL WAS SURPRISED AND TROUBLED when their line of horses headed east, directly into the furrow where the two arms of the Ubruulens met. He'd expected Nathan to lead them back the way he'd come and travel the lowlands south of the mountains. It was the sensible thing to do. Even at the height of summer, the peaks of the Ubruulens were snow-covered. The wind was strong enough to scour any exposed skin, and the hunting would be non-existent. And worse yet, the only way to cross the mountains was at Algid Pass.

The skin between Conall's shoulder blades itched at the thought of revisiting the site of his last stand as a ranger.

Nathan spurred his pony to catch up to Conall. "Cheer up, brother. The sun is shining. And if it gets too cold, we can always run as wolves."

"I would prefer that," Conall groused. "These ponies aren't fit to carry a grown man."

Nathan laughed. "They're sturdy enough, and they can pick a trail through the mountains as well as any goat."

He glanced behind them. Rudi rode next in line. He trailed a pack pony on a lead rope. Its bulging saddlebags were covered in an oiled canvas tarp. Conall had already asked what was so important that they'd bring another horse when they were aiming for speed and stealth. Rudi had just grinned and said, "Toys."

Garou had judiciously reminded him that he wasn't alpha of this group. The Rati knew the terrain and the enemy better than he did, and Nathan knew the Rati. That meant following Nathan's lead, and he didn't seem concerned by the extra rations and time a pack pony would take.

They left the tranquil valley late on the first day when they turned onto a narrow passage that rose in a steep incline. They rode in single file. The sun beat down without mercy. Conall was glad for the modified Ebos robe that covered his head and the dun-colored scarf that kept the constant wind from scouring his face.

They climbed the trail all afternoon, navigating switchbacks and several steep slopes. The ponies proved their worth by scrambling up these impossible trails without hesitation. Gravel slid under their hooves. Conall's mare shied as she lost her footing, but she caught her stride and continued the climb. After that, staying on horseback took all of Conall's attention.

From the front of the line Ailen whistled for them to stop. "Rest and drink, Captain?" he called back. Nathan waved his approval. The path was too narrow to gather as a group, but Conall managed to pull his mount next to Nathan's.

"What's with the others calling you captain?" he asked.

Nathan shrugged. Had the wind burned his face red or was he a little embarrassed?

"They wanted a human designation. I just liked the old timey feel of it. Something unique, I guess."

Nathan hadn't risen past the rank of maven in the rangers before Wrede's men left him for dead, and captain wasn't even a ranger designation.

"It's because of that book, isn't it?" Conall couldn't hide his grin. "What was it called? You obsessed over it for a year."

"Captain Cosmos," Nathan said. "And so what? He was a hero. I needed a hero back then, and we could aspire to worse things now."

Ianna had brought the antique book with full color drawings home from Briar Market. Nathan read it cover to cover a dozen times. He would recite from it by candlelight when they were supposed to be sleeping, and while they hid in the cellar he made up his own tales about the dashing and heroic Captain Cosmos.

"I just hope they don't expect you to leap tall buildings," Conall said.

"Ha ha. Nothing taller than a cottage, I assure you."

Their banter was cut short as Ailen whistled for them to march again.

Nightfall found them all huddled against the mountain with only the ponies for a windbreak. Conall pulled his saddle blanket over him as a gust of wind whipped up the trail. He could see snow on the nearest peaks. It was bitterly cold, and there was no wood for fire.

"Haven't you got any of those ley-stones?" He rubbed his hands together, trying to push warmth into them.

"We do, but it's too dangerous to use them up here," Nathan said. "The Taiga monitor these passes. We don't want to attract their attention."

Conall huddled into his cloak. The cold was preferable to the fierce warriors who occasionally came to raid from over the mountains. Since the last war when New Torwood's rangers had decimated the gaunt population, Taiga raids had become more frequent.

Nathan saw his scowl. "Don't worry, little brother. The Rati have an agreement with the Taiga. We helped to release their people from Wrede's black site and they have long memories."

"And yet, you won't light the ley-stones for fear of attracting their attention."

Nathan smiled. "There's no point in chasing after trouble." It was something their mother used to say. "And besides, the Taiga aren't the only predators around here."

Conall didn't have to ask what he meant. He knew exactly what kind of monsters roamed the mountains. He'd fought a war to beat them back.

Before settling in to sleep, he rose to check his mount. The mare had eaten a bag of oats and was resting with eyes half-closed. She didn't seem to notice the chill. Conall lifted each of her feet, inspecting them for stones lodged in the soft soles. Satisfied that she was sound, he gave her an extra handful of oats.

Rudi was fussing with the pack pony. He pulled off the tarp to reveal two large, basket-shaped saddlebags. One was full of weapons—rail guns, knives, bows and quivers of short arrows.

The second basket was packed with mechs of varying sizes and uses that Conall couldn't even guess at.

Rudi patted his stash. "For you, our weapon."

"I'm the weapon?" He could feel Garou's wolfish amusement.

"Yes, yes. Captain Nathan is our brains, Irva is lumina, Ailen is guide, and Kelli and Cob are muscle. You are weapon."

Conall grunted. This wouldn't be the first time he'd been pointed at an enemy and expected to fight, but this enemy was elusive and ephemeral. He wasn't even sure there *was* an enemy. They might make it to the Warren and back without ever encountering a fight, but his extra sense—the one his mother had called his wolf sense—knew that was naive.

"If I'm your weapon, I hope your aim is good."

Rudi seemed to think that was hilarious and he slapped Conall on the back as he wheezed out a laugh. "You are funny, Old Wolf."

Conall cocked his head at the little Rati. "Why is your English so good? All the Rati seem to speak better English than most Ebos."

"Tellllllliiiiiiveeeesion." Rudi drew out the word. Conall didn't understand and he clarified, "It's human mech."

"You mean television?" He'd read about such a thing. It was moving pictures that people used to watch. Stories that played out on a screen. Captain Cosmos had loved television. As a child, Conall had accepted it as fantasy. As an adult, he couldn't really see how television had been possible.

"We Rati have many ancients mechs. Times, long, long, long gone. But I make them work. Yes, yes! Televisions, telephones, computers. No mech too old or too new for this Rati."

Conall was still confused by his mech talk, but that seemed to be the normal state of affairs between them. Rudi reached into the weapons bag and pulled out a rail gun. He put an eye to its scope, then handed it to Conall.

"Here, here. This one for you."

The gun was longer than normal, but light. Conall hefted it, his fingers easily finding the safety and trigger. The balance was good. He looked through the sight and nearly jumped back. The scope saw farther than anything he'd ever used. He could pick out an individual rock on the highest peak over a mile away.

He primed the gun and it whined for only an instant before it was ready to shoot. Turning it off, he handed it back to Rudi.

"It's a fine weapon, but I prefer a crossbow. It's more reliable."

Rudi nodded. He tucked the rail gun back in the saddlebag and pulled out a bow and a quiver of bolts.

"These will suit. Yes? Yes."

Conall took the bow. It was solid and made of a lightweight metal he didn't recognize. The draw weight was a bit less than he was used to. Probably not so accurate as the one he'd left behind in New Torwood, but it felt good to have a bow in hand again. He pulled out a bolt. It was sixteen inches long with a thick head that tapered to a wicked point.

Rudi pulled another bolt and caressed its red fletching like they were the feathers of a favorite pet. "Punches through gaunt plating." He held up two fingers. "Two seconds after impact…" He gave Conall a side-eye and his hands opened. "Boom!"

"Boom? It explodes?"

"Yes! Everything gone, from here to here." He widened his arms to show a six-foot radius.

"Boom, indeed."

Conall examined the bolt again. What would they have done for these in the last war? So many human lives would have been saved.

"How many do you have?"

Rudi's eyebrows scrunched. "Only these two. Very hard to make. Very magically potent. Luminas work for months on one arrow. Do not waste, yes? Yes."

Conall nodded and slung the quiver over his shoulder. Two shots. He could work with that.

"What other wonders have you got in there?"

Rudi bounced on his toes.

"Guns, knives, traps, decoys. Many, many wonders." He pointed to the second basket. "And toys for the Warren. If any mech left to examine, we crack its secrets!" He threw a tarp over the saddlebags and tied it down, then stood back and seemed satisfied with his work.

"We keep hidden. Ebos do not ride with mech, do they? We hide, yes? Yes."

"Are you expecting to be attacked?"

"Always, Wolf. Always."

He slept fitfully that night and woke with a kink in his neck.

We're too old to sleep on cold rock, Garou groused. *And there won't be any hares for breakfast either.*

Conall ignored him while he ate his meal of caribou jerky and nuts. Garou continued to grumble about the loss of hot and tender hare meat.

Too soon, they were mounted and moving again, winding along the mountain track like ants crawling across a wall. They stayed below the snow line, but the road was rocky and narrow. The pack pony struggled with its burden and they stopped several times so Rudi could coax it forward.

The air was thin and crisp. Above them, snowcapped mountains glittered like shards of glass. For three days they followed this routine: wake, eat, ride, eat, sleep. On the fourth day, the trail began to slope downward again.

From the moment they'd headed north from Rivu, Conall had dreaded crossing the Algid Pass, and now that they'd arrived, ghosts pounded at the door of his memories.

The road widened as they neared the pass. Sheer rocky scarps caged them on both sides. Nathan spurred on his pony to catch up with Conall as he crested the hill and stopped to look down at the bottleneck ahead.

"Is it just how you remember it?" he asked.

"Fewer corpses." Conall squinted into the sun. Ten years ago, bodies had been piled three deep. The smell of blood and decay had lingered in his hair and on his clothes for days. He closed his eyes and could still hear the cries of the dying.

"You know they call you the Wolf of Algid Pass?"

Conall nodded. "I know."

"Ianna always said you'd be famous for something. Even as a child you wore the shadow of greatness like a cloak."

It was the first time Nathan had mentioned their sister since their reunion.

"No one would call what I did great."

"That's not true. Even in Rivu, I heard the stories of the wolf commander who led his squad to safety before disappearing into the wilds, never to be seen or heard from again."

"That's not the story most people tell."

"Oh, I heard the other part too. The part where you narrowly missed the bolt from your general's gun as you leaped on him and tore out his throat. Sounds to me like he had it coming."

Conall grunted. General Naylor had never been a fit leader. He was lazy and selfish, caring more for his comfort than for his troops. Conall and the other commanders had mostly made up for his lack of leadership skills, but in those last days of battle, many of his fellow officers were killed and Naylor had been forced into a more hands-on role. His fear was as evident as his ineptitude. He called for the troops to dig in and hold the pass when the gaunts outnumbered them three to one. And when Commander Jani complained, Naylor shot her. Conall had been at the Norsap outpost when the news of Jani's death came to him. He'd left his post and run back to the pass. Rangers swarmed past him, some sporting wounds made by rail guns. They shouted at Conall to turn around, that the general had gone mad and was shooting his own soldiers.

Conall hadn't retreated. He'd fought against the tide of fleeing rangers and then against the straggling gaunts who'd made it through their barricade until he faced Naylor. The man was red-faced and foaming at the mouth. He shook a rail gun that smoked in his hand, its rails clearly burned out.

A body lay at his feet, dead eyes open and caught in an expression of surprise. One of their own.

Something inside Conall snapped. The veil between man and wolf dissolved. He didn't even feel the change. He leaped from human feet and landed on Naylor with wolf paws.

Staring at the empty pass ten years later, he could still taste the hot iron of Naylor's blood. He glanced sideways to where a broken gatepost poked through a pile of debris, all that was left of the barricade that had held off the gaunts. For a while.

"Where did they all go?" Conall asked.

"The bodies?" Nathan asked. Conall nodded. "We burned them, after giving their bones the proper rites."

"The rangers should have taken care of it."

"Should have, yes. But the fighting moved south and then there were no more gaunts. Or at least no more than the usual few that always roam the Meadows. The rangers didn't waste resources cleaning up after their mess. But we," he waved a hand at himself and then to the Ebos behind them, "we need this pass to travel from Benni to the eastern Meadows. And we would not let their bones rot in the sun without recognition."

"Do the rangers know you took their dead?"

Nathan shrugged. "Norsap Outpost was manned for many years after the war. Someone must have returned here. If they have complaints about our cleanup, they never expressed them."

Conall continued to scan the ground. It was all so familiar and yet…not. He saw the faces of his squad, drinking and eating around small fires. He saw them dirty and bloody, defending the one road into the Meadows from the horde that would overrun their homes. No one knew where the monsters had come from, or why they'd arrived in such huge numbers. It didn't matter in those days. It only mattered that they held the pass.

He felt Nathan's hand on his arm. "Do you need some time?"

Conall shook his head. There was nothing here for him.

Ailen and Kelli took the lead through Algid Pass.

"We go single file from here until we reach the outpost," Nathan said. "Follow behind me closely. When Ailen stops, we stop. Don't leave the trail."

Conall dropped behind Nathan and kept his voice low. "Are you expecting an attack?" The Taiga were more active in the spring when their stores were low after a harsh winter. They shouldn't be expecting the raiders now.

"No. Taiga have been spotted in the region, but they mostly leave us alone. Ebos scouts booby-trapped the pass. It keeps the riff-raff out of our valley." Nathan grinned. "Don't look so worried, little brother. Ailen knows the way."

Conall grunted. It didn't escape him that Nathan had said "our valley." He truly considered himself one of the Ebos now. Conall wasn't sure how he felt about that.

As they rode on, the path grew cluttered with debris—discarded rails from guns, broken crossbows, and rusting mechs. His pony carefully stepped around a pile of wood posts. Conall stared at the pile realizing it was all that was left of the guardhouse that had once stood on this site.

A shiver rippled over him. He couldn't help feeling that an attack was imminent. Wariness of this place was ingrained in his muscle memory.

Ailen and Kelli stopped to confer at another seemingly random pile of debris on the road ahead. Conall's Essian vocabulary wasn't growing fast enough to understand them, but their sharp hand gestures told him something was wrong.

"What's going on?"

"Ailen says something has changed since his last visit here," Nathan said.

"What kind of something?"

"I'm not sure." Nathan listened as Ailen explained, pointing to the rocks that seemed to hold some significance.

"He says those were part of a tower. It was rigged to come down on anyone who tried to go inside it."

"Someone triggered it." Conall studied the tumble of stone. No one would have survived under all that weight.

"And recently. There are scuff marks in the gravel. They were here since the last rains."

"Scuff marks? You mean hoof marks?"

Nathan shook his head. "Boots."

"Saints teeth." That could only mean the Taiga. Conall glanced upward and slowly turned in his saddle, scanning the high points on the cliffs for scouts. "Should we keep going?"

"I think we have to." Nathan was also squinting at the cliffs.

They walked on, passing the fallen tower and leaving behind the memories of war as the trail led them into the Ubruulen lowlands.

The feeling of being watched never left Conall, but he was glad for the easier road. He didn't have to spend as much energy and attention keeping his seat on the pony and he could stretch his senses wide. He scented the air and listened to the wind, looking for signs of the Taiga.

Hours later, they passed Norsap Outpost without stopping. Two rangers watched them from the tower, their rail guns primed and ready to shoot.

Conall met the eye of one of those rangers—a boy with frightened eyes and a nervous finger on the trigger. He was glad when they turned a corner and left the tower behind.

They saw no other rangers.

"Looks nearly abandoned," he said. The fort could hold five hundred rangers. Where were they?

"Rati sources say they went south. To Oxeye. Something about needing reinforcements after a gangra outbreak."

Conall nodded. He'd seen the effects of that outbreak. Oxeye needed the resources. But leaving Norsap with only a few greens to hold it? That was tweaking fate's tail.

They made camp in the long twilight, about two miles south of Norsap. They were all exhausted, but Nathan ordered the ponies cared for and a perimeter set up before they rested. The guards, Kelli and Cob, stood watch. Conall helped Ailen gather wood for a small fire and Nathan put water on for hot drinks.

Irva found a stick and drew a line in the dirt, encircling the whole party, including the ponies. She plunked herself down in the center, legs crossed and hands flat on the ground. A fist-sized ley-stone was cradled in her lap. With eyes closed, her lips moved rapidly as she repeated the mantra that would call magic from the earth. After a few moments, she opened her eyes, then rose and stretched.

The trip through the mountains had worn her down. Dirt highlighted creases around her eyes and on her forehead. She saw Conall watching her and smiled.

"Was that a ward?" He pointed to the line scratched in the dirt. He'd heard of magical wards, but never seen one in action.

"You might call it such, though I have not ignited its power." She spoke slowly, as if carefully choosing each word. "I make preparations only. A ward is hard to keep up. It takes much…life force to sustain. I am a strong lumina, one of the best in Benni." She spoke these words without pride. They were simply fact. "But even I can only keep a ward for a few hours. So I prepare, hoping we will not need it."

Kelli shouted a warning seconds before a Taiga berserker dropped from the cliffs above—right in front of their camp.

30

THE ENEMY OF AN ENEMY

A MONSTROUS APPARITION ROSE IN front of Conall. The warrior raised his spear in the air and let out an ululating cry. Tanned hides covered him like a cloak, the ragged edges flapping as he gesticulated. Smears of black ash circled his eyes, giving him a skeletal air. His lips were blackened too and pulled back to reveal teeth filed to points. A dozen similar warriors lined up behind him. The cacophony of their calls was deafening.

A spear whizzed through the air and missed Conall's shoulder by an inch. Garou snarled. The Rati burst into sudden motion. Kelli and Cob jumped down from their watch points with spears ready. Rudi threw open the cache of weapons on the pack pony and tossed a rail gun to Nathan. Conall had his knives out and primed.

Irva dropped to the ground. She took up the meditative posture Conall had seen inside the Pit—eyes closed, back straight, palms to the ground—and she pulled energy from the earth itself. The hairs on Conall's arms rose. Magic sizzled around the lumina's fingers and shot outward, zipping through the grass like lightning.

Another spear flew toward them, but it bounced off an invisible barrier. Irva had turned on the ward. The flare of magic had also ignited the Taiga's wrath. They stomped their feet and pounded their spears just outside the ward's perimeter.

Nathan approached the barrier with his hands held open. The Taiga quieted. He spoke rapidly to the warrior in the center of the crowd.

Conall didn't understand a word of Taiga, but he wasn't surprised that Nathan could speak it. His brother was a genius. He'd taught himself to speak

Spanish and French from ancient books. He spoke Essian like an Ebos. Now he stood tall and negotiated with barbarians. The Taiga leader stared back with his blackened, inscrutable eyes.

After a few minutes, Nathan retreated to the center of the ward.

"He won't listen to reason." Nathan rubbed a hand through his short hair.

Another spear hit the ward. Irva shuddered.

"How long can she hold that?" Conall asked.

"I don't know." Nathan glanced at the Taiga who had returned to shouting and pounding their spears on the ground. His expression was pinched. "If they knew we were Rati, they'd probably leave us alone. We were allies with them once."

"So tell them!"

"It is forbidden," Rudi said. "Rati work in secret. We are safe only because enemies don't know we exist. Yes? Yes. Like shadows in the Meadows. We shout our name to every friend, our enemies find us."

Garou snarled and Conall agreed.

Nathan turned and crouched in front of Irva. The lumina's face was sheened with sweat. A vein in her neck strained.

"You were there. At Wrede's first black site when they wiped it out."

Irva nodded once. The effort cost her.

"Do you remember their names? The Taiga? Any name?"

Irva's lips moved, and one ghostly word came out. "Therrin."

"Therrin," Nathan repeated.

She nodded.

Nathan approached the invisible ward again. He raised his hand and shouted the name: "Therrin!" His voice barely rose above the berserker din.

"Therrin!" He screamed it again and again, until the lead Taiga finally took note. He lowered his spear and the others fell quiet.

Nathan spoke in Taiga again. His voice was raw from shouting. The warrior neither acknowledged nor dismissed his words. The two men faced off for a long tense moment. Irva whimpered, but the ward held.

Finally, the Taiga barked a command over his shoulder and one of his warriors took off at a run. The others crouched and sat on their heels, not relaxed but no longer menacing.

Nathan turned to Irva. "Let go." She dropped the ward. "Be watchful and ready to lift it again if they move." Irva nodded. She was trembling. Kelli rushed to her side with a water skin.

"Now what?" Conall asked. The wolf was close to the surface and his skin itched with the need to change.

"Now we wait." Nathan gripped his arm. Conall saw Misha glinting in his eyes too. His diplomatic brother was still a predator. Good to know.

The standoff lasted an hour. The Rati sat within their ward, not moving except to drink water. The Taiga were still as stones. Wind blew down the pass. It had the chill of the Fanfaronade, reminding them that their time in the mountains was limited.

Garou heard the faint crunch of feet on gravel before Conall did. It didn't come from the north and the pass through the mountains. It came from the south. The Taiga were in the Meadows, and with no one posted at Norsap, they were free to roam. The rangers in New Torwood needed to know about this incursion.

Moments later, the runner came loping up the trail. A second Taiga ran behind him. He was dressed similar to the other warriors, though his face paint had faded. He looked more human and friendlier, until his lips spread in a grin, showing those sharpened teeth.

He glanced at Nathan, then at his crew. Conall got the feeling this new Taiga didn't miss anything. He'd assessed them in a split second. The leader of the original group rose to greet the newcomer.

"Is that Therrin?" Conall whispered.

"I think so," Nathan said. They looked to Irva for confirmation and she nodded.

"Are you sure he's a friend," Conall asked.

"No." She rose and stood on wobbly legs beside him.

Perfect. Conall stretched his arms and back, readying for the shift to wolf.

Nathan and Therrin spoke briefly, or rather Nathan spoke and Therrin answered with guttural grunts. Then he turned to the other Taiga and conferred with their leader.

Irva's hand clung to Conall's arm. He glanced at her, hoping she was strong enough to raise that ward again. She swayed a bit, but her color was better.

When he turned back, the Taiga had faded like ghosts into mist. Only Therrin remained. Even Garou hadn't heard them leave. The wolf grumbled. He didn't like being out-stealthed.

Therrin spoke. The Taiga language sounded wet and came from the back of the throat. Conall could barely pick out individual words. Nathan listened and nodded. Then he made a gesture with his fist, as if he held an invisible spear that he pounded into the ground. Therrin showed his teeth once more then strode down the path. Within seconds, he disappeared into the landscape of stone and brush.

"What did he say?" Conall asked.

Nathan rubbed his forehead that was slick with sweat.

"He said they honor us as not-enemies." He smiled. "I don't think they have a word for 'friends.' But they remember how we fought to free their people and they will escort us to the Warren."

Conall glanced at the empty trail ahead. "They will?"

Nathan laughed. "You won't see them. Your wolf won't even be able to smell them, but they'll be there." He scanned the sun that was low on the western horizon. "We'll rest only as long as it's dark. We've lost too much time already."

31

SCENE OF THE CRIME

THE CONFRONTATION WITH THE TAIGA left Conall steeped in adrenaline. As they rode through the foothills, his tense grip on the reins made his mare shy off the path. Her hooves skidded on gravel and Conall squeezed with his knees to hold on. The pony took offense to this and bucked.

"Easy, brother." Nathan pulled his mount to the side to avoid flying hooves. "You're holding reins, not a knife."

Conall realized his knuckles were aching and he relaxed his grip.

"I don't like leaving a fight unfinished." He scanned the trail ahead. "And I don't like being watched." They rode through rough country between the mountains and the Meadows. Outcroppings of stone, scraggly bushes and swelling hillocks gave predators too many places to hide.

"The Taiga won't attack again," Nathan said. "That's not their style. They hit hard and fast, take their booty and run. They know we're armed and have little to give up. They'll move onto easier, more productive prey. Besides, Therrin gave me his word."

Conall wasn't sure how much the word of a Taiga was worth, but Nathan seemed at ease. He shook out his hands one by one. The mare snorted and he patted her neck. The poor beast probably wondered why she got stuck lugging around the large, tense human when the other ponies got lithe elves on their backs.

You give too much credit to a dumb beast, Garou said. In the animal kingdom hierarchy, horses were way below wolves.

They continued eastward, coming out of the lowlands. In the distance, a herd of bison spread across the Meadows. As they skirted the herd, Conall

245

pulled his scarf over his nose to filter the dust stirred up by thousands of hooves marching across the over-grazed land. His crossbow was never far from his reach and he checked the bolt. The bison would spook and stampede if a gaunt attacked, giving them plenty of warning, but there were other predators in the Meadows—silent predators that could be watching them right now. He felt his shoulders tensing again.

Half an hour later, he felt justified for his apprehension when they found the tail end of the herd. A titan eagle swooped from a clear blue sky and snatched a juvenile cow in its massive talons. The bison screamed. The eagle's golden feathers glinted in the sunlight as it carried off its meal.

Garou howled in predatory alliance.

Conall saw the moment that Kelli realized their ponies were smaller than that cow, and the eagle could have easily snatched one. Her face went pale under her hood and her pony pranced, feeling her fear.

Ailen grinned and patted the younger guard on the shoulder. He spoke a few words of encouragement, and the guards armed their bows too.

They rode on.

The August sun flirted with the mountain ridges, never rising high overhead, but never sinking low enough for full dark. Even after sunset the sky only turned an eerie purple-gray. They rode through this gloaming until hunger and exhaustion forced them to stop. Without the sun, the wind had an icy edge. They made camp and found enough kindling for a small fire.

"The Fanfaronade is early this year," Rudi said as he rubbed his hands before the flames.

Conall tucked his cloak around him and leaned against his saddlebag. He'd be more comfortable in wolf form, but he'd take his cue from Nathan.

His brother seemed thoughtful. He stared into the flames as if looking for answers. Conall wondered what the questions were.

The rest of their party was quiet. Irva sat apart with her hands pressed to the earth and eyes closed. Ailen ate his cold tack with glassy eyes. Kelli was on watch and Cob already slept. Kelli would wake him in a few hours to take over. Conall could feel sleep coming for him too.

"Tell me again about your time at the Warren." Nathan's voice jolted him back to wakefulness.

"I told you already." His voice was gravelly from breathing in road dust all day.

"Go over it again."

Conall sighed and propped himself upright. He took a big swallow from his water skin, wishing for Murdoch's water-to-wine knack just for one night.

"We decided to go to the Warren because of information we'd gathered at the oasis."

"What information?" Nathan asked.

"Some journals from Dr. Banerjee. They indicated that there was another site—a black site—called the Academy. And Denny, the surviving scientist confirmed it."

Conall had promised to keep Denny's survival a secret, but Squad 54 had traveled with the Ebos, and he had no doubt that Dalkyn had reported everything to Omika and the Rati in detail.

"We needed proof of the regent's complicity in the murders at the oasis, and Denny said we could find it at the Warren. I didn't trust him. Still don't, but the Warren was our only lead. So we went." He paused. A new suspicion occurred to him. "Is Denny one of yours? A spy, I mean." It would explain the kid's cageyness.

"No. We were in contact only with the scribe and Dr. Banerjee."

Conall nodded thoughtfully. Denny continued to be a nagging mystery, a thorn in the tangle of his thoughts. He shook his head to clear it and continued telling the tale of how they survived that one long night in the Warren, finishing with Orson's attack on Rowan.

"The scribe had been cursed with some kind of geas. I'm not really sure what that means."

"In a normal human geas would be a curse," Rudi said. "But a scribe? It is all ones and zeros."

Conall furrowed his brow and Nathan translated.

"Computers work like binary switches. Combinations of ones or zeros are the base of all programming."

"Zero, one, one, zero, zero, zero, zero, one." Rudi beamed.

"That's the letter 'a,' lower case." Nathan confirmed.

Conall shook his head. His world was just fine without knowing about ones and zeros.

"Whatever. Once it was clear that Rowan would survive the night, he attacked her."

"A switch in his head. Yes?" Rudi said.

"Maybe. I didn't see it."

The thought still left him cold. He hadn't been there to protect her. Denny, the one man he didn't trust or understand had stopped Orson by bludgeoning him with a rock.

"Go back to the part where you found Wrede's camp." Nathan spoke without looking at him. Instead, he stared into the flames as if seeing Conall's words play out in them.

Conall tried not to sound impatient as he went over the details of finding the abandoned lab again. He described the empty cages full of bones where Wrede's scientists had kept the gaunts-in-training. He detailed the half-ruined tents full of broken mechs.

"It looked like they'd pulled out in a hurry, only bothering to take the most important mechs. There were cables everywhere, overturned tables and smashed bottles. In the sleeping camps, the cots had blankets thrown back as if personnel had been woken up in a hurry." He closed his eyes, remembering the images in detail. Garou supplied the smells. Burned flesh from a pyre of gaunt corpses, ash from still-warm campfires. "They hadn't been gone long. And I knew they would be watching the site, waiting for us to come investigate."

"And that's all?" Nathan asked. "You mentioned a cave."

"Not a cave really, just a hatch to an underground…something. We didn't have time to investigate."

Nathan glanced at Rudi. "Could the signal be coming from underground?"

"Yes, yes. With a booster."

Nathan turned back to Conall. "Do you think you can take us back there?"

Conall nodded. Garou would find it. Even weeks later, the pyre of burning gaunts would make a stench trail easy enough for a pup to follow.

"That's the plan then." Nathan rubbed his hands together then stuck them under his armpits to warm them. "We go in quietly, find the underground bunker and whatever is making that signal."

"Do you think Banerjee is really alive?" Conall asked.

"I believe someone turned on that signal. Someone who wants us to come investigate." No one commented that "someone" could be Wrede and they could be walking into a trap, but as the fire burned low, they were all thinking it.

Two days later, the sky was overcast as the stone labyrinth came into view. The Warren jutted from the middle of the plains like a giant mech button waiting for the gods to press it. What would the button do? Split open the world like a walnut? Make it spin faster like a child's top?

You are easily amused, Garou said. *Like a pup with a ball of string.* He'd been quiet for most of the journey, sending only infrequent thoughts about unfamiliar smells or sounds. As they approached their destination, he grew more alert.

Despite what awaits us there, you can't deny this place is beautiful, Conall said.

Garou harrumphed but didn't answer.

The labyrinth *was* beautiful. The last time Squad 54 had been here, they'd approached it from the lower side and at night. He hadn't appreciated how the stone glittered like quartz. Intricate patterns on the walls made it shine like a faceted jewel. He remembered Denny's words about it being an unnatural phenomenon that scientists hadn't been able to explain.

The Warren had appeared in the tumultuous years after the Resurgence when magic swirled in the air like a miasma, eating away at city structures, shaking and splitting the ground, and reshaping the landscape to the whims of some new god—or perhaps an ancient god, long forgotten but newly awakened. Ancient ruins erupted from the broken earth. New Torwood City had been founded on such ruins. It wasn't a stretch to believe the Warren had been built by ancient masters for some higher purpose that was lost to time.

As they rode across the plains, the graphium locket warmed on Conall's chest. The urge to shift his attention to Rowan's message was overpowering, but they were vulnerable in the open. He left the locket alone and continued to scan the open Meadows with a bolt locked into his bow.

They circled the massive outer stone wall until they found the crack that Squad 54 had used as a door. Kelli and Irva stayed with the ponies. The rest of their group crept through the narrow passageway on foot.

Once inside, Conall let Garou's instincts take the lead. That night with Squad 54, the fights with gaunts and the incognito soldiers had left an indelible mark on his psyche, but the memories blurred together, and he was soon lost in the maze of stones. Light filtering down between the high walls only confused him more. They walked through shadows, into patches of light and back into shadow with every turn. It was disorienting and his eyes had no chance to adjust. He relied solely on Garou's nose and ears. Nathan was also listening to his wolf. His eyes sparkled with a ferocity that only came out when Misha was in control.

That stink of burned gaunt clung to the stone walls, but it was fainter than he remembered. The only sounds came from the occasional gabble of a crane somewhere in the Meadows and the constant wind buffeting stone.

A beeping noise made him turn and grip the knife at his belt. Rudi held out a mech device. It was square and small enough to fit in his hand. He studied the glowing screen. The mech beeped again and lights flashed.

"Put that away!" Conall hissed. His nose told him they were alone, but he hadn't survived this long as a lone wolf because he was rash.

Rudi smiled sheepishly and tucked the mech into his pocket. "Last signal was near here. Banerjee is close."

"Or someone who wants us to believe Banerjee is alive," Nathan reminded him.

"Yes, yes," Rudi conceded.

Conall pointed to a natural stone staircase. "Those will take us up top. It's easier to navigate the maze from there, but we'll be exposed."

Nathan considered it. "Can you find your way without going up?"

"I think so."

"Then we stay below. For now."

As they ducked under a natural stone bridge, Conall's foot slipped on slick stones and he recognized a new, acrid-sweet smell. Guano.

A flock of bats burst from the shadows under the bridge. Wings battered him. High-pitched cries assailed his ears. He ducked and covered his head.

"Bloody saints!" Nathan flailed his arms as wings battered him. The bats screeched out their complaints for being disturbed and flew off to find another nesting spot.

When they were back under the open sky, Conall sneezed to rid himself of the nose-blinding scent of guano.

"That was fun." Rudi grinned and pointed to a white smear on Ailen's shoulder. The scout grumbled something unintelligible and wiped his shirt with a handkerchief.

They continued at a steady pace. Conall was confident they were heading toward the center of the maze, but when they'd been walking for nearly an hour, they rounded a bend and hit a dead end.

Rudi let out a groan of frustration. Conall felt it too, but he'd lived too long alone in the Meadows to vocalize his emotions like easy prey.

Somewhere behind the clouds, the sun was setting. The light lost its edge, and the world seemed flatter.

While Rudi and Nathan argued about turning back, Conall stepped up to the wall that blocked their path. A protruding bit of rock gave him a foothold. He ran hands over the stone until he found a lip wide enough to grasp and hauled himself up. The days on horseback and nights sleeping rough caught up to him, and his muscles creaked with the effort. He pushed on. Higher up, the handholds were more distinct, as if they'd been chiseled into the rock.

"This way," he urged. The others turned to find him clinging to the wall like a spider. "We're close now." He pulled himself up another notch, and another. The wind pulled at his hair as he topped the wall.

By the time the others had made their way up, he'd oriented himself. The gaunt cages were just ahead. Beyond them lay niches used for sleeping quarters and then the lab.

He crept across the top of the stone wall, keeping low to make a small target, but his nose was already telling him they were alone. The others followed silently, except when they passed the cages full of bones left by the gaunts. Cob let out a small muffled groan.

By the time they reached the lab site, the stone walls had shrunk to only eight feet high and they easily jumped down.

Cob and Ailen scouted the area, poking their spears into collapsed tents and turning over burned logs in the fire pit. Conall headed right to the opening he'd found with Clem all those weeks ago. A door cobbled together from wood planks and discarded canvas partially covered the hole.

Had that been there last time? Conall couldn't remember. Memories from that night were cloudy. He bent to move the door aside, revealing a staircase that descended into darkness.

Rudi held out his mech again, scanning the ground. The lights flashed as he studied the screen.

"Signal comes from here." He pointed into the hole.

Nathan's expression was grim. "I guess we're going down."

32

ECHOES

AFTER HEARING THE NEWS THAT Roger was finally awake, the trip from Temple Jocasta to the palace seemed unbearably long. Market vendors were leaving the city and their carts jammed the streets. A stalled cat in the alley just before Hightown forced Rowan to backtrack and come at the palace from the back entrance. She flew past the keeper barracks and the quartermaster's hall, through the main atrium and down the long halls to the royal wing. She was panting by the time she reached her rooms. Elias, who was barely winded, swept open the door.

As she stepped inside a scratchy humming sound greeted her. Phalian was perched on Roger's head. The valet was bent over the coffee table. His new right arm held a stylus and it scribbled on a stack of papers.

Rowan peered over his shoulder. The page was filled with numbers and graphs. He finished one page and flipped it to a growing stack on the right, then started on a fresh sheet. It took a moment for Rowan to realize the new sketch was an anatomically correct heart. Possibly human. He finished and flipped the page again, filling the next one with incomprehensible graphs.

"Roger, what is all this?"

"Data."

That was all he would say when she pressed him.

She watched for over an hour, until the stack of clean papers dwindled to nothing. Then he paused and said, "Paper?"

Rowan had more paper brought up from the quartermaster. He would gripe about the expense, but she didn't care.

Roger scribbled for four days. He went through reams of paper and

Rowan replaced his stylus three times.

On the fourth morning, Rowan dozed on the couch. She'd tried to sleep in her bed the night before, but she kept getting up to check on Roger and decided to stay nearby.

It had been two weeks since she'd visited Grotto and met Harry Hightower. Two months had passed since Conall had left the city, long enough that the brief hours she'd spent with him felt like a dream.

Saints, she wished he would come home. She understood his need to learn all he could about his brother, but as time went by, she began to wonder if there wasn't more to it. Could a lone wolf ever be happy unless he was running free in the Meadows? Maybe he wouldn't come back. She gripped the graphium locket. She hadn't received a message from him in days, not since he'd written to say he was leaving Benni for the Warren. She had no idea why, no idea what he'd found in Benni, or what he expected to find at the Warren, and his silence was ominous.

Then Rowan realized that the room had gone silent too. Roger had stopped scratching away. He put down the stylus and rolled over to the couch. Rowan sat up. Her mind was fuzzy from lack of sleep.

"I have finished sorting through the information on the cachet, Princess. I copied out all the data files."

"All the files? Are they relevant?"

"Sandra Kane believed so."

"Okay." Rowan glanced at the stacks of paper on the table. She didn't know what to do with them. "What about the journal entries?"

"I can write those out too." Roger spun toward the table.

"No!"

Roger paused. He seemed to cock his head as if listening for instructions.

"How many journal entries did you tag?"

"Two hundred and forty-six. Shall I recite them for you?"

That was a lot, but she didn't see another option. "Yes, please."

Roger's eyes slowly pulsed with light as he began to recite in that high-pitched voice that represented Sandra Kane.

March 2, 590

*The team from Dowchester arrived today. Minister Wrede
accompanied them from New Torwood. Dr. Banerjee and his
assistant Elsie Myer seem competent enough. We'll see if they can
survive in the wild. Elsie, in particular, didn't seem too happy
with the accommodations. The rest of the team had a get-togeth-
er before dinner. Mostly junior science geeks who blink at bright
sunlight when they lift their noses from their books. There is one
potential guy. His name's Denny Feist, but I think he swings
for the other team. That's too bad. I've been out here a month
already. I could use a good roll in the mud…*

"Roger, skip that entry." Rowan didn't need to hear about Kane's sexual dry spell. She knew all about that kind of frustration.

March 3, 590

*While the new crew set up their labs, I followed Denny into the
field where he observed the female gaunts in the hollow by the
watering hole. Before leaving, Minister Wrede took me aside
and reminded me that my loyalty is to New Torwood, not the
Dowchester team. I told him I don't need a lecture about loyalty.
He made some disturbing comments about the disposability
of scribes, which I will be taking up with the Abbot Archivist
when I return to the city.*

The next several entries were detailed accounts of Kane's observations in and around the camp. She repeated several conversations verbatim. She detailed the work that the scientists were doing, though from a layman's perspective, since she didn't understand the science. Rowan listened for hours.

A maid came in and left breakfast on a tray, but Rowan only picked at it. Roger droned on. Only the entries about Denny really interested Rowan. His friendship with Kane grew as the months went by.

When Roger came to the end of yet another entry where Kane complained about the food and the weather, Rowan called a stop. This was getting her nowhere.

"Roger can you skip to the last tagged entry?"

The valet's eyes pulsed and he began again.

June 20, 591

They're here. I have only minutes before they find me. Banerjee suspects betrayal. I have copied as much of his data as I can. They took him. I do not know if he is alive. Now I must hide his work. For the good of New Torwood. Saints, for people every-where.

To whoever archives this record. Please, do not ignore my warn-ings. Bring this information before the Abbot Archivist. Miron Wrede is a traitor to New Torwood. He will bring only death, war and betrayal. Elsie Myer is his creature. Do not be fooled. She let them in. Oh, saints, I can hear them howl. She let them come for all of us. You can't help us, but don't let the saints forget us!

Spoken in the high-pitched voice that Roger used to mimic Sandra, the urgency of the message became almost farcical. Or it would have been had Rowan not seen Sandra Kane's desperation to hide the cachet and the record of the crimes she'd witnessed. Kane had seen the others torn apart by Wrede's pet gaunts. They'd all been murdered. All except three missing bodies.

One of those missing had been Elsie Myer.

Conall had suspected that the gaunts had been let into camp by someone. Now Rowan had confirmation of the traitor.

Jesus and Jupiter. Conall was on his way to the Warren. Had he found some information that brought him back to that horrible place? Was he walking into a trap?

She pulled out the tiny graphium and wiped away her last message, then wrote: *Myer works for Wrede.* She waited several long minutes, but the other screen remained blank. She had no way of knowing if Conall had received her message.

Thunder rumbled across the Meadows and rain began to tap at her window. She sighed. She had nothing better to do.

"Roger, continue with the tagged entries, working backwards from the last one."

For the next twelve hours Rowan listened to the slow betrayal of the Dowchester scientists.

33

THE STUDENT FORGES THE TEACHER

GAROU RECOILED FROM THE HOLE in the ground.

Holes should smell like dirt and bones and damp rot, he groused. This one smelled like lightning and hot metal. And human sickness.

Nathan spoke into a vox. "Irva? Are you there?"

The vox made a series of clicking sounds, then Irva spoke with a tinny uncertain voice.

"Yes, Captain."

"Are the horses secure? The Meadows clear?"

"All is quiet."

"Good. We're going underground. We may be out of contact for a while."

"Yes, Captain." More clicks and the vox went silent.

Ailen headed down the stairs first. Nathan followed, then Rudi. Conall brought up the rear, and Cob stayed topside as lookout. His eyes were big and dark in the dim light.

"No heroics." Cob responded with a shaky smile. Conall pointed to the guard's spear. "If they're close enough to use that, you need to run." Cob nodded and started scanning the tops of the Warren's walls.

Conall stepped onto the first stair. Damp air and unease enveloped him as he descended.

The others waited in the shadows at the bottom. Nathan pulled a thera lighter from his belt and lit a lamp that hung on the wall, filling the space with pale purple light. Rudi held his mech device at waist level, his eyes fixed on the screen.

They stood in a sort of antechamber, a big empty cavern with a low ceiling.

Dull stone tiles lined the walls and floor. A few dead leaves cluttered one corner, but other than that the space was empty. Conall swiped a hand across the wall and it came away covered in fine dust. He crouched to examine the floor. The same dust covered it, unmarred by any footprints. It was looking more and more like they were alone.

"Which way?" Nathan's voice was too loud in the quiet.

Rudi motioned with the hand holding the mech scanner. "That way." The screen showed a steadily throbbing green light.

Only one corridor opened from the antechamber. Conall placed his feet carefully but couldn't avoid the crackle of grit under his boots. Even the stealthy Ebos made scuffing noises. Thera lamps dotted the ceiling, but only one near the end of the hall was still lit. They moved toward it.

Conall waited with his bow cocked while Nathan pulled open the first door along the corridor. They found only a storage closet, mostly empty. There were a dozen more doors. They stopped to carefully pry each one open. Some were offices, others held broken crates and bottles of lab supplies.

When they finally reached the end of the corridor, they were met by another door with a grimy window at about human eye height. A faint glow emanated from it.

A new noise pricked Garou's ears. After a moment Rudi heard it too. He stopped and held up a hand as they listened.

A shuffle. A grinding of rusty gears. A bang of metal on stone. Silence.

Rudi's brows furrowed in confusion as the chorus of odd sounds repeated like a drum beat.

Nathan peered through the window.

"Jupiter!" he hissed, and Conall wasn't sure if the god's name was spoken in amazement or as a curse. Nathan pushed the door and it swung inward on well-oiled hinges.

The smell of rotting flesh and feces hit Conall like a slap in the face. He struggled not to cover his nose and to keep his crossbow pointing into the shadows.

The repeating noise—*shuffle, grind, bang!*—grew louder.

Conall stepped through the door, pointing the crossbow right then left in a quick scan. There were no immediate threats. He lowered the bow but left the bolt nocked and ready.

His eyes took in the sight, not really understanding what he saw.

Rows of desks lined the space. Each had that monitor and mech combination he'd seen in the Pit. Computers, Rudi had call them. But these were not computing. The screens were dark and the mechs covered in dust. A faint light came from deeper in the room.

Rudi let out a low whistle and lowered his scanner.

"Can you access these?" Nathan pointed to the dark mechs.

Rudi scratched his beardless chin. "Maybe. One must work, yes? Yes." He set the scanner on the table and examined the first computer.

A mech valet emerged from the shadows at the back of the room. It was humanoid, as tall as an adult Ebos with a complexion of rusted metal and a mouth like the bumper of a wind cat. Enormous eye sockets were filled with metal eyes that swiveled out of sync with each other. The grinding noise came from its joints. With every ponderous step, gears grated. Conall followed the mech with his bow, but it walked by them, seemingly oblivious to their presence, until it hit a wall. Its metal skull banged against the stone, then it backed up slightly and…*shuffle, grind, bang!* It repeated the odd dance.

Conall lowered his bow. The valet was just an abandoned piece of mech, left to rust into ruin when Wrede's crew had cleared out.

Ailen stood by the door. His spear pointed into the room but his eyes were caught on the malfunctioning valet as if it were the bogeyman.

"This one is dead," Rudi said, pulling Conall's attention back. He turned in the chair. "Maybe I access the memory, but maybe I check the others first." He moved over a chair and began his examination on the second computer.

"Do whatever—" A cough interrupted Nathan.

Conall spun, aiming his bow at the back of the room. Rudi ducked, as if he could hide under his mechs. Ailen's spear came up. Nathan waved at him to wait, then motioned for Conall to take the right side of the room while he took the left.

Conall moved along the row of desks until he came to a narrow aisle. The valet was still trying to brain itself on a nearby wall. The sound of its banging head and grinding gears masked any other noise. Conall stepped carefully past it and rounded the last row of desks.

One computer was lit up with green numbers scrolling on a black screen.

Sitting before it was a woman with the dusky complexion of a northerner and short black hair matted to her head with dirt and grease. She raised her eyes as he approached. The green glow from her screen made her seem ghoulish. Garou's nose twitched. He smelled blood. And sickness.

The woman grinned. "I wondered how long it would be before the rats showed up." She raised a hand that gripped a small rail gun. The distinctive sound of the mech priming filled the quiet. She pointed it at Conall, then pivoted to Nathan.

"Don't come any closer." Nathan froze. Conall's finger paused on the bow's trigger. He could take her out, but not before she got a shot off at Nathan.

"You Rati, just like vermin, always slinking out of the shadows." She wheezed and coughed, but her eyes never left Conall.

"Who are you?" he asked, but the woman only smiled. Sweat dripped down her face.

"She's Elsie Myer," Nathan said.

Dr. Banerjee's assistant, the one whose body they'd never found at the oasis.

"Why are you here?" Conall asked at the same moment that Nathan said, "Did you send Banerjee's signal?"

She wheezed out a laugh. "So predictable. You think we don't know about your spying? Miron isn't afraid of you. Little rats. Go back to your holes." She lifted her other hand and made a scurrying motion with her fingers. Blackened tissue spread from fingertips to wrist. "Little rats who only ever get crumbs. You have no idea how big the pie really is." Her shirt was torn at the shoulder and the bloody cloth stuck to blackened skin.

Elsie smiled, then bent over her desk, coughing until she spat a wad of phlegm on the floor. She wiped her mouth with the blackened fingers, then jerked the gun up again.

She smells like rot, Garou said. *We could take her as easily as a pup.*

Yes, we can. Let's see what she has to say first.

Elsie saw his glance and smiled again. Then her expression twisted in pain and she slammed the gun to the desk. Nathan jumped forward, but Elsie grabbed the gun again and waved it in his face. Nathan backed off with empty hands held high.

"Stay back. I'll kill you, I swear. What have I got left to lose?" She laughed. It was a phlegmy sound that ended in another coughing fit.

She's mad.

Like a rabid coyote, Garou agreed.

Movement caught Conall's eye. Rudi was quietly and methodically working his way from desk to desk, checking all the computers, while Ailen guarded his back.

"What do you want?" Nathan said.

"What do I want?" Elsie huffed out a sour laugh. "I want to finish my doctorate in mech biology. I want to travel the world, see Shythe and Dowchester and even sail across the ocean. I want to make a name in my field, and maybe enough money to move my family out of Squall's End. All those things are in the past though. Now all I want is to prove myself. To him." She shrugged her wounded shoulder.

Behind her, the valet hit the wall, turned and walked toward them with heavy paces.

"I want to be recognized for my contributions. I want—" A sob hitched in Elsie's throat. Tears and snot leaked down her face and she didn't bother to wipe them away. "I want to be noticed. I want *him* to notice. All my sacrifices and hard work…Everything. All of it." She sniffled loudly and rubbed her nose. Then she sat straighter and sucked in a deep breath. "But all Miron notices is results. So that's what I plan to give him. Banerjee, that fucking coward destroyed all his records, but I pulled them out of his damned brain. Not everything, but enough. It's all here." She tapped the computer monitor. "And you're too late. I already sent it to Miron—the missing piece he needs to build his fucking army of gaunts. And I hope he chokes on it." She wilted into her chair, wheezing out a pathetic laugh.

"Is that what Wrede's doing?" Nathan asked. "Building an army? Why?"

She leaned forward and spoke in a stage whisper. "This is not the part where I tell you everything. This is the part where I kill you." She sat back with a grin and the chair creaked under her weight. "To be honest, I'd hoped you'd bring more of your little rats. But this will have to do."

She raised the gun and fired. Nathan ducked. The bolt hit the wall. Elsie's eyes went wide and a metal spike jutted through her neck.

The mech valet that Conall had dismissed as harmless stood behind her with spinning eyes. Elsie gurgled and spat blood. Her fingers flailed against the spike as blood flooded her lips. Her eyes glazed. She slumped in her chair.

The mech yanked out the spike, tearing through flesh and bone. Elsie slid sideways and toppled out of the chair. Her body hit the floor with a thud and lay still.

The mech valet dropped the spike to the floor with a clang. Then it turned and bowed, eyes goggling in different directions.

"I am Dr. Banerjee. Thank-thank you-you for answering my call." The valet's head jerked right with each stutter. He raised a hand and made a fist. His joints creaked, then he pounded the fist into the side of his head. His eyes stopped their crazy waggling.

Rudi approached with his scanner held before him. "You sent the signal."

The valet bowed again with a grating of gears. "I am Dr. Banerjee."

"Is this possible?" Rudi pulled out another mech device from the bulging pack over his shoulder and started turning dials. The mech beeped and chimed as he made adjustments. He waved it in front of the valet from head to toe. The mech who would be Banerjee stood still for the inspection with only his eyes following the glowing scanner.

"What is it?" Nathan asked.

Rudi lowered the scanner. "I'm not sure. The shell is just an old valet, yes? But the core…that is something else. Something I saw once before, when we dissected that scribe a few years back."

That news shocked Conall. Nathan had told him of Wrede's crimes, but he'd hoped the Rati would be above such evil doings.

"How? Why?"

"It was during the war. A lot of scribes went missing. Don't look at me like that!" Nathan held up his hands as if to fend off a strike. "Look, we didn't kill the scribe. We only took advantage of a found body and an opportunity to learn more."

"And what did you learn?"

"Not much," Rudi said without taking his eyes off the scanner. "Scribe blood, bone and organs… full of tiny mechs, each with a speck of thera dust—mechs so small, yes? Cannot be seen with the eye. We found them, yes?

Yes. Follow the flow of thera. I call them nanomechs." He seemed inordinately proud of this name.

"What does that have to do with the valet?"

Rudi grinned. "After scribe, I trained scanner to detect nanomechs. They flow through our new friend."

"Is he human?" Conall asked.

"No. Yes. Maybe." Rudi frowned. "Scribes not really human either. Not anymore. Their bodies and minds change with nanomechs, yes? Change to something else. Something new. Valet is not the same, but also the same, yes?" He held the scanner to the side of the mech's head until it beeped then nodded. "Nanomechs."

"The student surpassed the teach-teach-teacher." Banerjee's head jerked again.

"The student?" Nathan frowned. "You mean Elsie?"

With a grinding of gears, Banerjee-mech nodded.

"She did this to you?"

Another grinding nod.

"Is that even possible?" Nathan turned to Rudi.

"In theory." Rudi scratched the back of his head, making the hair stick up. "Scribes record thoughts to cachet. Logical jump says all thoughts, all feelings could be loaded to cachet, then transferred to…" He glanced at the mech. "To a host."

"That's more than a jump. It's a giant leap," Nathan said.

Leaps in logic didn't sit well with Conall. "Are you saying this mech has the brain of Dr. Banerjee?"

"Not brain, but his memories, yes? Yes. Maybe emotions. It is fascinating."

"Fascinating." The whole idea left Conall feeling queasy. "But I don't believe it. And you shouldn't either. All you have as proof is some code sent by signal, and the word of this valet. I've seen a lot of mechs in my time. Even pneuma mechs made by Harry Hightower, and none of them could show emotion."

"Maybe redefine idea of emotion?" Rudi said. Conall growled at him. The sound came directly from his wolf.

It smells wrong, Garou said. *If you can't eat it, it's not alive.*

Nathan stepped between his brother and the Rati before the argument could escalate.

"Since we have no way to test it, we should operate on the theory that this mech does, in fact, hold Dr. Banerjee's memories. The next logical question would be why?" He glanced from Conall to Rudi, but it was Banerjee-mech who answered in a gravelly voice.

"When the soldiers came-came-came…" He paused while his head jerked. "Elsie said they were sent to save us. But I already knew-knew-knew." He spun around and bumped into the desk, backed up and rammed it again. Elsie's corpse fell out of the chair and landed on the floor with a thud.

"What did you know?" Nathan gripped his arm. Banerjee-mech faced him. His eyes were spinning wildly.

Banerjee pounded a fist into the side of his head. He turned to Conall and opened the fist. His articulated fingers gripped Conall's shoulders. The rough touch worked its way down to his wrist. Banerjee lifted Conall's hand to his face and stared at it, as if fingers and knuckles could hold the mysteries of the universe.

"I have no tactile sense." Banerjee touched one of Conall's fingers with his own. "I see this connection. Flesh to met-met-metal. But I don't *feel* it. How bizarre."

Conall pulled his hand away.

"I don't feel it at all!" The valet banged a fist into his head again.

If Dr. Banerjee truly lived in the mech's mind, he'd retreated. They were getting nothing more from him for the moment.

The valet turned and strode away with an unhealthy hiss of pneumatic pistons.

Nathan studied him with hooded eyes, then turned to Rudi. "Did you get anything from the computers?"

Rudi had pulled a chair over to Elsie's monitor and was already plugging mechs into her computer. He didn't raise his eyes from the symbols scrolling across the screen. "Nothing solid, but maybe…" He pounded a fist on the desk. "Yes, yes! There it is. All her data. How pretty." Scrolling green numbers reflected in his eyes as he studied it. His fingers flashed across the keyboard.

"Save it for now. We have to go," Nathan said. Rudi plugged a mech into the computer and the screen on the device began to glow with the same scrolling data.

"What about him?" Rudi jerked a thumb over his shoulder at Banerjee-mech.

"We're taking him with us."

34

DO MEMORIES MAKE THE MAN?

RUDI SAID THE DOWNLOAD FROM Elsie's computer would take several hours. Conall wasn't sure exactly what "download" meant, though he'd tried to explain.

"A transfer protocol, yes? Speed depends on oscillation rate. Binary…um, incantations, yes? Yes. Incantations broadcast through web of neurons, like projections of photonic noodles, yes?" The chair creaked as Rudi leaned back. He was getting into it now. He clasped his hands together and shook them. "Mutual agreement achieved—hello between machine and receptacle—then requesting machine discharges hypertextual demands. Binary sequences deliberately mis-ordered and reordered with code. Then… ZAP! All Elsie's research history stored in this little box." He patted the mech device that glowed on the desk. "Except zap takes five hours, yes? Yes."

Conall turned to Nathan. "Did you understand any of that?"

"About one in four words. I think he's deliberately obtuse to make his work sound more important than it is."

Rudi grunted. "*Esyup.*"

Nathan grinned. "He just called us ignoramuses."

"Been called worse." Conall couldn't help thinking how this mech would fascinate Rowan. Saints, he was a fool to think he could simply leave her behind. She should have been here. If nothing else she could have made sense of the Banerjee mech.

Rudi waved them away. "Go beat up something. Much work to do."

Nathan went up top to use the vox. If they were going to be stuck there for the rest of the night, he wanted to let Irva and Kelli know.

Banerjee-mech had dawdled over to the wall and was quietly banging his head on stone.

Conall went searching for food. From the arrangement of desks, it looked like the underground lab had once housed a couple dozen mech-mages, not to mention supporting staff. They had to have facilities for feeding them.

A door at the back of the lab had bent hinges that left it slightly ajar. Conall pushed it open and peered into another short corridor with more doors lining it on either side. Light shone weakly from the first room on the left. He stepped over broken crockery and other refuse. The lit room was a small kitchen with counters along two walls and a table in the center. Four chairs had once been around the table, but three were broken. He stepped forward to set the last one back on its legs. Glass crunched under his feet.

A thera lamp had been left burning on the counter, but it was nearly exhausted and the light barely filled the room. His nose told him that he wouldn't find anything edible here. The sickly-sweet smell of rotting fruit was strong.

A large mech butlery sat beside the counter. He opened the lid and the rot smell hit him like a fist. The thera chip had long burned out and the box was no longer cold. He let the lid drop. A quick search of the kitchen revealed moldy bread and a bottle that could have been wine. The cork was gone and only a few sips of rancid liquid remained. Conall wasn't thirsty enough to chance it.

He left the kitchen and headed down the hall. It branched at the end, turning right. There were no lamps in this corridor. Darkness stretched away from him, unfathomably deep. He stood for a long minute, staring into it and listening.

He considered exploring, but decided that splitting the group further wasn't a good idea. He retraced his steps and found that Nathan had returned. He was busy drawing runes on the walls of the lab with a piece of charcoal.

"There's a storm coming," Nathan said. "We might as well wait it out down here. I left Ailen on watch at the bottom of the stairs."

"What about Irva and Kelli?" Conall asked.

"They're going to bring the ponies inside the Warren, but they'll remain there." Nathan finished the last rune with a flourish and dropped the charcoal to the floor.

Conall pointed at the runes. "Protection?"

"Insurance." He wiped his hands on his pants. "We should get some sleep while Rudi does his thing. But help me get that out of here first." Nathan nodded toward the crumpled corpse of Elsie Myer.

Conall took the feet while Nathan grabbed her under the arms.

"She's surprisingly heavy for such a slight thing," Nathan said as they lugged the body out the back door.

"Death adds weight," Conall said. They dumped her in the kitchen with the other rotting meat. He found a rag near the butlery and wiped his hands before tossing it to Nathan. Conall turned back for the lab, but Nathan paused. He stared down at the dead woman.

"I feel like we should say something. We can't bury her, but maybe a few words…I don't know."

Conall turned back to the corpse. The gaping hole in her neck was nearly masked by congealing blood.

He thought about the last funeral he'd attended. An unmarked grave in the Meadows. Squad 54 spontaneously breaking into song for a dead ranger. A useless death.

He crossed his arms over his chest. "How's this: Here lies Elsie Myer. She gave her loyalty to the wrong man. Let the rats take the rest of her." He could have spit on the corpse, but he wouldn't waste the fluid.

Nathan frowned.

"You've become a hard man, little brother."

"By necessity."

Nathan looked like he wanted to say more, but he'd always known when not to push. Instead he pointed down the hall.

"Where does that lead?"

Conall shrugged. "Not sure. More labs, maybe a back entrance. If we were staying longer, I'd explore it."

A shudder went through Nathan. "Leave it for now. We need sleep. Hopefully the storm will pass and Rudi will be finished by sunrise."

In the main lab Conall settled on the floor, leaning against the wall next to the back door. If anything came down that hallway, he'd hear it before it reached the door.

He felt like this was the first moment of rest he'd had in days. Then he remembered the graphium and pulled it out to read Rowan's message.

Myer works for Wrede.

Garou snorted. Conall wasn't surprised she'd figured it out too, but he wondered how. Had she finally cracked the scribe's cachet?

A new impatience seized him. He was stuck down here in the dark when big things were happening in the world. He could feel it, like the shifting of winds before a storm.

He took out the tiny stylus and wrote three words on the graphium.

Coming home soon.

The thought of seeing Rowan again was the only bright light in that storm.

Nathan sat on the floor beside him and rested his head on the wall, eyes closed. Rudi was still staring at the computer screen.

"Is he reading or asleep with his eyes open?" Conall asked.

"Not asleep," Rudi said without moving.

Nathan opened one eye.

"Anything interesting so far?"

Rudi swiveled in the chair to face them. "The science is…difficult. Biology is not my best. Much here about gaunts…many experiments and all different. Some gruesome. But we know about those, yes?" He paused and made a disgusted face. "Other records appear too. Coming up now. Monetary records."

"What does that mean?" Nathan asked.

"It means that someone was paying Wrede a lot of money to carry out those experiments," Conall said. "Does it say who?"

Rudi tapped the desk with his hand. "No. Not Clear. They use code names, but maybe we track transactions, yes?"

"Yeah, follow the money." Conall suspected it would lead right to the regent's purse.

Rudi nodded. "Follow the money. There is more." He glanced at the screen then to the valet who was examining his fingers with the attention of one looking for the secrets of the universe. "I understand what Elsie did to Banerjee. Maybe. She documented much details, but science is complex."

"Explain it to me like I'm a five-year-old," Nathan said.

"In this, we are all toddlers, yes?" Rudi smiled and pointed at the screen. "Here is best I understand. She used scribe technology, but, hmmm, corrupted, yes? Yes. Corrupted science of scribes to transfer Banerjee's memories."

"His memories or his psyche?" Nathan asked.

Rudi splayed his hands in front of him. "What difference? Give a mech lifetime of memories for one man and mech becomes the man, yes? Yes."

Conall ground his teeth until pain stabbed his jaw. He was too much the wolf for esotericism.

No meat on a memory, Garou agreed.

"But why would she do that?" Nathan asked. "If she could download his memories, she would have the details of his research. Why stick him into a valet?"

The valet finished his inspection of the wall and strode toward them with measured steps. Each of his movements came with the grinding sound of rusted gears. He stopped next to Rudi and stared at the screen of scrolling data.

Rudi rolled his chair out of striking distance. Banerjee turned his head toward Nathan and Conall.

"I knew Wrede was coming to kill us. I had sus-sus-suspected for weeks." When he spoke, his mouth didn't move, but his head jerked with each stutter.

It's not natural, Garou said. *You should kill it.*

"I burned everything," Banerjee continued in that stilted voice. "All my journals. All my work-work-work. I thought that would be the end-end-end. But they wanted me. My knack. And so Elsie…stole my mind, my thoughts, my mem-mem-memories. But she could not steal my knack." The valet made a wheezing noise. It took Conall a moment to realize he was laughing. Mechs didn't laugh.

"You're saying your knack didn't get passed onto the valet?" Nathan said.

The valet stomped toward them, his hand stretched out. Conall scrambled to his feet and reached for the knife on his belt, but the mech's fingers barely brushed his cheek.

"So odd," came the mechanical voice. "I see the stubble on your face, but I can't-can't-can't feel it." He gripped Conall's arm. "I can feel the weight, but not the flesh. It's enough to drive one mad."

Conall had his own opinions about the mech's sanity, but he kept those to himself.

"Are you really Banerjee?"

The valet cocked his head. His eyes swiveled in their sockets.

"I think-think-think I must be. I remember my mother. She called me *shishu*. Am I shishu?" The fingers gripped his arm hard enough to hurt. Conall pulled away and put some distance between them. The valet's fingers reached for the wall and started tracing the line of tiles again.

"I didn't know shishu or Banerjee," Conall said carefully. "But I read his journal. If you're really him, you would remember more than was written there."

The valet was silent, except for the hiss of pneumatic gears as his arm stretched to reach the upper tiles.

"You wish to test me. Go-go-go on."

Conall thought back. He'd read most of Banerjee's journal that Rowan had found in the oasis, hoping that it would lead to some insights into Wrede's whereabouts or intentions. It hadn't. The journal had been written the year before Banerjee arrived at the oasis and centered mostly on the prep work that had gone into the journey north and setting up the camp.

One detail stuck out in his memory. The journal had alluded to a rift in Banerjee's family, but it hadn't gone into details.

"Before you left Dowchester, you visited your family home. Someone there was upset. Tell me why."

Gears whirred. The valet dropped its hands.

"My youngest sister, Jaya. She cried. Mother said it was because I was leaving but that wasn't true. Her cat had died."

Conall didn't care about facts. If it was true that Elsie had somehow filled this mech with Banerjee's memories, then he would know the answer. Conall wanted to know if the mech could access emotion.

"And how did that make you feel, to leave your family, your sister?"

The mech cocked his head and seemed to consider the question, but for all Conall knew, he was considering sticking that spear through his neck too.

"Jaya is special," the metallic voice said. "So child-like. I promised to bring her a new cat. A meadow cat. I am sad that I have failed her in this."

Banerjee turned his mech gaze on Conall.

"Did I pass your-your-your test, Commander West?"

"How do you know my name? I never met Banerjee."

The mech took his own head in both hands as if he might pull it from his shoulders.

"There is more in-in-in here…It seems that my former assistant stuffed this unit with much information. Banerjee's memories—my memories and the other data don't-don't-don't sync well. I fear I have only a few moments before they clash and then this voice gets lost in all the others. Listen to me please." He lowered his hands to grip Conall's arm again. For once, his eyes stopped moving and they focused on Conall's face.

"Go on." Conall didn't try to pull away.

"He wants my knack."

"He who?" Nathan said.

"Miron Wrede. I thought he was a benefactor. He brought my team-team-team to the Meadows, set us up with the camp and the funds to continue our studies. He said our work would benefit all mankind and I believed him because I wanted to. I wanted to believe that what-what-what we did had meaning."

"Denny Feist said you were studying the moment that a species evolved," Conall said. "The moment that the gaunts went from feral monsters to a community."

"Denny…dead now like all the others." The mech voice lacked intonation, but Conall detected regret in those words. He didn't let him know that Denny was still alive.

"Feist was a good field tech, and he was right. It was a profound moment to witness. But its benefits to the greater good?" The valet's shoulders rose. His chin lowered. The mech version of a shrug.

"So why did Wrede kill them all?" Conall asked.

"The data. We-we-we collected hundreds of hours of observations, blood samples, cellular examinations. Wrede wanted that data."

"To what end?"

"To corroborate what his own experiments were already beginning to show. That gaunts were once human. And that humans are slowly becoming gaunts. All because of thera. He-he-he wanted confirmation. And he wanted the data destroyed."

"Why?" Nathan said, but Conall already knew. He'd been to the southern cities, seen how thera was prized even though it was too rare for general use.

"New Torwood is the only producer of thera," Conall said. "It only grows in the Ikon River. Theracine Corporation is poised to launch it into the southern cities. They fully expect Dowchester and Scythe to embrace thera like New Torwood did. To become addicted to it."

"And since they control thera production they'll make a fortune," Nathan finished.

"But not if someone proves that thera is dangerous first. It will be all over for Theracine." Conall turned to Banerjee. "Will you testify to this before the Regent's Council?"

The valet's eyes spun. "I will, if you make one promise."

"Go on."

"I will return to your city, speak-speak-speak to your ministers, but when I am done, you dismantle this body and burn-burn-burn it."

His words met with silence.

Conall cleared his throat. "You want us to kill you?"

"Yes." The mech head swiveled to Conall. "Will you kill me, Commander West?"

"Yes."

Banerjee bowed with a hiss of gears, then leaned his head against the wall with a gentle bang and stayed there.

Conall met Nathan's eyes over the valet's shoulder. He knew his brother would try to talk him out of killing the mech. The philosopher in him wouldn't be able to help it.

"One more question," he said. "What is your knack? Why was it so important that Elsie would stay behind and turn you into…this?"

Banerjee kept his forehead against the wall, but turned his head to look at Conall.

"My knack is…was…molecules. I could see them. Like a microscope, but more. I could hear them. Feel them. I cannot explain. It made me a scientist. Now I am just…this." He lifted his head and let if fall against the stone.

Nathan opened his mouth to speak, but he was cut off by a howl. Conall held up a hand.

"It's just the wind," Nathan said. "The storm is raging up there."

Another howl. This one louder. Closer.

"That's not wind."

A scrabble of claws against tile came from the hallway by the kitchen and a gaunt burst through the broken door.

35

THE GLASS BOOT

ROWAN LEFT THE CHARTER HOUSE of the Weaver's Guild in high spirits. She'd just made a deal with the guild leaders to speak at their next convention. They were happy to expect bigger crowds with the draw of a royal keynote speaker, and Rowan was happy to have a forum where she could garner new supporters.

Her hand found the locket under her shirt and she pressed it to her chest as she hurried through the streets of Bailey.

Yes, it was a good day, made even better by the message she'd found on the graphium. Conall was coming home. Home. That word was significant for a lone wolf. Did it mean he planned to stay? She dared to hope.

With Elias as her escort, she made her way toward Squall's End. It was past midday. The sky was dark and foreboding, making it feel later. She stopped at a pub situated at a three-way intersection. The main artery ran from Bailey to the docks with shops and restaurants on each side. The offshoot wound along the border of Squall's End and would take her past Grotto and then to the West Gate, but she wasn't going that way. Today, she was here for the pub—The Glass Boot.

Bretta's building had undergone a transformation since it was a tearoom. The large front window had been boarded up, and a new sign hung over the boards. It was a mech contraption of metal—a mug of ale shaped like the outline of a boot. Ball bearings on thin wires rose from the top of the boot and spilled over the edge, giving it the appearance of overflowing beer. The mech was a repeater and every few seconds it reset, pulling the ball bearings back into the boot so they could spill again. Stained glass filled the metal outline of the boot and a thera lamp was hung behind it.

It was a beautiful piece of mech and Rowan stood admiring it for several minutes.

In truth, she was a little nervous about going inside. Her promises to visit Denny and Bretta had been forestalled by events in the palace. She'd neglected her friends. Even today, she only came because she needed something. She needed to do better.

With a sigh, she pushed open the door and entered the pub. Elias followed her in, and the door closed heavily behind them.

Inside, the pub was quiet, dark and homey. Bretta had installed a long bar of gleaming cherry wood. A dozen tables with club chairs were scattered around the room. Padded partitions gave some tables privacy. A hearth filled the back corner and a few soft chairs and end tables were placed in a conversational setup. With the windows boarded, the only light came from thera lamps in sconces on the walls or hanging over the bar. A mech janitor trundled around the tables, sweeping dirt into its dust bin.

Rowan had timed her visit to miss the lunch and supper crowds, so the place was mostly empty. Only one table had customers and these were two old men who played cogs and crowns, though the cards were mostly ignored while they nursed mugs of ale.

Bretta came out of the kitchen carrying a tray of sandwiches. She set it on their table and turned to greet the new arrivals.

"Rowan! Elias!" She limped over and threw her arms around Rowan's neck, then pulled Elias into the hug. Rowan felt her face grow warm as she endured the affection.

Bretta pushed Rowan and Elias back gently. "How is it you're here together?"

"Elias has joined my personal guard." Rowan felt a little silly saying it. A grown woman shouldn't need twenty-four hour supervision. But Bretta nodded.

"That's good thinking. Conall was worried you wouldn't have anyone you could trust in the palace."

"You saw him?"

"Only once. Before he left."

"Of course." He'd told her that, but for one glorious second, Rowan had thought he was in the city.

"Let me get a good look at you both." Bretta squinted one eye as if examining a work of art. "You're too thin, but you always were. And Elias, you need a haircut."

"Yes, Striker!" Elias saluted. Bretta had been their striker for only a few days, but she'd been the mentor who'd taught them to be rangers.

She looked different too. The hair loose around her shoulders softened her. A streak of gray had appeared along her right temple, but it seemed more like an adornment than a blemish. Rowan's eyes drifted down to her foot. She couldn't help it. Even after living with those who gaped at her mech arm for years, she had to see the glass foot.

Bretta had been caught in the backlash of Lena's knack while they fought a walrus titan. Lena had turned the titan to glass and the foot with it. Bretta stretched out her leg, turning the appendage side to side. She wore a leather boot on the other foot, but the glass one was bare. Rowan supposed it would be hard to find a boot that fit well. The glass shone dully in the dim light. It hadn't taken a scratch in all these weeks.

"It's holding up well," she said.

Bretta tapped the glass foot against the bar. "Solid as diamond. And it makes a great attraction. They come to gape at the glass foot and stay for Gus's kidney pie and peach cobbler." She leaned in and spoke in a lower voice. "I do miss shifting though. I never ran much as a bear, but now that option is gone, and well…I miss it."

Rowan nodded as if she understood, though of course she couldn't. She had no idea what it meant to be a shifter or to have that ability blocked.

"But I keep hoping and trying. One day the bear will overcome the glass. And in that spirit let's raise a toast to meeting old friends!" She went around the bar and poured draughts into glass tumblers.

Rowan lifted her drink and examined the glass. It was exquisitely faceted to let light catch the amber liquid inside.

"Beautiful, isn't it?" Bretta laid down the jug with a smile. "It's Lena's work. She left the service and opened a glasswares shop."

"I guess that's fitting." Rowan sipped her drink and fire rushed down her throat. She coughed and set the glass down. Elias gulped his and slammed the tumbler onto the bar with a grin. Bretta moved to pour him another, but he shook his head.

"Got to be alert to protect the princess."

"Good man." Bretta put the bottle down. They chatted for a few minutes about other mutual friends. Rowan told her about Noah working at the temple. Bretta said Murdoch had been posted to Oxeye.

"Probably learning a hundred new ways to cook up those nacara mussels. And where's that bird of yours? Can't remember ever seeing you without it."

"I had a meeting at the weaver's guild before coming here. I left Phalian at the palace. He can be…disruptive."

"I bet. Nothing like a nosy metal bird to throw a spanner in negotiations."

"Exactly. And what about Clem? Where was she posted?" Clem still had more than a year left on her mandatory military service.

"Oh, she's around." Bretta's lips pressed into an angry line. "Got transferred to the keepers after a little accident at her last posting."

"Was she hurt?"

"Dislocated shoulder. She's on the mend. If you ask me, they'll just put her in one dangerous situation after another, hoping the stress will make her shift into a bear and then they'll have a reason to expel her."

"That won't work." Clem and Bretta were half sisters, but she wasn't a shifter. Rowan thought the ban on shifters in the military was unfair anyway.

"Doesn't mean they won't try. At least they officially promoted her to scout. I just hope she can withstand their efforts to break her." Bretta slapped the bar with her palm. "Now, tell me what brings you all the way to Squall's End."

Rowan squirmed in her seat. She wished she'd come for this—a simple drink with old friends. "Actually, I need to speak to Denny."

Bretta's eyes clouded. "He's over there by the fire. Where he is every day."

Rowan turned on the bar stool and now that she was looking for him, she spotted Denny curled up in the farthest chair beside the big hearth.

Bretta gripped her mech hand. "I tried to get him to go home to Dowchester, but he's convinced there's nothing for him there. I think he's just afraid of the journey. Maybe you can talk to him."

They'd stashed Denny here to protect him. As long as Atherton and Wrede thought all the scientists from the oasis were dead, they would think their secrets were safe. But the assassination attempt proved that her enemies were not sitting idly by. It was time to stop hiding.

"I'll see what I can do."

"Good. If he stays here, he'll mope himself to death. The boy can drag down an entire room full of happy customers with his brooding. He needs something to occupy his mind."

Rowan turned to Elias. "Give us a few minutes, okay?"

Elias nodded.

"I'll bring you out something to eat," Bretta said, "and you can tell me all about those Ebos friends you brought back. Clem says they're amazing."

Rowan left them and headed for the back of the room. Denny watched her approach, but didn't get up.

She handed him a knotted piece of string.

"I thought you might want that back."

It was the talisman he'd given to her as a good luck charm. His fingers flicked out like a snake's tongue to grab the string. Immediately, the knots began to unravel by themselves. That impressive talent was the lesser of Denny's two knacks. His magic potential had to be off the charts.

"Aren't you going to say hello?"

"Hello, Princess." His smile was wan.

"Don't call me that. Not you."

When they'd linked their knacks with Noah in order to erase Orson's memories, something profound had happened. Denny was an impact empath. He didn't just feel emotions from others. He could affect them too. He'd been the vessel that drove them into Orson's mind while Rowan's knack blasted the thera in his blood and Noah mended the damage she'd left behind.

During that short struggle, they'd joined together as one mind, inseparable and indistinguishable from each other. Breaking the connection had felt like one egg splitting into triplets. She'd missed them immediately. And they would forever be linked by the bond they shared.

She felt no emotions coming off Denny now. He was holding onto his knack with tight reins, but she didn't need it to see he was miserable. The bruise on his face had healed, but his eyes were ringed in dark circles. His pale complexion, large eyes and messy curls made him seem waifish rather than roguish.

"When was the last time you felt the sun on your face?" she asked.

Denny shrugged.

"Bretta says you're bored."

"Bretta is a mother hen."

"You could do with some mothering."

Denny shrugged again.

"I know you don't want to go home to Dowchester, but you can't stay in hiding forever." Denny's secrets had become hers when they'd linked minds. She'd kept those secrets to herself, not even sharing them with Conall because she respected Denny's privacy. His family was…complicated, and he preferred a long distance relationship with them. His love for science had given him the opportunity to leave the south, and he'd jumped on it. Now he was forced to choose between hiding or going home. He was stuck, but she knew exactly how to unstick him.

She leaned over to force his gaze up. He watched her like a scared rabbit.

"I deciphered Sandra Kane's cachet. Or rather Roger did."

That made him sit up in his chair. His feet hit the floor with a thunk.

"What does it say?"

"A whole lot. Most of it I don't understand. But I've been to see Noah too and we have a theory that thera is slowly mutating humans into gaunts. Again."

Denny sat back in his chair.

"You're not surprised."

He didn't answer and she pressed him.

"Is that what you've been trying to hide all this time?"

Denny shrugged. "I suspected, but I had no real proof. I confronted Elsie Myer. She told me to keep my theories to myself and not waste Dr. Banerjee's time."

"Elsie was working for Miron Wrede. Maybe she still is. We never found her body."

"That figures." Denny let out a shuddering sigh.

So Noah's theory was true. Thera was slowly killing them all. Or worse, it was turning them into monsters. She gazed at the innocuous thera lamps on either side of the hearth. It seemed impossible that something so beneficial to their city could be so deadly.

"Dr. Banerjee and Elsie were working on some kind of test that would prove the link, weren't they?" she asked. "That's why Wrede was interested in their research."

Denny nodded. He looked miserable, as if the genetics of humans and gaunts were all his fault.

It always came back to Miron Wrede. And where was he now? Hiding in some black ops site making his army of gaunt hybrids? An army needed a target and it was only a matter of time before Wrede made his target known.

Rowan leaned in and forced Denny to meet her eye. "I know you're scared, but I could really use your help. There's a lot of information on that cachet, and I understand about one word in three. If you come to the palace, you can go through it all and maybe find that link we need to Wrede and Atherton. Put an end to all this. I'll keep you safe, I promise."

Denny was shaking his head. "No, no, no." He covered his face in his hands and rocked in the chair. Rowan hated doing this to him. He'd faced monsters in the oasis, and it seemed they were still chasing him.

Rowan squeezed his hand. "Look. I can bring Roger here, if that would make you feel better. But there's another reason I want you to visit the palace. It's Ethan."

Denny lifted his gaze and stared into her eyes. She tried not to flinch. He knew all about Ethan. She had no secrets from him.

"The doctors say he will never wake, that there is no activity in his brain, but I don't believe it anymore. Lately he's been restless, like he wants to wake and he can't."

"You want me to read him?" Denny sat perfectly still, like a rabbit ready to bolt.

"Yes."

He nodded and sucked in a deep breath that made him seem taller. "I'll come for that. And I'll look at the data while I'm there. But I'm not staying."

Relief flooded Rowan. Sharing her worries with Denny eased her burden, and reminded her why she needed her squad.

"Thank you."

Denny gave her a small smile. "If you were anyone else asking, I'd refuse."

"I know, and I'm grateful. I'll send Elias to get you tomorrow. Would that work?"

"Yes."

"Where is she?" A loud voice came from the front entrance. Rowan grinned. She knew that voice. She rose and turned as Clem came barreling through the pub. Her left arm hung in a sling, but the other clasped Rowan in a hug.

Clem looked exactly the same—brick-red hair pulled back and tied in a ponytail. Freckles spattering her face like abstract art and a full mouth that was made for grinning, which she did as she took in Rowan's posh, if subdued dress.

"Aren't you a fancy pants. It suits you better than that old ranger uniform."

"You think? I miss my cap."

"That's because you did such a shitty job cutting your hair. Don't you have stylists at that palace of yours?"

"I do. They despair for me."

"I bet."

Bretta brought a bottle of honey mead to the table. A mech server followed with a tray of tiny savory pies. Elias joined them by the fire and for the next hour the remnants of Squad 54 drank and ate and reconnected. No one mentioned Conall or the other missing members, but Rowan could feel them like a silent presence.

As she stood outside the pub to say her goodbyes to Clem, a ley-line surge rocked them.

"Bolt down your brassworks, folks!" Clem grinned as they rode the trembling ground. Someone from the square screamed. A thera lamp on the corner exploded.

The surge lasted less than a minute. People in the street had stopped to crouch in place as if that could protect them from the earthquake. They straightened now and went on with their business. Just another quirky day in the city.

"Is it just me, or are those getting to be a pain in the ass?" Clem asked.

"It's not just you. I sat through one while dining with the Dowchester ambassador. He nearly wet himself."

"I would have liked to see that!"

A thought struck Rowan.

"Why don't you join me in the palace. I've been given leave to take on a full honor guard. You could finish out your service there and no more reckless jobs for you."

Clem cocked her head. "Bretta's been filling you with tales again hasn't she?" She lifted the arm in the sling. "This was mostly my fault. Can't really blame anyone else. And I kind of like being a ranger. I get to shoot things."

"Still, I could use you in the palace."

"I'll think about it."

Someone in the square shouted. Then another cry came from further up the road. People started running, not toward Bailey or Squall's end, but up the alley that led to the West Gate.

Clem grabbed a woman who looked panicked as she ran by.

"What happened?"

The woman's eyes were wide and she held a hand to her mouth. "It's Talos. He's fallen and taken out the wall!"

36

HEART OF A MECH

ROWAN RAN. IT WAS BAD. She could see that even from a distance. Elias followed, but Clem led the way. Her keeper's uniform helped them to push through the gathering crowd.

The West Gate was the second busiest route into the city. Homesteaders used it to bring their wares into markets, and travelers from down south drove their caravans the extra miles to this entrance rather than try to get through the busier one at the docks. The gate itself was made of massive wooden panels that opened on rails wide enough to let two wagons pass at once. Towers rose above the wall on either side where keepers armed with rail guns kept watch.

The right-side tower was on the verge of collapse. There was a hole in the wall beside it, and a cloud of dust lingered over a pile of massive stones where it had caved inward. Talos's metal hand lay immobile in that gap. People were crying and screaming. Some were bloody from being hit by flying debris. Others were disoriented and wandering around covered in dust.

Rowan's heart sank even as her feet sped up. Clem bullied and pushed until the crowd parted for them. Keepers were already forming a line at the gap. When Rowan tried to get through, they stopped her.

"Stand back, ma'am. It isn't safe."

"I need to get to Talos!"

"No one's going out there."

Rowan sputtered. With the adrenaline rush and shortness of breath from the run, words failed her.

Clem stepped up. She glanced at the one bar on the keeper's shoulder and turned so her own two bars were visible.

"Do you know who this is, Keeper?" She pointed to Rowan.

"No, sir."

"This is Princess Rowan Elizabeth Cecilia Andula, heir to House Andula and way above your pay grade. Other than the fact that she can have your ass thrown in jail, she's also the only mech mage in the city qualified to work on Talos. So either you let her through or you spend the rest of your service hours mopping toilets." She leaned right into his space. "In the palace dungeons."

The keeper gaped at Clem, then at Rowan, but he let them through.

"Not a mech mage," Rowan muttered as they started to climb over the rocks.

"Close enough. And titles are important. You never appreciated that."

"I'm learning."

Conversation became impossible as Rowan concentrated on finding safe footholds on the rocks. From afar, the tumble of stones hadn't been daunting, but now that they were climbing, she realized the distance had been deceiving. She was perched on a tower of fallen stone that shifted dangerously under her feet.

A pang of cold fear seized her.

"Wait." She stopped and sat. Her breathing came in short gasps.

Clem saw her panic. She took Rowan's arm and whispered, "Not here. Don't let them see you sweat."

Rowan nodded and climbed to the top of the rocks. On the other side, she jumped down then bent over to let blood reach her brain again.

"I'm sorry." She clutched her mech arm to her chest. Her heart was pounding furiously. "I lost my arm in a rock slide and that was…I don't know."

"Triggering," Clem said.

"Yeah." But Rowan was already getting over it because the sight of Talos lying like a big metal corpse filled her with a new dread. He sat with his back to the wall, one arm folded behind him and legs stretched out. Part of the tower had collapsed over one knee. His copper and bronze face had never been animated by expression, but now it seemed even darker. His eyes were empty and somehow sad.

She turned to Elias. "Run back to the palace and bring my mech kit. The one I keep in my rooms."

Elias shook his head. "Minna will flay me alive if I leave you alone in the city."

"She's not alone," Clem said. "Tell old Minna that the princess has a new guard, and she's starting right now."

Elias grinned and scampered over the rock pile.

"You'll do it? Really?" Rowan gripped her arm.

"What the heck. Trouble seems to follow you around, so I'll probably still get to shoot things." Clem hoisted her rail gun and pointed at the gap.

"You should probably be pointing that at the Meadows," Rowan said.

"Nah. The keepers on the wall will stop anything coming out of the grass. I'm more worried about some fool trying to make a name for himself by killing the princess."

"There seems to be a lot of that going around."

Clem cocked an eyebrow at her. "Really? I'm going to like being your guard."

Rowan shook her head. Clem wasn't trigger happy, and she could handle herself.

"I'm going inside. Stay here. I'll come back for my tools when Elias arrives."

"Yes, Striker."

A bit of warmth returned to Rowan's guts. She didn't put much stock in titles, but she liked that one.

Standing on the giant mech foot, she dug out the key that she always kept on her belt and unlocked the door on Talos's ankle.

Inside, she crawled along the ladder—which was somehow more difficult than the usual climb—until she reached his hip, then she found the second ladder and began to climb his torso. It was too dark inside. The only light came from the open door and a faint glow above her. When she reached his chest, her worst fears were realized.

Talos's heart was going out.

The giant amber structure that housed the glowing orb seemed smaller, like it had wilted, and the orb itself was only a faintly pulsing rock.

She climbed a little higher until she was level with the orb. For the first time, she was able to get a really good look at it. Normally, the glow was too bright, making it impossible to see the mech work around it. Now she could see the orb pulsing slowly as if it breathed, and that breath was failing. The ichor-filled cables hung limply. One had been ripped away from the amber sack. It hung across another cable, its end dripping golden ichor.

She hung on the ladder, feeling weightless and burdened with the weight of her city at the same time.

Without his sympathetic magic, the city's water pumps would be silent. The council would speed up their plan to install thera pumps and Talos would become a relic. His great form would be left to rust in the Meadows.

She had no idea how to fix him, but she knew someone who did.

First, she had to do a little triage. She pulled out the ribbon that tied her hair and grabbed the bleeding cable. After a brief struggle while she tried to hang onto the ladder and the cable at the same time, she tied it off with the ribbon, pulling the knot tight until it stopped leaking ichor. The cable ended with an odd plug. It was oval, but pinched like an infinity sign. Her fingers instinctively brushed the underside of her mech arm, where a matching port was covered by her glove. The ports were a Harry Hightower signature.

She shook the cable gently to make sure the ichor was secure, then wrapped it around the ladder to keep it in place. It was little more than a bandage on a mortal wound.

She scrambled down the ladder, determined to use all her power as the royal heir to drag Harry Hightower out of his cave and into the sun.

37

WHAT'S UNCOVERED IN THE MIST

CONALL WAS UP AND MOVING with air knives in each hand before his mind even registered the threat.

The creature loomed six-feet tall, and stood in a simian stance with long arms hanging to the floor. Black scaled plating covered it from head to toe. A heavy brow ridge shadowed sunken eyes. Its square jaw opened in a roar to reveal meat-ripping teeth.

Conall shoved Nathan aside and leaped. His blades scissored across the gaunt's chest, but his momentum took him too far and the blades only scored the heavy plating. The beast roared and raked a claw down Conall's shoulder. Pain lanced him. He skidded to a stop, turned and kicked out the back of the gaunt's knee. It stumbled and he jumped on its back, driving it to the ground.

"Barricade the door!" he yelled even as he got the beast in a choke hold. He had no time to see if Nathan obeyed. The gaunt bucked and snarled. Its teeth found his arm and bit down. Conall screamed and drove a knife into its ribs. The thera-boosted blade ripped through it like paper. He yanked downward and felt bone give way. The beast howled and shook its head. Conall loosened his hold long enough to draw the second blade across its throat. Blood and spittle sprayed over him as the beast thrashed. He hung on until it went limp.

Rolling away, he lay panting on his back, still gripping a blade in each hand. They'd cost him a fortune, but they'd just paid for themselves a thousand times over.

More howls rang out from the corridor. He sat up to see Nathan and Rudi piling desks and chairs against the door. Banerjee was frozen with hands cupping his head and eyes spinning erratically.

A gaunt hit the door with a reverberating thud.

"That won't hold them for long," Conall panted. The howls turned to snarls and then came the wet sounds of a carnivore devouring flesh.

They'd found Elsie.

Conall closed his eyes and swallowed down the gorge that rose in his throat. He opened them to find Nathan hastily scratching a rune beside the door.

Too many to fight, Garou said. His sensitive ears picked up at least four more predators.

Too many, Conall agreed. Even if they had the mech valet on their side, they couldn't beat four gaunts, and Banerjee seemed to be spiraling into madness again.

Conall rose to his feet and wiped the bloody blades on his pants before sheathing them. "We have to go."

"But the download," Rudi said. "I need more time!"

"Take what you have," Nathan snapped. "We leave now."

Rudi looked like he might protest but a vicious growl from behind the barricade changed his mind. He pulled wires from Elsie's station and dumped his mechs in a large pack.

Conall shoved Nathan toward the main door. "Get topside."

"What about you?"

"I'll be right behind you. Go!"

Nathan pulled Rudi with him, and they ran across the lab. Conall turned to Banerjee.

"We have to go. Can you run?" Most mech valets had speed modes, but they were designed for maneuvering through crowds in the market, not outrunning gaunts.

"Banerjee, can you hear me?"

The mech's eyes rotated in their sockets, but he was otherwise still. Banerjee was no longer in charge.

Leave him, Garou urged. *He is not pack, not even flesh. He will only slow us down.*

Conall bent and groaned as he hoisted the mech into a shoulder carry. His wounded arm screamed at this abuse, and he staggered toward the door.

He made it to the bottom of the stairs before he had to dump Banerjee in a heap and rest.

His breath came in ragged heaves. Pins and needles ran up his arm and his hand was slick with blood.

Morning light filtered down the stairs from the open door to the Warren. Behind him the snarls of gaunts rose to a terrifying crescendo. They were followed by banging sounds. The gaunts had finished devouring Elsie Myer and were battering at the barricade.

"Conall!" Nathan half-ran, half-slid down the stone steps. He grabbed Banerjee under the shoulders and hauled him upward. Conall shoved from below, ignoring the shriek of pain in his shoulder.

Up top, they set Banerjee on his feet. The mech swayed but stayed upright. Dawn was upon them, and the air heavy after the rain. Mist settled between the walls of the labyrinth.

A howl came through the open door, far away but not far enough.

They ran for the nearest wall. Ailen helped Rudi up to the ledge, then together they hauled up Banerjee.

"Go with them," Nathan said. "Get as far away as you can."

"No!" Conall grabbed his forearm. "I'm staying with you."

Nathan looked ready to argue, but a howl stopped him. A gaunt leaped up from the stairwell.

Ailen shot it, his arrow piercing its eye. The beast went down screaming.

"Do it now!" Conall stepped away.

Nathan crouched and buried his hands in loose sand. His knack pulsed through him, and he bucked as if he'd been shot. Conall caught him before he fell over.

At first nothing happened. Then a muffled *whump* sounded, followed by a rumble like thunder. The ground shook as Nathan's runes were activated. Nearby stone walls collapsed. Conall dropped into a crouch. The wall they stood beside shook but held.

A sloughing sound began as the ground disintegrated, then a crater opened where the lab had been. The wounded gaunt fell into it with a screech and was buried under dirt and stone rushing to fill the void. A cloud of dust rose into the air.

Nathan stood and wiped a shaking hand across his face. His eyes were dark against his dust covered skin.

He grinned. "Just like the wolverine dens back home. Only bigger." Nathan stretched, cracking neck and shoulders. "It's so rare that I get to use my knack."

Conall clapped him on the back. "It has its moments. Now let the saints deal with the rest." He hoisted his brother up the wall and followed, ignoring the pain in his shoulder.

They ran across the top of the labyrinth until they found the hollow where they'd left Kelli and Irva.

"You're hurt!" said the lumina when she saw them.

"I'm fine," Nathan said, then jerked a thumb at Conall. "He's not. And don't let him tell you otherwise. See what you can do short term, but healing will have to wait until we're out of here."

"That might be difficult, Captain."

Something in Irva's tone stopped Conall in his tracks. The lumina wasn't given to theatrics.

"We have visitors." She pointed toward the Meadows. Conall peered through the gap in the stone wall. Nathan bumped him as he got a look, then he swore in several languages.

The sun was rising across the Meadows, burning off the mist to reveal a swarm of gaunts.

38

UNDER A HOLLOW SKY

Conall counted twelve gaunts. They stood in a line, vibrating with the need to run, like dogs restrained by invisible leashes. Conall's little squad numbered only seven. Nathan, Rudi and Irva weren't fighters. That left four to deal with twelve beasts. Not good odds.

Ailen joined him to study the horde. The gaunts knew they were there. Their eyes were fixed on the small gap in the rocks. One shifted, kicking up a cloud of dust. Another twitched like it couldn't bear to stand still, but none broke formation.

"Not natural," Ailen said.

Except during uprisings, gaunts rarely gathered in packs bigger than five or six and cooperation lasted only as long as their prey survived. These were Wrede's beasts and their handlers couldn't be far behind them.

Then a human stepped out from behind the last beast. Wrede hadn't wasted any time. He'd already improved upon his experiments. Instead of one handler to one gaunt, a lone soldier now controlled a dozen beasts. A rush of angry despair washed over Conall.

Damn the saints. He'd been so close to getting back to her. He'd finally understood that his place was by Rowan's side, and she would never know. She would think he'd died on a wild goose chase, that he'd put his peace of mind above his love for her.

He retreated back inside the Warren.

Rudi was already pulling weapons from the pack pony's basket. He thrust a crossbow at Conall and a quiver that held a dozen bolts, plus the two red-fletched arrows.

"Make them count." Rudi's expression held none of its usual humor. Conall nodded. The others kitted up too. Kelli and Cob put down their spears for crossbows. Rudi handed a rail gun to Irva and whispered a few words of encouragement. The lumina's face had gone white, and she gripped the gun too hard. Conall hoped she knew how to use it. Nathan strapped two knives to his belt and also picked up a gun. As he checked the rails, Conall gripped his arm.

"We don't have to do this, brother. We can hide in the Warren. Find another way out."

Nathan faced him. The wolf glinted in his eyes. "Do you think they will give up so easily? Do you think they aren't watching the other exits? We do this now and then I'm going home to Soffi and Jula."

Conall simply nodded. He had no better words of inspiration.

When the others gathered around, Nathan looked each in the eye and said, "Let's go kill some monsters." Then Conall's sweet, scholarly brother let out a battle cry and ran into the Meadows, firing his gun.

Conall ran after him. His first bolt released even as his foot hit the sands outside the walls. It struck gaunt plating and the beast staggered back. The gaunts flanking it dropped and lunged on all fours in that ape-like shamble that was impossibly fast. Conall nocked bolts and fired. And fired. A gaunt went down, a bolt through its throat.

"Kill the handler!" he yelled.

Garou howled in the back of his mind.

Nathan threw down his gun rather than reload it and tore through the line of beasts. Conall watched him, stunned. Sometime in the last ten years his brother had learned to fight. He slid along the gravel, slicing tendons behind a gaunt's knee. The beast went down and Nathan speared it through the throat. He jumped up and tackled the human handler. Conall lost them in the melee as a gaunt jumped a twelve foot gap to land in front of him.

The beast opened its massive jaws and roared, spraying Conall with spittle. It backhanded him, but Conall turned away in time, taking the brunt of the hit on his shoulder. He had no time for the lancing pain. Using the momentum of the strike, he spun away. A rail gun bolt struck the gaunt, piercing its nose and driving halfway into its skull. Conall dropped his bow and finished the beast with his air blade, jabbing it in the throat, and raking upward so the thera-infused blade did maximum damage.

Cob was down, but his blade was still flashing. Irva stood by the gap in the wall. Her rail gun was out. She struggled to pull the rails. A gaunt ran at her. Conall grabbed his bow, nocked a bolt with his hand that still gripped a blade, and let it fly. The arrow punched through the gaunt's armor plating and it fell, only steps from the lumina.

Conall stood heaving for breath, the crossbow braced on his right arm and a blade gripped in his left hand.

The sound of wind cats running on thera engines filled the space between the screams and grunts of the fights going on all around him.

He turned and shielded his eyes. A cloud of dust filled the eastern Meadows. It slowly resolved into dozens of cats, each carrying at least six soldiers. Coming fast. More gaunts ran alongside them.

"Jupiter and Jocasta." The plea to the saints came through ragged breaths.

They weren't going to win this fight. It didn't matter that Irva was brave enough to fire a rail gun or that his brother had somehow become a master fighter. They would all die here.

A brazen shout came from the mountains.

At the same moment, Ailen screamed and fell on Conall, tackling him to the ground. Ailen's shirt was torn and bloody. A gaunt leaped after him. Conall pushed Ailen away and staggered to one knee. The gaunt swiped a hand, its claws missing Conall's face by a breath. Conall jammed the crossbow into its chest and shoved. It fell back, giving Conall precious seconds to stand. The beast raised claws again and Conall swiped his blade across its elbow, severing bone and tendon. The gaunt shrieked and fell to one knee, cradling the useless arm. Conall spun, plunged his blade into the back of its skull, and yanked it free.

The gaunt fell.

Ailen didn't move.

Conall panted and bent over. The pain in his shoulder was blinding now. His empty stomach heaved and he spat onto the sand.

The exultant cry had grown louder. He lifted his gaze and saw dozens of warriors coming over the hill, screaming and shaking spears.

The Taiga had come.

Conall staggered forward, wanting to help them, but knowing he had little fight left.

Gaunts fell under the swarm of berserkers. The Taiga slammed into cats and pulled soldiers from their seats. The screams of the dying were terrible and drowned out even the Taiga's war cries.

Conall watched the carnage as he fought for breath. Then one cat pulled away from the others, fleeing the way it had come. It could have been a scout, rushing back to command with news of a defeat. It could have been a coward, running from the fight, but in his heart, Conall knew. It was Wrede.

He tucked away his blade and pulled the two red-fletched bolts from his quiver. His left shoulder ached and his fingers struggled to load the bolt. Finally, he raised the crossbow with his right arm, holding it steady by sheer will. The cat was nearly out of range.

Conall let it loose. The bolt sailed through the bloody melee and hit the ground beside the fleeing cat. The boom sent up a shower of rock. Conall was already firing the second bolt. It went right through the cat's back window.

The vehicle exploded.

Conall dropped the bow and shucked off his clothes, shifting before he even hit the ground. The pain in his shoulder nearly made him lose consciousness, but the shift healed all, and when Garou leaped across the body of a fallen gaunt, he did it on four solid legs.

He ran, dodging Taiga, gaunts and soldiers, bursting through clouds of dust and screams of the dying. He mounted the rise where he'd last seen the cat and found pieces of twisted and smoking metal. A tire had rolled some distance. Garou leaped over it. He put his nose to the ground and sneezed from the smoke filling the air. He found the first body under what was left of the cat's back end. She was badly burned, half her face ruined. Her one good eye stared at him blankly.

Garou left her and circled the cat. Another body had been thrown from the vehicle, and it lay in a crumpled heap twenty feet from the smoking ruins. The wolf snuffled it, flipping it over with his muzzle to be met with a pale blue stare.

Blond hair was matted to a cut on his forehead. One ear was blackened and the smell of burned hair was sickening.

That's him. Miron Wrede, Conall said. They'd only seen the former minister once, when Conall had first gone to New Torwood. He'd been a keeper then, before the war broke out. Wrede had dined with the regent and some hoity-toities from down south and Conall had been on guard duty at the gala.

This man was older, his blond hair faded to white. He had the ruddy complexion of a fair-skinned man who spent too much time outdoors. His eyes were just as hard as Conall remembered.

A rail gun lay beside Wrede, but he made no attempt to grab it. Garou put two paws on his chest and snarled, letting him have a good look at his fangs.

Wrede wheezed. He was laughing!

Garou snapped his jaws an inch from his nose.

Don't kill him! Conall urged.

"You can't win this fight, Commander West." Wrede's voice was calm. A brightness shone from his eyes—the light of confidence. Or madness.

"Tell your princess. She doesn't even want to win. Not really. She's just naive and confused. I bring progress. She brings only the misery of the past. Tell her to let it go. Let it go and I will let her live." The last words faded out in a hiss as Garou's weight sank into his claws that pressed on the traitor's chest. A growl vibrated through his bones.

"I'm coming for you, Wolf. And your princess." Wrede grinned, and then he was gone. His shift was as quick as breath. One moment he was a man, pinned under Garou's feet, the next he was flying away on sturdy black wings.

Garou's paws slammed to the hard ground. Conall let out a frustrated shout. *He's a Wildblood!*

Garou snorted and pawed the ground. He was angry to lose out on the kill. He turned in circles and whined.

Stand down. He's gone.

Garou lifted his nose to the sky and howled.

39

THE CURSE OF A LIFETIME

ROWAN CONVINCED GENERAL LIND TO supply her with an escort of keepers. They descended into the dark tunnels of Grotto, sacrificing stealth for force. She would feel guilty about that later, but for now, Talos was most important.

When they reached the Rustworks, it was deserted. Harry Hightower's warehouse looked like it had been abandoned for years. She left a note in his workroom, asking that he contact her at the palace, but she didn't have high hopes that he would answer it.

Over the next few hours, things got bad. There were only a handful of wells with manual pumps inside the city. Keepers were posted nearby to ration water. The crowds grew ugly, and more keepers were sent in.

The regent declared a state of emergency and made work on the thera-fueled water pumps a priority, but the mech mages estimated another month to completion. Rowan no longer blocked the council's decision. They needed those pumps. She'd concede to that defeat, but not to Talos's demise. Not until she had exhausted all avenues for his rehabilitation.

That night, under the yellow glow of her antique ley lamp, she pulled out the graphium and looked at Conall's latest message. Again. She'd read it a hundred times already.

Coming home soon.

A few words that changed her world. Conall was coming. It might be days or weeks, but he was coming.

She had advisors and friends in the city, but no one with whom she could share her deepest fears—the nightmares where her family and friends paid for her failures. But now, when she faced Atherton, Conall would stand at her side. She had no idea how long it would be before he arrived, but it didn't matter. Just knowing that he was coming eased her burden.

She tucked the graphium away. It was the only bit of thera she allowed in her rooms, and when Conall returned she would give up even that.

Thera was turning into a thorn in her side. She studied the schematics of the new water pump system. Dale had procured them from…well, she didn't really want to know how they'd gotten the plans. Dale made it clear that their work as her secretary involved a good dose of spying, and she was better left in the dark about that side of things.

She was no mech mage, but the plans seemed simple enough. A pump was primed with magic resonance. It was lined with thera that would need to be replaced every four weeks—at a steep cost to the city. The price wasn't the real issue though. The water supply would run right through this thera-laced structure.

She thought of those poor patients in Noah's ward.

Thera would steep in the drinking water. The people of New Torwood would drink this deadly tea unknowingly. They would cook with it and wash in it. How many more would end up in Noah's ward? How long would it take for the human population to sicken and die from thera exposure?

She'd argued for more time to study the problem, to come up with a safer solution, but now they were out of time. Riots had already broken out in Squall's End. The city needed water.

If only she could find Harry Hightower.

She'd sent runners looking for him. They checked every inn within the city walls and even inns along Kanta Highway, but Harry had admitted that he went by many names. In Oxeye, he'd been Halstead. She also remembered him as Hermie and Homer. He could be anyone, anywhere. She'd told the runners to look for an older innkeeper, with gray hair and a limp. It wasn't much to go on, and not surprisingly, none of the messengers had come back with good news.

Auntie Bella had been no help. When Rowan asked if she could contact her old flame, Bella laughed.

"Oh, darling. Never. Harry is a *god*." She'd said it the way a young girl gushes over an infatuation, then waved Rowan away so she could listen to her theragraphs in peace.

The mood in New Torwood City darkened by the day. Rowan read Dale's reports each morning with growing dread. More riots. Another unexplained illness broke out in Squall's End. Guilds squabbled for extra water rations. A mounting sense of unease hung over the city.

The guest suite beside Ethan's room had been turned into offices. As an official member of council, an office was allocated to her in the council wing, but she preferred the privacy of her own section of the palace. Privacy went only so far though. Atherton knew what she was up to. Just like she had spies among his courtiers and secretaries, he had eyes watching the royal suites.

A dozen pages worked for her now, and as Dale had moved into a more advisory position, they'd taken on a new secretary, a young man named Avram. He was quiet and sharp with round glasses and a bowl cut of straight brown hair. Privately, Rowan thought he looked like an owl just learning how to be wise. A mech valet followed him everywhere, holding a dozen agendas, charts and notebooks.

Rowan, Dale and Avram breakfasted together on the fifth day after Talos's fall.

"There were more riots in Bailey last night," Dale said before sipping from a large mug of hot tea. "Though the striker in charge says she thinks the main disruptors came up from Squall's End."

Rowan's breakfast sat untouched. Food didn't go down well these days. "How many wells still work in Squall's End?"

Avram sorted through some papers and handed one to her. "Only two, Evani." They'd all taken to calling her by the Ebos title. She didn't mind it so much anymore. "The third one is contaminated."

"Deliberately?"

"It's unclear."

"Hmm." She took a small bite of a scone just so she could tell Minna that she'd eaten something. "What about the palace water?"

Avram shuffled his papers again, but Dale answered. "Don't worry about that. The palace has its own well and pump, separate from the city's supply. It's an old system, but…"

"But sometimes older is better."

"Sometimes," Dale agreed.

"Is there a holding tank?" She pulled off a chunk of scone and tossed it to Phalian who was prancing around the table. The mech bird couldn't eat, but he enjoyed pecking it to pieces.

"Twenty-five thousand gallons," Dale said.

"I want half of that sent to Squall's End."

"That will take days to replenish," Avram said. "Atherton will be furious. The cook too."

The council could mandate city laws and allocate city resources, but she had full authority over the palace. Everything within it belonged to her family. If she wanted to give away her water, she could.

"I don't care about Atherton or the cook. We'll eat unwashed vegetables if we have to. And once the holding tank is replenished, I want another twelve thousand gallons distributed in the city. We'll keep that up until this crisis is over."

Dale nodded. "I'll make sure they know it comes from the palace directly, not the council."

Rowan waved away that idea. This wasn't about politics, but Dale would spin it whatever way they wanted despite her protests. It was Dale's job to protect her and they did so in a myriad of ways, including garnering support among the general population.

That thought brought up the next topic on their morning agenda.

"Did you speak to Docker?"

A vote from the Minister of Guilds could sway the council if it came down to a fight between Rowan and Atherton, and that battle was coming sooner than she'd hoped.

"She could go either way," Dale said. "She has no love for Atherton, but the guilds are deeply invested in thera. She won't support you unless you support Theracine."

Rowan sighed. The influence of Theracine Corporation grated like rust in her gears. They had too much influence and it was only getting stronger. They'd invested in many of the city guilds to the point where they were bankrolling most of the new businesses and construction in the city.

But she had a plan.

"We need to buy out some of those guild contracts."

"We can't do that," Dale said. "Not without approval from the council. Atherton would never go for it."

"I'm not suggesting we use council money. We'll use my money."

Dale and Avram gaped at her.

"What? I must have money. I know my mother left me some."

"She did and your father too. It won't be enough."

"Bella will help. She has more money than she knows what to do with. I'll talk to her."

Dale nodded. "I'll put out some feelers. See who's unhappy in their current contract. I bet we could get the farmers' guild interested. Construction on the new market in Bailey has stalled. My informants tell me that Atherton's conscriptions to replace workers in Oxeye hit farmers the worst. We could start there."

"Good."

Ferlan had been standing guard by the door. He stepped aside as Alice came into the room. She glanced at the Ebos and didn't even flinch. Maybe Omika had been onto something when he sent Minna and Ferlan to the city.

"Evani, there is someone here to see you. Says his name is Denlyn Feist."

"Denlyn?" Rowan's mind was blank. She didn't know any Denlyn. Then Dale whispered, "Denny. I rebooked your appointment for today."

"Of course. Send him in, Alice."

She'd asked Denny to the palace last week, but with all the commotion around Talos and the water pumps, she'd had to postpone.

"Uh, hello?" Denny appeared around the corner of the door. An attempt had been made to tidy him up, and Rowan suspected that was Bretta's doing. His hair was combed, though the unruly curls still fell over his forehead. He wore a clean but simple tunic over loose pants.

Roger rushed over from the corner with his arm upraised. He bumped into Denny's feet, whirled and bumped him again.

"Denny this is Roger. He won't remember you."

Denny smiled and crouched. "Uh, hi. I hear you're coming home with me for a bit."

In a clear voice the mech said, "Roger that! I look forward to working with you."

Denny raised his eyes to Rowan with a quizzical look.

Rowan shrugged. "I had his voice module fixed."

"That's amazing." Denny patted Roger's head and stood. "Well, where do you want to start?"

"We're finished here aren't we?" Rowan looked to Dale for confirmation. Dale nodded, then began packing up notebooks and scrolls.

Rowan said, "Roger, show Denny your data output."

Denny followed the valet as he rolled toward a side table. Roger held up the first sheet in several stacks of papers. "Data entry one of three hundred and eighty-two."

Rowan was probably anthropomorphizing again, but the mech looked like a proud artist showing off his work.

Denny took the sheet and studied it. His forehead crinkled in a frown. He picked up another sheet, and another.

"Does that make any sense to you?" Rowan asked.

"Some. But there's a lot here. More than I expected. I'll need time to go over it all before I can even start deciphering this data."

"I understand. You'll have anything you need. I meant it when I said you're welcome to stay here. You can have the room next to mine. Two keepers stand guard on the floor, and Minna, Ferlan, Clem and Elias are always on rotation."

Denny didn't look convinced. "I'll think about it. Let's visit your brother first."

Denny sat quietly beside the bed. Ethan appeared as he always did, stuck somewhere between a boy and a man. His bony chest rose and fell with regularity. Cheek bones cut sharp lines on his face that no longer held onto baby fat. He was gawky and pale as porcelain.

Phalian scampered up the covers to nuzzle his hand. Ethan's fingers didn't twitch, even when Phalian's sharp beak pecked him.

A spider dropped from the ceiling and landed on the pillow.

Denny drew back.

"It's okay. That happens. It won't hurt Ethan. Insects have always been drawn to him. That's his knack. When he was awake, he could sometimes get them to do his bidding."

Denny nodded, but looked pale. "Can we remove it for now?"

Rowan swept the spider into a handkerchief and tossed it out the window.

Denny settled on the chair. He didn't speak. He didn't touch Ethan. He simply sat with hands folded in his lap and his eyes closed.

Rowan watched them for a few minutes, then her mind wandered to the dozens of problems that faced her. She was doing everything she could for the people of New Torwood City, but it wasn't enough.

Was this what governing was like? Somehow the histories and fairy tales always left out the part about the ruler feeling inadequate, about the need to choose daily between bad choices and worse choices.

"Has Noah seen him?" Denny's words brought her back to the present.

"No. Dr. Renata has been his physician forever."

Denny nodded. "Since the accident?"

"It wasn't an accident. And yes. Dr. Renata is the one keeping him alive. Why? Do you think something's wrong?"

"I don't know. I sense…emotions."

"What kind of emotions?"

Denny pinched his lips together as if unwilling to speak.

"Come on, Denny. This isn't the time for your games. I need to know. Is my brother alive in there?"

Denny sighed. "He's definitely alive. I sense sorrow. And frustration. And anger. He wants to wake up, but doesn't know how."

As if responding to their words, Ethan's breathing quickened. His back arched and legs bucked. Moths appeared from nowhere and fluttered around his head. Phalian squawked and launched from the bed to fly around the room.

"What's happening?" Rowan grabbed Ethan's hand, but the seizure ripped it from her grasp. "Help us!" She yelled toward the doorway, hoping someone would hear.

Grant rushed in. The big nurse took in the situation with one glance and barked at an orderly in the outer room.

"Get Dr. Renata. Now!" The orderly ran off. Grant held Ethan's shoulders gently but firmly as the seizure calmed to trembles.

"What's happening?" Rowan asked, but Grant just shook his head. When Ethan finally calmed, Grant stood up with a frown.

"That was a bad one." He swatted at the moths, then straightened Ethan's shirt.

Denny retreated to the other side of the room as if he needed to get as far away from Ethan as possible. He sat on the couch with his knees drawn up to his chin and eyes wide.

Ethan lay like a wrung-out rag on the pillows. His breathing was shallow, and his skin had a sickly gray cast. Grant bathed his forehead with a cool cloth and plumped the pillow.

Rowan paced.

Dr. Renata finally swept into the room. She glanced at Rowan and Denny and dismissed them as unimportant, then listened to Ethan's heart. She took his pulse and grunted a few times as if confirming thoughts she hadn't spoken aloud.

Rowan lingered at the bedside.

"What happened?" she asked.

Renata brushed her aside, then leaned over Ethan and laid her hands flat on his bare chest. Rowan crossed her arms and covered her mouth with one hand, before she said something she'd regret. She could forgive Dr. Renata's rudeness if it meant she saved Ethan.

Her mech hand tingled as it always did when mage work was being done. After a moment the doctor sucked in a breath and slumped. She looked shrunken and old.

Renata took a deep breath and stood straighter. "There. That will hold him for a time." Deep lines scored the edges of her mouth and her lips trembled slightly. "He sleeps soundly for now. Perhaps if you didn't bother him so much, he would be more at ease."

"Perhaps you shouldn't speak to the princess like that," Denny said. Renata whipped around as if she hadn't seen him lurking in the corner.

"Who are you?"

Rowan intervened. "He's a friend." She put herself between Renata and

Denny so the doctor had to focus on her. "I thank you for your service again, Dr. Renata."

The doctor sniffed and left the room.

"Minna is right," Denny said. Rowan stared at him for a second, letting his words sink in. Then she turned to Grant and asked him to leave them.

"Of course, Princess." Grant patted Ethan's hand and left.

As soon as they were alone, Rowan hissed, "What do you mean Minna's right?"

"I mean that doctor may be keeping Ethan alive, but she's also holding him in some kind of spell. And she reeks of spite, anger and hate."

That last part Rowan had figured out herself. She stared at her brother lying in the bed. What had once seemed peaceful, now seemed helpless.

What if he was alive in there, struggling to wake up? What if Dr. Renata was part of some great conspiracy to keep Ethan in a coma?

"You should get Noah here to see him," Denny said. Rowan nodded, too numb to answer.

She sent Alice to find Noah, then retired to her room to rest. Denny followed, and he settled in the study with a stack of Roger's data sheets.

An hour later, Alice returned with a message.

"Medic Noah Sommerton says he will come as soon as his shift at the hospital is over."

Rowan nodded her thanks.

Denny worked all through the afternoon while Rowan tried and failed to occupy herself with one of Dale's history books. Dinner was brought up, but neither touched it.

It was well into the evening before Noah arrived and Rowan brought him straight to Ethan. Denny and Clem accompanied them. Rowan sent a page asking for Minna and Dale to join them too.

Before leaving, Grant had shaved and bathed Ethan. Dr. Renata would not be back for a few days unless something went amiss. Only one nurse sat on duty outside the prince's room, not one that Rowan was familiar with.

He rose as the princess arrived, trailing an entourage.

"Milady, your brother is resting."

"He's always resting," Rowan said.

"Yes, but, this is an ill timed visit. Dr. Renata said—"

"I don't care about Dr. Renata's orders, and since he sleeps round the clock, I don't think Ethan will mind."

"Yes, milady." The nurse looked unhappy.

Rowan spoke quietly, only for Clem. "Stay out here. Don't let him leave. Don't let anyone else in."

"Will do." Clem tilted her head side to side, cracking her neck, as if readying for a fight. She was in full uniform with a rail gun looped over her shoulder. The nurse slowly sat down and tried to make himself look small.

Noah, Denny and Rowan clustered around Ethan's bed. It was the first time they'd been together since Squad 54 had broken up. Having them there eased some of the worry that had been making her muscles tense for the last weeks. Now if only their commander were here.

He was coming home. She held onto those words like a charm against evil.

All this went through her mind as Noah examined Ethan.

Minna arrived. Dale came too and they both waited quietly by the door. No one spoke. Rowan barely breathed.

Finally, Noah sat back. A deep line creased his brow as it always did when he fought with his knack's backlash.

"Well, I can't find anything wrong with him." Noah wiped sweat from around his eyes. "He seems in perfect health, except that he seems…stunted. I'm not sure that's the right word. He's actually in exceptional shape for someone who's been bedridden for this long."

"The nurses take care that he doesn't develop sores," Rowan said.

"It's more than that. He grew up in a coma. His muscles should be atrophied. He should be deformed. But he's not. Not really. If he woke right now, he might not be able to walk, but it wouldn't take long."

"So when you say stunted…"

"I mean blocked. It's like something is holding him back. That's all I can sense."

"I can see the spell on him, Evani," Minna said. "It hangs over him like a dark miasma."

"And you agree with this?" she asked Denny. He nodded.

Dale had been spot on. Atherton wanted to rule and an incapacitated heir gave him unlimited powers. Renata was complicit in this treason.

Rowan sank into the chair beside Ethan's bed. Could they be heartless enough to leave a boy in this hell of a limbo for twenty years?

Yes, they could.

Rowan sank into the chair beside Ethan's bed. Could Atherton be so heartless that he would leave a boy to exist in this hell of a limbo just so he could rule in New Torwood?

Yes, he could.

And she'd let it happen. She dug her fingers into her scalp as if she could massage her brain and get it working faster.

When she finally looked up, she found all eyes watching her.

This was it. This was the moment when she went from being a princess to being a queen, even if she never ended up wearing the crown.

"Here's what we're going to do. Dale, set up a meeting with Chancellor March."

"And General Lind," Dale said. "He's on our side and if we plan to arrest Dr. Renata," they paused and glanced at Rowan until she gave her nodding approval. "If we want to hold Renata, we need the backing of the keepers."

"Good. Do it." Dale looked shaken by the news of Ethan's state, and she was glad to give them a job to occupy their attention.

"While Dale puts that in motion, the rest of us need to find a way to wake up my brother."

Minna stepped forward. "Evani, that is ill advised."

"Why? You said that Renata was holding him under a spell. Let's break it." She was so close to seeing her brother alive again, she didn't want to put it off any longer.

"The doctor has cursed him, Evani, but she is also keeping him alive. Have you seen how each time she heals him, she seems diminished afterward?"

Rowan nodded.

"That is because she gives a little of her magic to the prince. It is his only sustenance, but it is powerful. And this magic is all tangled up with the curse. One cannot be broken without the other. At least I cannot do it."

"And if we break both the curse and the spell keeping him alive?"

Minna shrugged. "I don't know. Maybe nothing. But it will take time for the curse to wear off and without Renata's healing spell, he may not survive it."

Rowan ground her teeth, thinking in circles around Minna's perplexing explanation. "So you say we need to break the curse but not the healing spell. And you can't do that?"

"Not me, Evani. I am the least of the mages in my family. My magic is but a bone shard compared to a femur."

Rowan blinked. Minna's metaphors were always a little gruesome.

"But that means you know someone who could do it."

"Yes, Evani. There are a few luminas in Benni with the knowledge. My brother Dalkyn is one. And I suggest he does it soon because Dr. Renata's bones are brittle."

"I will think about it." Sending a message to the Ebos would take time. "But first I think we have a minister to arrest."

40

BETWEEN REAL AND IDEAL

Nathan and Therrin conferred, then the Taiga chief called to what was left of his fighters, and the warriors loped away like half-wild beasts, shouting and singing their victory.

"He claims their debt to us is paid," Nathan said. "But if we plan to go to war against the humans, they will fight with us."

They were standing in the open Meadows with the carnage from their fight drying in the sun. The crows were already feasting.

"War against the humans," Conall said. He'd not thought of it that way. Could Atherton and Wrede set them against the united front of Ebos and Taiga? He'd been worrying about war for weeks now, but he assumed it would be between New Torwood and the southern cities. The scale of the pending conflict was growing.

"I have to get back to the city," he said.

Nathan nodded. "I know. I wanted to go with you, but Omika must know what happened here. We'll travel south with you for a day, and then turn west."

"Thank you." Conall felt his chest tighten. He'd just found his brother. He wasn't ready to lose him again.

Nathan nudged him with his shoulder. "Maybe we can run as wolves before I leave."

Conall spoke past the roughness in his throat. "Better than riding those saints-damned ponies. My legs are cramping just thinking about it."

Nathan laughed, but it was humor in the face of death, and the brothers turned back to the gruesome task of sorting through the dead.

There were more gaunts than humans on the killing field, a few Taiga...and Cob. Irva cut off his hand, wrapped it in a cloth and tucked it into her saddle bag. They buried him where he'd fallen after a short ceremony.

They didn't disturb the slain Taiga.

"They can be touchy about their dead," Nathan said. "They'll be back to carry them home."

After thoroughly searching the fallen soldiers and gaunts, they were left to rot in the sun. They found several trigger devices that the soldiers had used to control the gaunts.

"Their mechs are evolving quickly," Conall said as he handed the devices to Nathan. "This is already different than the one I saw a few weeks ago." Nathan passed the devices to Rudi. The Rati would deconstruct them and hopefully find a way to block or break the connection to the gaunts.

There were some injuries in their crew. Kelli needed Irva's healing for a gash across her stomach before they could move out. The others were banged up and bruised, but everyone agreed they wanted to get away from the smell of death, which was already hanging over the clearing.

Everyone but Banerjee.

He was already regretting his promise to travel to New Torwood and speak in front of the council. Mechs don't ride. The articulation in his legs let him walk, jump and squat, but not straddle a pony. In the end, they draped him over the back of Cob's pony and strapped him down. Neither the pony nor Banerjee were happy with this arrangement.

"I feel most undignified," Banerjee said. His head rested against the mare's flanks while his feet dangled over the other side.

"Sorry, old chap," Nathan patted the mech's back. "You'll slow us down if you walk."

Banerjee made a pneumatic hiss of displeasure.

It was already well past midday when they set out. Nathan and Conall shed their human skins and ran as wolves. As they headed south, the grass became longer and they made a game of darting through it. Misha pounced on Garou and they tumbled, growling and snarling.

"I wish you two would stop that," Rudi grumbled. Garou pranced beside Rudi's pony with his tongue lolling. He dashed into the grass to scatter a flock of buntings. Conall urged him on with a whoop. They hadn't felt this free in years.

Their brother was alive. And they were going home.

Ailen had hidden a bad puncture wound, and it had festered. Late in the afternoon, he dropped from his horse like a stone. They made an early camp while Irva poured her healing into him. Afterward, the lumina ate from their rations before curling up on her bedroll. Healing took a toll. Kelli was on watch. The others sat beside the small fire they'd made more for comfort than warmth, passing around a flask of yenni.

There wasn't much wood and the fire burned low. Conall and Nathan reminisced for an hour. Conall caught him up on his visit to their old homestead, ending with Lydan's gift of burial for Ianna. That put a damper on the nostalgia and conversation died with the fire.

Conall glanced at Banerjee. The mech sat on a rock in a brooding pose, with his feet wide and forearms resting on exposed knee joints. His hands hung down as did his head. His eyes had stop spinning, but they seemed closed off, as if the mech were lost in deep thoughts.

What do mechs think about? Garou asked.

Oil cans and circuit boards, I suppose.

Conall noticed that even though the Rati didn't have the usual Ebos aversion to mechs, they kept out of Banerjee's way. Rudi, in particular, kept throwing glances at Banerjee as if he might leap up and murder them all.

Banerjee shifted on his rock. The hiss of his gears sounded like a snake creeping through the grass.

Rudi shot him a dark look.

"Were there mechs like him on Essa?" Conall asked.

"Worse." Rudi shook his head.

Everyone knew that the elves came through the veil during the

Resurgence, but Conall had never heard stories about the how or the why.

He tossed the flask to Rudi. "We told you our stories. Now it's your turn. How did the Ebos end up here?"

Rudi looked up and scrunched his face.

"To Benni? Or to the Meadows?"

"To this world. Why did you leave Essa?"

Rudi stirred the fire with a stick. The flames reignited, lighting his face with a ghoulish glow. "There was a hole. We did not make it." He tilted his head and hummed. "Or maybe, yes. I do not know. Our people were mostly lost by then. Some jumped to this world. Too few. Hundreds maybe, yes? But not more."

Conall let that sink in. It was probably rude to ask, but he wanted to know. "How did your people die out? Nathan said something about mechs destroying cities, but I can't see how that could happen."

Rudi scoffed. "We were like you once. Farmers, hunters, gatherers, yes?" He smiled. "We were better at it. Our archers would beat your rangers. We were artists, poets and musicians. Our world was not perfect, but it was…" He seemed at a loss.

"Perfect adjacent," Nathan supplied.

"Yes, yes." Rudi made finger guns and pointed them at Nathan. It was such an oddly human gesture from the elf.

"We broke perfection. We created mechs that could think, yes?" He tapped his head with a finger. "Intelligent mechs. They learned."

"That's not possible," Conall said. Rudi looked pointedly at Banerjee.

"Possible, yes. We did not stick memories inside mechs like Elsie. Maybe we should have, yes? Yes. Our mechs were intelligent but without coho-ne-teno. Soulless. They learned. We fed them knowledge, lore, stories, histories. Everything." Rudi fell silent and mimicked Banerjee's brooding.

Nathan picked up the story. "Remember when we were kids and Ianna brought home that ancient book about the robots that took over the world?"

Conall remembered the book—*Robot Law*, or something like that. Robots had risen up and learned to make weapons. They were fast and nearly indestructible. And when one fell, they were replaced with two more. Robots who'd been created to serve humans soon decided that humans were the scourge. They systematically tried to wipe out every living thing. The book had given Conall nightmares for weeks.

"It was like that?"

Nathan grinned. "Not at all, but you should see your face!"

Conall wanted to punch him but they weren't kids anymore, so he settled for kicking dirt over his shoe.

"You'd think that would be how it ends," Nathan said. "But the truth is much more prosaic and much worse. When the mechs learned everything they could from the Ebos, they started teaching themselves. But there was a flaw in this learning. They were taught creative thinking to solve problems, and being creative means learning to lie. Falsehoods slipped into their programming. At first it was simple things—a recipe used saw dust instead of flour. A book list had made-up titles of famous authors. Silly mistakes that were easy to spot. But what about a list of edible plants that contained one deadly herb? Or a children's song that promoted violence? Or a home-cleaning solution that mixed bleach with vinegar?"

"I can see how those would be a problem. But couldn't you fix the programming?" Conall asked.

"We tried." Rudi looked solemn. "Mechs already surpassed our learning. Three errors compounded to six, yes? So fast. Then twelve and twenty-four. Simple math, yes?" He shrugged.

"From what I understand the tipping point happened faster than anyone imagined," Nathan said. "They didn't react until too late. Suddenly their mechs were spouting nothing but nonsense. And since Essa was linked by computers, the disease spread in minutes."

"I still don't see how that could destroy a civilization," Conall said. "So you go back to living without mechs."

Rudi shook his head. "Dams collapsed with no computers to regulate pressure. Cities flooded, yes? Power grids exploded. Boom!" He lifted his hands to the sky, mimicking an explosion. "Nuclear plants melted. Ships fell from sky. Trains…smashed." He pounded his fists together. "And no more doctors to heal wounded and sick. Only mechs." He spat on the ground. "Mechs who attacked patients. No healing. The end came, yes? Yes."

"*Not with a bang but a whimper*," Nathan said. "T.S. Elliot."

Conall nodded. He vaguely recognized the name from when Nathan went through his ancient poets phase.

They were quiet for a long moment, each envisioning this horror in the small flames of their campfire.

Nathan finally broke the silence. "And so the Rati remain vigilant against the mech threat."

"Is that why Omika is determined to have Ebos in the city?" Conall asked.

Nathan nodded. "The threat was minimal when mechs were made with ley-line magic. They were labor intensive and more art than machine. Thera changed that. Mech use has risen exponentially. They are for now, purely machine—vehicles, clocks and messengers. But the drive to make mechs intelligent is still there. Just look at Wrede and Elsie. These people have no conscience backing up their lust for progress." He nodded toward Banerjee. "The Ebos fear—we fear that another leap to intelligent mechs will destroy this world too."

Banerjee spoke without lifting his head. "Progress without con-con-conscience becomes extermination. Society devours itself from within."

That thought killed all conversation. They watched the fire burn out. Rudi began to snore. Nathan lay down with his back to the fire. Conall stayed where he was. The shift healed most wounds, but his shoulder still ached, and he was more comfortable sitting up. The stories he'd just heard kept him company like unsettled ghosts.

The locket warmed on his chest. He pulled it out, eager to hear from Rowan, but her message sent a chill through him.

Help. Urgent. Bring Dalkyn.

41

WALKING IN THE KING'S SHOES

ROWAN CROSSED THE LARGE ATRIUM in front of the Hall of Rule. As children, Ethan and Dale had rolled toy cats across its flagstones when court wasn't in session. Rowan's favorite memories were of common days, when the king listened to petitions from the general populace. People came from all over the city, bringing gifts for the royal family, hoping to curry favor for their causes. The hall had been full of life on those days—people, chickens, goats, mechs, children, and as much excitement as the harvest fair. And the sound she remembered most was her father—his booming laugh and his stern voice when he meted out judgments.

The regent refused to lower himself to hear common petitions. People had to put claims through his office, and that meant going through a league of underlings and a mountain of paperwork.

The Hall of Rule sat empty now. Rowan hurried past it. She entered the long corridor that led to the wing devoted to city government. Offices along this route held minor officials busy with their particular tasks—small tasks that built one on top of the other to form the mighty workings of the city. This East Wing was where things happened. Ministers met here. Deals were made. Petitions signed.

An office had been assigned to her along this corridor, but until now, Rowan had never used it, preferring her more private offices near her rooms. Still, there was something to be said for being seen, especially with the right people. And with Atherton away on a tour of the Titan Thera Mines near Old Torwood, it was time to solidify the support she'd been courting all summer. The battle for the council was coming much sooner than she'd anticipated.

The busy schedule of meetings occupied her mind, so she didn't dwell on the nightmare waiting in the royal wing.

She'd failed Ethan. They all had. For years they'd left him caged in his own mind. If she stopped to think about it, the horror of that failure would undo her. But she wouldn't weep by his bed. Instead, she vowed to fix things, to see her brother take his rightful place on the throne. Only then would her guilt be assuaged.

She showed up fifteen minutes late for her first meeting, just enough time for the gossip mongers to find out who waited for her. No doubt news of this interview was already circulating through the East Wing.

Good. It was time to stir things up.

Avram walked so closely behind that he bumped into her when she stopped at the office door.

"I want you to take notes. Of everything. Every word she says, every look she makes. If a fly lands on her head, I want it documented. Got it?"

The secretary's Adam's apple bobbed as he swallowed hard. "Yes, Evani."

"Good." She took a moment to smooth down her tunic. She wished Dale was by her side, but they were busy arresting Dr. Renata.

She'd met with General Lind before breakfast. He'd been reluctant to detain a prime doctor and sitting minister, but Rowan had laid out all her cards. Lind was a loyalist, and when he learned of Renata's treachery in keeping the prince incapacitated all these years, he'd immediately promised to assume responsibility for the arrest. Rowan thanked him and sent Dale along to be sure the warrant was done by the books.

In a matter of hours the news would be public. Rowan hoped to have several alliances secured by then. This next encounter would go a long way to meeting that goal.

She entered the room and found two men waiting for her, each sitting on opposite sides of a conference table.

Rowan frowned. One of the men rose and extended his hand.

"Princess Andula. I am Kenneth Smith."

"I know who you are. I was expecting to meet with Flora Bosman." Smith was Flora's secretary or advisor. Rowan wasn't exactly sure what his position was within the Theracine hierarchy, but she wanted to speak with someone who had the authority to make deals.

"I apologize, but Ms. Bosman is in Old Torwood, touring the thera mine with the regent."

Of course she was. Rowan hesitated before sitting at the table.

"I assure you, that I have all the authority required to meet any requests you may have." Smith was smooth. A practiced politician. Pale hazel eyes contrasted with his dark skin. He was attractive, but tended to blend into the background until you noticed those eyes. Instead of windows into his soul, they were doors that kept everyone out. *Dead eyes,* she thought.

She glanced at the other man seated at the table.

Remy Padgett shrugged. The ambassador seemed wholly unconcerned by this turn of events.

"Fine. Let's get started." Rowan sat at the table. Avram sat a few chairs away. He immediately pulled out his notebook and started scribbling. Smith frowned at the secretary but said nothing. Rowan smiled. He was probably wondering why she wasn't using a scribe, why she preferred to go old school.

Let him wonder.

She cleared her throat. "I'm planning on making a proposal in council within the next few days…a proposal that will require a vote. I would like assurances, that when that time comes, Theracine's vote will fall on my side. Theracine and those ministers who are beholden to the corporation."

Smith's eyebrows rose.

"Ministers beholden to us?"

She didn't want to mention names though she was fairly certain that Minister Docker was in Theracine's pocket. But it wasn't those she mentioned so much as those she left out that would let Smith gauge the efficiency of her spy network. Or Dale's spy network. So she simply nodded.

"I see." Smith steepled his fingers and tapped them on his chin. "And I would assume this proposal will be…life changing?"

"It is."

They all understood what they were talking about. Rowan had said the words in her mind a hundred times, though never aloud. Treason. Rebellion. Coup. She was mobilizing the overthrow of her own government.

Kenneth Smith smiled. "And what will Theracine get in return for this vote?"

Rowan bit her tongue to keep back the words she really wanted to say—that in her father's time no corporation would ever have had a vote on the council. Instead, she smiled sweetly. "What do you want?"

Smith squinted at her. "They all told me you were stupid, shallow. A silly girl who wasn't right in the head." He tapped a finger against his temple.

Rowan didn't bother to ask who "they" were. She knew how most of the nobles saw her.

"But I see they were wrong," Smith said. "Or they were lying. Instead of making me an offer, you ask what I want. Most of your ministers don't understand this basic rule of negotiating. Don't give away what you don't have to. Fine. I'll play along. I want the water pumps. Stop blocking their construction and installation."

Interesting. "I want." Not "we want" or "Theracine wants." She was beginning to wonder about this Kenneth Smith. Maybe he wasn't Flora Bosman's underling at all.

Rowan chose her next words carefully, not wanting to tip her hat and give any indication that she knew about thera's dark side. But there was no way she would let her city's water supply be contaminated either.

She smiled. "I will find a way to revive Talos."

Smith spread his hands. "You might. It's a long shot, but even if you succeed, what will be the cost? How long will you let the city go thirsty?" His lips spread in a wide smile, showing off impeccably white teeth.

"I agree. It isn't an ideal situation. How about this. I won't block the construction of the thera pumps. Or the installation…as a back up system. When Talos comes back online, the thera pumps take a back seat."

Smith didn't lose his smile, but he sat back in his chair. "It's not enough. Not for what you're asking." Again they skirted around using that word—treason. Smith waved a hand "Some vague assurance that the city might need our thera pumps in the future. It's not enough."

"I thought you might say that. Which is why I asked Ambassador Padgett to join us."

Smith narrowed his eyes. Rowan couldn't be certain of how the ministers would vote, but neither could Smith, and Rowan was about to show him that she had support outside the council.

"Ambassador Padgett and I have become friends in the short time he's been here, haven't we?" She gave his arm a friendly pat. Remy's eyes lit up. He liked a good game.

"Indeed we have. It turns out that the princess and I have a passion for fine dining. In fact I have invited the princess to visit our great city in the south to sample some of the finest cuisine in the world."

"To which I replied that I would love to travel to Dowchester, if only the journey weren't so long. And Remy…" She feigned embarrassment for being so informal. "I mean Ambassador Padgett has pledged his city's support for the new highway in order to make my journey more comfortable."

"Indeed I have put the proposal before King Erskine and Queen Tabina and they've ordered me to approve it." Remy opened a folder and passed a document to Smith. It outlined the new highway, the bridges, the lumber rations required, and even the soldiers pledged from both cities to keep travel along the new road safe. Rowan tapped the empty space beside Remy's signature that was scrawled across the bottom of the last document.

"All it needs is the regent's signature," she said, "which I'm certain will be no trouble to obtain…in two days time."

Smith's grin faded, but not because he was angry. He was assessing her. "And you're certain. In two days, the regent will sign."

"With your support, yes."

Smith drummed his fingers on the table and frowned. He was just realizing that he'd been played. The highway was bait he couldn't resist. Negotiations for the new road had stalled, with King Erskine making demands that no one in New Torwood could meet. Of course, that had been a stalling tactic.

Those pale eyes gave nothing away, but Smith said, "You will have my backing. In two days time." He made a motion to rise, but Rowan stopped him.

"Perhaps a sign of goodwill from Theracine in the meantime? Just so the, uh, regent will know to count on your promise?" Before he could balk, she added. "Water. That's all I want. Commit to using your resources to bring water from the river into the city until the thera pumps are online. I promise that all the credit will go to the Theracine Corporation. Goodwill can go a long way."

Smith shook his head and let out a rough sound that might have been a laugh. "They were definitely wrong about you." He left without making that final promise, but Rowan had high hopes that the city's thirsty residents would soon be getting some relief by way of the Theracine Corporation.

"You play a dangerous game," Remy said. "This man, this corporation, they hold too much money in your city. All that wealth in one pocket is power. And now you give them more power by bringing them the goodwill of your citizens. If you're not careful, there will be no room for a regent or a monarch in New Torwood."

"I know. But I have to do something. We need water and I need their vote."

Remy handed her the treaty. "As soon as this is signed, I will be heading south. It was no joke, my offer. There will always be a safe haven for you in Dowchester."

She had no doubt he meant it, but Rowan was learning that no entity, not a corporation, not a guild, not a minister or even an ambassador granted any favor without wanting a reward. She wasn't sure she could give Remy the reward he wanted.

"Thank you. I do hope to see your fantastic city one day, but not as an exile."

"Of course. I will wait for the treaty to be signed. Goodbye, Princess." He bowed over her fingers and kissed each of her knuckles. Maybe it was a southern thing.

Clem waited for her in the atrium.

"You have visitors."

"Visitors? Who?"

By her calculations, Conall couldn't arrive for another three days. She hadn't even heard from him since she sent her desperate plea for help, but she knew he often ran as the wolf and it could be days before he saw it.

Clem didn't answer. She just smiled and started walking toward the West Wing. Rowan followed. When they reached the west atrium, she stopped to hand the signed highway treaty to Avram. "Take this back to my office and lock it up." Avram nodded and headed straight through the atrium toward the offices. Rowan followed Clem down the right-hand corridor toward her private rooms. Now she was intrigued. Who would Clem bring to her private suite?

Clem opened the door and they were greeted by a strange mech valet. He was as tall as her shoulder, with a rusted helmet for a head and crazy eyes.

"Greetings, Princess Andula. I looked forward to meeting you-you-you." Except for the stutter, the mech spoke with strangely human articulation. His language module was even better than Roger's. Then he bowed, smacking his head on the door. He rose, turned and slammed his head into the wall again before heading back into the room.

Rowan turned a questioning look on Clem, but she only shrugged and watched the odd mech with a faintly amused expression.

Minna wouldn't let anyone dangerous in, so Rowan stepped into the room. Minna stood by the seating area with two Ebos she didn't recognize. They all turned to her as she entered, but Rowan had eyes only for the other figure in the room, standing by the balcony with his back to the door. She knew the cut of those shoulders and that shaggy blond hair.

"Conall!"

He turned with a smile that lit him from the inside out. In seconds, she found herself in his arms and the rest of the world faded.

42

PRINCESS EVIL WENCH

ROWAN HAD CHANGED. CONALL COULD see it from across the room as she stood in the doorway with confusion wrinkling her nose. She stood taller, as if she no longer tried to hide from the world. Her hair had grown out and someone had styled it to fall in graceful waves around her shoulders. She wore her own version of high fashion, taking the elements of current trends such as embroidered collars and sleeves, but pairing them with flowing pants and a long tunic in navy blue that was both regal and saints-damned sexy as it hugged her curves.

For a second, he wondered if his princess—the one who preferred ranger caps to tiaras—was still in there somewhere.

And then she was running across the room and he remembered how perfectly she fit into his arms, as if that crook in his shoulder had been made for her. He was home.

Everyone else in the room suddenly had somewhere else to be. Clem whistled for Phalian who was squawking and flapping around the ceiling. Rudi even ushered Banerjee out the door.

"I thought…" Rowan cut off her own greeting with a kiss as if she needed the connection more than words. He realized he was clutching her shoulders too tightly and eased his grip. Her body, in that flimsy material, pressed against the length of him. Garou made a happy noise and it rumbled from Conall's throat as he leaned into the kiss. His lips were chapped from too much sun and wind. Hers were soft and yielding. His beard scraped her, and he tried to hold back, but she pulled him closer, her fingers twining in the hair at his nape.

When they finally came up for air, Rowan leaned her head against his chest. He kissed the top of her hair. She was shaking.

"Hey!" He tipped her head up, ready to brush away tears, but saw that she was laughing. Her chin was rubbed raw from his beard and her eyes flashed with the fire he remembered. His princess.

"What are you laughing about?"

Rowan brushed away a stray tear. "You need a haircut. And a shave. And you smell like road dirt and horse. And saints, I missed you so much."

He kissed the end of her nose. "I missed you too. Maybe, milady could show me the way to the bath?"

Sometime later, after Rowan had convinced her maids that she was quite capable of turning on a faucet all by herself, and no, she didn't need help washing or drying or laying out fresh clothes, and yes, they should leave her alone with the dangerous-looking stranger…after all that, they were finally alone.

Conall undressed hurriedly. She examined every inch of him as she struggled to undo the ties at the back of her tunic.

"You're thin," she pronounced. "And you're favoring your shoulder." Then she huffed out a breath of frustration as the ties refused to come undone.

"Let me." He turned her around and swept her hair aside, then planted a kiss on the delicate curve of her neck. His fingers fumbled at the tie until the tunic finally fell away. His lips worked their way down her spine, coaxing little moans from her. She shimmied out of her underclothes and leggings and stood naked before him.

She wouldn't meet his eye, but instead reached over and turned on the faucet. Hot water started filling the tub and steam kissed her skin. He couldn't mask the hunger in him as his eyes ranged all over her lithe body. She was perfect—long limbed, supple, soft in the right places and strong where she needed it.

Sitting on the tiled edge of the tub, she lowered her eyes. She was blushing!

"What's the matter?" This wasn't their first time. Had he done something wrong? Something to make her turn away from him?

With her left hand she squeezed her mech wrist.

"It's just that, I have to take this off. For the bath. No one but me has seen my arm in a long time—or what's left of it. I guess I'm shy about it."

She lifted her chin, her expression halfway between fear and defiance. Garou scowled in the back of his mind. Their mate should never be made to feel less than perfect.

Conall crouched and spread her knees so he could brace them on either side of his hips, then he held her gaze.

"Never hide from me."

Two spots of pink stood out on her cheeks. She touched the inside of her mech arm—three fast taps, two slow—and repeated it on the outside latch. Something clicked and hissed. She turned the mech and pulled it away to reveal a rounded pink limb with two silver disks implanted on either side. He lifted her elbow to his mouth and kissed it. His fingers massaged the sensitive skin, while his lips moved onto her breast. He took her nipple in his mouth and sucked. Her back arched. He rose bringing her with him. She wrapped her legs around his hips, and he carried her to the settee in the corner. His lips never left her skin. And while the room filled with steam, he rediscovered every crease of elbow and knee, every dimple, every fine line that made her special.

Sometime later, they remembered the running water and turned it off before the tub overflowed. Conall sank into the blissfully hot bath and Rowan climbed in behind him. He leaned against her and she soaked him with a sponge before lathering his hair with lavender-scented soap. He groaned as her nails dug into his scalp, sending shivers right into his legs. He reached back and cupped her breast, slippery from the soapy water.

"Now you're just being greedy," she said.

"It's been a long couple of months. Greed isn't the only thing I'm feeling." He tried to pull her into his lap.

"Not yet! You'll get me covered in suds."

"You're already covered in my road dirt."

She let her right arm drape over his shoulder. He turned his head and kissed her on the inside of the elbow where a small port normally connected to her mech.

"You were already a very dirty girl."

She let out a gasp of outrage and pushed down on his shoulders. The tub was big enough that he slipped underwater and came up sputtering.

"You evil wench!" He grabbed her around the waist and pulled her into the water with him.

"Just trying to rinse your hair, and that's Princess Evil Wench to you, Commander!"

An hour later, with their passion sated once again, they lay in the tepid water with no desire to get out and get dressed. Rowan sat between his legs with her back to his chest. He played with her wet hair, making curlicues where it fell across his arm.

"How did you get here so fast?" Rowan asked.

"When I got your message we were already halfway to Oxeye."

"But I thought you were in Benni."

"We had a change of plans." He paused. There was so much to tell her, he didn't know where to start. "I sent Nathan back to fetch Dalkyn, but Irva and Rudi and I came right here. We were lucky enough to get a boat out of Oxeye. That cut the travel time in half."

Rowan shifted to look up at him. Her body slipping against his caused him to stir again, but the serious look in her eye shut down any thoughts of more romance.

"Nathan? You found your brother?"

"I did. And yes, he's alive. He'll convince Dalkyn to come, but in the meantime, Irva is also a mage. Maybe she can help, if you finally tell me what was so urgent."

Rowan sighed and fell back against his chest. "It's Ethan. Minna suspected and Denny confirmed it. He's not in a coma. Dr. Renata—and I assume the regent too—have conspired for years to keep him in that state, under some kind of curse."

"Fucking bastards." The profanity was not strong enough for the rage that her words ignited in him. His fist hit the water, sending up a spray. A boy's life had been taken. A man's destiny played like a pawn piece.

"What do you want us to do? Tell me everything."

So she did. She told him how they needed Dalkyn to break the curse and keep Ethan alive long enough to come out of it. She told him about arresting Renata, about visiting Noah at the temple and their theories about thera. About Roger's new programming and what he'd found so far on the scribe's cachet.

"That's how we learned that Elsie Myer was working with Wrede."

Conall grunted. They'd come to the same conclusion at about the same time.

"The problem is, Sandra Kane was a scribe, not a scientist. Roger has decoded her files, but most of the time, she was recording things she didn't understand. I don't know how helpful those recordings will be in front of the council."

Conall thought about Banerjee and the wealth of information stored in his broken memory.

"I can probably help with that. And I have so much to tell you, but your fingers are turning to prunes and I think Irva should see Ethan as soon as possible."

"I don't know. Minna says the curse is beyond even her capabilities."

"Short of Omika, Irva might be the strongest mage the Ebos have. If she's willing, I think we can wake your brother tonight."

Rowan burst into tears. It was sudden, like a summer storm.

She wiped her eyes with a wet hand and smiled shakily.

"I'm sorry, it's just been…hard. So much has happened since you left. I feel brittle under the weight of it all." The storm was over as quickly as it began and Rowan was once again the tough, strong princess. But he'd seen the fear and despair underneath that mask, and he vowed that he would never again leave her to face those alone.

43

BETWEEN THE GEARS AND THE GRIND

DALE LOOKED UP AS ROWAN entered Ethan's room with Conall and Irva following.

"Have you been here all day?" she asked. They looked like they'd slept in his clothes.

"Mostly." Dale ran a hand over their eyes. "But I did as you asked. General Lind is preparing the warrant for Renata's arrest. She should be secured by this evening, long before Atherton returns." Dale glanced at Ethan. "Then I had to come here. I had to try to reach him."

Dale's eyes were deeply shadowed, hollowed out from lack of sleep and proper nutrition. The collection of insects on Ethan's pillow was a testament to how much Dale's presence agitated her brother. She had to put a stop to it.

She circled the bed and tugged on Dale's arm.

"Leave him be now. It's going to be okay. This is Irva." She pointed to the slight Ebos who lingered in the doorway. "She can help Ethan. We're going to get him back and everything will be all right."

Dale shook their head. "It won't be all right. It can't be. We left him like that." They pointed at Ethan with a shaky hand. "For *years*! Oh, saints, how could we have left him like that?" Dale crumpled into the chair again, shoulders heaving with the effort to hold back tears.

Rowan patted their shoulder. Dale had always felt things too keenly. Not that she didn't have guilt over Ethan's condition. She did. It woke her before dawn most days with a clawing anxiety that had no release. But she used that guilt to fuel action, to propel her forward in this dark game of politics that had been thrust upon her.

328

Dale seemed to have given up. Did that mean Dale loved Ethan more than she did? Maybe. Or maybe the truth about that fateful day when they were children had finally cracked the careful shell Dale had built as protection from those horrors. And maybe that was a good thing. Ethan and Dale could now heal together.

Phalian circled the room near the ceiling, silent except for the click of his wings. Rowan let him be. He was sensitive to stress, and this room stank of it.

Irva was already examining Ethan. She was a thin figure. Coupled with the Ebos stature, she seemed almost childlike, until you looked into her eyes. They were dark blue and fathomless, as if they held the wisdom of ocean and sky. She didn't wear the usual Ebos robe but a plain tunic and loose pants. The bone piercings and jewelry were also absent. Rowan noted the same austere dress on the other Ebos. Conall had introduced him as Rudi, and she wondered where he'd found these most unusual elves.

Irva picked up Ethan's hands and pinched each fingernail until it turned red. Then she felt the bones of every knuckle, squeezing up toward his wrist, then his elbow and shoulder. She brushed aside a beetle and pressed hands to his chest, then bowed her head as if listening. She stayed like that for a long time until she finally lifted her head. Tiny lines framed her mouth when she smiled.

"The curse is very strong. It has been worked into his blood and bones for many years, like vines suffocating a tree but also holding it upright. It will not be easy to untangle these vines. And when I do, we must be ready to support the weak tree that will emerge."

"So you can do it? You can break the curse?" Rowan asked. Dale's hand snaked out to grip hers and she squeezed it.

"Yes." Irva stood straighter. "I am confident I can break it."

"Is it dangerous?" Dale asked.

Irva frowned and the creases around her lips deepened. Rowan's mech hand creaked as she clenched it in a fist.

"There is always danger when curses are involved. They are like…" She turned to Minna and muttered a word in Essian.

"They are like bombs," Minna said.

"Yes, like bombs." Irva made an opening motion with both hands. "They can explode and hurt more than just the cursed one."

Rowan pulled Minna out of the room.

"Do you trust her?" she asked.

Minna nodded. "Before Irva became one of the Rati, she was a great lumina in Benni. She taught Dalkyn and me when our bones were still soft."

Rowan had heard Minna use that expression before. It meant when they were children.

"What is the Rati?"

"It is…" Minna seemed at a loss for words. "It does not matter in this place. Irva is a better mage than even Dalkyn. That is the only importance."

Rowan sucked in a deep breath and returned to Ethan's room.

"All right. We're going to do this. What do you need from us."

Irva looked around the room. "Fresh water. The prince will be thirsty when this is over. A sharp blade, sterilized. And bandages."

Minna sent Alice running for the supplies. Rowan lingered beside the bed. Dale was clutching Ethan's hand.

"Are we in the way?" she asked. "Should we leave?"

"No. Stay by your brother. He knows you are here. Touch him if you will. It will help him to find his way back to the living."

Rowan nodded though Irva wasn't looking at her. The lumina's attention was fixed on the pulse on Ethan's neck the way a starving vampire hunted its next feed. Then Rowan could feel the pulse too, thrumming under her mech fingers that gripped Ethan's wrist.

Alice returned with a tray holding the supplies and laid it on the bedside table.

"Please make sure we aren't disturbed," Rowan said. Alice gave a fumbling curtsy and dashed out the door, closing it behind her. Minna put her back to the door. Irva stood on one side of the bed. Dale and Rowan crowded the other side, and Conall lurked behind them, a solid presence propping up her resolve.

After a few minutes of intently examining the veins on Ethan's arms, Irva picked up the small blade from the tray.

"I am sorry," she said. "This will hurt. There is no other way."

Rowan hesitated, then nodded.

Irva opened a red line across Ethan's forearm. He didn't move. She dipped her fingers in the blood and dragged a line down his arm.

Ethan's eyes twitched behind closed lids.

Irva drew out more blood. A low hum resounded through the room, and Rowan thought it was coming from the mage. Her eyes were closed and her fingers made intricate movements in the blood as if she were twisting fibers into yarn.

Something hit the window. Rowan turned to see a swarm of insects battering the glass—flies, bees, moths, beetles. That was the source of the hum. Phalian tried to fly through the window and hit the glass with a bang. Conall pulled the curtains closed, and Rowan called the bird to her. Phalian's claws skittered on her shoulder and dug in. The stab of pain was grounding.

Rowan's mech fingers clutched Ethan's hand and they itched as magic filled the room. Her other hand reached back for Conall and his fingers interlaced with hers.

Irva began to chant, a low droning sound that matched the hum of insects. Her voice rose to a piercing pitch. Ethan's legs bucked out. His back arched. A dozen beetles shot from under the blankets and scattered. Outside, insects battered themselves against the glass. Ethan's head rolled back and the veins on his neck stood out in rigid lines.

"Stop! You're hurting him!" Dale lunged at Irva.

"No!" Rowan threw her arms around Dale's waist and dragged them back. She pushed Dale toward the chair and they collapsed into it, moaning in despair.

She reached for Ethan's free hand again as the chant died away. Irva bowed and her hair draped around her face. Her shoulders heaved as she tried to catch a breath. Ethan lay against his pillow, once again still as a corpse except for the line of sweat dripping down his temple.

The chant began again. Conall wrapped his arms around Rowan and they stayed locked like that, swaying to the sound of Irva's magic. The lumina lifted her head. Hair clung to her damp cheeks. Her eyes seemed to sizzle with blue fire. She opened another line of blood, this time on Ethan's chest, next to the thin scars that had marked him on the day he'd fallen into the coma. Irva dragged her fingers through blood, painting swirls of red over his skin.

Her voice rose to a crescendo and died.

Rowan held her breath until her heart ached. Irva wasn't done. She sucked in another breath and began again. Her face was red, her eyes bulging. Every time she cut him, Ethan's body bucked and fell limp.

Dale whimpered. They could no longer watch. Rowan couldn't tear her eyes away.

Another crescendoing cry, another seizure. Irva collapsed over Ethan, who slept on.

Rowan thought that was the last of it. Irva had nothing left to give. Her breath came in ragged gasps. Minna stepped forward. She parted Irva's matted hair and tucked the bloody locks behind her ear.

"Essami, please let me help."

The lumina nodded and sat up. Minna's hand rested on her shoulder. She smiled at Rowan and held out her other hand.

"Let us give what we can, Evani."

Rowan clutched her fingers.

Irva began the chant. Her voice was raw and faded out. She opened another cut on Ethan's chest. When she leaned in to dip her fingers, she nearly fell over. Minna held her upright.

The air buzzed as if lightning had just struck, and Rowan felt…something. Like a string of electricity had just been pulled through her arm into Minna's grip. She nearly jerked her hand away, but Minna's reassuring smile stayed her.

"It hurts, Evani. But only a little. Close your eyes and think of your brother, of your love for him."

Rowan nodded. She tasted blood and realized that she'd bitten her tongue. With eyes closed, she felt that electric draw of magic through her again.

Irva's voice was rising.

A new voice joined her. A man's voice.

Rowan's eyes snapped open.

Ethan's frail body seized, twisting and arching. His eyes sprang open. A scream erupted from his lips.

Rowan gasped. Tears fell unchecked down her cheeks, but she wouldn't let go of Ethan or Minna to wipe them away.

Ethan fell back on the bed, unmoving.

The room fell silent, except for Dale's hiccuping cries.

Irva was lying across Ethan's outstretched arm with her head turned toward them. She looked dead. Blood was smeared across her cheek and clotting in her hair. It stained the sheets in a large red blossom.

Dale slumped into the chair, staring blankly at the still forms on the bed. Irva hadn't moved. Ethan was just as still. Rowan laid her ear against his chest.

There it was. A steady heartbeat. His chest rose to meet her ear and she let out a sound that was half-laugh, half-sob.

Irva finally stirred. She sat up and wiped blood from her face.

"Quickly. The bandages. Before he loses too much blood."

Minna took over, wrapping Ethan's arm firmly. Rowan wadded another bandage and pressed it to his chest.

Irva stood and swayed, then fell into a chair. She poured herself a glass of water with shaking hands. Conall stepped around the bed to help.

"Thank you." Irva's smile was wan. Her eyes had lost some of their luster.

"Did it work?" Rowan asked. "Why doesn't he wake up?"

"It worked. The curse is broken." Her voice grated like chalk on sand. "I was able to pull it from his blood. There may be residual effects for some time, but if he is strong, he will be able to fight those off."

"So when will he wake up?"

Irva shook her head. "When he is ready. We must have patience. His body has been asleep for years. His mind must remember how to wake up. It may be hours. It may be days. But he will wake." She took a roll of bandages, dipped it in her glass and wiped the blood from her face and hands.

Rowan finally remembered her manners. "Thank you. We will wait with him, but you must be exhausted. Please let me have someone show you to your room."

Irva nodded. Her legs buckled as soon as she rose. Minna took her arm and spoke in low Essian as she helped the lumina from the room.

Denny and Noah had been waiting outside. Noah cleared his throat and approached the bed. He examined Ethan and nodded.

"He's already stronger. It worked. He'll wake up soon."

Rowan nodded and didn't speak. She felt like a new spell had been cast over them. A waiting spell.

The door burst open and Dr. Renata stormed into the room.

"What is the meaning of this?" She saw the blood and her eyes blazed. "What have you done to him? Get out of here! All of you."

Rowan took a deep breath, but instead of facing Renata, she turned to Conall.

"Commander West, would you mind detaining Dr. Renata?"

Conall grinned. "You know, I'd really like that." He grabbed a roll of bandages from the side table, then pulled Renata's arm behind her back. Renata snarled and tried to squirm away, but Conall grabbed her other hand and tied them together. He spun her toward the door.

"Unhand me you…you stinking beast!" Renata sputtered. She was holding on to her ire, but it thinly masked fear.

"Dr. Renata, you are under arrest," Conall said. "You will be tried for treason against the crown for your part in keeping the prince and heir incapacitated."

"That is a lie! I saved him!" Renata shook herself, trying to break Conall's grip. "This is insanity. On whose authority can you do this?"

Renata's hair had come loose from its combs and fell over her face.

Rowan leaned in. "On my authority. Get used to it."

Conall dragged Renata out the door and Rowan followed them to the atrium where two keepers stood guard.

Rowan stood before the first keeper. "Please escort Dr. Renata to the dungeon. She's under arrest."

The guard's eyes bulged. His throat worked up and down as he tried to speak. "I, uh…I can't…" He glanced wildly around the atrium, looking for help.

"You can." Rowan's tone forced his gaze back to her. "Send a runner to General Lind if you need confirmation. But be quick about it."

The guard nodded, and his partner took off at a run.

While they waited, Renata filled the atrium with her poisonous diatribe.

"You will fall for this. You will be shown as the treasonous ones! You will all hang!" Noah walked back to Ethan's room and returned with another roll of bandages.

"You're fools! All of you." Renata shouted, spraying spit with her rage.

"You will let him die for your foolish…"

Noah shoved the roll into her mouth. She choked and her eyes nearly goggled from her head, but she was finally silent. Bless the saints.

"Thank you, Maven," Conall said.

"My pleasure, Commander."

A few minutes later, General Lind arrived with more keepers. They took Renata away, but the General lingered, watching Renata fight against every step.

"It has begun, then," Lind said.

"It has," Rowan answered.

"Is the prince awake?"

"Not yet, but he will be. Soon."

"And you're ready for what's to come?"

Rowan wanted to say, *no, I'll never be ready,* but she wouldn't show any weakness, not in front of the general.

She lifted her chin. "I am."

"Let Saint Mars watch over you, then."

Rowan swallowed hard and nodded. Mars was the patron saint of the keepers, but it didn't elude her that he was also once the god of war.

General Lind followed his keepers out of the atrium.

Rowan let out a slow breath and felt herself deflating.

"So what does come next?" Conall asked.

"I don't know." She ran a hand over her hair, pulling it from the ties that held it back. "There's been so much. Weeks of planning. Curve balls I didn't expect, like Talos. I still don't know what to do about him. And tomorrow, Atherton will challenge me when he finds out about Renata."

Conall took her hands. She could feel them shaking in his grip.

"One storm at a time," he said. "Just like out in the Meadows."

She bit her lip and nodded.

"Good, then I might be able to help with Talos. There's someone you need to meet."

44

HEART OF A MECH

CONALL DIDN'T UNDERSTAND EXACTLY WHAT had happened in Ethan's room, but there'd been some transfer of power between Rowan, Minna and Irva. It took a lot from Rowan. She was shaky and pale. He got her comfortable on the couch in her room and asked the page to have food brought up. Then he put a blanket over her lap and pushed a glass of honey wine into her hand.

"You're treating me like I'm sick."

"Not sick but maybe in need of some spoiling. And some sleep."

She is a warrior, Garou said. *She will sleep when the war is done.*

"Garou says you are a warrior. He's very proud of you."

Rowan smiled and sipped her drink. It put a bit of color back into her cheeks.

"Tell him he's the hero. He saved my life, after all."

Conall could feel Garou's pride like a tail wagging in his brain.

"His ego's big enough already."

Garou harrumphed.

When the food came, Rowan only nibbled at it. Conall left to find Banerjee. He was in the suite set aside for the Rati, along with Roger and Denny.

Rudi put his fingers to his lips and pointed to a closed door. "Irva is sleeping."

Conall nodded and turned his attention to the others.

"Hello, Commander." Denny lifted a hand in greeting.

"Denny. Glad to see you're well." The kid's gaze still struck a chord in Conall. There was just something...unknowable about the empath. He wasn't cagey, exactly, but hidden. Conall didn't like it.

336

"I've been helping Roger decipher the data on the cachet," Denny said. "Though Rudi here seems to know more about it than me."

"Ones and zeros," Rudi said.

"And Dr. Banerjee has narrowed down our search immensely," Denny said. "We have actual graphium memos between Atherton and Wrede."

Curious. Denny seemed to have accepted Dr. Banerjee without question.

"Is it enough to convict him?" Conall asked.

"Along with all the other evidence? Possibly." Denny fidgeted with his ratty old string. His nervous gesture wasn't reassuring and Conall frowned.

"We'll keep digging," Denny said.

Banerjee was sitting in the corner with Roger at his feet. The smaller mech's head was tilted back, and he gazed at Banerjee like a puppy waiting for a cookie.

"Right. The princess needs to speak with Banerjee and Rudi, but let's take this slow. One at a time. Banerjee, would you come with me?" The mech nodded and ponderously waded across the room. Roger zipped along behind him. Conall wondered if there was a bit of mech hero worship going on there.

When he ushered Banerjee into Rowan's suite, she put aside her wine and rose, letting the blanket fall to the floor.

Her eyes sparkled. He'd seen that look when she found Roger in the Meadows and when she stood on the wall to inspect Talos.

"Where did you find him?" She approached Banerjee who watched her with his unsettling eyes. "I saw him when you first arrived, but with everything that's happened, I forgot."

Conall cleared his throat. This wasn't going to be easy. "Princess Rowan Andula, may I present to you, Dr. Banerjee."

Rowan had been reaching for the mech, but she stopped.

"Hello, Princess." Banerjee made an attempt to bow, and his joints wheezed.

"I don't understand." Rowan stared at the mech valet with the spinning eyes. Conall knew exactly how she felt. It seemed impossible. Ludicrous, even.

"It's some dark mech-magery by Elsie Myer."

"You mean to say that this…this mech is Dr. Banerjee? The one from the oasis? How is that possible?"

"It's all very complicated. Rudi would give you some convoluted explanation about the principles of programming, nanomechs and circuits or some such nonsense."

"Rudi, the other Ebos you brought? How can he even be in the same room with such mechs? Even Minna still cringes when she sees Roger."

"He's a Rati. They're different." Conall ran a hand through his hair. He was making a hash of this.

"Look. I don't know the mechanics of it. But this valet has all of Banerjee's memories, and he can feel things. Like the way Phalian can sense your emotions. Call it magic. Or mech. Or some bastard hybrid of the two. It doesn't really matter. All you need to know is that Elsie Myer transferred Banerjee's…consciousness for lack of a better word."

Rowan opened her mouth to speak, then shut it again and frowned. Phalian jumped from her shoulder and landed with a scrabbling of metal claws on Banerjee's shoulder. The mech's head swiveled with a hiss and he stared at the bird. His hand rose and he awkwardly patted Phalian's head, metal clanking on metal. Phalian didn't seem to mind.

Banerjee turned his attention back to Rowan.

"I am very glad-glad-glad to meet you."

"Thank you. May I?" She held out her mech hand, ready to touch the valet. Banerjee swiveled his head down and up, in a jerky nod.

Rowan laid her hand on his chest and closed her eyes. Conall knew she was reading the flow of magic through the mech-work. Eventually, she let her hand drop.

"It is you." Simple as that. Her knack cut through the doubt and confusion. It had taken him days to accept the valet was actually Banerjee, but she confirmed it with a touch.

"What happened to you?" she asked. "I mean why couldn't you keep your…your original body?"

It was a good question, one that Conall hadn't thought to ask.

"I got in the way. At the oasis. Elsie was supposed to kidnap-nap-nap me, but I suspected her betrayal even then. I helped Sandra Kane escape and a gaunt mauled me. Wrede was furious. He wanted my knack-knack-knack."

"Your knack? Why?"

"Banerjee can, or could, read cells down to their molecular level," Conall said.

"It is a form of empath magic," Banerjee explained. "Very effective for the kind of experiments Wrede is doing."

"But you can't do that now?"

Banerjee held out his metal fingers. "It was all in the touch. I lost that sense along with my knack."

"I see, but could you train another empath to do it?"

The pistons in Banerjee's arms ground as he lifted his hands in an attempt to shrug.

"Maybe."

"Well, if nothing else, we need to get you cleaned up. Those gears are stiff. And let's see if we can do something about that stutter."

"You must tell-tell-tell them." Banerjee's hand bumped against Rowan. He was trying to grip her arm. Conall stepped between them, but Rowan held onto Banerjee's hand anyway.

"Tell who? Tell them what?"

"My king. Erskine. He must know of the betrayal."

Rowan squeezed the mech's hand. "I have already done so. Your ambassador knows what happened. You may speak to him yourself. And I vow that those responsible will be brought to justice."

Banerjee was still for a long moment. It was hard to assign human emotions to that blank expression, but Conall thought he was assessing Rowan. His eyes were still and he looked more like a statue than a mech. Then his eyes started to spin and he stood back, breaking the connection.

"Wrede wanted my research. Only after I was wounded did they realize I had destroyed all of it. Suddenly, they needed me alive, but it was too-too-too late. They believe I hold the key in here." He tapped his head. "That is the real reason Elsie…did what she did."

"They key to what?"

"To finally cracking Wrede's own research. To making a human-gaunt hybrid, an indestructible soldier that can be controlled. So far he has been successful only to a certain degree. The gaunts are…unmanageable."

"It's true," Conall said. "We saw that in the field. Kill the human controller and the gaunt goes berserk."

Rowan frowned and Conall realized he hadn't told her about all his trials in the Meadows yet.

Banerjee's head tilted to the side, in a pose that Conall had come to recognize on the mech. It was his way of smiling since his lips no longer moved. "Berserk. Yes. All that strength and rage-rage-rage. It cannot be cured by magic alone."

"And you could cure them of this rage?" Rowan asked.

"Probably not. It is in their DNA. My knack allowed me to study such things, but altering them? I do not know. But Wrede will not stop until he has worn out every avenue. He doesn't care how many gaunts he mutilates or how many humans he murders."

"And do you hold the key?" Rowan asked. "If they get a hold of you or your research, will they succeed?"

Another hiss of pneumatics as he shrugged. "I don't-don't-don't know."

Rowan paced across the room, chewing on the end of her thumb, before pacing back to them.

"Okay. Let's put the problem of Wrede's experiments aside for now. We have Sandra Kane's cachet. Roger has been deciphering it for weeks. What I need is proof that Wrede murdered your team. And proof that Atherton approved that mission. If we have that, the rest doesn't matter."

"Your friend Denny and Rudi have found such proof. Sandra Kane-Kane-Kane documented much, and I believe a scribe's word is law in your city."

"And Banerjee has promised to testify in front of the council," Conall said. "Rudi too. The Rati are very knowledgeable in all things mech."

"I keep hearing that name," Rowan said. "Who are these Rati? Why don't they wear bones like the other Ebos? And how can they be so cavalier around mechs?"

"It's a really long story." Conall ran a hand over his eyes. They'd traveled nonstop for three days to get here. He'd barely slept on the boat from Oxeye because a storm had tossed them all night long. Now he was feeling the effects of exhaustion. And Rowan was nearing her limit too. There was a tightness about her eyes that hadn't been there before. They'd both been through the works and the big showdown was only beginning.

"Look, I'll tell you all about it, about finding Banerjee, the gaunts, and the Rati. Everything. But what's important to know right now is that with Sandra Kane's cachet and the information inside Banerjee's memory, we can prove that Atherton and Wrede conspired to kill the scientists at Eklridge and that they tried to kill us."

Rowan glanced over at the mech who watched them with his unnatural stillness.

"Will it be enough?" she asked.

"It will have to be."

Banerjee chose that moment to display his less savory qualities by turning on his heel to bang his head on the hearth. Phalian squawked and flew onto the mantle.

Rowan raised an eyebrow and stared at Conall.

"Uh, he does that sometimes. A bit of corrupted…something or other, Rudi says."

Roger wheeled over to Banerjee.

"Do not worry. I can find the corrupted memories and fix them. Would you like me to access Dr. Banerjee's system?"

"That's new." Conall frowned. The last time he'd seen Roger all the little mech could say was a squeaky, "Roger that!"

Rowan smiled. "He got an upgrade to his voice processor."

Conall admired her ability to roll with all this mech talk. He still stumbled over words like computer and processor.

Roger's wheels spun him around. "Please sit down."

Banerjee's head jerked downward to take in the smaller mech. Roger lifted his arm. The rusted bolt was gone and a sleek silver appendage had taken its place.

"You are too tall for me to reach," Roger said. "If you want my help, you must sit."

With a hiss, Banerjee's knees bent and he clanged to the ground, settling his back against the wall.

Roger's arm rose and a device like a key poked out of his hand. It joined to a port on Banerjee's chest. Conall could hear the connection whirring.

"How long will it take?" Rowan asked, but both mechs had gone silent.

"Come on." Conall took her arm. "Let's leave them to it."

"Yes, I should check on Ethan anyway."

Conall thought rest would be a better idea, but he could see a sort of manic determination in the set of Rowan's jaw, and he gave in. He'd made a vow to himself that he would protect this woman, but he was starting to realize that meant protecting her from herself too.

"All right. A quick visit, then I'm dragging you to bed."

She ran a finger along his jaw. "You are an insatiable wolf."

"To *sleep*, Striker."

She saluted. "Yes, Commander."

45

A Lifetime in Minutes

As they left her suite, Rowan heard raspy yells coming from Ethan's room. She ran down the hall. An anxious group of people hung around his doorway—Noah, Denny and Alice among them. Avram and Rudi were there too. Dale's panicked voice came from inside the room.

"I'm so sorry! Please forgive me." It was more blubbering than words.

Rowan skidded to a stop just inside the door. Ethan was curled in a ball at the top of the bed, naked except for his underwear and a sheet that he clutched to his chest like a lifeline. He clawed at the bandage on his arm. His eyes were huge and round in a face that was all sharp angles and dark shadows. Dale clutched at his foot, the only thing within reach, and continued to plea for forgiveness—forgiveness that Ethan, in his current state was unable to give or even understand.

"Denny! Help Ethan!" Rowan rounded the bed and grabbed Dale by the shoulders. Dale fell into her arms, sobbing. Rowan wasn't having it. She pushed them away. "Stand up! Stop this right now. You're upsetting Ethan!"

Dale sucked in a breath, hiccuped out a last sob, and wiped their nose with a handkerchief. That was better. She didn't know what had gotten into them. Her whole life, Dale had been her rock. The one who stood stoically by her side when they told her about her father, about her missing arm, about Ethan never waking. Until Squad 54 came along, Dale had been her only friend. She'd leaned on them so often, and now? Now she wanted to shake some sense into them. All these years, they'd held in this fear, anger, and sadness. Ethan's waking was like the cork popping on all those emotions.

Maybe it was time to let Dale lean on her.

She took the handkerchief and wiped their cheeks. Dale sniffled and looked lost.

"Go get cleaned up. Have something to eat and sleep."

"I…I can't."

"You can. I'll have food and valerian tea brought to your rooms. Now, go." She shooed them toward the door. Dale looked back at Ethan.

"I promise he'll be here when you wake, but you're no good to him like this."

Dale nodded and left the room like they were off to their own execution.

Rowan turned to face her brother. Denny was sitting beside him, cloaking Ethan in calming vibes. Ethan had uncurled, and he lay on his side. He gazed at Rowan with eyes full of wonder. A butterfly had landed on his head. How did they even get inside? She brushed it aside, smoothing his hair at the same time.

"Mother?" He gazed up at her in wonder.

She shook her head. "No, Ethan. It's me, Rowan."

He reached for her hair where it rested on her shoulder. "But you look just like Mother." His voice rasped and he put a hand to his throat.

She took his hand in both of hers and squeezed. His eyes locked onto her mech arm and widened.

Oh, saints. There was so much to tell him. Where did she even start? How did she fill him in about the life he'd missed?

Conall had come into the room and he sat in the chair where Bella usually sat.

Bella! She'd have to tell her aunt about Ethan soon. If she heard it from anyone else, she'd be furious.

Rowan turned to the others waiting at the door.

"I would like some time alone with my brother, please."

Noah nodded and turned away, taking Avram, Rudi and the others with him.

Denny squeezed Rowan's shoulder.

"Don't go too far," she said. "In case I need you."

Denny nodded and left.

Conall rose from the chair, but Rowan urged him to sit.

"Stay, please?" She tried to fill her eyes with the need she felt. She had no idea what she was doing. The grand plan she'd had for taking back their birthright had bloomed into something huge and chaotic. She was scrambling to hold onto all the pieces, and she couldn't do it alone.

Conall smiled and sat down again. "Take your time. I'll be right here."

Simple words, but they were the crutch she needed.

Denny's calming influence still held, and Ethan's gaze drifted to the faint light coming through the window. Gently, she let go of his hand and sat on the edge of the bed.

"Ethan?" Her voice croaked. "Do you know where you are?"

"It's all wrong." He lifted one hand to his face and turned it to examine his palms. He ran a finger along the roughness of his unshaven cheek. "All wrong."

Rowan pulled his hand away.

"You were hurt. Do you remember?"

His haunted gaze latched onto her.

"An accident?"

"No. Not an accident."

This wasn't going to be easy. While her brother had slept, he'd become a man, but he gazed at her with the eyes of a child—hopeful, trusting, and confused.

She took a deep breath and began to speak, taking him down the long journey that would lead him from that fateful day when men had pretended to be gaunts to kill the prince, to today, when she'd finally understood that they could wake him.

"Enough." He cut her off and turned his head on the pillow.

"Ethan, I want you to know…"

"No more." His voice was barely above a croak. "I want to sleep."

Rowan glanced at Conall who nodded.

"Of course. You rest. We'll talk more when you're feeling better."

She tucked the blankets around his thin shoulders and left him staring at the twilight coming through the gap in the curtains.

46

A GOD BY ANY OTHER NAME

Out in the hall, Rowan left Conall to deal with security. She didn't trust the palace guards to keep Ethan safe. Conall had promised to work with Clem and Elias to be sure someone stayed by the prince's side day and night.

Bella's suite was next to Rowan's and far enough from the sick room and the new offices that the elder princess was probably unaware of the commotion surrounding Ethan's awakening.

She knocked and waited. When there was no answer she crossed the hall and opened the big double doors to the King's Suite. A scratchy tune drifted from the library, and thera light shone through the open door. Bella's lilting voice followed along with the music, sounding like a lost ghost.

Rowan found her lying in a heap of silk skirts on the small reading couch. Sometime in the last few days she'd made an effort to dress properly, but her hair had come undone and it hung down her back in a long coil of gray shot through with red.

With the curtains closed, the room was dim and Bella's face was hidden in shadow. The moment Rowan told her about Ethan, Bella would run to his rooms. She needed information first, but how could she broach the delicate subject of Harry Hightower, the only man Bella had ever loved?

Bella waved an empty glass. "Be a dear, and get your old aunt a refill?"

Rowan took the glass and placed it under the elaborate mech decanter that had been one of her father's prized possessions. It was shaped like a monkey standing on a barrel. His hands were cupped in front of his groin, and when you pushed on his top hat, whisky shot from between his hands like a stream of urine. The king had thought it was hilarious. He claimed it was a Harry

Hightower creation, though having met the famous mech mage, Rowan couldn't believe he had such a childish sense of humor. Or any sense of humor.

She filled the glass and handed it back to Bella.

"Wasn't that a gift from Uncle Hermie?" Rowan pointed at the monkey.

"Hmm?" Bella sipped her drink and swung the arm holding the glass in a grand sweeping gesture as the music came to a crescendo. The song ended and the air filled with scratchy static. Rowan turned off the mech. She needed Bella's full attention.

"Oh, yes. Hermie gave it to your father for his wedding. Your mother hated it."

"It seems so whimsical for Uncle Hermie."

Bella's hand dropped to her lap and whisky sloshed over her skirt. "You would know? You were a child when he went away."

"I mean from what you've told me."

Bella watched her with a small, sly grin. "Do you want something? Another corpse needs prodding perhaps?"

Rowan shook her head and sat on the edge of the couch. She pushed Bella's skirts away to make room and took her hand. It was dry and leathery and cold.

"Listen, Auntie, things are happening. Things I need to tell you about, but I need something from you first."

Bella smirked. "Are you finally giving that Atherton a good trouncing then? It's about time."

"No. Well, maybe. But not yet. I need to put some other pieces together first. Like Talos."

"Ah, yes. Such a shame about the old mech. It seems like all the good things from past days are gone now." Bella wilted against the couch.

"Not gone. Not yet. I can fix Talos, but I need to find Harry Hightower."

Bella opened one eye, then the other. She sat up marginally straighter.

Rowan shook her hand. "That's why I need you, Auntie. I know Hermie and Harry Hightower are the same man. You must know how to contact him."

"Oh, child. You don't just contact Hermie or Harry, or…whatever. He's a *god!*" Bella laughed. It was not a happy sound.

Rowan watched her for a moment, frustration and the need for patience warring inside her. "You said that before. I thought you were being flippant."

Bella sat right up until her face was inches from Rowan's.

"There is nothing flippant about Harry Hightower. He is the god Vulcan. Or Hephaestus. Polymetis to the poets. Khalkeus to the smiths. Whatever you wish to call him. He *is* a god and cannot be hailed by the likes of us."

She crossed her arms over her thin chest and sat back.

Rowan's teeth tugged on her bottom lip. Bella seemed tough, but that hard exterior was thin and brittle.

There was no help for it. She had to come clean.

"I met him."

Bella's eyes widened.

"In Grotto. Well, below Grotto actually. In the old mech boneyard. But I think…" She rubbed her temple. Saints, she was tired. "I think I met him before, at an inn outside of Oxeye."

"He was always partial to inns. And smithies." Bella's hands clasped hers. "Tell me, what did he look like?"

"Old. Not ancient, but mature. Wise. He had gray hair and a beard. He walked with a slight limp."

Bella nodded. "He prefers this form. Plain. Unassuming. But he can take any, you know. He could be as handsome as Adonis if he wanted. Young or ancient. Blond or dark. Only the limp stays every time. That was a gift from his mother, and he can't ever change it." Her eyes narrowed. "How is it you remember him? He once told me that only one who truly loved him could remember him if he didn't wish it."

"Minna had an herb. It blocks memory magic."

"Hmm. Your Ebos friends serve you well."

Rowan tried to bring the conversation around again. "So, how can I contact him. I went back to the Rustworks. He wasn't there."

"He is everywhere and nowhere. You could search for a thousand years and never find him, then turn around and he'll be right behind you. Harry appears as Harry wills and no mere mortal can command him."

Bella sank into silence.

Maybe she was right. How did one command a god? It was a laughable idea. More than laughable. It was treason. The founders of New Torwood City had outlawed the worship of the gods for a good reason. Where had the gods been when magic surged through the world, opening rifts that let in monsters, knocking down cities and transforming landscapes with cataclysmic storms?

The gods had let it happen. All the gods, old and new. Gods prayed to by millions of Christians, Muslims and Jews. Gods forgotten by fallen empires and those start-up gods with shrines dotted all over the world. None had come to help the humans when magic tore the world apart.

So why should a single god come to a lowly princess when she called? It was not for her to understand why the gods acted as they did. Still, he'd helped her before.

"If I wanted to…call him. How would I go about it? A blood sacrifice?" Rowan didn't like that idea, even if it meant saving her beloved Talos.

"A sacrifice, yes. But Harry was never partial to blood. He will want something much more dear. Something you can't do without." Her eyes were nearly black in the dim light, black and piercing, like obsidian blades. "You can find him in the gardens of Jupiter's Temple. Not the new one in Hightown. The first temple that was erected at the same time as the Old Bailey."

Rowan knew the one. It was an ancient building dedicated to Saint Jupiter, and it housed a smaller temple for Vulcan, the saint of mech mages.

"Behind the main temples, there is another, more of a shrine than a temple. That is Harry's heart. Vulcan's shrine. If he chooses to hear your call, that is the place to make it."

"Thank you—"

Bella cut her off. "But that is treason, child. If you do this, you must go alone. Take no one, not even your handsome wolf. Trust no one."

Rowan nodded. She was learning that there were degrees of treason. As long as no one was hurt, she would find Harry. And despite Bella's words, she knew Conall would follow her. No matter what laws she broke.

"Auntie, there's something else you need to know. Ethan is awake."

47

PRECIOUS

JUPITER'S TEMPLE IN BAILEY WASN'T fancy like the one in Hightown that with the water clock. That temple had marble columns, granite floors and large, clean halls to accommodate hundreds of visitors a day. This temple was smaller, and it housed workshops pledged to Vulcan, the saint of blacksmiths, inventors and mech mages.

Rowan and Conall approached at sundown. It had already been a long day. The longest of her life. Conall had wanted to wait until they were rested, but Atherton would return tomorrow. They were running out of time.

The flat light of dusk hid much of the temple's wear, but even full darkness wouldn't cover its derelict untidiness completely. There were scorch marks on the front steps where some mech mage's experiment had gone awry. The columns holding up the portico were cracked and chipped and looked like an ill-timed sneeze might bring them down. Many of the windows were boarded up because the glass had often blown out during experiments, and the mages no longer bothered to replace it.

The main temple and mall where mages and smiths sold their wares was also closed for the night, though a crowd was gathered outside, standing around a fire in a metal drum.

Rowan and Conall snuck through a rusting wrought iron gate in the shape of a peacock and hid in the shadows.

"Looks like a bunch of apprentices with too much time on their hands," Conall said.

One of the mech-mages whooped and the flames shot skyward in spears of red, green and purple. Something exploded inside the drum, creating a

350

bang and a cloud of smoke. Then the shouting began.

Conall shoved Rowan ahead of him.

"Hurry! While they're occupied."

They ran for the yard behind the temple. Smoke billowed above the roof, but they ignored it. Vulcan's temple was set on fire at least once a month.

Rowan's eyes were slow to adjust after the bright explosion, and she stumbled over debris on the ground. Broken bits of mech lay abandoned around the garden. It was hard to tell if they were old installations left to rot or new installations in progress. Either way, they cast deep shadows, and the air sizzled with spent magic.

She jerked backward, banging into Conall when a rat jumped into the light. It sat on hind legs to examine the intruders, then hurried on its way. Phalian swooped after it, silent except for the clack of his tiny talons as he threatened the retreating rodent.

Conall squeezed Rowan's shoulders and her rampant heartbeat slowed.

They moved deeper into the garden, leaving the remnants of mech mage failures behind. The path became overgrown with brambles and end-of-season wildflowers. Rowan grabbed a clump of thorny vines with her mech fingers and pulled them aside. Ahead, more vines blocked the way. Frustration filled her with ice. She rubbed her arms, then pulled out the small map of the temple grounds that Dale had found in the archives.

"I'm sure it's this way." She tapped the map and pointed to the brambles blocking their route. She was thinking about zapping the foliage with her galvanic magic, but wasn't sure that would accomplish anything.

"Let me." Conall stepped forward. He pulled two knives from his belt and flicked his wrists. Rowan had seen the air blades during their Meadows excursion, but that had been in the midst of fighting off titans or gaunts and she'd never really seen them up close. The magic vibrating from them set her teeth on edge. He cut downward, one blade then the other. The vines seemed to melt away. He grinned and moved forward, hacking at the foliage. They were cutting a swath a toddler could follow, but she doubted any of Vulcan's adherents would be looking this way tonight.

It was darker under the trees. The night was quiet except for the swish-swish of his blades and a few shouts from the hidden streets. The city seemed very far away, even though the temple garden didn't extend more than a block in any direction.

A light appeared ahead. As Conall worked his blades, moving toward it, Rowan realized it was moonlight shining through an opening in the dense canopy. Conall stopped and tipped his head so the light shone on his face. With his eyes closed, he breathed deeply as if he could absorb the moon into his lungs. He seemed to be more vibrant suddenly, and bigger, more solid, like his normal self was only a pale smudge of his true self that came out in the moonlight.

"Is that a wolf thing?" she asked.

He turned to her and smiled. Bathed in the blue light, he was beautiful and her heart ached watching him.

"The moon? I don't know. I've always liked it." He shrugged. "Could be a wolf thing. I have nothing to compare it to."

"You must be tired after clearing all those vines. We should rest here."

"Nah. I'm fine. The moon feeds me. But I think here is where we're supposed to be anyway. Look."

For the first time, she noticed that he stood beside a rock formation. He pulled away the vines choking it to reveal an oddly-shaped black rock.

"Is that…"

"An anvil." Conall grinned. "There's no more fitting shrine to Vulcan or Harry. Whatever we're calling him these days."

"Do you think it matters what we call him?" she asked. "Bella said he would only hear us at his shrine. But what if we use the wrong name and only annoy him?"

Conall's brows lowered, shadowing his eyes. "I'd like to say that a god should read what's in our hearts. That's most important, after all. But I don't believe they care enough to look that closely" He took her hands and she stared into the shadows where only a glint of his eyes could be seen. "Are you sure you really want to do this? We can find another way."

"There is no other way. But if you're worried about being accused of treason for attempting to treat with a god, I can do this on my own." She tried to pull her hands away, but he hung on.

"You know that's not what I'm worried about. Saints, it won't be the first time they've tried to pin treason on me. Probably won't be the last if I hang around with the likes of you."

His grin took the sting from his words, but they both knew it was true. The road before Rowan wasn't going to be an easy one, and every signpost along the way would be marked with treason, treachery and betrayal. All the more reason she needed to revive Talos. Without him, the Theracine Corporation would seal their stranglehold on the city.

Thanks to Roger and Banerjee, she had the proof she needed to upset the council cart and remove Atherton. Talos was the last piece of her strategy that would cement her place as the new regent until Ethan was well enough to be crowned.

She would give up a lot to see that happen.

"So what do we do?" Conall asked as he turned in a circle, taking in the sight of the old shrine. Rowan swatted a mosquito and Phalian went after a moth disappearing into the branches overhead.

"I think we should clear the space first. Show our respect by putting his altar in order. And here. You need to chew this." She tucked a wad of surrow weed into her mouth and handed the pouch to Conall.

He eyed it skeptically. "What is it?"

"Memory wort, I think. Minna calls it surrow. Chew it but don't swallow."

Conall put some of the weed in his mouth and made a face.

Rowan smiled. "It's bitter, I know, but it works." She'd filled him in about meeting Harry in Rustworks and about the time he'd stolen their memories in Oxeye. Conall hadn't liked the idea of someone playing with his memories.

They cleared overgrown vines from the anvil altar and found a brook running behind it. The water trickled slowly and silently. It pooled behind the giant anvil then leached away into the undergrowth. Following it, they found a small structure that had once been a hut. Its thatched roof was rotted and the door was missing. There were no windows. They could only surmise that it had been the original temple put on this place before the city walls had even been erected. When the bigger temple was constructed, this small shrine had been forgotten.

They cleared enough space between the anvil and the hut to kneel. The ground was damp and rich with decaying greenery. Rowan's knees sank into it. She steadied herself with the tips of her fingers and closed her eyes. She was aware of Conall kneeling beside her and Phalian watching from the trees. She felt silly. How did one pray? She'd read about it in old books, of course. Her tutors had always made it sound frivolous or foolish even, but prayer had been very real to the people in those stories. Somehow, she had to make it real today.

Lord Vulcan, hear my prayer.

She didn't speak the words aloud. The books all said that wasn't necessary. Gods were omniscient. He could hear her thoughts, but would he? It seemed to her that being able to hear the thoughts of everyone on earth would get tiresome pretty quickly. Maybe that's why gods didn't listen to prayers. Maybe there were just too many voices to pick out only one or two. But she had to try. Surely, in this city, she would be one of the few speaking directly to Vulcan.

Lord Vulcan, god of smithies, son of Jupiter, hear my prayer.

That seemed too formal. She tried again.

Harry Hightower, if you can hear me, please…come forth. Manifest or do whatever it is you do. I need you!

She continued like this for some time. Water soaked through the knees of her pants. Her back ached from the awkward kneeling position and still she sent her silent calls out into the universe, hoping the god would answer.

He didn't.

Frustrated, she called out in a sing-song voice, "The hunt is done, shadows run!" It was an old verse that children sang when playing hide-and-seek, a call to come home. It was a long shot, but she was out of ideas.

"This isn't working." She rose and stretched.

The moon had shifted and half the altar was now hidden in shadow.

"Maybe Bella was right and you need a sacrifice," Conall said.

Rowan nodded. "From what I read, the newer gods abhorred blood sacrifices, but Vulcan is an old god, from a time when blood was given freely and frequently with prayers."

"So what? We come back with a goat or a chicken."

Rowan didn't want to kill an innocent animal on the off-chance that some old god might like the taste of blood.

"No. I think it's the intent that matters. Blood was sacrificed back then because it was the most important thing to the prayerful. Later, grain was given or water, two things the people needed to survive. It showed how much they were willing to give up for the goodwill of their god. And Bella said Harry would want something else. Something precious to me."

She stepped to the altar and began pulling at the glove that covered her mech arm, one finger at a time. Conall jumped up and gripped her human hand.

"No. You can't."

"I can. Harry Hightower gave me this arm. It turned my sadness into curiosity and sent me down the path to tinkering with mechs. I was alone before that, with nothing on my horizon but more loneliness. Harry's mech gave me something to reach for. So yes, it saved my life. It's precious to me and giving it up will be more significant than spilling blood."

Phalian squawked overhead and she hardened her heart to the sound. The bird and the arm were linked in a way she'd never understood.

Conall pointed at Phalian. "What about him. You would give him up too?"

Fear and sadness nearly choked her. She gripped his arm. "You didn't see them, Conall! All those sick people in Noah's ward. All addicted to thera and dying slowly and painfully. That's what Theracine would do to everyone in New Torwood. I won't have it!" She stamped her foot. "I would give up Phalian and more to save my city. I would give my life." She sucked in a breath and it hitched in her throat.

Conall held her gaze until she thought she might crumble under it, then he nodded and stepped away.

"That's why you will make a great queen. I hope I'm around to see it."

"Regent, not queen." Ethan was king, and she would make sure he wore that crown.

With her left hand, Rowan found the pressure points on her right elbow and tapped them. The arm released its grip on her flesh and she twisted. It came free. The residual limb felt strangely cold and vulnerable in the night air.

She laid the mech on the anvil in the last ray of moonlight, and shouted, "Harry! Come and get it!"

For a long minute, nothing happened. Then Phalian squawked and shot into the shadows. As Harry Hightower limped into the light, Phalian landed on his shoulder.

"Stop banging on my door, human, or I will make sure you don't remember my name, elf magic or not. And it won't be pleasant." He spoke quietly, but his voice seemed to boom in Rowan's head.

He turned to walk away.

Rowan rushed toward him.

"No! I need your help. Please! To save Talos." Desperation fueled her and she grabbed his arm.

You dare!

He hadn't spoken aloud, but the voice reverberated in her head. It was echoed by a distant rumble of thunder. A force jerked her off her feet, and she flew across the clearing, landing hard in the stream.

Conall roared and lunged at Harry.

"No!" Conall would defend her and it would cost him his life. She scrambled to her feet and found him immobilized, suspended in mid-leap with his hands outstretched, ready to strangle the god. His teeth were clenched and lips parted in a frozen snarl.

Rowan grabbed his hand, but he didn't move.

"What have you done to him? Release him!"

"You come with too many demands, little princess. Say what you came to say, and if I'm feeling generous, I will leave your wolf unharmed."

Logic battled with emotions inside her. Rowan's instinct was to protect Conall, but she'd sacrificed enough to get the god to notice her. She couldn't give up this chance to have him hear her petition.

"Talos has fallen," she said. "His heart has dimmed. It's almost gone out. Please, you created him. You can fix him."

"And why should I?"

"Because he's dying!"

"Everything dies. Even the gods. Eventually."

Rowan considered that cryptic message. Was he saying that Talos was a god? Or that he, Harry Hightower, could die? Or *was* dying?

She tried a different tactic.

"Without Talos the city's water pumps have failed. The council has commissioned new pumps that run on thera. You understand the dangers of thera. I know you do. My father was against it and that was your doing. You even told me that you left New Torwood because the council embraced thera."

"You should not remember that conversation."

"But I do. I promise I won't tell anyone how to find you. Please, just come to Talos and heal him. No one has to know."

Harry picked up her mech arm and turned it over. It was so odd to see it as something separate from herself. It looked fragile and alien.

"This was a good piece of mech," he said. "One of my best." He tossed it to her. She caught it with her other hand and clutched it against her chest.

"Fix your own problems, little princess. You have everything you need." He brushed Phalian from his shoulder. The bird fluttered in the air, metal wings clacking as Harry disappeared into the shadows.

"SQUAWK!" Phalian flew around her head in a frenzy.

Rowan sagged against the anvil, clutching her mech arm to her chest. Phalian scrambled onto her shoulder and his metal beak pecked her arm just above the truncated elbow, hard enough to draw blood.

"Ow!" She rubbed her arm. She deserved that. "I'm sorry." She leaned into Phalian and he bobbed his head against hers, a rare stymphalian kiss.

Conall burst into motion, knives out.

"Where is he? What happened?" He snarled and growled. The wolf was ready to erupt from him. He darted into the bushes, looking for a fight that he couldn't win.

Phalian settled down and shifted to a mouse. Rowan rubbed her forehead. Her head was throbbing. The side of her tongue was numb from the memory wort. She spat it out and wiped her mouth.

They'd committed treason, begged a god for help, and still they had no answers.

She could hear Conall cursing and slashing at foliage. Harry was long gone, but Conall needed to work out his rage. It couldn't sit well that the god had so easily incapacitated him.

She slipped her arm into the mech. The connection clicked home and she felt whole again. Phalian scurried down the arm to his charging port, and Rowan watched him settle into his cradle.

Conall returned. His expression was dark as thunder.

"What did Harry say?" she asked. "Something about having everything I need?"

There was a solution here, but she was exhausted and her brain was too sluggish to find it.

"I don't know." Conall shook his head tightly. He was still pissed. "I couldn't hear anything. It was like an avalanche was rumbling through my head."

She squeezed his hand. "Come on. Let's get home before the mech mages find us trespassing in their garden. I need to sleep on it."

The next morning, Rowan woke feeling energized. Had she dreamed that she'd spoken to a god? No. She hadn't. Harry had come when she'd called. And his words hadn't been as unhelpful as she'd first believed.

She did have everything she needed.

Conall was asleep beside her. When she shook his shoulder, he mumbled and rolled away.

"Wake up!" She shook him harder. "I know how to fix Talos! I need to speak to Irva. And Rudi. And Denny. Saints, we need everyone here."

Conall opened one eye. "Did no one ever tell you that wolves aren't morning creatures."

She shook him again. "Get up! We're going to fix Talos. We're going to fix everything."

48

WATERWHEEL OF THE SOUL

CONALL WATCHED IRVA CLOSELY. SHE blinked like an owl in the morning light when Rowan explained her plans for Talos. He'd been traveling with the lumina for long enough to recognize that she was hesitant.

They were seated at the breakfast table on Rowan's balcony. Minna stood by the doorway, frowning. Conall had cautioned Rowan to keep the meeting small for now, at least until they understood if her plan was feasible.

A maid came in and served tea and pastries. Irva sipped from her mug and smiled. "Your tea is better than anything we have in Benni."

"Definitely," Conall said. They'd had only Benni rations for the trip home and he'd been glad to get back to civilized tea.

"It's brought in from the south," Rowan said. Her smile was tense. He could tell that she was desperately impatient to hear if her idea could work.

"I have not had the chance to examine your giant mech man, but Minna explained the dilemma," Irva finally said. "I believe the solution to his recovery lies with the ley-line beneath your city. Please tell me what you know of Talos's magic."

Rowan put her cup down. Her mech fingers drummed the table and Phalian ruffled his feathers from his perch above the door, a sure sign that Rowan was agitated.

"Talos is the, uh…battery that fuels the water pumps. You might say it's his knack, if mechs could have one. Minna explained it as mimicry magic. I take it you know what that is?"

Irva nodded and Rowan looked embarrassed.

"Of course you do. Right, well, it was a new concept for me. The way I understand it, the circuit that Talos makes around the city walls isn't just for show. It serves the deeper purpose of this sympathetic magic. Like a magic waterwheel."

It was a new concept for Conall too.

"A simple analogy, but not without merit," Irva said.

"Right. So Talos's continuous circuit is the magic that turns the engine that makes the pumps go. When Talos fell, he broke that link. If we restart his heart, get him up and walking again. Then…" Her mech fingers creaked as she gripped the arm of her chair. Conall put his hand over hers and squeezed. "Then we hope the magic link kicks in and the water flows."

Irva listened to her explanation with lips pursed in a frown. That wasn't encouraging.

"You think it won't work," Rowan said.

Irva's expression softened. "It can work, Evani. Your city was built on a ley-line, a cunning plan by your founders. Talos is indeed a battery. His steps are the waterwheel, as you say. If you restart his heart he will walk again." Her smile faded away. "But starting his heart will not relink Talos to the ley-line. That magic is beyond your skills, Evani."

Conall had known it wouldn't be easy, even when Rowan's excitement had gotten them up before dawn.

"Can you do it?" he asked.

Irva smiled, but her eyes were fixed on Rowan. "Should the Evani ask it of me, I should be required to try."

"Okay. What does that mean?" Rowan said.

"It means that Omika has charged us—me, Rudi, Minna and Ferlan—with the task of helping you, Evani. If you ask this thing, I will do it."

"That makes you sound reluctant. Is it dangerous?"

"Yes, Evani." Irva folded her hands in her lap and looked composed.

"Dangerous as in it could kill you?"

"Yes, Evani. Ley-line magic is finicky, but I am well trained. If you wish, I will act as the link between Talos and the ley-line."

"Thank you, Essami," Rowan said. Conall had heard Minna use that title and he assumed it was a mark of respect.

Rowan continued, "I would consider it a great favor if you could try."

"Very well. I must see these water pumps and Talos."

Minna stepped forward. "I can take you. Rudi will want to see them too."

As Irva rose to leave, Rowan stopped her. "How long will it take?"

Irva frowned. "I cannot be sure until I inspect the ley-line, but once we begin, I will need two full days to prepare."

"Thank you, Essami."

Irva gave a short bow and left with Minna.

"Am I asking too much?" Rowan said. "She looks exhausted already. Maybe fixing Talos right after waking Ethan is too much for her."

"Minna would tell you," Conall said. "Rudi too. Let them do their research and we'll know more. Rudi has been dying to see inside Talos anyway."

Conall had finally explained the Rati-Irivu and their lost home world. Rowan had taken that information in stride. Nothing, not even killer mechs seemed to faze her.

Our mate will be queen, Garou said. Conall didn't disagree, but he knew her feelings on that subject.

The wind blew in from the north and Rowan rubbed her arms.

"That's the Fanfaronade, for sure."

"Do you want to go inside?" Conall had a knee-jerk reaction to seeing her in any kind of distress, and he had the sudden urge to bundle her in blankets.

"I'm fine." She tapped his hand with her fingers. He liked that. It was as if she needed a connection between them. Being away from her had been brutal, but it had shown him exactly where he needed to be. Right here at her side.

Later that afternoon, they would confront the council with Atherton's crimes. He would stand by her side then too.

They ate quietly, waiting for Dale to show for a last review of their case before the council meeting.

"Where are they?" Rowan grumbled. She called for Alice. "Go find Dale and tell them we're waiting."

"Yes, Evani." The girl bobbed and disappeared into the suite.

"I still think I need to question Renata." Rowan sipped her tea and looked defiant. Conall didn't see the advantage to that interrogation, and he didn't want Rowan exposed to that woman's venom. They'd had this argument once already, but Rowan didn't want to let it go.

"It's my duty. I called for her arrest. I should question her, see what she has to say for herself."

"That's fine, but you don't have any experience with interrogation. Let me handle it. I interrogated prisoners during the war."

Rowan shot him a perplexed look. "You interrogated gaunts?"

"No, Taiga warriors. There were rumors that the Taiga were behind the gaunt uprising, though I doubted it at the time." He doubted it even more now after meeting the Taiga.

"Even so, Renata isn't some barbarian from over the mountains," Rowan said.

"Barbarians would be easier to break than that old bird." Conall hadn't forgotten how Renata had trapped him into service for the regent.

"You just want revenge." Rowan softened the accusation with a smile.

"Not at all. Renata might have tricked me, but I think that little adventure turned out all right. Don't you?" He dipped a hand under the table and ran it across her thigh, which was covered only in a thin robe.

"It's had its perks." Rowan squeezed her thighs together, trapping his hand. Her eyes bore into his, sparking the desire they'd just recently sated. That was one of the hundreds of things he loved about her. She never slapped his hand away or feigned surprise when he touched her. Of course, he didn't abuse that power and kept his affections for when they could be properly explored. And right now, they had business to attend to. So he let his hand retreat and sat back in his chair.

"We need Renata's testimony." Rowan sighed. "Dale said we might not have enough votes without her."

"So what? You plan to torture her into confessing?"

Rowan lifted her chin. "If I have to."

Conall smiled and shook his head. He had no doubt she would do it too.

"She won't give in easily. Renata has known you all your life and she still thinks of you as a child. She doesn't respect you."

"She'll learn to respect me." Rowan pounded her fist on the table, making the spoons jump. "I just tossed her ass in jail. When I'm through with her, she'll lose her house and her medical license."

"She still won't break. The only thing that will sway her is the offer of a pardon."

"No!"

He gripped her fingers. "Look, I'm not keen on it either, but you have to consider it."

Rowan shook her head. "No way. She kept my brother in a coma! For years. How can I just let that go?"

"Because to her it wasn't personal, and she'll use your emotions against you. They all will. Atherton, Wrede, Docker. The ones who play the game best don't let it become personal. You can either get revenge. Or you can win. You can't do both."

"Seems to me, revenge should be the reward for winning."

Conall nodded. "It should be, but that's rarely the case. Sometimes the bad guy—or bad old lady—gets to go free."

Rowan slumped in her seat. She clutched a cup of tea against her chest as if it could warm her. A gust of wind tossed her hair across her cheek. She brushed it aside and met his eyes.

"So what exactly are you suggesting?"

"We go in together. Let me ask the questions. You stand there looking impatient and imperial, like you would rather have Renata's head taken off than spend another moment in the dungeon. Let me make it clear what's on the line."

Rowan nodded. "Okay. But make no promises. Not yet."

"Bring Phalian. She has a weakness for pretty mechs. He can distract her while we dig for the truth."

Alice returned and bobbed a curtsy. "I'm sorry, Evani, but I couldn't find Secretary Shannock anywhere."

Rowan looked distressed. "Where are they?"

49

THE DEVIL'S INVOICE

WHEN THEY OPENED THE CELL, the doctor was standing with her back to the door, tall and straight and seemingly unbroken. She turned angry eyes on them and Rowan wasn't fooled. Renata might look fierce and unbending, but she suspected the stance in the middle of the room was simply so no part of her touched the dingy walls.

Phalian sailed around the tiny cell, his flapping wings sparked on the stone walls. Renata's eyes tracked the little mech.

Rowan crossed her arms and leaned against the wall by the door. Glancing around she noted the single cot and a commode in one corner. A bedside table held a thera lamp and a stack of books. It wasn't the luxury the prime doctor was used to, but neither was it the rat-infested holding cell she deserved.

Conall stalked into the room, moving like a predator, all lanky muscle and suppressed energy. Renata's eyes widened slightly when she saw him and then a sneer curled her lip.

"You brought your dog. Where's his leash?" Renata folded her hands together and let them fall in front of her, pretending to be at ease. Her hands trembled.

"I'm off my leash, Doctor." Conall showed his teeth. "But you won't be." A keeper entered the room and Conall nodded toward the prisoner. The keeper grabbed Renata's hands and bound them with shackles, then locked the chain to a cleat in the wall, leaving Renata on a leash of about three feet. He gave the chain a tug, making her stumble and left without a word.

Renata lifted her metal bound hands and let them fall with a clang. "This is unnecessary."

Rowan made an angry noise. Conall gave her a look and she tried to relax and let him do his job.

"Since you've been poisoning the prince with your touch for years, I think it's very necessary," Conall said.

"I *saved* the prince. I kept him alive!"

"Those are two different things. You kept him alive, yes. But saving? There was no saving going on in that sickroom. You cursed a child to a half-life. You forced him to live in the shadow of his birthright, never alive enough to take it, but not dead either. No. Because a dead prince would mean a dynastic shift. An incapacitated prince was much more useful to a regent who wanted to rule. How much did Atherton pay you to keep the prince not dead but not alive? How many of your bejeweled mech clocks and lizards were paid for with that cursed money?"

"You can't prove any of it." Renata's lips pursed, setting off a spray of deep lines around them.

Conall leaned in. "Oh, but we can. We have two accounts taken from dead scribes. Cachets that we deciphered. They have impartial evidence to prove Atherton's crimes—and yours by association."

This was only partially a lie. They hadn't found any direct evidence on the cachets linking Renata to Atherton.

Renata's eyes flicked to Rowan, then to Phalian who was perched on her thera lamp, then back to Conall.

"I don't believe you. The council won't believe you either." The chains on her hands rattled, then she fell still again.

"Maybe not." Conall grinned. "But they'll believe the prince. Ethan is awake. And he has quite the story to tell. You see, he was aware all this time. He knew what you were doing. In his mind, he screamed for you to stop. But you didn't. You visited that horror on a child, and watched him grow into a man. And now he'll be king. How do you think he will remember your time together."

Again, most of that wasn't true, but Renata believed. Rowan saw the moment when her haughtiness turned to jelly.

"What do you want from me?"

It was time for Rowan to step in. She pushed away from the wall.

"I want your vote. Today."

Renata narrowed her eyes. "You're going after Atherton. Stupid girl. Do you really think you can run this city on your own?"

"I'm not on my own. I have General Lind and Chancellor March on my side. And I have my own advisors." She glanced at Conall and he winked.

"And what do I get in return?" Renata asked.

Rowan almost said, "You get to live, bitch," but if she was going to be the regent, it was time to start acting like one.

She took a deep breath and willed her voice to sound strong. "What do you want?"

50

SECRETS IN LEATHER AND VELVET

TIME WAS TICKING AWAY. DALE hadn't slept all night but spent it searching the archives instead. They hadn't found any hint of the missing ledgers. Two days ago, they'd even hired someone to search Atherton's townhouse in the city, and before dawn Dale snuck into the regent's office and swept it again.

Sitting in Atherton's chair, Dale gazed around the office. There was nothing here.

Every time they closed their eyes, Ethan's first words in twenty years haunted them. He'd looked right at Dale, and whispered, "I hurt inside." Then he'd lain there helpless and confused. The thought stoked rage already burning in Dale's heart. They had a chance to make amends.

Atherton wouldn't get away with it. Not this time.

The regent was due home today. Rowan needed those ledgers. It was time to stop the self-pity party. The only place Dale hadn't thoroughly searched was Atherton's bedroom. It was time to do the deed.

Coming through the servants door, Dale paused. The suite had been recently cleaned, awaiting the regent's return. Fresh flowers filled a vase by the main door. A basket of scones was arranged on the table in the sitting area. Dale waited a beat to confirm they were alone, then strode to the bedroom.

Sighing deeply, they pulled on gloves. For Ethan and for Rowan—for the people they loved, Dale would search the regent's butt plugs.

51

A CROWN GAMBLE

ROWAN SAT IN HER FATHER'S chair in the council chambers. She'd dressed carefully, aiming to look regal and somber in a long dress of deep blue. It was embroidered on the shoulders in Andula house colors of gold and maroon. She'd left Phalian in her rooms and felt naked without the mech bird fluttering around her head.

Rowan's chair creaked loudly as she shifted in her seat. Dale sat on her right. They'd come through with a big win that morning. Her fingers rested delicately on a leather-bound ledger. The book was a bomb ready to go off, and she was the trigger.

The Infinity Clock ticked away to its mysterious end on the wall, but that was the only sound in the room, despite the fact that almost every minister was in attendance.

Chancellor March sat next to Dale with the Ministers of Defense, Generals Lind and Kranson. March and Lind had assured her of their votes, and Kranson usually sided with Lind.

Beside them sat Flora Bosman, CEO of Theracine Corporation. Her official title on the council was Energy Minister. She'd brought her secretary with her. The mysterious Kenneth Smith had no official role in this forum. His presence was a boldface reminder of Theracine's undue influence.

Marylyn Docker, Minister of Guilds, sat on the opposite side of the table. Docker was mentioned several times in the ledger and had always been a staunch Theracine supporter. Rowan could no longer expect help from her.

Abbot Archivist Wiktor and Minister of Foreign Affairs Stella Keiffer sat with their heads together, whispering like co-conspirators. They had little love for the royal family in general and Rowan in particular. Rowan hadn't forgotten that the Pincer assassin had named Keiffer.

The Temple Liaison, High Orator Lucian, sat beside them with a scowl on his face. He'd backed her at the last council meeting, but his vote could go either way. Gene Hayes, acting Minister of the Purse, was the last one at the table. He looked ready to bolt, but Dale had assured her that Hayes was on board.

Anyone counting votes right now, would assume a six to five tally in the regent's favor, but Rowan had a couple of extra daggers in her boot.

A scribe entered the chamber and took her seat at the small desk provided for her. Avram was already there, taking notes for Rowan. The scribe didn't acknowledge his presence in her booth, but simply shoved his notebook and papers aside when she sat.

Rowan hadn't requested a scribe when she'd booked this emergency meeting. That oversight was a slight to the Temple of the Word, and a proclamation about Rowan's intent, going forward. She glanced at the Abbot Archivist. Wiktor smiled. He wasn't going to let her banish the scribes without a fight.

Atherton's new secretary popped his head into the room and goggled at the assembled ministers then fumbled through an explanation for Atherton's tardiness.

"The…uh, regent…uh, Atherton has been on the road this morning. He's only just…uh, arrived."

"Minister Bosman also arrived this morning," Rowan said. "But she managed to be on time."

The secretary muttered something that could have been an apology and fled.

Sitting to her right, Dale grinned. Their professional pride couldn't help being amused by the new secretary's graceless ineptitude.

Ethan's waking was a blessing, but also a shock, and Dale had taken it badly. They were already prone to bouts of dark melancholy, and when they'd disappeared for over twenty-four hours, Rowan feared the worst. But Dale had shown up in her rooms only an hour ago, looking disheveled and hollow-eyed from lack of sleep, and bringing her the best gift of all.

Rowan's mech fingers spread protectively over the leather cover of the ledger. She should never have doubted Dale's conviction. With Dale as her anchor and Conall as her shield, she thought she might just survive the next hour.

The room fell into silence while they waited. News of Renata's arrest had leaked, and the ministers kept glancing at the doctor's empty chair.

Rowan's honor guard spread around the room with Minna taking her usual spot behind the princess. Clem, Elias and Ferlan were also in attendance. Alice had done wonders in a short amount of time and created a sort of uniform by dressing them in the traditional dun tunic and leggings of the Ebos, but adding a belt and scarf in gold and maroon.

Conall surveilled the gathering from the far corner. His only uniform was a glower that made most of the ministers look away. Noah stood beside him, looking uncomfortable. She'd asked him to be in attendance in case there were questions about Ethan's care and recovery. Denny had opted to stay with the prince. His empath knack was the only thing keeping Ethan from spiraling into constant panic. Rowan worried that Ethan wasn't adjusting well, though Denny and Noah both assured her that it was too early to make assumptions.

Conall saw her frowning and tipped his chin upward in a question. She smiled to show that she was fine. Her fingers drummed on the ledger.

A stir of activity outside the doors indicated someone's arrival. All eyes turned that way.

Bella strode into the room. Rowan's first hidden dagger had arrived. The princess's hair was swept into a towering beehive. Darker red outlined her ruby lips. Her maroon and gold dress was sumptuous but austere.

She didn't greet anyone, though her fingers trailed across Orator Lucian's shoulder before taking the seat beside him. The temple liaison winced at such a public display of affection.

By law, every first generation relative of the monarch had a seat on the council. Bella had never claimed that privilege before, but she hadn't needed much urging from Rowan to claim it today. After she'd seen Ethan last night and learned of the curse that had kept him imprisoned in his own body for two decades, Bella had needed to be restrained. She'd wanted to kill Atherton. When she'd learned he wasn't in residence at the palace, she'd retreated to her rooms, cursing the regent with a dozen foul names.

"Good morning, my poppies," Bella said cheerfully. "Are you ready to serve our people today, or shall we all just jack ourselves off as usual?"

Orator Lucian gasped. Olan March grinned. Several of the ministers fidgeted in their seats. It was uncommon enough to have someone other than the regent call a meeting, but they were beginning to suspect that something far more momentous was happening.

Rowan caught Flora Bosman's eye and smiled. The Theracine director didn't look any worse for her recent travels. Her short, dark hair was cut in a straight fringe across her forehead. It made her look hard, and Rowan guessed that was the intent. She wore no makeup, but her perfect skin needed none, and her wide-set eyes were an icy blue that seemed to reflect the light and hide her emotions.

Rowan's gaze trailed to Kenneth Smith. He smiled blandly. Rowan had the irrational feeling that he could read her thoughts.

When all this fuss was over, Rowan vowed to have Dale look into the workings of Theracine Corporation. Something wasn't right there.

Atherton finally appeared, looking annoyed. He'd washed off the road dust, and his hair was slicked back into a shiny helmet. The regent's chain of office hung over a silk suit in eggplant purple with silver pin stripes and a fuchsia tie.

"What is this I hear about Minister Renata being arrested? How dare you presume to do such a thing without consulting me? I demand to know what the charges are."

Atherton loomed over Rowan's chair. Up close, she could see that his delay in arrival had been so he could perfect his makeup. Even Bella didn't wear so much foundation, and was that…yes, he'd added a faux mole beside his left nostril.

Rowan caught Conall's eye roll.

How nice of Atherton to dress up for treason, she thought.

"Faustus, sit down so we can get this meeting started," Bella said. "I have whisky to drink and money to lose at cards."

Atherton spun and glowered at her. "What's she doing here?"

"I have some announcements to make," Rowan said, "and I felt it was important that the eldest royal be in attendance."

Bella smiled and flashed her middle finger at Atherton.

With nothing else to do, Atherton sat in the regent's seat on Rowan's left.

Rowan pushed back her chair and rose.

"I will explain Dr. Renata's arrest shortly, but first, I have some very exciting news to share. Prince Ethan is awake."

There was a moment of stunned silence, then the ministers all started speaking at once. Marilyn Docker's voice rose above the others. "Prove it! No one has seen the prince in years."

Rowan had expected this dissent.

"I visited my brother this morning," she spoke loud enough to be heard. "Just as I have visited him nearly every day for the last nineteen years." Rowan tinged her voice with bitterness and the ministers fell silent. "But you don't need to believe me. Prince Ethan is recovering quickly and soon he will be ready to make a public appearance. In the mean time, General Lind and Chancellor March can confirm that he is well."

Both ministers nodded.

"I have seen the prince," Chancellor March said in his rumbling way. "He is awake and in good health."

"Thank you, Chancellor." Rowan turned her attention to the others. "That is the good news. The ill news is that Dr. Renata has admitted to her part in keeping Prince Ethan in a magic-laced coma all these years."

More stunned gabbling erupted from the assembly. Rowan laid her hands flat on the table and gave them a moment to digest this news, though she suspected for some, it wasn't news at all. Orator Lucian looked particularly outraged. That was encouraging. She'd need all the support she could get for this next part.

She held up her right hand. All eyes went to the black-gloved mech and the confusion quieted.

"I find it impossible to believe that a prime doctor would commit such a heinous act," High Orator Lucian said. "How do we know Renata's confession wasn't coerced?"

"All that will come out in a trial," Rowan said. "We have confirmation of the curse from two people with magic sensitivity. And when Prince Ethan is well enough, he will be able to confirm Dr. Renata's treasonous act."

That brought a thoughtful nod from the High Orator.

Rowan took a deep breath and continued. "However, we have to consider that Regent Atherton either knew about Renata's activities, which would make him complicit, or he was ignorant of them, which makes him simply incompetent. Either way, Faustus Atherton should be removed from this council and I, as Prince Ethan's only sibling, should be made regent until he has recovered from his ordeal and can take his rightful place as king. I ask that Regent Atherton call the vote or I will."

The last part of her proclamation was lost under the shouting.

Atherton jumped out of his chair, and Rowan saw Clem move to intercept him, but she held out a hand to stall her. Atherton wasn't going to attack. He shoved his chair back violently, then turned and stalked to the wall. He stood with his back to the room for several seconds then turned.

All eyes were on him.

"I am still regent here. And if we must go through this ridiculous formality, I will be the one to oversee it. Before I do, I would remind all of you that King Reynar was my friend. I wept for his loss and vowed to care for his family and his city. And for the last twenty years, I have done exactly that. I built trade. I won a war. And perhaps most importantly, I made alliances with our southern neighbors. And what has the princess done? Until last month, she was a child tinkering with her toys in the palace basement."

He sucked in a breath, puffing out his chest, then ran his hands over his suit jacket.

"The princess and I will, of course abstain from voting. All those in favor of Princess Rowan Andula as Regent of New Torwood City, say 'Aye.'"

The two generals spoke up immediately.

"Aye."

"Aye."

She had been expecting that.

"Aye," said Chancellor Olan March. That too was no surprise, but she needed six votes.

"Aye," said Bella.

Rowan's heart beat loudly in her ears, and she realized she was holding her breath. She let it out slowly. Her eyes roamed around the table.

Minister Docker glared at her. Abbot Archivist Wiktor was solemn. Keiffer crossed her arms over her chest and said nothing. She hadn't expected help from this crew, but Orator Lucian refused to meet her eye too. That was a blow. She thought his sympathy for Ethan had swayed him.

Then Gene Hayes raised his hand. "Aye."

Rowan fought to keep the relief from her face. Dale had worked magic to get that vote.

That was five votes to five. She was hoping that Lucian would side with her so she wouldn't have to use the other dagger hidden in her boot, but he refused to even look at her.

Rowan nudged Dale. They produced an official-looking document and read its contents.

"I have here a signed proxy vote from Prime Doctor Renata. She casts her vote in favor of Princess Rowan Andula."

A stunned silence followed. Rowan's guts were in turmoil. Then Atherton started to laugh. It was a fake and haughty laugh that he coupled with clapping hands as if he had just watched a pantomime spectacle.

"That was a very good try, Princess, but once again, you've proven that you know nothing about the city you wish to rule. Proxy votes are not legal in this chamber. Only ministers in attendance may vote."

Rowan felt the floor fall away from her. She glanced at Dale but they seemed uncertain. She couldn't disprove Atherton's claim. Not now, and later, it wouldn't matter.

She looked around the room again, searching for the help she knew she wouldn't find.

Atherton clasped his hands behind his back and puffed out his chest. "So if there are no more 'Ayes' we can dismiss this charade." He was about to turn away when Flora Bosman lifted one finger.

"Aye."

Relief flooded Rowan's veins in a hot flash. She'd hoped but hadn't truly believed. Bosman voted for Rowan only because she held the highway treaty with Dowchester hostage, but she didn't care. A vote was a vote.

All color drained from Atherton's face. Rowan waited for him to make the proclamation that she was now regent, but he simply stood dumbfounded.

"Thank you Faustus. Your services are no longer required in this chamber."

Atherton's top lip trembled with a suppressed snarl. She turned her back and addressed the council as regent.

52

A COMMAND SHIFT

ROWAN WAS AMAZING. CONALL THOUGHT of all the times he was able to watch her without her knowing, and this was the best. She was a natural, standing up to the petulant ministers. Making Atherton call the vote on himself not only made the regent implicit in his own downfall, it followed protocol so there could be no appeal to the ruling. It had been a masterful move.

The ex-regent stood beside the open doors looking lost. Sweat clung to his brow, melting the thick make up. The line of his jacket rumpled under his hunched shoulders. His hands were clenched into fists, and a vein stood out on his temple. He looked like a man who'd been shot but had forgotten to fall down.

Do not overlook a trapped rat, brother, Garou said. *They are dangerous.*

Conall narrowed his gaze. Was Garou right? Was Atherton working himself into a rebuttal or something worse?

Rowan turned her back on the regent to address the ministers. Garou rumbled another warning.

"I thank you for putting your trust in me," she said. "It has come to my attention that Miron Wrede is not dead, so my first act as regent is to indict Wrede for the murder of thirteen scientists and staff at Eklridge Oasis, and one ranger." She paused but the ministers had nothing left to say, so she went on.

"Minister Wrede will be tried in absentia. If he is found guilty, a ranger squad will be sent to capture him."

Minister Keiffer finally found her voice. "You can't just put a minister on trial without proof!"

"Of course not. We have ample proof." She glanced at Conall and he gave a tiny shake of the head. They'd discussed this. Rowan had wanted to bring Dr. Banerjee in to speak to the ministers today, to solidify their position against Wrede. Conall had argued that it was too much for the ministers to take in all at once.

Rowan must have conceded because all she said was "We have an eye-witness account and the cachet of a dead scribe that details the last moments before the attack at Eklridge. The scribe was one of the victims but managed to hide the cachet before dying."

Abbot Archivist Wiktor jumped to his feet, slamming his hands on the table.

"That cachet belongs to the temple! How dare you tamper with it. The word of a scribe is sacrosanct!"

Across the room, Clem hid her grin behind her hand. Conall coughed to cover his own laugh.

Stay vigilant, brother! This fight is not over yet!

Garou's words jerked him back to attention. He pushed away from the wall and scanned the room.

Nobody had moved from their seats except the Abbot. Atherton, though dismissed from council duty, had not left the chamber and everyone seemed to be ignoring this breach of etiquette. He watched the proceedings with a glazed look.

Rowan continued as if the abbot hadn't spoken.

"Minister Wrede was…and is at the forefront of a secret cabal that is carrying out heinous experiments on humans and gaunts."

This brought a flurry of comments. The abbot didn't sit down, but he lost some of his bluster. Flora Bosman shifted in her seat, uncrossing then recrossing her legs. Beside her, Kenneth Smith frowned.

That one has the eyes of a predator.

Smith looked up, met Conall's gaze, and smiled as if he'd heard the wolf's words.

Rowan tapped her mech hand on the leather-bound book in front of her, bringing everyone's attention back to the front of the room.

"We don't yet know the exact nature of these experiments, but I assure you, we will find out." She gave Flora Bosman a sharp look that said, "I'm coming for you."

Garou rumbled happily. *Mate is fierce.*

"And this rot goes much deeper than Miron Wrede." Rowan raised her voice a notch to be heard over the murmuring. She opened the ledger and started flipping through it. She stopped at a particular page and ran a finger down the columns of numbers.

"Here we go. Five-thousand chips paid to Dr. Renata on the fifteenth of this month." She flipped the page over. "An identical transaction last month and the month before. I suspect if we examine this ledger, we'll find these payments go back many, many years, perhaps for a service rendered? A service such as maintaining a curse on the prince?" Rowan tapped the book, then turned to the Minister of the Purse. "Tell me Mr. Hayes, would I find these transactions go back that far?"

To his credit, Hayes didn't try to backpedal. "Yes, Princess. But that is not the official purser's ledger. This is." He tapped a similar leather-bound book on the table before him.

"You're right. This one was found among former regent Atherton's…uh, personal effects. It tells a very different picture than your ledger, doesn't it?

Hayes hung his head and nodded.

"And in your capacity as acting Minister of the Purse, have you recently performed an audit of the royal treasury?"

Hayes nodded again, then cleared his throat and said, "Yes."

"What did you find?"

"The funds in the treasury do not match the official records. Some two million chips are unaccounted for."

"Liar!" Atherton raised a fist and Clem stepped forward, her hand on her knife hilt. Atherton glared at her. He turned, paced across the room, and pounded his fist on the wall. He stayed like that with his head bowed. The attention of the ministers swiveled back to Rowan at the other end of the room.

Atherton was closer to Conall now and the wolf could smell fear on him.

Rowan touched the page. "There are a lot of other unexplained transactions in here. Payments to guild leaders, foreign assets and even some ministers at this table. In fact, the loss could have been much worse than two million, but there are also incoming payments that have no explanation other than the tag, TC. " She smiled at Flora Bosman. "I can't confirm what these mysterious transactions mean, but I will find out."

Smith leaned over and whispered in Bosman's ear again. She pursed her lips, gathered her notes and rose. Without a word, the two Theracine officials left the council chamber.

When the door boomed closed behind them, Atherton seemed to shake off the lethargy that had stunned him.

"You stupid, little fool!" He jabbed a finger toward Rowan. Spit frothed in the corners of his mouth. He dragged his hands through his hair, leaving it sticking straight up.

"You'll ruin everything! The city is in crisis. There is no water and you just alienated the only people capable of getting those pumps back online. You are not fit to rule!"

His hands made fists as if imagining his fingers around Rowan's neck. She stood defiant in the face of his wrath, but Conall, who knew her so well, saw the tight spots of color on her cheeks.

"This ledger is written in your hand, Faustus. It's enough to indict you for treason. And perhaps the most telling entries are the payments to Miron Wrede. How will King Erskine feel when he learns you bankrolled the murder of Dowchester citizens?"

"You…little…" Atherton didn't get to finish that thought. His face turned a bruised shade of purple, and he seemed to shrink into his clothes.

Garou felt the magic before Conall did. He howled, forcing the shift on them even as Conall's mind was trying to understand what he was seeing.

Atherton's suit collapsed as he disappeared into it. In an instant, far faster than any shifter he'd ever known, a fully formed fisher cat jumped onto the table and hissed. The creature was as big as a bear cub with the undulating body of a weasel covered in coarse brown fur. A long, thick tail snaked out behind it. The blunt snout and ears were ursine, and when it hissed, it showed off wickedly sharp fangs.

The fisher shrieked, arched its back and leaped over Abbot Archivist Wiktor. Ministers screamed and chairs fell over as they tried to run. One more lope and the fisher cat pounced, claws reaching for Rowan's neck.

Garou's shift was also lightning fast. Need to save their mate spurred the magic. Pain exploded through his bones, then he was running, shaking it off just as he shook off the human garments that clung to his legs. In three bounds, he leaped over the screaming ministers, over the chairs and the table to tackle the fisher just as its claws raked across his mate's throat.

Wolf and fisher landed on the floor in a scramble of fur and flying claws. Garou clamped his jaws onto the fisher's spine and pinned it. The creature shrieked and thrashed, twisting like a snake to snap at Garou's ears. The wolf snarled and let go, but only so his teeth could latch more deeply onto flesh and fur.

In the back of his mind, Conall was screaming to leave Atherton alive, that they needed him to answer to justice.

Garou shook his head, snapping the weasel's spine.

The wolf had no patience for human justice.

53

The Chains of Office

Rowan pressed a hand to her neck and it came away bloody, but she felt no pain.

Garou was devouring Atherton's remains on the floor. The snap of breaking bones and the wet lapping of blood was the only sound in the room.

Atherton was a fisher cat? How could he have hidden his knack for so long?

She had to address this disaster, but shock tangled her tongue.

Minister Keiffer shoved back her chair and pointed at Garou.

"Murder!" The other ministers were too stunned to react. "Murder!" Keiffer shouted again.

Bella was the only one who hadn't risen during all this commotion. She stood now, only to step around the dazed ministers and slap Keiffer.

"Don't be such a fool, Stella. We all saw Faustus attack the princess. Look! She's bleeding. Commander West was only protecting her."

Keiffer's eyes blazed. "Then a trial should prove his innocence, but Regent Atherton deserves at least that much!"

Bella sighed dramatically. "You always were a dumb twat. Atherton's actions attest to his guilt. What would be the purpose of trying Commander West? Just because your nipples get hard when you think about putting him in jail? What would that prove? I'll tell you what. It will expose every secret in that ledger." She jabbed a finger toward the book, now laying open and forgotten. "A trial will expose it to the whole city. Every detail. Every transaction. It will let everyone know what corrupt pieces of shit you and your cronies are. Is that really what you want?"

Minister Keiffer looked away and didn't answer.

Bella flopped into her chair. "Saints, I need a drink."

Rowan adjourned the meeting. There was no point in trying to further her cause today. Everyone needed time to process the shock and the new rule of things.

Chancellor March gripped her shoulder on the way out and glanced at Garou. "Will you be all right?"

Rowan squeezed his hand back and smiled. "I'll be fine. Thank you for everything."

The old chancellor's smile weighed heavily in his eyes. "Your father would be proud of you, Regent Andula."

When everyone was finally gone, Rowan asked Clem to secure the chamber doors and leave her in peace for a while. Only Bella refused to leave. She pulled a flask from somewhere in the folds of her dress, took a swig and handed it to Rowan, who drank deeply. The whisky burned feeling back into her limbs.

"How long is he going to be at that?" Bella nodded toward Garou.

"Until he's satisfied. The wolf is a little over-protective of me."

"I saw that. I'm glad for it too. Makes me worry less about what's coming for you. I bet some of those ministers will be changing their plans because of that wolf too." Bella let out a shrill laugh. "Did you see that old fart, Abbot Wiktor, when Atherton leaped right over his head." She sniffed the air. "Yep, he definitely shit himself."

Rowan felt a laugh burble up inside her, but when it emerged, it felt more hysterical than humorous. She sucked back another draught of whisky.

"Keiffer, Docker and Wiktor are all in that ledger."

Bella sighed. "Ah, that makes me sad, mostly because that means Lucian's vote against you was nothing more than his conscience. I thought better of him."

Rowan wasn't worried about the temple liaison. He was the only one who didn't seem to want her dead. "It means I'll have to fire them from the council. It could get messy."

"Nonsense dear. Wiktor and Docker will probably quit to keep their secrets. And Keiffer is Atherton's puppet. Nothing more. She hasn't had an original thought in twenty years. But now she can be your puppet."

"Maybe. I'll think about it. She *did* try to kill me." She took another swig of whisky. Maybe Bella was right. Pincer assassins seemed like the least of her worries right now. "The amount of money in that ledger is staggering. How will the city recover from its loss?"

Bella took another sip from the flash, then said, "It could have been much worse."

Rowan nodded. "I think Atherton started paying Renata and some of the others with treasury funds, but in recent years I suspect Theracine has picked up that tab for those bribes. It will take a while before I understand just how strong Theracine's hold is."

"Put your little friend Dale on it. They have a knack for ferreting out the truth."

They sat in the silence of old companions who were thinking the same thoughts.

"They'll come after you now," Bella said finally. "Bosman and her cronies."

Rowan sipped the whisky and handed the flask back with a nod.

"Wrede is making an army of gaunts and Flora is funding him. We have proof. They're not just making monsters, Auntie. They *are* monsters."

Bella stared at her, then nodded. "Fucking monsters." She took another gulp of whisky. "Makes me glad you have your own monster to protect you." She jutted her chin toward Garou, then rose. "Well, that was the most fun I've had in years, but perhaps too much excitement for these old bones." She tipped Rowan's chin upward and stared into her eyes, then inspected the cut on her neck, just above the collar bone.

"Make sure you clean that well. Saints only know what kind of filth was under Atherton's claws."

After Bella left, Rowan sat for a long time staring at the Infinity Clock. Eventually, she felt a nudge and her hand fell to Garou's soft head. He put his muzzle in her lap and she stroked his ears. She didn't even care that he was covered in blood.

He draped something long and dangling over her knee, then licked his lips. It was the regent's chain of office. Rowan wrapped it around her fingers. She leaned down, kissed Garou right between the ears, and whispered, "Thank you."

54

The Bones of a Mech

Rowan rode in a palace cat. Conall drove. Minna and Bella sat in the back seat. Conall had coordinated with General Lind and an army of keepers kept the street clear. Without water, the city was at a standstill and people had too much time on their hands. Time and worry. Many came every day to pay homage to Talos. Others were looking to cause trouble. Rowan ignored the cheers and the angry shouts that were thrown at them. Bella enjoyed the attention and threw kisses at fans and dissenters alike.

Clem was on duty at the gate, coordinating the keepers who held the fragile peace by forcing the crowds to stay behind barriers.

"Stop the cat," Rowan said.

"Not here," Conall said. "It's not safe."

"Stop or I'll jump out."

Conall swore and slowed the cat to a stop. Rowan stood up on her seat, and swept her gaze over the crowd.

Voices called out. *Is the prince awake? Is the regent dead?* Then the voices were drowned out by hundreds of others yelling and cheering.

Rowan held up a hand until the crowd quieted.

"It is true. Your prince is awake!" She smiled and waited for the cheering to die down. When it didn't, she shouted over the din. "Prince Ethan will address the public soon." The crowd quieted. Everyone wanted to hear what she had to say. "I hope my term as regent will be short, and that I leave the city a better place for my brother and for you. My first act as regent will be to set Talos on his rightful path and restore the city's water. May the saints bless him and you!" She waved again and sat down. The noise was deafening, and the onlookers pressed against the barricade.

Conall hit the pedal and the cat lurched forward. Clem waved them through the gate, and then called for the keepers to close ranks behind them.

The noise of the crowd chased them into the Meadows. They rolled past the tumble of stone that marked the fallen tower. The gate had been hastily repaired. It wouldn't hold against an army of gaunts, but it was sturdy enough to keep the crowd from following their cat. There were other gates though, and another crowd waited outside the wall behind a hastily erected barricade. The keepers had also cleared the wall on either side of the gate, but hundreds of brave souls had climbed the stones to watch from farther down the wall.

Conall slowed the cat and Clem caught up to them. She pointed to the spectators on the wall.

"Should I have them cleared?" she asked.

"Yes," Conall said, at the same time as Rowan said, "No." She laid a hand on his arm. He was tense.

"They're out of arrow range, aren't they?" she asked. Conall gave a reluctant nod. The crease between his brows was as deep as cat tracks in the mud. "Then let them stay. Whether things go right or wrong, we'll need witnesses to this day."

"Then you should have brought along a scribe." He knew she abhorred the whole idea of scribes, but she let the jibe go. He took her security personally, and his ranger sense was telling him that this whole procedure was a titan-sized risk.

They parked the cat and got out to walk the rest of the way.

Talos lay against the tower as if he'd sat down for an afternoon nap. Rowan shielded her eyes and stared at his face. There was no flicker of light behind his eyes.

Someone called to her from the watching crowd, but she ignored them and turned her attention to the smaller group of people gathered by Talos's outstretched foot.

Noah was there and Denny too. Ferlan and Elias had joined Clem to patrol the crowds. Minna conferred with Rudi and Irva. Rowan couldn't make out the words as they spoke Essian, but by Rudi's gestures toward Talos, he was expounding on the virtues of the mech or his abhorrence for it. With the Ebos, it could go either way.

Only Dale was missing. They'd volunteered to stay back at the palace with Ethan. The prince was too weak to walk, and he had developed panic attacks when left alone. His new physician was a young Jocastan doctor suggested by Noah. She was relentlessly optimistic about Ethan's recovery. Rowan chose to believe her. For now.

She needed to focus on the job at hand or Ethan would have a very different New Torwood to rule.

The thera pumps were progressing under the city. Soon the water would be back online, and the city would become beholden to the Theracine Corporation for its basic needs. The people—her people—would be forced to drink water steeped in thera. Rowan refused to let that future take hold. They had to get Talos up and moving.

"Are you ready?" Noah wiped sweat off his brow. The day was already hot. It would be even hotter inside the metal mech.

Rudi seemed to have worn out his argument with Irva.

The lumina sat beside Talos's foot and crossed her legs.

"Are you comfortable, Essami?" Minna said. Irva reached up and touched Minna's cheek with affection.

"I am comfortable. Thank you." She laid her palms flat on the ground and closed her eyes. Blue veins showed through the almost translucent skin of her throat. After preparing this spell for two days, she seemed fragile, like a porcelain vase teetering on the edge of a mantle.

Rudi kicked at the sand and stalked away.

"Is everything all right?" Rowan asked Minna.

"It will be, Evani."

Rudi strode toward them and poked Conall in the chest with a finger. "This will kill her. You kill her!"

Phalian squawked and flew at the Rati, banking right just in time to avoid hitting him. Rudi swatted the air as if Phalian were a giant fly.

Rowan frowned. "Irva assured me she could do this magic. Are you saying she was lying?"

Rudi scrunched up his face. "Lumina do not lie. She will do it and it will kill her."

"Can you stop her, if she goes too far?"

Rudi shuffled his feet. "I do not know."

"I will stay with Irva," Minna said. "She is the anchor to the spell, but I will be her anchor."

"If you think this spell is too much for her, you'll pull her out?"

"Yes, Evani. If that is your wish."

"My wish is that no one dies today!"

"Yes, Evani. We will do our best to honor that request."

Rowan felt a growl rumble in her chest. She was so deep in this mess, she couldn't see the surface anymore.

Conall took her mech hand in his and held the gloved fingers to his lips. "That goes for you too, Striker. No one dies today. We can find another way."

She nodded, not trusting her voice. They both knew the stakes here. It wasn't just about Talos and water. It was about taking back her city, about letting the people see their princess do something extraordinary. To remind them of why the Andula family had ruled here for three hundred years.

Minna approached. She carried four white crystals on long leather cords.

"From here on, Irva cannot be disturbed. She talks to the ley-line even now. The link is fragile and easily broken. Put these on." She handed one to Noah, Denny, Rowan and Bella. A similar crystal hung around Minna's neck. Rowan draped the cord over her shoulders. The crystal was diamond-shaped with rounded edges. It was heavy against her chest. She ran her mech fingers over it and they buzzed with potent magic.

"Do not remove them until the spell is done," Minna said. "No matter what. They link us to Irva. Break that link without the proper guidance and… it will hurt." Minna frowned. For once she found no humor in the situation, and that scared Rowan more than anything.

"I will act as Irva's second," Minna added. "If things go wrong, I will break my ley-stone, but that will…"

"We get it," Noah said. "That will hurt."

Rowan gripped Minna's hand. In the few months since their return from the Meadows, Minna had become more than her bodyguard. She was her friend.

Minna met Rowan's eyes. "I assure you, Evani, all will be well. I feel it in my bones."

Rowan nodded. There was no more positive prediction from an Ebos.

Minna gripped her ley-stone. "There is another such ley-stone attached to the water pump under the city. Irva has spent two days priming these stones with magic. Think of them as a trigger to start the spell. They link you together, and all of you to Irva. And Irva to the ley-stone. She is the center—the conduit. The magic will flow from her to you, and from her to the water pumps under the city. Do not fear the force of this magic. It will feel overwhelming. Trust in your colleagues. Together, our bones are strong."

Rowan suspected that saying sounded better in Essian.

Minna turned to Rowan. "The only piece missing is Talos."

Rowan nodded. "I understand." Linking Talos into the loop was her job.

"Good," Minna said. "When the time comes, you must all push your magic into the stones. Do not hold back."

"How will we know it's time?" Noah asked.

"You will know," Minna said darkly.

"Terrific." Noah gripped his ley-stone and turned away.

They still had a few minutes while Irva prepared herself. Noah and Denny sat beside her, forming a rough triangle. Minna turned to join them, but Rowan stopped her.

"Thank you, my friend. For this and so much more."

"You are welcome, Evani." She glanced up at the sleeping Talos. "He may be a mech, but his bones are important too."

The crowd on the wall was getting rowdy. Conall pulled Rowan aside. "I'm going up to the tower to make sure they have enough keepers. I don't want this whole thing going to shit because of a few rabble-rousers."

Rowan nodded. Her mouth was suddenly dry. His eyes softened, and he ran his thumb along her neck, past the bandage from the fisher cat's scratches and up her jawline. She leaned into the touch until he cupped her face in his hand.

"I'll be back before you get started. I promise. Just let me…" He cleared his throat and tried again. "I wish I could be in there with you. I wish my knack was more helpful."

"It was helpful in the council chamber." She touched the bandage. "You saved my life. Again."

"And now I have to let you go save the city." He grinned. "It's not always easy being consort to the regent."

She laughed. "Is that what you are? Consort? Sounds dirty."

"It could be." His lips covered hers. It was a brief kiss, far too brief. They still hadn't talked about what Conall would do once things settled. Would the lone wolf take to the Meadows again? She wanted him to stay, but now wasn't the time for that conversation.

With his mouth against her ear, he whispered, "Go be the hero. They're all watching. Show them what a princess can do."

He strode off toward the tower.

Rowan's legs felt weak. She filled her chest with a calming breath and turned her attention to the job at hand.

Hero, indeed.

Rowan climbed onto Talos's foot. She shielded her eyes with one hand and waved to the crowd with the other. It looked like half the city stood on the wall watching. Someone cheered. Someone booed. Rowan clenched her mech hand in a fist and the cheers won out.

She unlocked the door in Talos's ankle and turned back just in time to see Conall returning from the tower. His face was lost in shadow, but he raised a hand. A greeting and a farewell.

Phalian followed her inside the iron giant. His wings sparked as they hit the metal wall.

"SQUAWK!"

"You don't have to come," Rowan said. "Stay with Conall, if you want." But the bird landed on her shoulder. His prickly claws scratched through her shirt and Rowan was glad for the grounding sensation that kept her thoughts from flying in every direction.

It was hot and dark inside the mech. With Talos sitting, she had to crawl blindly until she reached his waist, then she grabbed the ladder and started to climb. A faint blue aura shone from the ley-stone. It did little to light her way, but she didn't need light. She knew every rivet and every rung on that ladder.

The metal creaked and groaned as it took her weight. She'd never noticed it before. When Talos was up and walking the sounds of hydraulics and gears drowned out everything else.

When she reached his chest, she looped her elbow around a ladder rung and hung on, catching her breath. The heart seemed to glow very dimly, but she couldn't be sure it wasn't simply the reflection from the ley-stone. She tucked the stone into her shirt and waited until her eyes adjusted again.

Yes. It was as faint as a forgotten dream, but it was there. Talos's heart hadn't burned out yet.

The cables that joined the heart to the ichor reserve hung slack. She found the one she'd secured and removed the ribbon that bound it. Gold liquid oozed from the end of the cable. Rowan plugged it with her mech finger. Her hand sizzled with energy. The ichor was unlike anything she'd felt before. It was more magical than blood. Even more than the thera-laced blood she'd sensed in the scribes. If Harry Hightower was Vulcan, did that mean this ichor was the blood of a god?

Before second guesses stole her courage, she removed the glove on her mech arm and opened the port on the underside of her wrist—the one shaped like an infinity sign.

A flash of memory stung her. The first time Conall had held her mech arm, he'd wondered about that port and she'd had no answer for him. She'd never known its use. Now she did. Harry had built a connection to Talos right into her arm. It was almost like he'd expected this day to come. Maybe he had.

She patted the metal wall affectionately. "Here's hoping Harry was right and I do have everything I need to fix you."

She plugged in the cable.

The magic in the ichor bit into her nerve endings and she jerked. Phalian jumped down to her wrist and pecked furiously at the cable.

"Stop that!"

The bird pranced. He was clearly agitated.

"It's all right. I'm all right." After that first jolt, the magic had leveled off. "You shouldn't stand there, though. Just in case. Why don't you stay in my pocket." She tried to shoo him away, hoping he'd shift, but he just squawked again and landed on her shoulder.

The ley-stone pulsed. The lash of magic nearly knocked her off the ladder. She pulled the stone from her shirt. It was glowing bright blue now. Another pulse of magic throbbed through it, making her knees weak. She wrapped her left arm around the ladder to brace herself and gripped the ley-stone in her fist. Her mech arm hung suspended in the air by the cable—a full circuit.

It was time.

She pushed with her magic—magic that until a few months ago she'd credited to her mech arm. Now she felt it flow both ways. Down her arm to the cable and into Talos's heart, and outward through the ley-stone to Irva and the others.

The stone pulsed again, a deep throb that echoed in Rowan's bones. Talos's heart surged with light and went out.

More! We need more!

Rowan focused her cry into the ley-stone.

The pulses came faster, drawing on her magic and...

...and suddenly she wasn't clinging to the ladder in the dark. She was standing on a flat ground surrounded by blue sky. No, not sky. The blue came from the glowing ley-stones. Noah's, Denny's, Bella's and hers. They formed a circle with Irva at the center. Her ley-stone shone like a star moments away from exploding. Minna stood beside her—a rock in the current of magic.

Rowan turned in wonder. A laugh bubbled through her lips. The magic flowed through her, giving as much as it took. It felt *good*.

She saw Noah laughing too. He was lit from inside. So were Denny and Minna. She could see their bones and the delicate weaving of veins and capillaries. And more. Tiny flashes of electricity wove patterns in their heads.

It's their thoughts. I'm seeing the working of their minds!

Irva's voice came like a flash of lightning. "Now!"

Rowan pushed with everything she had. The magic felt cool and comforting…until it didn't.

The surge reversed and wildfire seared her veins.

Something was wrong, so desperately wrong. She could hear herself screaming and could do nothing to stop it. Phalian's squawk added to the cacophony. Rowan's skin was being flayed. Muscle tore from bone. Bones crunched under the heel of unforgiving magic. She was nothing—no body, no mind, only red-hot pain.

She heard Minna scream, *No Essami!*

A tsunami of magic engulfed her.

A life exploded, its magic like shards of glass cutting her soul.

Rowan blacked out.

Awareness came back to her as she sucked in breath. She didn't know how long she'd been out. Seconds, maybe minutes. Her lungs felt like shredded rags. A whimper escaped her lips. She licked them and tasted blood. Everything hurt.

Her ears rang and then the noise resolved itself.

She was hearing gears turn.

And the painful squeal of hydraulic pumps coming back to life.

And the incessant squawking of a very angry bird.

She blinked away dark spots in her eyes. Talos's heart hummed with light.

Phalian's screech finally demanded her attention. She shifted on the ladder. Her arm and one foot were caught in the rungs. How had she not fallen?

Phalian. He held the end of the cable in his beak. At some point, it had come unplugged from her arm and he'd wound it around her, securing her to the ladder.

Rowan let out a sob. Phalian landed on her shoulder and made strange cooing noises she'd never heard from him before. She poured every ounce of gratitude she had into their connection.

The ladder lurched sideways.

Talos was getting to his feet! Gears screamed. After so much downtime, they needed grease. Slowly, ponderously, the right leg swung forward.

When his foot slammed to the ground, it rattled Rowan's teeth, and she thought she'd never heard anything so beautiful.

She hung on the ladder, sobbing and laughing and sobbing again. She'd given everything to the spell and had barely enough energy to keep from falling.

And then it came back to her. Those last seconds before she'd blacked out. Minna's cry and that horrible explosion.

Oh, saints. Irva!

She untangled the cable and tied it off so the ichor didn't leak away. Then she hurried downward. Her foot slipped, and her chin slammed into the metal rung. She dangled in midair with only her mech arm gripping the ladder, a dark and dangerous drop below her. Her feet scrabbled to find the rung and she began the descent, slower this time.

Too slow! She cursed. Every second she wasted, Talos was walking away from Irva and the others.

The door at the bottom hung open, a beacon of daylight. She dashed outside with Phalian swooping beside her. She clung to the handhold beside the door and blinked in the bright sunlight. Behind them, the gate loomed, nearly a quarter mile away already. The crowd of onlookers on the wall was just a dark smudge.

She was too far to see Irva and the others.

When Talos put his foot down again, she leaped from it and took off at a run.

Her legs jellied under her and she stumbled more than ran. Stones and clumps of crabgrass tried to trip her. She fell, tearing the flesh of her palm and her pants at the knee, then rose and kept moving.

Someone was rushing out to meet her. Conall. He waved his arms as if she were a runaway horse.

"Rowan! No!"

She was close enough now to see them. Noah was on his knees, screaming out the effects of his knack. Denny stood beside him. There were two other figures hunched together.

Ferlan dashed from the gate, screaming as he ran.

Conall tried to stop her, to hold her back with the comfort of his arms. But she had to see.

She had to *know*.

She skidded to a stop just as Ferlan fell to the ground over the body.

Irva sat up, cradling Minna in her arms. The lumina's eyes were red and tears flowed freely from her cheeks onto Minna's.

Irva rocked back and forth. Her eyes met Rowan's.

"I am sorry, Evani."

55

THE MARROW REMEMBERS

ROWAN SLEPT FOR TWENTY-FOUR HOURS straight, waking only when Conall insisted that she eat. On the following morning, she lay in bed, feeling like she was recovering from an illness.

"How's Ethan?" Her throat was raw and her voice croaked.

Conall sat on the edge of her bed and brushed the hair from her forehead. "He's getting stronger. Don't worry about him. Just rest."

"And…the others?" She couldn't bring herself to say their names, not when a very important name would be missing.

"They're resting too." Conall kissed her forehead. "Drink this. Irva says it will help to replenish your magic." He handed her a small vial.

Rowan pulled the cork and downed the bitter liquid.

"How does Irva have the energy to make potions?" The lumina had taken the brunt of the spell.

"Rudi's been helping her when he's not tinkering with Talos."

"Oh, good." She flopped back on the bed. At least she could tick Talos's tune-up off the list of worries that stuffed her head like wet wool.

"Go back to sleep." Conall tucked the blanket around her. "I'll be right…"

But she didn't hear the rest as darkness took her.

Irva's potion helped, and Rowan woke in the middle of the night, feeling alert. Conall snored softly beside her. Not wanting to wake him, she lay for

395

some time, watching the play of light from the window and fiddling with the wound from the fisher cat's claws. The scab made a dotted line from her collar bone to her chin, but the worst of it was healing well.

She thought about Atherton and the pure hate she'd seen in his eyes before he shifted. She thought about the work that still needed to be done to heal the city. She thought about Ethan.

And Minna.

She wanted to be happy. They'd beaten the odds. The water pumps were back online. Ethan was awake and Atherton would never hurt anyone again. Even Theracine Corporation had been put in their place, though she knew that couldn't last.

But Minna's death overshadowed any joy. Her life had been the price for those accomplishments and Rowan couldn't help feeling the cost was too high.

It hit her team hard too. Irva had said that Minna was the victim of a ley-line surge, the kind that had been plaguing the city for weeks. The spell had worked. Talos's heart had restarted and relinked to the ley-lines, then before Irva could disconnect, the surge had overwhelmed her. That much magic would have burned through all of them and consumed Talos's heart if Minna hadn't blocked it.

Minna, their anchor.

Simple ill luck and bad timing, Irva said, but Rowan knew the truth. Rowan had ordered Minna to protect Irva, and she'd obeyed her Evani. She'd saved them all.

Rowan had been regent for only a few days and already her crown was heavier by one soul. She couldn't wait for the day when she could pass that crown on to its rightful owner.

Hunger finally made her get up. She found Elias on duty out in the hallway, and asked him to send someone for food. When she returned to bed, Conall was awake.

She smiled. "At least with you in my bed, the guards have agreed to stay out of my room. Minna used to insist on sleeping…" She trailed off.

Conall pulled her close. Wrapped in his arms, she had the strength to accept the grief inside her, and she wept.

"Minna was right to be worried. Why didn't you tell me you'd been targeted by Pincers?" He kissed her neck to soften the rebuke.

"Oh, that." She hiccuped as her crying faded. "I guess with everything else going on, I sort of forgot. Sounds crazy, I know. It just wasn't a priority. Besides, with Atherton dead, the contract is probably void."

"Maybe." Conall didn't sound convinced. The maid arrived with a tray of tea and sandwiches. At Rowan's request, she set it on the bed and left quietly through the dressing room.

Rowan ate two sandwiches and drank an entire cup of tea before speaking again.

"Remind me not to let my hands get close to your mouth when you're hungry." He grinned. "I might lose a finger."

Rowan stuffed an entire quarter sandwich in her mouth.

"Such a princess."

She stuck out her tongue.

"Do that again and I'll make you use it."

She swallowed and licked her lips, very slowly.

"Now you've done it."

His voice was dark and he went spelunking beneath the covers to find that soft spot on her inner thigh that drove her wild. She grabbed his hand, not to push it away, but to urge it up her thigh. She needed the grounding of his touch right now. She needed him to banish thoughts of loss and worry for days ahead. Their intimacy was frantic and undignified, and when they finally came together, joy, pleasure, and pain erupted from her in one wretched scream.

At some point, the sound of the tea tray clattering to the floor brought them up for air.

Rowan swept back her sweaty hair and held in a giggle made from equal parts exhaustion and waning adrenaline.

"The maids will think we had a food fight."

Conall lay back and pulled her close so she could lay her head on his chest. Her mech fingers made circles in the hair on his damp skin.

"I feel like a bad person for doing…that today of all days. "I feel like a bad person for doing…that today of all days. But I really needed a break from my thoughts. They just keep bashing around in here." She tapped her head.

"That's my job as consort. To keep you sane."

Rowan huffed out a laugh. "Consort." She sat up and leaned on one elbow to look him in the face. "You know one of those many worries I can't dismiss is that you'll leave again. So I thought, what if I found you a proper position. Like ambassador to the Ebos?"

Conall shook his head, but she rushed on before he could voice his protest.

"Think about it. Omika wants an Ebos presence in New Torwood. Who better than you to foster that relationship? It would mean you could still travel, but your base would be here, and…"

Conall touched her lip with one finger.

"You wouldn't just be consort," her words were muffled around his finger.

"Hush." He leaned in to kiss her, then said, "I won't be Ambassador to Benni."

Her stomach clenched. She knew what was coming. The lone wolf needed to run free. She was stupid to think she could ever cage him.

His smile caught her off guard.

"Don't look so solemn, Striker. You won't get rid of me that easily. I've already thought of the perfect solution that will keep me here at your side. I'm going to be your new head of security. Minna was right. You need an official honor guard. You should have had one years ago. Ethan too. We know Atherton had his reasons to be lax in this area, but that stops now."

Rowan narrowed her eyes. "You're not just saying that? You'll really stay?"

"Yes."

"And Garou? He's okay with living in the city?"

Conall tapped a finger against his temple. "If I tried to run away again, he'd make my life hell until I turned my ass around."

Rowan kissed him soundly, then settled her cheek against his chest again.

"It's settled then. My new chief of security."

"There's just one thing I would ask." His voice rumbled through his chest.

"Hmm?"

"I want to go after Wrede."

Rowan squeezed her eyes shut and wished she *could* lock him in a cage and keep him safe. But that would be how she'd lose him for good.

"Of course," she said with forced optimism. "It will be our priority, and you'll have every resource you need."

They talked well into the night, discussing other necessary appointments and the arrangements for the ceremonies that would fill the next few days.

As dawn lightened the sky, they made love again—this time, lingering over every touch.

Alice woke her early.

Rowan stared bleary-eyed at the page. "Your meeting with the Ambassador is in less than an hour, Evani."

"Of course. Thank you."

Alice left and Rowan tipped her aching body out of bed. After washing and dressing she found Conall sitting up with the blankets tucked around him. He was listening to Roger recite the morning gossip from the palace. Conall had already been implementing some new security measures and Roger was one of them. Mech valets were ubiquitous in the palace and the city. No one paid attention to yet another mech rolling around, and Roger was able to glean information in the form of gossip.

Roger finished his report on movements in the keepers' barracks as Rowan came in.

"You're up early," Conall said. "Need back up this morning?" The blankets covered him to the waist, revealing rugged shoulders and chest grizzled with fur. His tousled hair stuck up and a three-day beard only highlighted his warm smile. She wanted to climb back into bed and feel that beard in places it wasn't meant to be. Instead, she draped the regent's chain of office over her shoulders. The pendant fell almost to her navel and felt like a millstone around her neck.

She turned and kissed Conall on the nose. He leaned forward to grab her, but she danced away.

"Go back to sleep. I have an early meeting with a handsome ambassador."

Conall fell back on the pillows. "Oh, thank the saints. I'm too old to keep up with you."

"Liar." Rowan let her hand skim down his chest. He caught her fingers and kissed them. "I'll be back in time for the ceremony."

"Ceremonies," Conall said.

"Right." It would be a busy day.

She turned to leave, then stopped.

"Have you heard from your brother?"

Conall nodded. "He sent a runner ahead. They'll be here later today. Dalkyn's coming too."

"Okay. That gives us time to prepare." But how did one prepare for telling a brother he'd lost a sister?

The Keeper's Yard was bustling with activity, but it all stopped when Rowan stepped outside. Rangers who'd been loading crates onto cats stopped to watch the procession. The mechanics stood up and wiped their greasy hands on rags. Others faltered in their steps. Some saluted.

Rowan sighed. Gone were her days of being inconspicuous. The chain of office was a beacon and so was the maroon and gold uniform of her new honor guard. She nodded to keepers and rangers as she headed to the gate where a small group waited beside three fully loaded cats.

Remy was easily distinguishable from the group as he stood six inches taller than most others. He threw back his head and laughed, the sound booming in the quiet morning.

Rowan's heart skipped when she saw who stood beside him. Denny. He smiled shyly as she approached.

"You're going home then?" she said.

Denny nodded. "It's time."

Remy clapped him on the back. "His sister will be glad to know he's alive."

"Your sister?" she asked.

"Of course," Remy said. "Didn't you know that your friend here is Queen

Tabina's little brother? The king and queen were heartbroken when they learned of his supposed death."

Denny turned a bright shade of pink and looked at the ground. His fingers were twined with his favorite fidget rope.

Rowan laughed. "Conall will be happy to know that I finally ferreted out your secret. Why didn't you tell us?"

"I thought you knew. After, you know…" He glanced at Remy, and Rowan understood. Denny assumed that after their bonding rite, Rowan knew all his innermost secrets.

"Right," she said slowly. "I knew you had a sister, and that you quarreled with her. I just didn't place her as the queen."

Remy was watching them curiously.

That one has a built-in lie detector, she thought. To distract him, she held up the treaty document. "All signed and official."

Remy took the document and looked it over.

"I never doubted you'd come through." He gently touched the scab on her neck. "Everyone is talking about the princess who stood with her wolf and defied the council. I wish I'd been there to see it." He waved the document. "King Erskine will be pleased. Work on the new road will begin immediately. Let it be a symbol of a new alliance with trade flowing to both our cities."

"Trade, yes. But be careful what you wish for ambassador. Not all trade is good."

Remy tilted his head and smiled. "That's strange talk from a new regent."

Rowan ground her teeth, deciding how much to say. What proof did she really have that thera was poisoning their people? She turned to Denny.

"You have a long journey ahead of you. Use it to fill the ambassador in. Tell him everything. And when you get home, tell your sister and brother."

Denny nodded. Remy arched his eyebrow.

"Some progress is not worth the price," Rowan said with a smile. "That has been my first lesson as regent. Safe travels Ambassador."

56

A COG IN THE RIGHT PLACE

CONALL WAS GRATEFUL THAT THE first of three ceremonies that week was over quickly. Rowan's official swearing in as regent was a private but formal affair. They met in Ethan's room so he wouldn't get tired out. Bella and Dale were in attendance, along with most of the ministers.

Flora Bosman and Stella Keiffer had sent their apologies if not their excuses for missing the event. As Bella had predicted, Marylin Docker and the Abbot Archivist had quit the council.

Conall had insisted that all the ministers be searched for weapons before entering the room. They hadn't liked that, and he couldn't care less. If they were allies, they would understand. If they weren't allies, they were learning that a new sheriff was in town and easy access to the royals was a thing of the past.

Ethan was dressed in a simple suit and sitting in a chair. A sheen of sweat glistened on his forehead, and the room smelled of closed air, sweat and a hint of vomit. A moth perched on the prince's gold epaulet and no one bothered to brush it away. Every few minutes, a wave of trembling overtook him. Grant stood by the door, looking concerned for his patient.

Conall leaned toward Chancellor March and whispered, "No bells and whistles today. Make it tight and clean."

March pursed his lips and nodded. Then, in a booming voice, he read out the rights and responsibilities of the office of regent.

"Do you, Princess Rowan Andula promise to uphold these laws, and represent your king to the best of your abilities?"

"I do."

"Do you, Prince Ethan Andula, accept Princess Rowan Andula as your representative on the council and in all matters of state until such a time as you see fit to dissolve the Office of Regent and ascend to the throne in its stead."

"I do." Ethan's voice warbled like he was still pre-pubescent and another fit overtook him.

"Everybody out!" Conall ordered. The ministers were happy to oblige and the room emptied.

Ethan was already fading. Rowan helped him lie down and tucked the blankets around him.

"Rest now. I'll be back later to get you ready." She brushed hair off his forehead. Ethan mumbled something and curled into a ball. He was asleep before they left the room.

Grant followed them out and Conall pulled him aside.

"If he's not up to making an appearance this afternoon, I need to know now."

The citizens of New Torwood had been overjoyed to learn their prince was awake, but after a week, they were getting impatient to see him. Ethan was scheduled to make an appearance from the palace balcony that afternoon.

"I'll see that he's fit," Grant said. "A good rest, some hot soup and starch in his shorts will get him standing."

Conall nodded. "We'll keep it brief, but I'd like you there, just in case."

Just in case Ethan fainted or started babbling, crying or ranting, things he seemed to do in abundance these days.

"Of course, Consort. I mean Commander." He titled his head. "Sorry, I'm not sure what to call you."

Conall grinned. "We'll figure out something."

"I'm sure. Whatever it is, I'm glad to have you around, sir."

"Thank you, Grant. The feeling is mutual."

Rowan was already next door in what Conall was calling their war room. He'd asked to have Noah and Banerjee waiting for them. Dale was there too. And Chancellor March. Noah was scowling at the chancellor, like he suspected some kind of intervention.

Conall sat and waited for Rowan to speak. They'd both agreed this was her show.

"Thank you all for taking time to meet. I know this is a busy day. I'll be brief." She turned to March. "Chancellor, I asked you to stay behind because I have some new appointments to make and you'll need to ratify them."

"Of course, Regent." March's mustache twitched as if he held back a grin.

"First, you already know that Dale will be my Senior Advisor. I'd like them to have all the necessary access to the archives, the quartermaster and the treasury."

The chancellor nodded. "They should have a suite in the West Wing too. Would you care for Atherton's old rooms?"

Dale hesitated. "Uh, sure."

"That's settled, then." The chancellor turned back to Rowan, waiting for her to speak again.

"Commander West will be taking over security for the palace." She paused when March raised an eyebrow. "I know this cuts in on your territory as chancellor. I hope you'll accept this new division of duties."

"With grace, my regent." He nodded in a short bow. "I'm getting on in years. That's no secret. Handing over security will be a relief, and in truth, it should have been done years ago, but I didn't trust any appointee of Atherton's."

"I know you'll give Commander West everything he needs to get started."

"I'm an old wolf myself in many ways," March said. "I'm sure we'll get along splendidly."

Conall met the chancellor's eye and nodded.

"Good. That's settled then," Rowan said. "Now, this is Medic Noah Sommerton. I want him to head a new commission that oversees the thera camps. If Theracine expects us to send conscripts, then we need oversight. Noah will start with a thorough investigation of the gangra outbreak at Oxeye." She smiled. "If he's willing."

Noah stood, his eyes wide. "Why me?"

"Because you have the medical knowledge to find the truth. And because I trust you. Will you do it?"

Noah nodded tightly. Conall had no doubt that Noah would dig through the dirt in Oxeye until he carved out the rotten core of Theracine's treachery.

"Good." Rowan clapped her hands. "That leaves just one more

appointment to be filled. Chancellor, you may have a hard time with this one, but I hope you'll trust me."

"Of course, Regent. As I trusted your father."

She walked over to Banerjee and took his mech hand in hers. "This valet holds both the physical and emotional memories of Dr. Sonny Banerjee. I believe he *is* Dr. Banerjee."

Roger had done an excellent job of cleaning up Banerjee's memory cells. The stuttering was gone and his eyes focused on Rowan with calm intensity.

"Thank you, Regent Andula." Even his voice module was more stable.

"Conall told me of your wish to be…decommissioned, but I would ask that you put that off. For a little while anyway. This fight isn't over and I believe you still have a great purpose ahead of you. Will you be my new Minister of Science?"

March's bushy eyebrows rose and his mustache twitched. He couldn't hide his surprise.

"My lady…I mean Regent, this is highly irregular."

"We live in irregular times, Chancellor." She turned back to Banerjee. "Will you do it?"

Pistons hissed as the mech nodded.

"Excellent! Then we once again have enough ministers for a quorum. Chancellor please draw up the papers to confirm these new posts."

Chancellor March agreed, but he was shaking his head. Conall took his elbow and walked him out.

"Not sure how I'm going to explain this to the other ministers," March said.

"My suggestion is, don't. Let anyone who has objections raise them in the council chambers. Rowan will shut them down."

March nodded. "She is a force to be reckoned with."

"Like the Mogra and the Fanfaronade blowing through town all at once. New Torwood may never be the same."

"I hope so, my boy. I certainly hope so."

Conall left the chancellor at the atrium, but before he returned to the war room, Banerjee stepped from the shadows to confront him.

"I hope you have not forgotten your pledge, Commander West. When this fight is over, I still expect you to end this mech life."

Conall spoke slowly. "I will hold to my promise. But you just pledged yourself to the regent. I expect you to keep to it as well."

"Indeed, I will. Until such a time as I am no longer needed. As proof of my new loyalties, I offer you a token of information."

"Go on."

"Elsie Myer trapped me in this body for a reason."

"You said it was because of your knack."

"My knack, yes, but also the data that knack has provided over the years. Wrede suspected that I knew the missing link between humans and gaunts and he was right." His joints creaked as he settled against the wall. "I have studied the DNA of many creatures, plants too. I can say with some assurance that Wrede will never be able to make a stable human-gaunt hybrid. Human DNA is too fragile."

"Is that why they turned to thera as a solution?"

"Perhaps. But long term thera ingestion kills 99% of its human victims. It is not a viable solution. Shifter DNA is."

Banerjee fell silent while Conall let that revelation sink in. His father had been an addict, but thera hadn't killed him. Was Banerjee right? Unlike humans, shifters could regenerate damaged cells. Was that the key?

"Does Wrede know this?"

"Not from me, but perhaps from Elsie. I don't know what she managed to transfer out of that cave."

Garou growled and the sound came out Conall's mouth.

"Then we'd better find Wrede. And soon."

57

NEW GEARS BITE HARDEST

ROWAN TRIED NOT TO GAPE at the crowd in the square on King's Way. Had people gathered like this to hear her father speak? She couldn't remember. Certainly Hightown hadn't seen the likes since his death.

Ethan played his part, though she knew it cost him. He waved and smiled and the crowd ate it up. Their magical prince back from the dead. Rowan pretended sisterly affection kept her close, but in reality Ethan was leaning heavily on her.

"Don't step aside or I'll land on my face." Ethan spoke from the corner of his mouth, still smiling.

A wave of trembles went through him and the smile faltered.

"I've got you." She circled her arm around his waist. He was as light as a child, and her time wrenching out rusted bolts had made her strong.

Ten minutes later, the crowd's enthusiasm hadn't dimmed. She eyed the ants and beetles clustering around their feet. Agitation always made Ethan's knack stronger. A fat bee circled their heads and then another. When the gnats found them, she called for Grant to take the prince back to his room. The spectators roared in displeasure, but Rowan took it in stride, smiling and waving for another few moments before following her brother inside.

The ministers had gathered to cheer on their prince and they clapped as Grant helped him into a mech chair and wheeled him away. Ethan could still only manage a couple of steps before his legs gave out, but he smiled at the reception from his ministers.

Rowan pulled off the heavy robe she'd donned for the performance and handed it to a waiting page.

"May I have a word, Regent."

Rowan almost walked by before she realized Flora Bosman was talking to her.

Right. I'm the regent.

"Of course. Would you like a refreshment in my office?"

"No. I'll be brief. The quartermaster tells me that he supplies your rooms with candles and even an antique lamp from the days of ley-line magic."

"Call me old school."

"Let's not pretend. You have no love for thera, just like your father."

Rowan lifted her chin. If Dale was right, this woman had been part of the plot that killed her father.

"You don't get to talk about him."

"No? All right then. How about the truth. Thera is here to stay. It's cheap and renewable. People depend on it. They won't go back to costly ley-line mechs or dirty oil lamps. You might as well ask them to live in the dark ages. Banning thera would cause city-wide turmoil."

Rowan waited for her to finish, then waited a moment longer, until Bosman started to look uncertain. She leaned in.

"Thera is killing people. You know it and you don't care. A few dead addicts doesn't affect your bottom line, does it." She leaned back and crossed her arms. Bosman wore a sneer. The other ministers had noticed the confrontation and were watching.

"How much profit did Theracine make last year?" Rowan asked.

"That is irrelevant."

"How much?"

Bosman shrugged.

"My accountants tell me it's somewhere in the millions," Rowan said. "And this year, even with the outbreak in Oxeye, it will be even more. In fact it is because of that outbreak. You don't have to pay all those expensive reapers. You can start with conscripts, pay them a fraction of the old salaries and start again. Your shareholders must be pleased. But nobody asks, at what point is enough money enough? Can you not already buy whatever you want? At what point can you say to your shareholders, we've made our profit, let's do some good with it? Or does good not even factor into your equations?"

Rowan caught her breath. Her heart was pounding.

"You're a fool and you will destroy this city with your backward thinking."

"Maybe. But wealth breeding wealth isn't the answer either."

Bosman shook her head, then she spoke very quietly, for Rowan's ears only. "You may be princess or regent or even queen one day. I don't care. Keep your titles. They won't block the blade coming for your throat."

Rowan watched her walk away. Theracine was a problem for another day. Still, her hand went to her throat where the gouges from the fisher cat's claws were only starting to heal.

The ceremony for Minna was more of a goodbye than a funeral. Nathan and Dalkyn had arrived the previous afternoon, only to hear the news of Minna's death from Conall. Dalkyn had insisted that his sister be taken home to Benni, so her coho-ne-teno could be properly celebrated.

Ferlan was going with them, though he'd promised to return.

Rowan stood in the Keeper's Yard outside the palace with the small group of people who knew of Minna's sacrifice. Rowan had ordered Alice to find an appropriate shroud to wrap the body. And Minna lay on a cart, bound in a maroon sheath stitched with gold thread. Rowan nodded to Alice when she saw it. The girl had done well.

Conall and Rowan had a few private moments with Minna before the others arrived. Conall bowed his head and said a small prayer, then left Rowan to greet the Ebos delegation that was just arriving.

Rowan spotted Dalkyn and Irva and a tall man who had to be Nathan. Conall stopped them halfway across the yard, giving Rowan time to say her last goodbyes.

She gripped her friend's arm through the cloth. Part of her wished that she'd never gone into the Meadows with Squad 54. Then Minna would be safe in Benni. But then she might never have learned about Ethan's curse. No, she couldn't wish for that. Perhaps it was best not to wish for an alteration to the past, but for a promise of the future.

"Your sacrifice won't be forgotten," she murmured. "Nor will it be in vain. Talos walks and the city is safe from thera for now. That won't be undone. Not in my time."

"It is a fine tribute for a warrior," Irva said. Rowan moved aside to give the lumina access to the cart.

Irva peered at the shrouded body. "Her bones will have a place of honor at my hearth." Her eyes shone with unshed tears. "A grandmother should not have to revere her granddaughter's bones. The world should turn the other way."

"Granddaughter? Minna is…was your granddaughter."

Irva sniffled and smiled. "Of course, *Essami* means grandmother."

Rowan wanted a hole to open up and take her bones away. Saints!

"But I called you Essami! Please forgive me. I thought it was a title of respect."

"It is." Irva took both Rowan's hands in hers, not shying away from the mech. "I would be honored to have another granddaughter to remember my bones one day."

Rowan nodded. "Thank you…Essami."

Dalkyn strode over. She would have preferred to avoid him, but Minna had whole-heartedly embraced the plan to bring humans and Ebos together. Rowan wouldn't sully her memory by slighting her brother.

"Omika sends his breath and his greetings." Dalkyn nodded his head in what might have been taken as a bow.

"Thank you. Omika is well?"

"Omika is old and should not have to bear the bones of one of his favorites." He looked down at his sister wrapped in the maroon shroud. "She should have trained to become Evafara. Not me. She was the best of us. But her coho-ne-teno was restless. She wanted to see the world and meet people from far and wide." He lifted his chin and looked down his nose at her. "I hope it was worth it, *Evani*." He spoke as if he no longer believed she deserved the title. Motioning for two Ebos to lift Minna, he turned and left with a swirl of his robe.

Rowan wanted to call him back, to beg for his forgiveness, but she was regent now. Begging and apologies had to be handled with diplomacy.

"Do not take his words into your marrow," Irva said. "Dalkyn's bones are well hidden."

Her heart felt tight, but Rowan smiled. "Dalkyn says *Evani* like it's a curse."

"Perhaps it is."

Rowan wiped her hand across her brow. "I wish to the saints you Ebos would stop being so cryptic and just tell me what Evani actually means."

Irva smiled. "It means…" she tilted her head and considered. "I don't think there is a word in your language. Prophet, perhaps. But more. It means one who will change the world."

"I suppose that's not so bad."

"Perhaps, but the Essian word for change is *kalpe*. It also means to break."

"Terrific. Rowan Andula, breaker of worlds. What a great epitaph."

Irva smiled. "Real change doesn't come easy, Evani. Often old habits and beliefs must be destroyed in order to make way for new growth." She squeezed Rowan's arm again. "I think you'll enjoy that. In Benni, there is a children's song about the Evani. It begins like this: *Evani golden crown, she burned the sky to ash. Bones all rattle. Cities all shatter…*" The song faded as Irva caught Rowan's shocked expression. "Perhaps such things are better heard through innocent voices. One day, when you come to my hearth, I will have the children sing it for you."

Rowan sucked in a deep breath.

"What will happen now between us?" Rowan saw Irva's confusion and added, "Between the Ebos and the people of New Torwood City. Will Omika call Ferlan back? And the others?"

She'd miss Ferlan. And having Rudi stay to oversee the much-needed maintenance on Talos meant that Rowan would be able to focus on restructuring the council and implementing new strategies for trade with the south.

"Omika sent a message," Irva said. "If the Evani is willing, he would like to send you a full honor guard of Ebos warriors, and perhaps a delegate from the Ossvara to act as ambassador to Benni. Would the regent find that acceptable?"

"Yes!" Rowan didn't even have to think about it. She would blame herself for Minna's death until her own dying day, but it seemed Omika didn't share that view.

"And perhaps once things settle here, we can send an ambassador of our own to you," Rowan said.

Irva nodded. "To Benni, yes. Not to me."

"You're not returning?"

"No. I choose to stay awhile."

Rowan nodded. "You are welcome to stay as long as you want…Essami."

Irva's eyes sparkled and she gripped Rowan's hands. "Thank you, Evani. I should like to be here to see you break the world."

58

A HOWL AT DAWN

"Safe travels." Conall gripped Nathan's shoulder.

Nathan thumped his back with a fist. "At least this time it won't be ten years before I see you again."

"No. I'll be there by month's end. I plan to make sure the Benni ambassador arrives safely in New Torwood. You wouldn't consider the job, would you?"

Nathan cocked his head. "Perhaps. I would love to show Soffi the city. But Omika might insist on a true Ebos taking the job. He has big plans for trade between the two cities, and having the face of an Ebos at court will go a long way to normalizing those plans."

"Minna has already done a lot to further that cause. The whole city will know what she did for them. The Ebos warrior will become part of the lore of New Torwood."

There was a moment of silence between the brothers. Then Nathan took Conall's arm and pulled him away from the others.

"Tell me the truth," Nathan said in a low voice. "Coming to Benni is just an excuse to hunt down Miron Wrede."

"Not an excuse. An opportunity. Right now, I have no idea where to start looking for that monster. I hope the Rati will help us." Conall ran his hand through his hair.

"Of course. Why do you think Rudi is really staying in the city? If we find anything, he'll let you know." He clapped Conall on the shoulder and grinned. "Just like old times, eh? The brothers are hunting again."

59

A CHAMBER OF CONCEALED WHISPERS

As FIRST ADVISOR TO THE new regent, Dale had been given a choice of suites in the West Wing. Standing in the doorway of Atherton's former suite, Dale wondered if this was the best choice. It was certainly the best suite of rooms, but it would need a full remodel and thorough cleaning to get out the stench of Atherton's sickening perfume.

Dale scanned the dim bedroom. The purple and black needed to go. So did the wall of fornication. Everything in it would need to be searched again and catalogued. They'd found the ledgers here, but what other secrets were stashed away among the clutter of mechs and toys?

A page arrived carrying two large crates.

"From the quartermaster, sir."

"Set them down by the door," Dale said. "And tell the quartermaster I'll need more of those. A lot more."

The page left and Dale decided to start with the sex toys.

Best to get the worst of it over with.

They had nearly emptied the rack of floggers when a sound made them turn, a cat-o-nine-tails dangling from their grip.

Princess Bella stood in the open doorway, her head tipped to the side as she scanned the room. She stepped over to a rack of mech dildos, picked one up and turned it on. The appendage vibrated in her hand.

"I never understood the appeal of such things. Give me real flesh and a man that can hum. It'll do the same job." Bella waggled the dildo with a grin.

Saints, kill me now.

Dale tried to put the image out of their mind, but the memory of ancient

Princess Bella jiggling a mech dick would haunt them for the rest of their days.

"Can I help you?"

Bella set down the toy, took out a handkerchief and wiped her hands.

"I heard you were taking over these rooms. There is something here that is mine. Something I gave to Atherton many years ago and I want it back."

"Whatever you want, it's yours. All this stuff will go to charity anyway."

Bella glanced at the crates full of sex paraphernalia. "I'm sure the orphans will be delighted."

Dale grunted. They were only dimly aware of the princess rifling through Atherton's dresser drawers until she said, "Well, look at these."

Dale glanced up. She held a packet of letters bound in ribbon.

"Faustus had a romance. How sweet." Bella dumped the letters on the dresser. "There it is!" She pulled a small box from the drawer. "Come and see this. It's true artistry."

Dale sighed and rose. She handed over the box that held a watch on a leather band. It didn't look like anything special, a little rough with wear, actually.

"It's very nice," Dale lied.

"It was my grandfather's. I gave it to Faustus when we were just teenagers. We were so young and stupid." Her eyes glistened with unshed tears. "I really thought he was the one, thought he'd be in my life forever." She laughed quietly. "And I guess he was, just not in the way I imagined."

She gazed at the watch, then closed the box. "You know he wasn't always so bad. Once upon a time, he thought he could do good. He had the ear of the king and he wanted to shape policies, to fix what he thought of as social injustices. That stemmed from his early years. He grew up in Squall's End until a rich old uncle died, leaving him a modest house in Old Bailey."

She looked at a picture of Atherton and Old King Reynar in a frame on the dresser. Dale had seen the picture on their first visit to the black and purple room. They'd thought it odd that Atherton would keep a picture of the man he'd helped to murder, but then Atherton was pompous enough to believe in his own righteousness.

Bella gripped Dale's hand. "Power corrupts. See that the princess doesn't fall into the same trap. It's your job now to protect her, even from herself." Her gaze and her grip were so fierce, Dale stumbled backward. She let them go.

"I never had to worry about such things, of course. My only corruptions come from a bottle and a deck of cards." She patted Dale's cheek in a grandmotherly way, then turned and strode out, leaving Dale bemused and slightly uncomfortable.

The packet of letters caught their eye. Not that Dale wanted to know more about Atherton's love life, but all avenues of intelligence needed to be exploited.

They slipped the first letter from the envelope and read. It was worse than they had imagined. The writing was feminine and dripped with sweet salutations. The woman whined for an entire page about how long she had to wait for their next assignation.

Dale was about to dismiss the letter as irrelevant, when they saw the name signed at the bottom: Angelina. They flipped over the envelope and sure enough, the letter came from Angelina Wrede, Miron's daughter. The return address said simply, Ashwood Lodge.

Dale's memories went spinning back to their days as a page, when Atherton had been a secretary to the chancellor. Dale had been assigned to Atherton during a trip he'd taken deep into the Meadows near the border of Wildblood territory. It had been only months after Ethan's attack and the fear of gaunts was firmly planted in Dale's mind.

The trip had been a nightmare and the party at Ashwood Lodge even worse—a drunken revelry of sex and drugs that had terrified young Dale. They'd hidden in the kitchens for the entire weekend and slept the last night in the back of their cat so they wouldn't get left behind.

So Miron Wrede's daughter had been Atherton's secret lover? Dale wondered if the girl knew about Atherton's darker proclivities. Probably. If she grew up in that lodge with her father's parties, she wasn't a wilting wallflower.

But none of that really mattered. Dale gripped the envelope tightly enough to crease it. What mattered was they had a place to start looking for Wrede.

60

GODS AND MECHS

PHALIAN LAUNCHED FROM THE MANTLE in Rowan's room and flew out the open balcony door. The sun was flirting with the southern horizon. In a few weeks it would set and not rise again until spring, but today it reflected sharply off Phalian's wings.

Up, up, up—those metal wings clacked. A strong wind tossed him sideways, but he caught the air stream and soared toward the figure sitting on the roof of King's Tower.

Harry Hightower lifted his hand to let the bird land.

"Hello, my friend."

"CHIRP!"

Harry winced. "We never did get that voice module right, did we? No matter." He patted the bird's head. "Oh, look. You're right on time."

Talos came around the corner. Harry scrutinized the giant. His gait was smooth. Each step fell with a satisfying hiss of pneumatics.

"She did well, your princess."

"CHIRP!"

Talos lumbered by and disappeared around the bend in the wall, but still Harry sat, looking over the city he'd helped to build. After Reynar's death, he'd gone south, but something kept bringing him back here. The city wasn't just a collection of walls and roads. It was alive. If he was honest, it was his greatest creation in a long line of marvels.

"You'd better get home before she misses you."

"CHIRP?"

"Me? I think I'll just sit here a while."

Dear Reader,

As a special gift to you, I created a unique card game: Cogs and Crowns. And I'm giving it away to all my newsletter subscribers! Join my reader's group at KimMcDougall.com/Readers-Group to get your game!

You probably know that authors love reviews, but do you know why? Reviews are important to every author, for the following reasons:

- They help other readers know what to expect from the book.
- They let me know how my books are received by readers.
- They help booksellers decide which books to show to new readers.

If you enjoyed this book I would be grateful for your honest review. It can be as short as you like. Even a few positive words will go a long way. And I'll try to make it as painless as possible. Use this link, KimMcDougall.com/Review-Mech-and-Magic to find the review site of your choice.

Be sure to sign up for the Readers' Group at KimMcDougall.com/Readers-Group to get updates on new releases. When you subscribe, you'll get two free ebooks plus a digital download game just for subscribing.

And check out The Knack Series page for character sketches, playlists, series FAQ and more. Visit KimMcDougall.com/Knack

Thank you for reading *Mech and Magic* and I hope you'll continue Squad 54's adventures with me.

What to Read Next?

A magical journey of second chances, hidden mysteries, and the unexpected enchantment of a small village—where love, loss, and the fae collide in the most surprising ways.

Elenna Kane gave her heart to Jamie, his farm, his needy rescue animals, and his rambling, impractical house. But after his death, she's left struggling to hold onto a life that feels increasingly impossible.

Just when she's ready to walk away, the village of Mullarkey Mills wraps her in its quirky embrace. As the seasons change, an old plow horse teaches her to hold onto joy. A wind phone becomes her bridge to Jamie's memory even as she cautiously explores the possibility of new love. And the whispering woods begin to reveal their hidden truths, drawing Elenna into a shocking mystery that will open her eyes to the dark splendor of the fae living right under her nose.

Black Annis Year is a new cozy fantasy from the author of the Valkyrie Bestiary. Grab it now for a tale that will leave you believing in second chances, love that transcends time, and the wonder that's always just beyond the trees.

Discover the small town with big magic—buy *Black Annis Year* today and start your adventure! Find out more at KimMcDougall.com/Black-Annis-Year

Books by Kim McDougall

The Knack Series
A Knack for Metal and Bone
Mech and Magic

The Fair Folk of Mullarkey Series
Black Annis Year

Valkyrie Bestiary Novels
Dragons Don't Eat Meat
Dervishes Don't Dance
Hell Hounds Don't Heel
Grimalkins Don't Purr
Kelpies Don't Fly
Ghouls Don't Scamper
Devils Don't Lie
Unicorns Don't Cry
Worlds Don't Collide

Valkyrie Bestiary Novellas
The Last Door to Underhill
The Girl Who Cried Banshee
Three Half Goats Gruff
Oh, Come All Ye Dragons
Thorn of Vioska

The Hidden Coven Series:
Inborn Magic
Soothed by Magic
Trigger Magic
Bellwether Magic
Gone Magic

About the Author

If Kim McDougall could have one magical superpower, it would be to talk to animals. Or maybe to shift into animal form. Definitely, fantastical critters and magic often feature in her stories. So until Kim can change into a griffin and fly away, she writes dark and humorous Urban, Epic and Cozy Fantasy from her little farm at the edge of the woods in Quebec, Canada. Kim's book series include Valkyrie Bestiary, The Knack, The Fair Folk of Mullarkey and Hidden Coven.

Visit www.KimMcDougall.com for more information about Kim's books and to join the her reading group.